The Last Uncharted Sky

The Last Uncharted Sky

CURTIS CRADDOCK

TOR

A TOM DOHERTY ASSOCIATES BOOK • NEW YORK

This is a work of fiction. All of the characters, organizations, and events portrayed in this novel are either products of the author's imagination or are used fictitiously.

THE LAST UNCHARTED SKY

Copyright © 2020 by Curtis Craddock

Map by Curtis Craddock

A Tor Book
Published by Tom Doherty Associates
120 Broadway
New York, NY 10271

www.tor-forge.com

Tor® is a registered trademark of Macmillan Publishing Group, LLC.

The Library of Congress Cataloging-in-Publication Data is available upon request.

ISBN 978-0-7653-8965-7 (hardcover)
ISBN 978-0-7653-8967-1 (ebook)

Our books may be purchased in bulk for promotional, educational, or business use. Please contact your local bookseller or the Macmillan Corporate and Premium Sales Department at 1-800-221-7945, extension 5442, or by email at MacmillanSpecialMarkets@macmillan.com.

First Edition: 2020

Printed in the United States of America

0 9 8 7 6 5 4 3 2 1

To Bujold, Heinlein, Chalker, Norton, Pratchett, Cherryh, and Dick, for showing me this world existed.

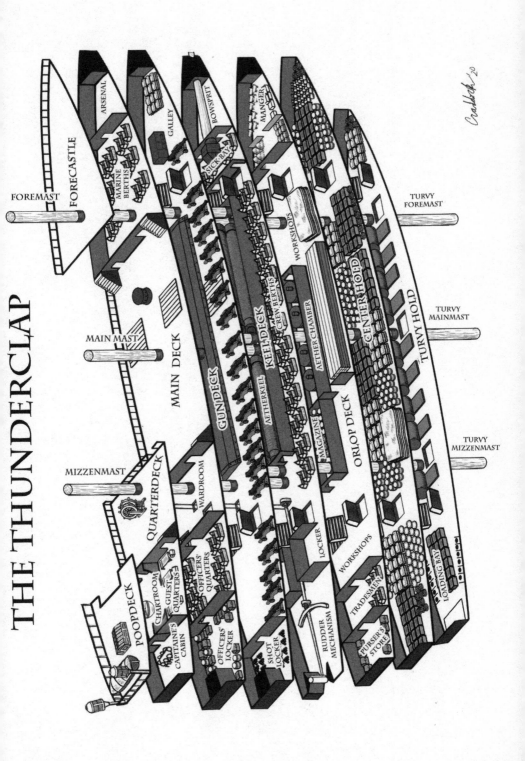

THE THUNDERCLAP

FOREMAST
FORECASTLE
FORECASTLE
ARSENAL
MARINE BERTHS
GALLEY
BOWSPRIT
MANGER
SICK BAY

MAIN MAST
MAIN DECK
WORKSHOPS
GUNDECK
AETHERKEEL
KEELDECK
CREW BERTHS
AETHER CHAMBER

TURVY FOREMAST
TURVY MAINMAST
TURVY HOLD
CENTER HOLD

MIZZENMAST
QUARTERDECK
WARDROOM
MAGAZINE
ORLOP DECK

TURVY MIZZENMAST

POOPDECK
CHARTROOM
GUEST QUARTERS
OFFICERS' QUARTERS
CAPTAINE'S CABIN
OFFICERS' LOCKER
SHOT LOCKER
LOCKER
RUDDER MECHANISM
WORKSHOPS
TRADESMEN
PURSER'S STORE
LOADING BAY

The Last
Uncharted Sky

CHAPTER

One

Draped in beggar's rags and leaning on a cane, Jean-Claude lurked at the entry to Three Brick Alley, awaiting his quarry. Loose strips of transparent linen covered his eyes, and his face itched under layers of the best stage makeup alchemy could provide. He'd been here through the tolling of an hour, precious time slipping through his fingers. Apprehending a shape-shifting spy was not something one could jot down on an agenda, but he had only one day left to manage it.

Passersby went about their business, steering well clear of the blind and stinking beggar. Jean-Claude trusted that his young co-conspirator, lurking in an even narrower alley across the way, had not become distracted. She had proven herself a professional despite her tender age.

The chatter on the street rippled, like a herd of cows muttering to one another at the scent of predators nearby, a swift rumble of noise and then watchful silence.

From up the street came a surly mob of Last Men, a particularly desperate breed of doomsday cultists. Young, lean, and angry, they wore long feast-day robes, but went with hoods thrown back to display shaved heads tattooed with row upon row of saintly icons, each one defiled. Their leader had a disfigured omnioculus—the Builder' eye, blind and bleeding—emblazoned on his forehead.

Jean-Claude stumbled from the alley wheezing, "Alms for the blind." He held out a tin cup and blundered headlong into the nearest tough. The cultist fell, Jean-Claude collapsed backward on purpose, and "accidentally" barked the leader's shin with his cane.

"Filthy whoreson!" the leader growled. "Break his legs."

His bodyguards stepped in to give Jean-Claude a kicking.

"Builder bless," Jean-Claude said, holding up his hands defensively and rocking wildly. "Builder bless. I mean no harm."

"The Builder's dead, vermin." The mob piled on Jean-Claude, punching and kicking, blows that would leave bruises but no worse thanks to his failing to be a easy target. Jean-Claude wailed quite piteously.

"Stop!" came a high, shrill voice. "Please stop! Don't hurt my papa!" A young girl, somewhere between eleven and thirteen squeezed through the press of men, fell to her knees, and covered Jean-Claude with her body.

"Out of the way, girl." One of the brutes grabbed her by the hair and dragged her off Jean-Claude. "You'll get yours next, I—Breaker's breath!" He leapt back and shook his hand, recoiling from the field of open sores and blisters that covered her face.

Jean-Claude sat up, the bandages on his face falling away to reveal blackened skin, cracked and rotting, dripping with pus. "Pox and plague take you all." He spit up the wad of rice and curds he'd been holding in his cheek.

"Pest! They've got the pest!" shouted one of the Last Men.

Jean-Claude lurched to his feet. "Boils and blisters on your balls!"

The first ruffian bolted, and the rest followed like a shoal of aerofish fleeing a leviathan.

Jean-Claude nodded to his young accomplice. They withdrew down Three Brick Alley until they came to a dark junction where several buildings didn't quite line up.

Jean-Claude's heart raced and his lungs burned from the exertion, but he looked down at the girl, Rebecca, and asked, "Package delivered?"

Rebecca was on loan from St. Josephine's Home for Foundlings, which was a front for the most lucrative urchin gang in the city. An incomparable pickpocket, Rebecca could steal a man's wooden teeth if he smiled at her. Alternately, she could play the part of a putpocket and plant a prize on a person.

Rebecca was already scrubbing the makeup off her face, or at least smearing it more evenly. "Of course. They was distracted enough I coulda taken their boots."

Jean-Claude pulled at a small vial of wood spirits and started scrubbing off his makeup goo. The stinging liquid chilled his face and left his skin raw. He handed the spirits to Rebecca. "Don't get it in your eyes."

Her nose wrinkled but she splashed it on her face and got to work peeling off boils and blisters to reveal a face full of freckles. "What's that marble thing for anyway?"

The contraband in question was a contraption that Capitaine Isabelle had contrived: small metal sphere, not much bigger than a marble, with a tiny sliver of chartstone inside. She'd actually gone on at some length to explain to him how it worked, showed him some very detailed technical drawings which he nodded at politely and completely failed to comprehend.

Jean-Claude arched an eyebrow at her. "Why do you want to know?"

Rebecca shrugged. "Weren't too long ago the Last Men was just a pack of nutters standing on street corners screaming, 'Builder's dead!' Used to throw rocks at 'em. Never bothered with their pockets 'cause they never had anything worth taking. Since Burning Night, they ganged up. Started recruiting hard and beating up folks who won't pay bribes. Makes lean pickings for me. Now you show up, la reine's man, and says, how 'bout we put these marbles in their bags. So I think what's they done to get the nobs mad at 'em?"

Jean-Claude grunted approval at this line of reasoning. Orphans grew up fast on these streets, but Rebecca was quick and bold even by those standards.

Jean-Claude drew forth his hunter's eye, a device that looked like a timepiece the size of his hand. He flipped open the lid and showed her the face. Instead of watch hands there were three needles with beads that could slide along their length showing distance and direction. All pointed in the general direction of Uptown, and the third bead was catching up with the first two.

"The marble was a prey marker," Jean-Claude said, which was more evocative to his mind than sympathetic resonance nodes, which was what Isabelle called them. "Works on the same principle as a ship's orrery. That black needle points to the prey marker you just dropped off. The other two are the ones we planted earlier."

"The ones *I* planted." Rebecca looked rather more skeptical than impressed at this fine bit of engineering. "If you want to know where they're going, why not just follow 'em?"

"I've been following them," Jean-Claude said. "The problem is, I can't be everywhere at once. Also, their new leader, Hasdrubal, is a Seelenjäger. He can hear you and smell you and get away before you ever catch sight of him." Jean-Claude wasn't fond of shapeshifters at the best of times, but since he'd started hunting Hasdrubal, he half believed he was chasing a ghost. Now he was running out of time. After months of preparation, Isabelle's ship was scheduled to loft tomorrow on an expedition to the top of the world, and Jean-Claude would be damned if he'd be left behind.

"So why's la reine care about the Last Men?" Rebecca asked.

"Because their leader is one of the men behind Burning Night," Jean-Claude said. A foreign spy and agent provocateur, Hasdrubal had helped the old roi's estranged son depose him. The usurper had come within a heartbeat of claiming the crown before Isabelle had stopped him.

Since Burning Night, all the rest of the conspirators had been captured, killed, or chased away, but Hasdrubal remained at large. Spymaster Impervia wanted him interrogated for his knowledge of the Skaladin spy network, and la reine herself wanted to mount his head as a trophy and send it to his master, the Tyrant of Skaladin, as a warning.

Jean-Claude levered himself to his feet, his knees creaking. "Thank you for your help."

"Where are we going?" Rebecca asked.

"We aren't going anywhere," Jean-Claude said. "I'm going to fetch allies. You are going about your business." Not that he liked the idea of sending her back to the orphanage. Children deserved to be raised, not just trained to fetch like dogs, but at least she had a roof over her head and some measure of protection.

According to his hunter's eye, the Last Men seemed to be gathering well outside their normal territory, and given their garb he thought he could guess where. It was time to muster his reinforcements, set an ambush, and hope Hasdrubal put in an appearance. Jean-Claude must catch him today.

Rebecca folded her arms and said, "I don't have to follow the marks. I just have to follow you. So you either have to waste time trying to lose me, which I'm betting you can't, or you can let me help."

Jean-Claude glowered at her. "I appreciate your courage, but these people are dangerous. Hasdrubal especially."

"Which means you need all the eyes you can get."

Jean-Claude bit his tongue on another rebuff. She'd already dug her heels in, he didn't technically have any authority over her, and there wasn't anything he could do short of stuffing her in a barrel that would keep her from following him.

"One question," he said. "Why?"

"Because they turned me inside out last week and I means to get my own back. Besides, maybe la reine needs a pickpocket."

Jean-Claude snorted at her audacity, but in truth l'Empire did need its share of sanctioned smugglers, thieves, spies, and other scofflaws. Perhaps he could find a place for her in Impervia's service.

"Very well," he said. "You can come with, but you're in the army now, and I'm your sergeant. You do as I say and no buts about it. Deal?"

Her eyes narrowed, "You're not just going to tell me to go away."

"Where we're going, I need someone who can stay out of sight and scout for me."

"Where's that?"

"The Uptown Temple," he said. Today was the Feast of Saint Cynessus and all the Last Men had been wearing feast-day robes. Given that they generally despised the Temple and defaced all ritual objects, it seemed a strange choice of raiment unless they meant to blend into the worship crowd and stir up trouble.

"Deal," Rebecca said.

⟶

The oration for the Feast of Saint Cynessus the Blind had already started when Jean-Claude, Marie, and Jackhand Djordji arrived at the temple with Rebecca in tow. The worship hall was packed like a pickle barrel. Jean-Claude's hunter's eye pointed to all three of his prey markers being inside. Yet with everybody in feast-day robes, many with hoods pulled up, it was impossible to pick the Last Men out of the crowd.

It was Marie who'd suggested they come around back. They could get a better view of the faces in the crowd from the balcony behind the dais.

A rectory was attached to the apse of the temple. Rebecca slipped in through a basement window and hurried to unbar the door. There was a time when Jean-Claude could have squeezed through that window. These days he'd get stuck like a cork in a bottle.

"What is it with you and strays?" Djordji said. "Never meets an urchin you doesn't coddle." As thin and knotty as an old rope, Djordji had trained the best fighters in l'Empire over the last half century. He'd also trained Jean-Claude, though he wouldn't admit to it.

"She just followed me home," Jean-Claude said. "I didn't even feed her."

"You bought her a fish pie on the way up here," Marie said in a voice that sounded like it was echoing through a misty graveyard at night. Her whole form was white and bright as the silver moon Kore, and her expression was as blank as a porcelain doll's.

"I offered everyone a fish pie on the way up here," Jean-Claude said.

"Only because she was hungry," Marie countered.

"It's not like she can't get her own," Djordji said. "She picks about a dozen purses."

Before Jean-Claude could retort, the door shuddered and opened, and the urchin in question poked her head out. "Come on."

Jean-Claude led the way through the clerical residence and along the passageway to the vestry behind the dais. A startled usher hurried toward them, "Messieurs, mesdemoiselles, what are you doing—"

Jean-Claude doffed his hat and said, "I'm so sorry we're late; the crowds were terrible."

"But—" said the usher.

"Has the sagax arrived yet? We were supposed to meet him for private instruction."

"No, but—"

"If he's not here, we'll just wait for him in the gallery. I think I see one of his attendants. Thank you. Builder keep you."

Jean-Claude's companions slipped by the usher while Jean-Claude kept him occupied. Djordji paused and peeked through the curtain separating the vestry from the dais. Beyond, the temple orator delivered the blind saint's Exhortation of Return in the Saintstongue. The congregations of the Enlightened faithful chanted along, speaking words they believed without understanding.

"Sharpshooters in the window," Djordji snapped. "Three by my count."

Jean-Claude abandoned the usher. "Marie, countersniper."

Marie unslung her twist gun. Jean-Claude peered through the draperies. The warm, golden light of ten thousand candles filled the temple instruction hall. On the dais, in elaborate golden vestments, the orator lifted the reliquary of Saint Cynessus from the altar and raised it over his head. The reliquary's box, made of the finest burlwood, was engraved with the icon of a winged key with a blind eye for a head.

Up behind the clerestory windows, men with profane symbols tattooed on their faces took aim and cocked their weapons.

Jean-Claude rushed through the curtain, vaulted the guardrail, and plowed into the orator from behind. "Down!"

The orator collapsed in tangle of heavy limbs just as gunshots split the air. The reliquary flew from the orator's hands, bounced off the altar, and arced toward the Enlightened worshippers, who shrieked in fear and confusion. A bullet spanged off the altar. The two temple knights who had been flanking the dais jerked and fell. Gouts of blood spurted from grotesque wounds.

Marie braced against the vestry doorframe and squeezed the trigger on her twist gun. Fire and smoke belched from the barrel. One of the assassins fell away. She ducked to reload.

Jean-Claude grabbed the orator and pulled him into better cover. "Why in Torment are the Last Men trying to kill you?" Killing an orator and terrorizing a temple service were the sort of thing a mad cult might do, but it was far too senseless for Hasdrubal.

"I have no idea!" the orator squealed, and covered his head.

Two dozen men burst from the crowd, howling like fiends slipped from the halls of Torment. They threw back their hoods to reveal their tattooed heads and produced a variety of weapons from under their robes. The frighted worshippers broke and stampeded, crashing through the main doors and into the street, trampling anyone who fell.

A half squad of temple knights raced from the side hall and charged the cultists. Gunshots from above sent one sprawling and screaming. A temple page sprinted for the reliquary. A mob of Last Men hurled themselves at the knights and drove them back. The chief cultist split the page's head with a meat cleaver.

Marie leaned out of the vestry and pulled her trigger. Another sharpshooter fell. Marie had always been fierce in her quiet way, but her progress since she started combat training was nothing short of terrifying.

Jean-Claude pointed the orator at the vestry. "Go. That way! Rebecca, get him out of here!" That would get her out as well.

A cultist pounced on the reliquary, held it up, and screamed at the fleeing crowd. "Heretics! The Savior is dead. He rose from the Vault of Ages and the Temple murdered him because they could not bear to be exposed as the charlatans they are! Today, see the first of the saints fall!"

Bafflement stumbled through Jean-Claude's mind. They had come for the reliquary?

"Behind the altar, get them!" The mob swarmed toward Jean-Claude's position.

Jean-Claude drew rapier and main gauche and heaved himself over the rail into the main gallery, landing with an inelastic creak of his knees.

Two cultists rushed him. Jean-Claude stepped into the one on the left, ducked his flailing club, and ran the main gauche between his ribs, then shoved him back as the second cultist swung a fireplace poker where Jean-Claude's head had just been. A flick from the tip of Jean-Claude's rapier slit the man's throat, but two more were already on him.

Two more gunshots banged, and the air around Jean-Claude's head clouded with gun smoke as Marie leapt on the altar and unloaded two of her six pistols into Jean-Claude's attackers. Both men went down and a space cleared up, but it was like blowing a hole in the water, for even more filled in.

"Get the one with the box!" Jean-Claude shouted. He stabbed a cultist whose eyes were green with glimmer oil. Too intoxicated to care, the man ran up Jean-Claude's blade to the hilt and stabbed with his knives. Jean-Claude let go of the rapier to avoid being perforated, decked the cultist in the face with his left hand and then bore him backward into his fellows.

Marie fired again, but Jean-Claude couldn't see what she'd hit.

A blade flashed to Jean-Claude's left and a cultist fell, moaning. Djordji appeared beside him.

"I see you loses your sword," Djordji said, skewering a cultist and guiding his body into the path of another. "You learns nothing I teaches you."

"Fight now. Critique later," Jean-Claude said, drawing his pistol and shooting a cultist who had climbed up behind Marie.

"Kill the heretics!" shouted the leader. "Gut them on the altar of their—"

Marie's pistol ball turned his shout into a splat and he pitched backward.

The crowd clogged up the far end of the worship hall, climbing over a pile of bodies they'd made in their panic. Two temple knights had been slain, though they'd winnowed the cultists.

Down from the shadows at the top of the octagonal dome stooped a great pyrebird, black oily smoke trailing from its charcoal wings. It landed next to the reliquary and spat tongues of flame that ignited tapestries to either side of the dais.

The pyrebird's form blurred. It billowed upward and outward and solidified into a shape that was almost a man, if a man had cloven hooves and the head of a black goat with long scimitar-shaped horns. He wore robes the color of fresh-spilt blood and a sleevelike hood that covered his face except for his caprine beard and scarlet eyes.

"Hasdrubal," Jean-Claude growled. "You're late."

The remaining cultists circled their leader. He crouched and hefted the reliquary in a large, blunt-fingered hand. Flames leapt from the tapestries to the old wooden beams.

Hasdrubal turned one scarlet eye to Jean-Claude. His voice was a bray. "Congratulations, Old Hand. You have failed, which was the most noble and correct thing you could have done."

"I didn't know the tyrant cared so much for old bones," Jean-Claude replied. Why did Hasdrubal want the reliquary? It wasn't as if they were particularly hard to come by. Nearly every temple he'd ever set foot in claimed at least one saintly remnant. Jean-Claude reckoned that the saints must have actually been snakes, judging from how many rib bones they'd left behind to be venerated.

Hasdrubal said, "I have done the tyrant's bidding and have seen your roi cast down, but it is not enough. You should take joy. The lie of lies has been exposed. I will bring an end to everything the Breaker has wrought." Hasdrubal made a sweeping gesture toward Jean-Claude and company. "Kill them."

"Marie," Jean-Claude called. Bullets were their best chance against a Seelenjäger. They couldn't shift shape while they had metal in their bodies.

"Empty," she replied, her voice toneless.

The Last Men charged. Hasdrubal changed into a chimerical form that was part mountain ape, part hard-shelled crackback and bounded away, crashing through the press of people still trying to get out the door and scattering them like autumn leaves.

Jean-Claude grabbed a banner pole and used it like a quarterstaff. He cracked a cultist's skull and swept the legs from under another. Djordji cut throats and punctured lungs. Marie plunged into the fray, slashing a man's belly open with her short curved blades.

The ceiling caught fire and hot ash rained down. A flaming timber crashed onto to the benches, setting them alight. The final few cultists broke and ran.

"Out, out!" Jean-Claude retrieved his good sword, and ran for the vestry with Marie and Djordji on his heels. He had to make sure Rebecca had escaped. He pelted through the residence then out into the alley and saw her nowhere. He prayed she'd gotten away cleanly. If Hasdrubal really was just after the reliquary, he'd have no reason to chase her or the orator.

He hurried around to the front of the building, calling Rebecca's name. At the front steps, rescuers were ducking into the burning building to pull out those who'd fallen. The heat grew like the inside of a furnace being stoked. Jean-Claude joined the smoke eaters, grabbed a groaning trample victim by his tunic, and dragged him out.

He left the victim with a group of rescuers at the bottom of the temple steps, then rushed back for another. The heat rolled over him like dragon's breath. If the temple didn't have such a high ceiling, he wouldn't have been able to make past the doors. Marie and Djordji helped rescue another handful, but when Jean-Claude turned to go back for more, the inferno defeated him. Three times he crawled into the smoke, trying to get under it, calling out for anyone still alive, but it reached into his lungs to smother and choke.

He could do nothing but watch as the roof collapsed, shooting embers into the darkening sky. They were lucky, he supposed, that Rocher Royale was the one city in l'Empire Céleste were the fire had almost no chance of spreading. Etched into the side of an immense cliff, the capital city was carved from stone: bas relief on an urban scale. All the wood in the temple had been imported, a tribute to the Temple's stately decadence.

Jean-Claude turned his attention to the stricken. He had seen many battlefields, but few where the victims were so bewildered. He sent runners to the royal infirmary, rallied the congregation, and moved the casualties to the temple outbuildings. They opened up the refectory and laid the worst cases out on the stone tables. He, Marie, and Djordji bandaged wounds and secured broken limbs. He applied every bit of battlefield medicine he'd ever learned until the doctors and surgeons from the infirmary showed up to do battle with death for those who clung to the brink.

A tight band around his chest loosened when Rebecca showed up with the orator in tow.

"I took him the back way in case the buggers chased us," she said. "Never saw one though."

"Well done," Jean-Claude said. "Get some water and see what Marie has for you to do."

Rebecca departed, and Jean-Claude turned his attention to the orator, a square man well padded and drooping round the edges. The orator dabbed at his red sweaty face with a cloth.

Jean-Claude said, "Learned one, what was so important about that reliquary that a Skaladin spy was willing to risk himself and sacrifice his followers to obtain it?"

"Oh." The orator's flesh sagged across his frame like a sail taken out of the wind. "That was the Hand of Saint Cynessus, a true reliquary, and now it's fallen into the hands of that thief. Saints forgive me."

"A true reliquary? As opposed to an untrue one?" Jean-Claude asked.

The orator winced and said, "Most reliquaries have been . . . adulterated over time, but the provenance of the hand is impeccable. It belonged to the gatekeeper himself."

"That doesn't explain why the thief wanted it. Does it hold some miraculous power? Will it restore a man's grip or make his cock hard?"

The orator fluffed up like an angry chicken and scolded. "That reliquary was sacred. To touch it was to touch the path to Paradise Everlasting."

"The Hand of Saint Cynessus has never produced a miracle, but I imagine the relic will be of great interest to the heretic's master back in Skaladin," said another voice, deep and grating, as if the gears of the speaker's voice box did not quite mesh. Up the aisle between the tables in the makeshift surgery strode a quaestor, one of the Temple's own hounds. Jean-Claude knew the man's rank by the pair of scythes sewn in yellow thread on his umber mantle. The hand sticking out of his right sleeve was made of quondam metal the color of bronze but filled with purple shadows that oozed and flowed like clouds of ink underwater.

The sight of the living prosthesis raised all the hair on the back of Jean-Claude's neck; the last man he'd seen wearing one of those had been the same one who cut off his beloved Isabelle's arm and nearly plunged the whole world into war. Yet this quaestor had no clockwork eye, and no hump on his back that might indicate the presence of a pickled head.

The orator placed his hands on his chest and bowed. "Quaestor Czensos, thank the saints you're here."

"Be about your business," Czensos said. "And reflect on your failures today."

The orator's face went red and he bowed himself out. "Builder keep."

Czensos did not respond in kind.

Jean-Claude didn't like men who bullied their subordinates. "So, Quaestor, you're saying this mummified hand has only sentimental value."

Czensos adjusted the line of his nose so there could be no mistake he was looking down it at Jean-Claude. "The Tyrant of Skaladin hates the Risen Saints with the terrible passion of a jealous lover. He knows salvation is beyond him and therefore seeks to deprive the Savior's gift to everyone else. He razes temples wherever he finds them, burns books of Enlightened wisdom, enslaves sorcerers, binds them to the lash and breeds them like pigs. It would give him great pleasure to destroy the last remnants of the saint who held the door to the Vault of Ages or anything that took part in Legend. Is that sentimental enough for you?"

Jean-Claude rubbed the back of his neck. "It seems a rather trivial prize for all the effort put in to obtain it."

Czensos folded his arms across his chest in a pose Jean-Claude silently dubbed "A study in imperious prickishness."

Czensos said, "You underestimate its political value. It is a victory the tyrant can parade in front of his own people or a token he can use against the Temple. Your failure to stop the theft cannot be excused by diminishing the value of the stolen item."

Jean-Claude laughed. "Ha! I'm no mangy dog to carry off your fleas. The relic was not my responsibility to keep. I'm only interested in the thief, not the bauble. If you want your worthless-yet-valuable trinket back, you'd be best served by lending your assistance to l'Empire in catching him."

"If l'Empire wishes to aid in capturing this Skaladin spy, l'Empire can begin by telling me his name."

Jean-Claude considered telling Czensos to go chase a falling rock, but even if he was of little direct use to Jean-Claude's pursuit, he might still make Hasdrubal's life more difficult, which was an indirect benefit.

"The thief's name is Hasdrubal," Jean-Claude said.

Czensos frowned. "A beast-man with the form of a black goat?"

"Not bad for a first guess," Jean-Claude said. How did Czensos know him?

"Then you are lucky to have survived the encounter. The black goat is a sanctified thrall from the Maze of Eyes. He is the tyrant's personal assassin and spy. I know you will not take my advice, but I am compelled by duty and conscience to warn you not to pursue this villain. You are not a match for him. The Temple will deal with him. Builder keep."

"So you're saying the Temple does not intend to coordinate with l'Empire in this matter?" Jean-Claude asked.

Czensos walked away without another word.

Jean-Claude watched the noxious little stoat out the door before stirring himself to look for Marie. It made sense that having failed in his bid to install a puppet on l'Empire's throne, Hasdrubal would like to have some secondary prize to bring home to his master by way of apology, but "I will undo all the Breaker has wrought," sounded rather more ambitious than a man running back to his master with his tail between his legs.

In all likelihood Jean-Claude would never find out what Hasdrubal meant by his enigmatic proclamation. Isabelle's ship would sail on the morrow and he'd have to turn this investigation over to Comtesse Impervia and her other agents. He did not want to think about the report he had to give her. Debacle did not begin to describe it. He'd managed to let Hasdrubal slip away, lost a true reliquary before he even knew he had it, and let a temple burn down. Impervia would march straight past disappointment and directly into sarcasm. Not the way he wanted to say goodbye.

Rebecca returned with a cup of hot cider. "Marie says you're to drink this."

"Merci," Jean-Claude said. He took the cup and considered the child, the orphan, the budding artist of misdirection and prestidigitation before him. Impervia would certainly take her in, train her to be an unstoppable thief, but children needed more than training. She wasn't a tool.

"How much does Old Spiderfingers take of your catch?" Jean-Claude asked. He knew the thief master from her days as master thief. These days she ran St. Josephine's. She provided food, shelter, education, and discipline to the biggest gang of orphans in the city. The powers that be tolerated her crew of underage pickpockets, housebreakers, and beggars because she was wise enough to direct her charges at foreign visitors, and because she made the orphanage largely self-sufficient.

Rebecca flinched. "Nobody calls her that anymore. It's Madame Ophelia."

Jean-Claude wondered when the old woman had started putting on airs. He said, "You didn't answer my question."

"I still owe her indenture," Rebecca said bluntly, meeting him with the sort of feral stare that suggested further inquiries in that direction would be considered acts of aggression.

Jean-Claude despised orphan indenture, a legal noose that obligated foundlings to pay back their caretakers for the expense of raising them, reducing many to perpetual servitude.

"What would you do if you didn't owe?"

Rebecca looked wary. "I don't know."

"I know a ship that's leaving soon, and it has need of a cabin girl." Isabelle's much-anticipated expedition to recover the *Conquest*'s lost treasure was due to set sail tomorrow. Isabelle could use someone like Rebecca, someone quick and clever to relieve Marie of her duties as handmaid. Likewise, Isabelle was incapable of not caring about people in her charge.

Rebecca's eyes went round. She leaned forward, yearning, but caught herself. "I can't."

"I didn't ask if you could. I asked if you wanted to."

She made a surly face. "What good's wanting sommat you can't have?"

"Because every good thing in the world comes from someone doing something they didn't think they could."

"That's why the world's such a shithole then."

Jean-Claude shrugged with a nonchalance he did not feel. She must feel he was trying to trick her. Offering bait for a scam she could not see. "It was a thought. I'll be on the ship. So will Marie and Djordji."

That gave Rebecca pause. "What about Madame Ophelia?"

"I'll deal with Old Spiderfingers, get her off your neck even if you don't want the job," Jean-Claude said.

"But I don't know anything about ships," Rebecca said.

"Neither does Jean-Claude. Difference is, he's got no excuse," Djordji said, coming up behind her. He held a long-stemmed pipe in his teeth, and the sweet and sulfurous smoke of dragonweed gathered under the wide brim of his hat.

Marie came with him. The smoke smudges and bloodstains on her clothes slowly faded to white over time.

"Isabelle already has a handmaid," Marie said. She and Isabelle had been living arm in arm since they were both in pigtails. Even when Marie had been turned into a bloodhollow, Isabelle had maintained their friendship, keeping her sane through twelve years of torture, and resuscitating her mind and soul when the whole world said it was impossible. You couldn't slide a knife between them.

Jean-Claude said, "If you're going to be her bodyguard, you have to stop being her handmaid."

"Jean-Claude makes good point for once," Djordji said. "You can't be tied down making tea and lacing bodices, and child's the kind who comes sharp but needs balance. She's cleverer than Jean-Claude was at her age."

Jean-Claude protested, "You hadn't even met me when I was her age."

"And when I does, you aren't as clever as she is now."

Marie said, "Have you told Isabelle about this, or is it going to come as a surprise?"

"It was a surprise to me when I thought of it, but what do you imagine the odds are of Isabelle turning away a plucky orphan?"

"About the same as a fish wearing mittens," Marie acknowledged tonelessly.

"If she wants to go," Jean-Claude said.

Rebecca's brow furrowed as if she were groping for a clear path through a thick wood.

"Which ship?" she asked.

Jean-Claude smiled on the inside. "The *Thunderclap*."

Rebecca's eyes rounded. "That new frigate? They say the capitaine is an abomination." This last was said in a tone of amazement.

Djordji chuckled.

Jean-Claude's anger came up at the mere mention of the insult, but Rebecca had not meant any harm. "Her name is Isabelle. She's a dear friend of mine, and I will advise you not to slander her that way again."

"No offense," Rebecca said without a trace of contrition.

Jean-Claude snorted. "So the question is, are you interested in applying for the position, or would you rather stay here?"

Rebecca took a deep breath before the plunge. "I want to go."

Djordji sat on one of the tables and took another pull at his pipe. "Now that's set, what does we do about Hasdrubal? Does that fancy timepiece of yours say which way he goes?"

Jean-Claude flipped open the hunter's eye, but the needles were loose and wobbled wherever momentum took them. "I deduce the prey markers were destroyed in the fight."

Djordji coughed into his hand, a deep cough that sounded like he was trying to shift wet leaves. Jean-Claude grimaced. Djordji had been suckling that pipe for sixty years, and it had its hooks in deep. Sticky black flecks covered his glove, and the reek of his breath diffused through the refectory, joining all the other infirmary smells. Marie touched his shoulder in worry, but he shrugged her off. Jean-Claude felt sick to his gut; he hated to see the old man in this state. Rebecca shied away.

When the fit finally passed, Jean-Claude relayed what he'd learned from Czensos and said, "I'll talk to Impervia and Isabelle, see if they know anything more about the reliquary."

By the time Jean-Claude was done, Djordji was already back on his pipe. "I puts the harbormaster on alert, and has a word with some fishermen I know."

"And by fishermen you mean smugglers," Jean-Claude said. Dodging excise officers and evading the port authority was the sport and livelihood of all the fisherfolk along the Towering Coast. It was amazing the sorts of things that fishermen pulled up in their nets. Not just aerofish, crackbacks, and reef krakens, but plenty of things that had no business in the open sky: bales of dragonweed, rum, rare spices, a cornucopia of "shipwrecked cargo," and the occasional fugitive.

Jean-Claude said, "So you think Czensos has it right and Hasdrubal will bolt?"

Djordji shrugged. "If he scarpers, we has to catch him now. If he doesn't, Impervia catches him later."

Jean-Claude allowed the logic of that. To Marie he said, "You take Rebecca and get Spiderfingers to sign off on her indenture."

Marie's porcelain-doll face could not change expression, but her answer was very careful, "I've never met Spiderfingers."

Jean-Claude grunted. He'd been training Marie for months how to talk her way through trouble and out the other side. She didn't take to it like she did to fighting.

He said, "Then it's time you did. She's a thief, used to be a good one, till she got caught and the city guard lopped off her right hand. She lost her nerve after that, opened up the orphanage. She's not likely to become violent, and she's very susceptible to bribes."

"Didn't you promise to do this?" Marie asked.

"Yes, and I am using one of the tools at my disposal, to wit, one apprentice. As much as you might like it to be otherwise, being a bodyguard involves much more talking than stabbing. You know the dance steps. Now you need to trust the music."

CHAPTER

Two

Isabelle had all but lost count of the number of times she'd stood before some judicial body that considered her an existential threat. This time it was a triumvirate of Fenice sorcerers, each clad in colorful feathers and iridescent scales that gave them armor as light as down but stronger than steel. The Fenice of the Vecci city-states had a blood feud against Isabelle's sire's family that stretched back hundreds of years to the Maximi, Fenice twins who had all but conquered the world. Isabelle had arranged this tribunal to bring that vendetta to an end.

At least this time l'Empire Céleste was on Isabelle's side.

Impératrice Sireen had lent her forestlike throne room at le Ville Céleste to the occasion and watched the proceedings from atop her throne, playing the arbiter of protocol but not currently asserting herself as the giver of law. For the time being, this was Isabelle's show.

She'd donned her naval capitaine's uniform, a burgundy jacket with silver trim, and a single loop of crimson braid that marked her as a sorcerer in l'Empire's military service, and stepped smartly into the arena to present her case to these ambassadors of ill will.

As support, she brought along Major Bitterlich, her friend and protector. He was dapper as always in his marine uniform, his feline eyes half-lidded, his cravat just so, a sheathed longsword in his hand. He surveyed the Fenice as a streetwise tomcat might evaluate a group of pigeons: fun to play with if too wormy to eat.

She also brought the newly minted Lord Chancellor Thibaut, borrowed from l'impératrice in a firm acknowledgment of her favor. He bore a white specimen box.

To the Fenice, Isabelle said, "You sought to end the line of the Maximi. That has been accomplished. My sister, Brunela, was the last to carry their memories. She tried to hand her memories down to me, but as many can attest, I crushed her vitera before it could implant them in my brain."

Isabelle's right arm, amputated just below the shoulder, had been replaced with her spark-arm, a manifestation of her unique l'Étincelle sorcery. It was a ghostly limb, made up of swirling pink and purple sparks and filled with luminescent clouds of lavender and rose. With it, she gestured to the white specimen box in which was displayed the crushed and desiccated body of an insect-like creature about the size of a plum. "There is nothing left of my ancestors."

This was not entirely true. Brunela's attempted usurpation of her skull had left Isabelle with the spiteful echoes of her past lives, an ancestral chorus. For the last three months a gibbering mob of other people's memories whispered in her ears, shouted from the shadows, and occasionally bled through to stain her vision with bits of the past that weren't really there. It was like having a whole troupe of ghostly actors stepping from behind the curtain to deliver random lines from a hundred different plays.

Don Pyros, the Fenice leader, was tall and broad, with a great crest of red-and-gold feathers that shimmered like flames under the harsh alchemical lights. His companions were similarly beplumed, though in shades of green and blue. How many lives had they lived, and what memories of their ancestors did they carry down the ages? Had any of their forebears actually witnessed the Great Betrayal that began this cascade of vengeance?

Don Pyros looked unconvinced. "Let me see your hair."

Both of Isabelle's honor guards quivered with affront. To demand a Célestial woman take off her wig was tantamount to commanding her to disrobe in public. It was a humiliation and a prelude to degradation.

Isabelle held up her flesh hand to restrain her compatriots. She'd been expecting this, counting on it in fact, and hadn't pinned her wig in place. She doffed her plumed hat and pulled off her raven tresses to reveal a head of knuckle-length mouse-brown hair, patchy on the right side where she'd been burned. It had been three months since she very publicly destroyed Brunela's vitera. If she was going to become a Fenice and carry on her father's line, she should have sprouted feathers by now. The lack of down or feather proved her claim was true.

She stepped forward and bent her head for examination.

All three of the Fenice moved in, combing her hair as if looking for lice.

He'll break your neck . . . gut him now . . . filthy vermin, growled Isabelle's ancestral chorus, a mélange of voices each talking over all the others. Between one voice and the next, the parquetry floor of Sireen's throne room disappeared, and in its stead was a heap of sandstone rubble on which lay the broken corpse of her brother, Nunzio, from some life long ago. She might have reached out and touched his feathery crest.

Isabelle squeezed her eyes shut against the hallucination, a ghostly stain of her ancestor's life that leaked into her mind like blood through cloth. It was maddening to see things she knew were false but that no amount of logic would allow her to dismiss. All of her senses insisted the corpse was there—the rotten meat stink of its decay got up her nose and made her gag—despite all the evidence reason could bring to bear.

She took a twice-daily potion that kept the chorus quiet and kept the ghost stains from leaking through, but the foul brew also made her thick-headed. She'd trimmed today's dose to let her think more quickly and clearly during the tribunal. Apparently she'd cut down a little too far.

Finally Pyros stepped back and frowned. "It seems you are telling the truth," he said, clearly disgruntled to find that his chosen prey had died without his help. How much of his life had he dedicated to this endeavor? How many lifetimes, just to find the job already done?

Isabelle opened her eyes. The ghost stain had faded, thank the saints. The chorus was still there, mumbling in the background like voices at a party consisting entirely of uninvited guests.

Isabelle put her wig back on. "Your relentless pursuit made Brunela desperate. Desperation caused her to make mistakes of which I was the beneficiary," she said, by way of offering a balm for his pride. She certainly took no joy in her sister's death. It had been entirely necessary, but killing was never something to be proud of, no matter how dire the need.

Pyros made the barest shrug, accepting this narrative without enthusiasm.

Isabelle said, "As a further proof of the deed and as a token to carry back to your people, I give you Primus Maximus's sword, Ultor." Isabelle gestured to Bitterlich, who stepped smartly forward and presented the blade in a newly made sheath across both his palms.

Pyros reached for the scabbard, hesitated, then lifted it anyway.

"If I may," he said, for drawing weapons in la reine's presence was generally a faux pas of fatal proportions.

"Gently," said Sireen, her voice smooth and mellow.

Pyros stepped back and drew the weapon partway. Even the smallest sliver of the blade would have been enough to testify to its authenticity. The metal itself was emerald green and honed so fine that light shone through the edges of the blade as if through an icicle. When it moved, it threw sparks and left a green smear in its wake as if cutting a bloody rent in the air. Arcanite blades such as this had not been crafted since the soul forges died after the Annihilation of Rüul, the city the saints had founded after emerging from the Vault of Ages.

Pyros stared at the weapon for a long moment, then closed his eyes, blew out his breath, and pushed the sword back into its sheath.

"A perilous trophy indeed," he said.

"You will trouble my subject no more, then," Sireen said, a decree rather than a request.

Pyros made a show of settling his crest. "We are satisfied vengeance is done. The Maximi are dead and shall not rise again. Capitaine Isabelle and her descendants have nothing to fear on that score."

"No one's children should have to grow up with the fear of being assassinated," Isabelle said pointedly. Not that she had children . . . yet. She certainly had the urge to motherhood, an ember of curiosity and fascination that glowed warm whenever she spent time with her women friends and their offspring. Yet it seemed a goal that should be pursued from a position of security and stability, which she'd never had and likely never would.

The tribunal broke up with all due ceremony. When the Fenice departed, Isabelle bowed to Sireen. There was no precedent for commissioning a woman as a naval capitaine, and so she had adopted the male protocols by default, much to the annoyance of her peers, who had been doing their best to pretend she didn't exist.

"Thank you, Madame," Isabelle said. Without Sireen's permission, this parley would not have been possible.

"You are most welcome. You were correct to point out that it would have done your mission no good to have them chasing you through the deep sky."

Isabelle's pulse thrummed in anticipation of her mission, of being aloft on a skyship again. Excitement kept one step ahead of her dread of fouling it all up.

She had been commissioned especially to lead an expedition to the top of the world. At the first glimmering of spring, when the Solar's light spilled into the Twilight Latitudes after months of darkness, she would sail north and challenge the Bittergale—a lethal tumult of tumbling stonebergs and a constant cyclone of hailstones the size and speed of cannonballs, an impossible, impassable barrier that chewed up ships and spat out flinders even more surely than a great fetch.

Yet beyond it, if she could clear the way, was the wreck of the *Conquest*, fabled flagship of Secundus Maximus's lost armada, and its legendary pay chest: the treasure of a century in coin and plunder. It was enough to make a pirate weep.

Of more interest to Isabelle and value to l'Empire was the Craton Auroborea on which the *Conquest* had crashed. If her guide was to be believed, it was a lush, green land ripe for exploration and colonization.

"Are you ready to sail?" Sireen asked. Her tone was casual and friendly, but the question was definitely in the official-business category.

Isabelle's conscience curdled. Was she ready? More to the point, was she able? She'd been wrestling with it for months. She had trained for this role, helped plan the expedition, recruited for it, and outfitted it with every tool it would need to get the job done. She was certainly as prepared as she was ever going to be.

She'd also be responsible for the lives of over four hundred men, attempting a dangerous passage into the unknown whilst seeing and hearing things. Yes, the potions had the chorus under control . . . except when they didn't.

Yet to stand down meant she would lose everything. The Célestial Parlement had already stripped her of her noble title. She had no right to own or inherit land. They'd done everything they possibly could to render her a legal nonperson. She'd even lost her family name. Making Isabelle a naval capitaine had been Sireen's way of getting around those restrictions while technically abiding the decision of her nobles.

Was it not better to sacrifice one life than risk disaster for many? Was it moral for her to proceed without telling Sireen about the voices in her head?

She will discard you like an old rag, her chorus whispered. *You will be confined, erased.*

Isabelle hated it when the chorus had a point. If she admitted to this privy council of lunatics, it wouldn't matter that she had them under control, Sireen would be obliged by good sense to relieve her of duty. Isabelle would fall. Even if Sireen gave her some sort of sinecure, she'd still be condemned to live as a ghost made flesh, haunting society without ever being part of it.

And she still had so much more to give. She'd been suffering these intrusions for months and she'd still managed to assemble the mission. She'd learned to captain the ship, mastered navigation, and kept up a schedule that had her officers panting to keep up. She knew she could handle this responsibility because she already was. Besides, she had Jean-Claude, Marie, and Bitterlich looking out for her.

She cast a questioning glance at Bitterlich. He returned her appeal with a confident nod.

Isabelle took hold of her fear, lifted her chin, and said, "I am prepared, and the expedition is ready to depart as soon as the weather clears." She could do this. She had done harder things before. She'd wanted to be gone weeks ago. The longer she remained tied up here, the more competition she was likely to have. Plus, the long spin of Craton Massif was carrying Rocher Royale south, farther from its goal.

If Sireen suspected any of Isabelle's inner turmoil, it did not show in her smile. "Good. I look forward to seeing you off, but I'm afraid there is one more thing I must require of you. Artifex Erdorad has been pressuring me to put a Temple sagax on board to minister to the spiritual needs of the crew."

"You mean he wants a spy on board," Isabelle said. "And you wouldn't be bringing this up unless you meant to foist one on me." Why would Sireen do that? The Temple loathed Isabelle, with her unladylike ways and her uncanonical l'Étincelle sorcery. In addition to whatever spying the sagax would be sent to do, he was sure to undermine Isabelle's authority with the crew. All her life such men had labeled her "the Breaker's get."

Sireen leaned forward, her posture more conversational than command-ing. "Correct, but you know it's rude to interrupt your sovereign in mid-foist."

"My apologies, Madame," Isabelle said. "Foist away."

Sireen resumed her regal posture and steepled her fingers, a gesture that reminded Isabelle of Grand Leon. "Because Erdorad is speaking on behalf of the Enlightened faithful rather than on behalf of the Temple in Om, I choose not to dismiss his request out of hand. I do, however, insist on choos-ing the sagax."

There came a rumbling from under the floor. Gears turned and springs unwound, opening a trapdoor. From this hole emerged a man in red-trimmed yellow robes with a mantle embroidered with the interlocking gears of the Builder's ineffable machine. His nose was hooked like a vulture's beak and he walked like someone who had learned to do so by reading a manual, each bit moving in sequence but not together.

A gut punch of recognition made Isabelle's bile rise along with her an-ger. "Sagax Quill. I should have thought you'd have been hanged by now."

"It's a pleasure to see you too, Capitaine Isabelle," Quill said, his voice as dry as wind through autumn leaves. "Congratulations on your promotion."

"I see you've met," Sireen said.

Isabelle said, "The last time I saw this man he was ensconced in the in-ner circle of the usurper Lael, deep in counsel with Lael's lieutenant, Has-drubal." She hesitated and faced Sireen. "Unless he was a spy of yours."

"Unfortunately not," Sireen said. "Or it might have saved us all a great deal of trouble. Also, we do not believe that Quill was in league with the usurper."

Isabelle wondered who that "we" consisted of, probably Sireen and Com-tesse Impervia, l'Empire's spymaster and Jean-Claude's sharp and pointy paramour. Isabelle would have to have a word with her before she set sail.

Quill twisted a thumb ring of quondam metal, the sort of trinket only a cleric might possess. "I was there on behalf of my master, the truth. Who is always a third party in matters of politics. I was not privy to Lael's thoughts or a member of his council."

Sireen said, "Quill is also a member of the Observationalist sect, cur-rently at odds with the ascendant Traditionalists in Om."

"On the verge of being labeled heretics, in fact," Quill said, "which will spark a civil war with no boundaries and no obvious conditions of victory."

"The only victory in war is not to have one in the first place," Isabelle said. She'd stood in front of two wars now and put both conflicts back on their haunches. "But that is not the business before us today. Why did you involve yourself in this mission?"

"Madame Sireen requested—"

Isabelle bristled at the first sniff of Quill trying to go around her authority. "Madame could have picked any number of clerics from any one of a half dozen different sects. You were once a Temple Seeker, someone who went out and investigated miraculous claims, not the sort of person who sits quietly in a garden like a leek waiting to have your head pulled out of the ground. I have no doubt you approached l'impératrice with some reason you should be included and convinced her it was worthwhile, but understand this: I am the capitaine of the *Thunderclap*. If Madame put you on my ship, she also put you under my authority, and I will not have anyone on my ship who cannot account for themselves."

Out of the corner of her eye, Isabelle saw Bitterlich's whiskers twitch with amusement.

Quill's gaze flicked to Sireen and back to Isabelle. He managed to bow to her without ducking his head, a dip of the shoulders like a chicken on the strut.

He said, "You are quite correct, Capitaine. When we met at the usurper's soiree before Burning Night, I had been invited because Lael thought he could make use of me to legitimize his coup d'état, just like you. Unaware of his ulterior motive, I answered his invitation because he was known to be an antiquarian. He told me he had just returned from the dig of a lifetime, and could I please help him make sense of what he had found. It took me not five minutes to realize that he had found the *Conquest*."

"You're not the only person to figure that out," Isabelle said. Lael had been quite tight-lipped about the discovery in life, but his death had been messy, and his fleeing allies had traded their knowledge of the wreck for sanctuary in various noble houses here and abroad. The last few months had seen a flurry of expeditions being prepared up and down the cratonic rim, all of which aimed to claim the wreck and recover the treasure.

"No, but I am the one who took the opportunity to recover all of Lael's notebooks, including the ones where he describes the menace that drove his expedition from the Craton Auroborea. It is quite likely that I know more about the dangers the expedition faces beyond the Bittergale than you do, even with your guide."

Isabelle had to allow that Quill might have a point. She had two advantages over her expeditionary rivals. The first was a sliver of behemoth bone from the bonekeel of the *Conquest*. Placed in a navigational orrery, it showed exactly where in the sky the wreck was, just not how to overcome the obstacles between here and there. For the obstacles she had a guide, Hailer Dok, a Gyrine Windcaller with a noticeable honesty deficit, who had taken Lael through the Bittergale and claimed to have discovered a path anyone could use, though how there could be a stable path through a constant vortex Isabelle could not guess. Dok further claimed that Lael's expedition had been driven off the wreck by a swarm of monstrous insects.

"You mean other than the bugs," Isabelle said.

"In addition to the bugs, yes," Quill said. "And I can help sift the wreck itself, extract and preserve that which is of historical curiosity in addition to monetary value."

"And what do you get out of it?" Isabelle asked.

Quill glanced at Sireen. La reine's expression gave away nothing of what she was thinking. Her bloodshadow flowed into a wide pool at her feet that looked thicker and wetter than any shadow should be.

Finding no guidance there, Quill shrugged, or possibly just twitched, and said, "You may recall that the *Conquest* set out to raze the City of Gears and cast down the tyrant."

"I recall reading about it," Isabelle said. No one outside her very small circle of intimate advisers knew that she had inherited any memories of her past lives at all, much less that she recalled bits and pieces of the Kindly Crusade itself.

Quill twitched as if he were on the verge of a great spasm, but it subsided and he said, "Yes, that is what I meant. To aid in the theological destruction of the irredeemable heretics, the Maximi took along Prime Architect Cassius of the Temple in Om. Cassius was on the *Conquest* the day it was lost. Needless to say, he never returned, but the College of Artifexes always keeps a seat for him at the conclave, and the Omnifex speaks with his voice and his vote."

"Which gives him two votes to everybody else's one," Isabelle said. "Of course, given the size of the College of Artifexes, one extra vote is hardly an insurmountable advantage."

"It's a keen symbolic advantage," Quill said. "Or, at least it will be until someone brings back Cassius's remains and his regalia from their long exile.

Then a new Prime Architect can be created, and the Omnifex's power as executor of the absent diminished."

Temple sniveler grasps at old bones, suckling for power like marrow, the chorus sneered. *A scavenger of great men long turned to dust.*

Isabelle had gotten good at not twitching when the chorus licked her ear, but their cynicism did inspire a question.

She asked, "You expect to be able to rescue his remains after centuries of neglect?"

"Not his mortal remains," Quill said. "But his regalia included an arcanite staff, every bit as adamant as the blade Ultor that you captured. Unless it fell into the Gloom, it will have survived. Furthermore, the ultimate purpose of this expedition is to start a colony, and l'impératrice agrees with me that it would be best if the colonists' spiritual needs are attended by a sect that builds from a foundation of observation and experiment rather than authority and obedience to doctrine."

Isabelle would rather the new colony eschewed religion entirely. Once one had a foundation of inquiry and a willingness to accept evidence, the very idea of doctrine and dogma became counterproductive. Alas, excluding the faithful from the colony was not a fight she was going to win, and while she trusted Quill no further than the width of a hair, the Observationalists were amongst the least offensive of the Temple's many sects.

More to the point, the chance of weakening the Omnifex and redrawing the political map of the College of Artifexes was not one Sireen would pass up.

"We sail on the first good wind when the weather clears," Isabelle said. "You'll be bunking with our other passenger. I imagine you will find his theology a fascinating study."

Sireen dismissed Quill, and Isabelle watched him all the way out.

Sireen made a small throat-clearing noise, and Isabelle whipped round to pay attention.

"Did you know your sparks flare up when you're angry? It's like pumping a bellows across hot coals, puff and flash and fall away as ash."

"I hardly notice them," Isabelle said. She had learned to ignore the cold sparks swirling around her in the same way she ignored her own heartbeat and the sound of her breath.

"You should be happy about Quill." Sireen's voice always had a musical quality. "His quest represents an opportunity to split the Temple and bleed away their power."

"Yes, Madame," Isabelle said.

Sireen snorted. "Do you know you never say 'Yes, Madame' to me except when you don't mean it? When you actually agree with me, you always have something more interesting to contribute. So tell me, what have I overlooked with Sagax Quill?"

"Not with Quill, per se," Isabelle said. "But with the idea of splitting the Temple. Our ancestors already tried that once, and we ended up with the Tyrant of Skaladin, which remains our mortal enemy nigh on a thousand years later. To defeat the Temple, we must make it unnecessary. The Temple feeds the starving and clothes the poor, so we must make sure nobody goes hungry and everyone has winter clothes. The Temple treats the sick, so we must build free infirmaries and train physicians in medicines that actually work. Civilization should be a gift that we give our children to be handed down and improved upon with each new generation. The Prophecy says that the Savior will come when we have prepared the world for him. I think that as we perfect the world we will turn around and discover we have saved ourselves."

"I think you underestimate the human ability to be dissatisfied," Sireen said, "and our need for spiritual allies and divine guidance."

Beliefs are but tools to leverage weak minds, her ancestral chorus pitched in, and the walls behind Sireen had turned to stone, moss-covered and pitted with age, with several half-decayed corpses in pilgrims' robes piled at their base. *Such is the fate of believers.*

Isabelle shook her head, refused to heed the macabre scene, and said, "I cannot imagine why anyone would want some invisible, intangible voice telling them what to do."

The audience concluded in short order, and Isabelle and Bitterlich bowed themselves out. They descended the spiral stair below Sireen's throne room. The steps curled around a shaft of quondam metal, one of the myriad strange and apparently senseless internal components of the Célestial Spires— immensely long tubes of adamant that rose from deep beneath the royal plateau several kilometers up into the clouds. The outer edge of the stairway's helix fell away into black nothingness.

Isabelle kept revisiting the conversations, looking for clues she'd missed, or angles she'd miscalculated. Even with her medicine dosage reduced, she still felt muddy-headed.

"Well done," Bitterlich said. "You definitely showed those peacocks you're not chicken."

Isabelle dragged herself out of her mental cyclone and bestowed him the glower he was looking for. "You've been waiting to say that all day, haven't you?"

Bitterlich contrived to look innocent. "I just thought it was another feather in your cap."

Isabelle resisted the urge to groan. As handsome and dashing and daring as Bitterlich was, his sense of humor drifted toward vile puns. The only way to deal with him when he got like this was to play dumb. She took off her hat and examined it carefully. "I don't understand. It doesn't have any more feathers than it did this morning."

Bitterlich glanced aside at her. "Since when did you become fusty?"

Isabelle replaced her hat and said primly, "I heard an atrocity being committed, and I stifled it."

"I have no egrets," Bitterlich said.

Isabelle refused to be flushed from cover. "I don't trust Quill."

"Do you think he was lying, or is this a manifestation of your generalized distrust of anyone in yellow robes?"

"Why are you assuming it can't be both?" she asked. "Will you follow him for me, see what he gets up to?"

"For you, mon capitaine, anything." He tipped his hat to her. "Is there anything in particular you suspect him of?"

"An ulterior motive," Isabelle said.

"The one he provided wasn't ulterior enough?"

"It seemed tailored to please Madame. Quill may not agree with the Omnifex or the Traditionalists, but I doubt he truly wants to fracture the Temple."

Bitterlich nodded and tugged at his lacy cuffs. "I'll follow him, but what about you? You seemed a little preoccupied. Are your passengers acting up?" He rubbed his temple with the catlike pad of his thumb.

"I just need a private spot to take my silence draught," Isabelle said, patting her belt pouch. She always carried some with her. "There's a difference between needing a little help and being helpless."

"I wasn't suggesting . . . I just don't want to abandon you."

Funny he should put it that way. He'd been on the verge of courting her when she told him about the voices in her head, and it was about at that point their blossoming intimacy had started to wither. Bitterlich was still funny, friendly, and ever so attentive, but he seemed more careful now and less playful. He certainly had never tried to kiss her again, despite her open invitation. He wore his reserve like a mask.

It wasn't hard to understand; nobody wanted to be intimate with a woman who might just be going mad. She supposed she couldn't blame him, as much as it grieved her, and as much as she felt a fool for keeping the lantern lit. She didn't want to go looking for someone else. She hadn't been looking for anyone when she found him.

"You haven't abandoned me," she said. Failing to come closer was not the same as leaving, and if an arms-length friendship was all she could get, she would take it and be glad. "I'll see you at the gala tonight. I'll even put on a gown."

Bitterlich's ears pricked up and his honey-colored eyes grew wide as if trying to lure this vision in from the future. "I pray that my quarry goes to bed early. I . . . uh. I had best be on my way." He backed up until only the tips of his toes were on the staircase and bowed to her. "Builder keep."

"Savior come," Isabelle replied.

Bitterlich fell backward off the stairs, a swan dive into the void that made Isabelle's heart stutter despite the fact she knew damned well he could fly. His whole body rippled like a flag in the wind, and he looped upward again in the form of a nightprowler bat, all black furry body and leathery wings. He orbited her several times chittering.

"One of these days you're going to turn into an ox by mistake, and I'm going to laugh," Isabelle said.

Bitterlich made one last pass and flittered away into the darkness.

Isabelle took a deep breath, let it out, and said, "All men are children."

"He is an animal, not a man." Isabelle found herself suddenly in a tunnel, long, dark, and narrow. Behind her, a great slavering beast howled for her blood.

Run! The urge nearly whelmed her, but she knew she was standing on a stair, surrounded by ways in which to fall to her death. She forced herself into a crouch, grabbed the pole for an extra point of stability, and waited for the errant memory to fade.

When at last she could find herself in space again, her right foot had nearly slipped from the step. The longer she went between draughts, the larger and stickier the ghost stains became, and the longer her hallucinations lasted.

Isabelle sat on the step, clinging to the quondam metal pole with her spark-hand, and waited for her racing heart to slow. Clearly her ancestors did not care if she lived or if she died. Most likely they were too broken and diffuse to care about anything. She had on occasion turned her attention inward and peeked into that mental space that her ancestral chorus resided. The Fenice called this space the everdream, and it seemed to exist at least partially strung out in some esoteric direction that had nothing to do with ordinary three-dimensional volumes. It was the same sort of construct as a Seelenjäger's soul vault, the place where they kept the soul skins of the animals they'd absorbed.

Yet whereas Bitterlich described his Seelengewölbe as carefully constructed and meticulously organized so that his soul strings didn't get tangled, Isabelle's head space was absolute bedlam. Bits of past lives swirled like shards of a stained-glass window in a vortex. When she chanced to touch one of the spinning panes, it sucked her in, immersing her in sudden experiences— she was a man, a woman, a judge, a fugitive, betrayed, triumphant—before flinging her out again. And every time the ghost shards took a little more of her with them.

Isabelle did not venture into the everdream anymore. Perhaps if she'd been brought up a Fenice, or had not ripped her sister's vitera out of the back of her head, she would have had the wherewithal to construct a useful framework for these memories. As it was, she had no option but to keep them locked away.

She took a silencing draught from her belt pouch, pulled the stopper, and tossed it down before she had a chance to spill it. Warm, slimy, and pungent, it was like slurping a decaying slug. Her stomach rebelled, as it always did. She took slow, steady breaths until the urge to vomit receded.

She pulled out her timepiece, marked the time in her notebook, then hauled herself to her feet. It generally took the stuff about half an hour to make her feel like she was walking through knee-deep water, then another half hour to muffle her ancestors to the point where they sounded like a distant snore.

As soon as she could straighten up, she marched down the stairs. Straight as an arrow or mad as a spoon, she still had work to do.

CHAPTER

Three

To catch up with Quill, Bitterlich the bat dipped and flipped through one of the many holes that ventilated the royal complex's current wooden infrastructure and flitted out into the ancient space it occupied. Le Ville Céleste was built inside one of five massive quondam spires, tubes of imperious metal that had survived the Breaking of the World. The insides of the tubes were not exactly hollow, the space being impinged by great buttresses of odd material and crisscrossed by cables and beams at angles that suggested no structural purpose.

More than anything else, the void between all these things was filled with darkness, old shadows that had witnessed the passing of centuries undisturbed, growing deeper with time until they seemed to stretch out of this world entirely.

Bitterlich kept up a string of clicks and chirps that ricocheted off the structures and painted for him a map of sound. It wasn't like sight exactly, coming in rapid bursts, with no sense of color but providing enough tactile acuity to guess if something was hard or soft.

Pipes, coils, and struts of strange materials spanned the void, some going nowhere, some twining together, a few sporting quondam artifacts like the fruit of some insane tree.

Most of the artifacts had long since died, killed in the Breaker's cataclysm or dying afterward like delicate plants in an untended garden. Still, a few hardy specimens remained, thriving like weeds, or maybe mushrooms in this old tomb. There were metals that throbbed with a dull inner light when seen from the corner of one's eyes, crystals that seemed to be constantly growing at their edges whilst shrinking into their own centers. There were fluids that clung to some surfaces and passed through all others, rippling to the rhythm of forces unseen.

Bitterlich had spent a great deal of time in this strange jungle in his youth. It was a setting good for both curiosity and despair, emotions he had experienced in abundance.

It was here he'd met Monsieur Belleaux, an empirical philosopher who'd spent his days exploring the spire, trying to quantify the strangeness. Bitterlich had helped his team navigate the quondam jungle, and in return Belleaux had introduced him to empirical philosophy. Looking back, Belleaux might have been the first Sanguinaire to instantly treat Bitterlich as if he was a full human and not some half-beast. Like Isabelle, he judged men by other standards, and never had time to waste on contempt, not when there was so much exploration to do.

"What we know about the world would fit in a thimble," he'd said. "What we know that we don't know would fill a bucket. What we don't know that we don't know is all the rest." He'd gestured at the whole of creation.

Perhaps that was how Isabelle had slid so easily past Bitterlich's defenses. She had that same ability to be captivated by reality. He hadn't expected her to be captivated by him.

He adored Isabelle. He hadn't meant to. He'd only wanted to like her because she was fierce and smart and cool under fire. He'd deployed witty banter, which was usually good at establishing rapport without provoking intimacy of feeling, but she'd foiled him by finessing secrets he'd sworn he'd never tell and helping him grieve for friends long dead. Banter had become flirting, and before he knew it, they were saving each other's lives and thwarting a coup d'état.

Even then, he might have escaped romantic longings, but she'd gone and kissed him, or rather she had beguiled him into kissing her. Not that there was anything wrong with the kiss. Indeed, it had been a prizewinning specimen of its type. He hadn't wanted it to stop. He'd wanted it to go on and on. He wanted to make her happy.

What he wanted didn't matter.

She'd all but sent him a gilded invitation to court her, to become her lover, her partner, dare he dream, her husband. She wanted children.

He couldn't give them to her. He needed to tell her that. Every day he didn't was a dereliction of friendship. He'd been derelict for months now, hoping that desire would fade on its own, without fuss or embarrassment . . . or shame.

Like a great wooden spiderweb spanning the gap between several large quondam pipes was a domed platform called the Middle Junction. Here most of the major pathways in le Ville Céleste converged. Several balconies opened up into the tube, giving visitors a chance to stare and wonder at the quondam landscape in which they were embedded.

Bitterlich darted through one of the arched openings, caught the air with his wings, and shot up to the domed ceiling, which was decorated with a suspended lattice like the spreading branches of a tree over a stylistic painting of a daytime sky.

Bat eyes weren't the best for big rooms, so he turned his attention inward and summoned a different shape. His animal shapes were all tucked away in his Seelengewölbe—a space within his mind that he was aware of in the same way he was aware of his limbs. Weaving a skin felt a bit like unraveling a bit of old cloth with one hand, stiff knotted threads bump-bumping as he tugged, whilst knitting a new shape with the other hand. There was a feeling of spilling away and then of tugging back together a shape one could anticipate but not really feel until the last thread was knotted.

Like knitting, it took real skill to improvise, and one had to be very careful to keep the skeins from getting tangled.

He landed on the suspended branches as a witch owl, a stout little bird with feathers the color of charcoal, huge eyes the color of embers, and excellent hearing.

At least a hundred people milled below. Courtiers and ambassadors, nobles, pilgrims, and scores of servants eddied their way across the floor. Several enterprising vendors had set up shop smack in the middle of the space selling buttered bread, mugs of soup, and the lemon pastries to which all native Célestials seemed to be completely addicted.

Quill moved through the crowd in fits and starts so as not to get bowled over by steadier pedestrians. Whatever had debilitated his body certainly hadn't stopped him from rising in the Temple. He was but one step below the exalted ranks. Such a man was not to be underestimated. He departed through the passage that led toward the foreign apartments where many honored guests were kept. What had happened to cripple him so?

Bitterlich flew back through the archway into the spires' interior and zipped ahead to the next major junction, where he combined the clinging pads of a gecko with the color-changing camouflage of a lesser reef kraken and slithered in through a small hole to await his mark. In this way, he forward-followed Quill to the guest quarters, where the sagax approached the suite given over to the Fenice delegation.

The thrill and terror of discovery raced up Bitterlich's spine. Did Quill have a master besides the Temple? He would not put it past the Fenice to send a spy after Isabelle, just to be sure, or an assassin to make the point moot.

The clayborn soldiers acting as door wardens recognized Quill on sight and pulled the curtain aside to let him enter. Bitterlich slipped through a crack in the wall and scuttled underneath the structure before creeping up again through a hole in the floor.

Bitterlich climbed up the back of a water jug as a mouse and surveyed the room over the lip. The guest rooms were usually sumptuously appointed with rope-sprung beds with feather mattresses and silk sheets, upholstered chairs, tapestries, and crystal lanterns. All of that luxury had been cleared away, and the rooms were as bare of ornament as a cowshed. The room was set up like the inside of an officer's tent, with bedrolls, backpacks, military standards, and camp stools. Given the Vecci predilection for extravagant display, Bitterlich speculated that this minimalistic approach was a deliberate expression of ostentatious austerity, an outward representation of their vow of vengeance against the Maximi and their descendants.

Bitterlich tried to imagine generation after generation of Fenice hunters undertaking a vow of poverty and enduring monkish conditions to complete a quest only to find that it had already been achieved. They might find that sense of purpose, especially in the absence of any other raison d'être, a little hard to let go.

Pyros and his companions had put away their *cappotto di piume*, the layer of close feathers and scales that covered their bodies and served as armor. Only their distinctive crest feathers remained to mark them as sorcerers. Ultor lay on a folding table, just enough of the blade showing to draw the eye.

Quill bowed his head and took a knee before Pyros, kissing his ring. Then he stood and assumed the posture of a subordinate giving a report. Unfortunately, he spoke in Vecci, a language opaque to Bitterlich. Pyros referred to Ultor at least twice, and both times Quill made a negating gesture. Damn but Bitterlich wished he had some idea of what they were saying. Was he Pyros's spy? What else could this meeting possibly mean?

The conversation did not last long. Quill knelt again, backed away, and departed.

Bitterlich squeezed himself out of the room and scurried along to follow the sagax.

—

Isabelle stood on a small wooden stool in Comtesse Coquetta's dressing room, while the comtesse's servants sewed her into a formal gown. Isabelle could have gone to tonight's gala in her uniform, but the event was in honor of her friend Gretl and the inauguration of her teaching hospital, and Isabelle didn't want to distract from the principal honoree by being any more outlandish than absolutely necessary.

Her head still droned with the voices of her ancestral chorus, but the silence potion had at least moved the party to a pantry in the back. She'd set her timepiece to alert her when the next draught was due.

Coquetta had put Isabelle in a deep-burgundy gown with just enough silver thread to flash in the presence of Isabelle's spark swarm.

Coquetta was a bountifully built woman with a pile of blond hair and a pale-blue gown. She spoke with a gossip's eager whisper: "Did you hear? Someone burned down the temple."

Isabelle's pulse picked up a little. News of the Temple was rarely good for her. "When?"

"Just a few hours ago," Coquetta said.

"Oh good," Isabelle said. "I have an alibi."

Coquetta huffed a laugh. "They will eventually get tired of hounding you and move on to pestering some other poor soul."

Isabelle said, "That sounds like punishment out of an old goblin story." She affected an old woman's cackle. "The only way you can be free of your curse is to pass it on to an unsuspecting innocent." She let her voice drop back to its usual register. "It sounds like what I should be doing is annoying the Temple so much that they spend all their energy trying to get rid of me. I can save some poor sod from getting his head chopped off for the crime of having an atavistic sorcery."

"Now you're just being dramatic," Coquetta said.

"Around you? Saints forefend." Isabelle said. "Do we know why it burned?"

Jean-Claude's voice rumbled from the curtainway behind her. "Hasdrubal turned into a pyrebird and set the place alight in the middle of the oration."

Joy lifted Isabelle's mood and she twisted to turn, which earned her a sharp squeak from the seamstress, who was trying to make Isabelle's skirt fill up naturally despite the fact that she had no hips to speak of.

Coquetta strode over to Jean-Claude and took his hands. "Welcome, my friend."

"Jean-Claude," Isabelle said. "Were you there? What happened?"

"The good news is, the hunter's eye worked like you said it would. We tracked three of the Last Men to the temple."

Pride in her creation bolstered Isabelle's spirit. "I'm glad it worked, but if that's the best news, what is the worst?"

"The worst is that people died," Jean-Claude said. He told them of the battle they'd fought and its aftermath. "The crowd was packed in and when the gunfire started they panicked; some died in the crush. Some died in the fire. We won't know how many until they've cleaned up the rubble."

Cold dismay settled in Isabelle's breast. "That's horrible."

"Poor souls," Coquetta said, and made a sign against evil.

Jean-Claude shook his head in the manner of a horse bothered by a stinging fly. "We gave aid and comfort where we could. Everything that can be done has been, save for the mourning. On matters yet unresolved, Hasdrubal managed to make off with the Hand of Saint Cynessus, a reliquary with an excellent pedigree."

Coquetta tilted her head. "Do you have any idea what he means to do next?"

Jean-Claude said, "He said he was going to unmake all the Breaker has wrought."

"That's . . . ambitious," Coquetta said.

Jean-Claude grunted. "He did not provide me with detailed plans as to what he meant by it. Isabelle is the only person I know who's actually talked to him, beyond the ritual exchange of insults and improbable threats. I was hoping you might have some insight."

Isabelle shook her head carefully so as not to upset the woman with the needle. "I only spoke to him the one time, and not at great length. All he did was tell me how Lael rescued him from a cruel master in Skaladin, a story which was almost certainly a lie."

She paused, considering her recent audience. "It may be just a coincidence, but I met Hasdrubal at the same place I met Sagax Quill. They were both at Lael's soiree, dithering over his research notes, and Madame just put Quill on my ship."

Jean-Claude's brow furrowed. "Does Madame know about that connection?"

"It was in my report," Isabelle said. "She believes that Lael was trying to recruit Quill into his coup just as he tried to recruit me, and with as much success."

Jean-Claude cast a glance at Coquetta. "Have your people heard anything?" Coquetta was Sireen's social adviser and gossipmonger. The high nobility kept her very busy sifting through a constant churn of scandal, sedition, and conspiracy.

"Hasdrubal doesn't get invited to many dinner parties," Coquetta said. "And Quill seems to be something of an ascetic. I'll see what I can find out, put on a small salon to raise funds to help those faithful who lost family in the fire, ask my clerical friends, chat them up about Quill and see what comes up. It will take time though."

"Thank you," Jean-Claude said. "Just pass the gleanings on to Impervia, and you might want to add Quaestor Czensos to your list of invitees."

"He's a snake, that one, but it would be rude not to invite him," Coquetta said.

Isabelle asked, "A snake how?"

"Cold-blooded, venomous, slithers into any hole," Coquetta said. "He's never met a non-pedigreed sorcerer he doesn't think is Breaker-touched, and his path is lined with gravestones. 'Better to slay a thousand innocents than risk a single abomination running free.'"

"Lovely man," Isabelle said dryly.

Coquetta said, "Poor Saint Cynessus. I always thought he got a bad deal." This got her a curious look from Jean-Claude. She continued, "Well, think about it. Iav betrayed the Builder and stole his power. The Breaker entered the world. The Primus Mundi shattered. The saints ran for the Vault of Ages. Saint Cynessus held the door for them. He looked out to see if there was anyone else coming and got blinded for his trouble. And after all that, now some wretched heretic has stolen his hand."

"He was blinded for disobedience," Isabelle said. She had always been suspicious of that parable; looking over one's shoulder seemed a trivial thing for the architect of all creation to be worried about when his great project was cascading toward ruin.

"In better news," Jean-Claude said, "I've found you a cabin girl."

A sharp and senseless dread filled Isabelle. "I don't need a cabin girl. I've got Marie."

"She's your bodyguard, not your handmaid," Jean-Claude said. "Besides, Marie agrees with me on this. She needs to spend more time on her training."

"Which just means you bamboozled her first," Isabelle said. She loved Jean-Claude like a father, but he was a very creative editor of the truth.

"I just pointed out that she can't be watching your back while she's straightening your knickers and fetching your tea. She's got to be free to move around," Jean-Claude said. "Besides, it's not like you won't both be on the same ship, sleeping in the same cabin."

Isabelle had to admit the logic of this, even if the thought of Marie drifting away made her sick to her heart.

"Who is this would-be cabin girl?"

"Her name is Rebecca," Jean-Claude said. "She's a pickpocket."

Isabelle scowled. "The last thing I need on my ship is a thief."

"I prefer to think of her as a plucky orphan," Jean-Claude said. "She impressed Djordji. She's smart, and gets fast under pressure."

Isabelle glowered at him. She didn't need surprise additions to her crew, but neither did she want to hold Marie back from the path she'd chosen.

"A delightful scamp," Jean-Claude prodded. "An adorable moppet."

"Now you're just larding it on," Isabelle said. She took a deep breath. "But as you say, I can't be tying Marie down. Bring Rebecca to the ship tomorrow. I want to tell her all the things you neglected to. I'm guessing you didn't sit down with her and make her understand the legal ramifications of swearing an oath, and what it means to serve under military law, and the fact that she'll have to complete at least ten years of service regardless of what happens to you or me."

Jean-Claude said, "We hadn't reached that stage of the negotiations yet. I didn't want to scare her off before I outlined the benefits of joining the navy, such as escaping her orphan indenture. She hardly believes escape is possible."

Isabelle remembered she had makeup on just in time to avoid rubbing her eyes in exasperation. "Out of the frying pan and don't worry about the fire?"

"You'll like her," Jean-Claude said.

"I'm sure I will," Isabelle said, "which means I need to give her a real choice and the whole set of facts."

—

Jean-Claude sat across a small table from Impervia in her receiving room. It was a casually decorated space with embroidered chairs and bookshelves filled with a selection of books, knickknacks, and conversational artifacts, assuming one wanted to start a conversation about foiled assassination attempts, cloak-and-dagger diplomacy, or the efficacy of various types of poisons. There was a portrait of Impératrice Sireen on one wall, signaling Impervia's allegiance to the new reine, and wide pastoral scenes on the other three walls, compensating for the fact that the room had no windows.

Impervia glowered at Jean-Claude over the top of the dram of emberwine she'd been nursing for the last half hour. "So you managed to burn down a temple, lose a true reliquary, and let Hasdrubal escape with no hint whatsoever where he's gone or what he means to do, and you have the nerve to walk away and dump the whole thing in my lap." Her bloodshadow rippled like a restive snake.

With Impervia it was hard to tell if she was actually angry with him or just practicing. In either case, it did no good to shrink before her. The thing she liked, the thing she needed, were people she couldn't intimidate.

"I wouldn't want you to get bored," he said. "Besides, without me, you wouldn't know the true reliquary was in play."

Impervia's half-moon eyes narrowed. "You have no idea how much I long to be bored. My excitement means danger to my empire and my reine."

Jean-Claude laughed. "If you couldn't find a conspiracy, you'd invent one just to keep yourself occupied. What I want to know is what the local Skaladin are saying about it." Despite the fact that the Tyrant of Skaladin was the great enemy, the penultimate evil just below the Breaker herself, the tyrant still managed to have agents all around the Risen Kingdoms. Impervia's counterspies kept track of them, and they usually provided some insight into the tyrant's plans: cloak, dagger, shadow, and whisper.

"Surprisingly little," Impervia said. She frowned. "I got the impression that the Maze's spymasters weren't informed of Hasdrubal's part in Lael's coup, which doesn't really surprise me. The Master of Eyes had every reason not to involve them. If they'd been exposed, it would have revealed Lael as a pawn of the tyrant and shifted the balance against him.'

"Speaking of the tyrant, I have received word of a great stirring in the City of Gears. The tyrant has called in his banners and there is word of a fleet assembling in the Sundered Isles. I've already passed this on to Fleet Command, but I thought you should know."

That news sent a shiver down Jean-Claude's spine. The Sundered Isles were Skaladin strongholds in the Hoary Gyre, well within striking distance of Isabelle's intended flight path.

"Do they know the *Thunderclap* is headed that way?" Jean-Claude asked. It had proven impossible to keep the existence of Isabelle's expedition a secret. By now it was nearly common knowledge that she was hunting the *Conquest* treasure. What l'Empire had managed to keep secret was where precisely that prize was located. Jean-Claude had heard many theories bandied about in the past months, but so far no one had guessed that the wreck might lie north beyond the impenetrable wall of the Bittergale. All of her competition would be playing catch-up.

"I must assume that they do know and will be hunting you. Hasdrubal might not have accompanied Lael on his trip through the Bittergale, but we have no reason to doubt he knew where his co-conspirator was going."

"So our only advantage is that we have Hailer Dok and the *Conquest*'s keel shard."

"I wouldn't be too sure about that advantage, either. The Skaladin keep Windcaller slaves along with every other type of sorcerer."

"Even if they do have a Windcaller, that doesn't mean that person knows how to penetrate the Bittergale."

"True, but if Dok figured out how to get through, someone else can as well."

"And the *Conquest* shard?" Jean-Claude asked.

"Just don't lose it."

"I'll tell Isabelle." Jean-Claude finished the last of his drink and set the glass on the table.

"How is she adjusting to her new role?" Impervia asked.

"She can handle it," Jean-Claude said.

"That sounds . . . incomplete." Impervia finally took a meaningful draw at her liquor. "I always have a hard time picturing her in the military."

Jean-Claude thought about Isabelle all the time, but he rarely had to tease apart his own understanding of her into discrete sentences. "She wants peace, but she's no pacifist. Still, I don't think she would have accepted the commission if she was being sent to war. She's in it for the exploration. She's really looking forward to getting aloft. The sailing she likes."

"And you?"

"Not looking forward to the flying-around bit," he said.

"Have you ever thought about staying behind?" she asked, a note of caution in her voice. "I could use your help."

He'd thought about it a lot. Thirty years ago, he'd missed his chance to make a life with Impervia, which was probably a good thing. They'd both gone on to build separate lives, raise their own children. Now they had a chance to be friends and lovers, support without dependency.

"Have you ever thought about coming along?" he asked.

"More than once," she said, and let out a long, soft breath. "But I'm not going and you're not staying. Oil and vinegar may taste good together, but they always separate."

"Life as a salad," he said. "One day fresh; the next wilted."

Impervia made a noise that was somewhere between a cough and a laugh. "I always planned to live a long life, but I never expected to get old. If I had, maybe I would have managed to fall into adventure when I was young. Instead I end up an old spider tied to her own web."

"Is that where you got your taste in bed play?" Jean-Claude asked.

She narrowed her eyes at him. "That wasn't an offer."

"My apologies," he said, and bowed his head over his hand.

"It wasn't a rejection, either." She slid off her chair and was hardly any taller sashaying toward him than she had been sitting down. She was a tiny woman, though by no means weak. She kept up a daily regimen that would have knackered someone half her age, and her bloodshadow could rip a man to pieces or reduce him to a soul smudge with barely a thought.

She stood before him arms crossed, one bronze leg peeking out from the slit in her skirt. "There's elderroot in the green bottle," she said. It was an aphrodisiac of notable potency. "If you're sailing off for months, I get your undivided attention tonight."

Now, *that* was an invitation.

The last time Isabelle had been in the Royal Agonesium for the Deranged it had been closed off and oppressive, covered in grime, dimly lit, and muted by cobwebs. Tonight it was bright, airy, and clean. L'impératrice had given the building and a large endowment to Isabelle's friend Gretl, a superlative surgeon, to turn it into a medical school.

This royal endorsement had the effect of providing Gretl and her apprentice, Darcy, with more prospective students than she could reasonably handle. L'impératrice would be her first student, along with some clayborn students brought in on merit, and a cohort of Sanguinaires called the Succoring Shadows, who had dedicated themselves to using their bloodshadows for healing, not harm. Isabelle, having been on the receiving end of more shadowburns than she cared to remember, still cringed at the thought.

Tonight, the hall was packed with comtes and ducs, the sugar on top of the upper crust. Sanguinaires dressed all in white to flaunt their bloodshadows were interspersed with a few Seelenjägers, including a huge man with the aspect of a boar and a woman who seemed to be half badger. There were also several silver-eyed Glasswalkers, or at least their espejismos, reflections that they'd cast through a mirror from wherever their bodies currently waited. The foremost Aragothic dignitary, one Duque Mendoza, captured Isabelle on the way in to convey regrets from the Crown that her former betrothed, Príncipe Julio, would be unable to attend.

"Something has stirred up the Skaladin on our antiwise frontier," Mendoza said. "It's probably just more of their internal politics boiling over the edge of the kettle, but the príncipe is attending the defenses, just in case. He does instruct me to say that he wishes you fair skies."

Isabelle dipped her head in understanding. "Please thank Julio and give him my regards." Could the stirring Skaladin be related to the troubles Jean-Claude was having with Hasdrubal? There was no way to tell at this distance.

Isabelle stood with Gretl in the receiving area, to help keep her company. Being deaf and mute hadn't stopped Gretl from amassing extraordinary skill as a physician and surgeon, but even at her own celebration, the high and mighty avoided her in favor of her slightly less objectionable assistant.

"How is your head?" Gretl's hands and body flowed in three-dimensional hand speech.

"About the same," Isabelle replied in the same language. "I let the potion go too long this morning. Had some hallucinations."

Worry and exasperation took turns parading across Gretl's face. "Don't do that. The brain takes a long time to heal, but it won't get better if you keep ripping the wound open."

"I know," Isabelle said. "I won't let it happen again. I'll be fine."

Gretl shook her head. "Liar. I know you. What you'll do is keep trudging, no matter how bad it gets, until you finally hit a wall you can't bash through with your forehead. Then it will be up to your friends to gather your pieces and stitch them back together."

"I haven't been given much choice," Isabelle said.

Gretl's eyebrows lifted. "Did you ask for another choice? I know you helped me get all this." She gestured to the agonesium cum teaching hospital. "You helped Valérie start her business. You helped Marie become a bodyguard."

"I had very little to do with that," Isabelle protested.

"You said yes," Gretl countered. "And you said it a lot. You said yes after other people said no, and you got other people what they wanted. If you really wanted your own university, Sireen would have given you one. You could have had your own garden and your own studio, and you could have worked on your mathematics and painted solarsets and gone sailing on your yacht. But you didn't ask. Madame said, 'Let's make you a frigate capitaine and send you to the far end of the world into dangers undreamt of,' and you jumped like a cricket. As much as you want to make everyone around you happy, you also want the adventure. I'm glad for you, but don't tell me you didn't have a choice. And don't go thinking you have to win or die, either. There's no Lael or Kantelvar out there trying to wreck the kingdom. If your head goes to pieces, let someone else take over and let yourself heal."

Isabelle frowned at this reprimand. Everyone seemed to think she was more stubborn than she really was. It wasn't as if she didn't take advice from those she trusted, but in this matter no one had advice she could act on.

"Do you think my head will go to pieces?" Isabelle asked worriedly.

Gretl hesitated, then made a careful reply. "The potion I gave you helps some people who have visions and hear voices. It seems to be working the way it should on you, but that doesn't mean your injury isn't unique. You literally yanked a Fenice vitera out of your brain. I don't know if your troubles are because of what it put into you or the damage it did coming out. As long as the potion keeps working, I'd say you should be fine, but that means you have to take it on schedule."

"I will," Isabelle said. "Even if I don't want to."

Social obligation called Gretl away. Isabelle moved around the crowd at the edge of the room, looking for friendly faces but remaining otherwise unobtrusive. Somewhat more than half the people in this room had voted in Parlement to strip her of her social identity, and she saw no reason to entertain them. Indeed, having congratulated Gretl she saw little reason to linger, and merely counted the minutes until it would be socially acceptable to leave.

A servant she recognized approached her bearing a tray of wine goblets in both hands. He was a resident of the facility, a man of middle years in black livery with a white sash emblazoned with a red blood drop. Isabelle met his gaze and saw battle scars in the rings around his eyes.

"Thomas," Isabelle said. She did not accept a cup. Wine did not mix well with her medicine. "It's good to see you up and about."

"A good day, Capitaine," he said, lifting his chin. "A good day."

Thomas had been an advocate until some calamity had shattered his mind and let a Torment in. Now he carried drinks in hands that quaked.

According to Gretl, the job and its uniform gave him a sense of dignity and purpose he'd been lacking. His life was improving, but it was like building a sand castle one grain at a time.

Isabelle watched him walk away, taking every step as if he were on a tightrope in a high wind. Would she end up like him, a shadow of herself, or worse as one of the blank-eyed muttering ones who knew no reality beyond nightmare?

The very idea filled her with a dread that no amount of reason could suppress. If she had one constant joy in life, it was the freedom of thought and reason. Without that, she was nothing.

Yet she had dealt with fear before. The only answer was to keep focused on the goal, to keep pushing forward even into soul-shivering terror, even through despair. If she was doomed to madness, she would race it to the horizon ere it caught her up.

"Madame Isabelle," said a voice as old and fruity as a shriveled plum. It heralded the arrival of an older Sanguinaire woman in a dress that set the standard for fussy, exploding with lace at every aperture like a pressure vessel captured at the moment of bursting.

"Capitaine," Isabelle said. Perhaps she would have been better off wearing her uniform. "I'm afraid you have the advantage of me, Madame . . ."

"Duchesse Belda du Lavaudieu," she said imperiously. "The one who paid for the *Thunderclap.*" Two of her servants posted themselves nearby, forming enough of a cordon to keep the rest of the celebrants away.

"I'm so pleased to meet you," Isabelle said, her courtier's smile asserting itself over her natural reticence. It was not unlikely that Duchesse Belda was amongst the cohort who had voted to strip Isabelle of her rights.

"Of course you are, dear," Belda said. "I just want to make sure that you have everything that you need for success on this expedition. I expect good returns on my investment."

"The ship and its crew are well prepared," Isabelle said. It was one of the great flaws of l'Empire's system that la reine had to lean on her nobles to pay for things like warships, which naturally encouraged said nobles to believe they ought to have some say in how the ships were used. It was entirely possible that Sireen had offered something in exchange for this civic donation, but if so, she hadn't told Isabelle what it was.

Belda leaned in and stared up at Isabelle, "Are you sure? I only want the best people on my ship, and I have heard rumors of undesirables."

"I selected my officers myself," Isabelle said in a tone that ought to have suggested this was dangerous ground. It had not been easy to find officers who would submit to a woman capitaine, even at double pay and a promise of promotion.

"Not all of them," Belda said. "From what I understand the Imperial Marines have their own chain of command."

"Yes, but I trust their commander implicitly," Isabelle said. Having Bitterlich serve as the marine commander was one of her chief reassurances against any possible mutiny.

The duchesse made a tsking noise. "Oh, but you shouldn't, my dear, I've heard the most horrible beastly things about him."

Anger flared in Isabelle's heart. The Sanguinaire generally looked down on Seelenjägers and thought of them as animals, but she'd never met a kinder or more considerate man than Bitterlich, and she would not have him slandered.

"Madame Duchesse," she said coldly. "I regret to inform you that you have been listening to the wrong people."

Belda's eyes narrowed and she lifted her fan as if to hide her words from lip readers in the audience. "Don't be so quick to dismiss. All men are beastly, but that Seelenjäger once tried to rape Comtesse Eulalie."

Isabelle felt like she'd been punched in the gut. What Belda suggested was impossible. Bitterlich had never shown anything but polite discretion around Isabelle and her ladies.

Careful of her tone, Isabelle said, "What evidence do you have to support this accusation?"

"Oh, it never got to an accusation," Belda said. "The beast-man—"

Isabelle cut her off. "Madame Duchesse, I will not hear unfounded accusations. Good evening to you." She stepped away smartly, bowed ever so slightly, and tipped the hat she wasn't wearing. "Builder keep you."

She did not wait to hear if the duchesse gave the proper reply, but strode off at a pace the old woman would not be able to match. Yet no speed could shake off the sheen of slime the duchesse had drenched her with. Yes, seemingly decent men could turn out to be fiends, but it was also true that rapists tended to be recurrent in their crimes. Bitterlich went out of his way to be inoffensive. He'd sought no power over her, protected her secrets, and had given her his own. Neither did he seem to have any interest whatsoever in sex, be it for power, procreation, or pleasure. More's the pity.

All men lie, but their secrets are your leverage, muttered the ancestral chorus, surging up like a shadow from the deep sky and then submerging again.

Isabelle checked her timepiece, but her next scheduled draught wasn't for hours yet. The chorus was just riled up because she was. Most likely Belda was trying to turn Isabelle away from Bitterlich so that she could suggest a replacement. The navy was the world's single largest repository of ne'er-do-well nephews, and putting one of her Sanguinaire relations on Isabelle's ship would give Belda insight into and influence over Isabelle's greater mission.

Yet why had Belda thought Isabelle would believe such a horrid lie? Surely if such a tale existed Isabelle would have heard about it by now . . . or if she hadn't, Coquetta would have.

Isabelle craned her neck and spied the gossipmonger plying her trade, drifting through the room introducing newcomers, doling out fresh ideas, and listening to chatter. She sifted the high court babble for the conversations being had beneath the surface of the language, the undercurrents that pulled society along.

Isabelle caught her gaze and tapped her own earlobe, requesting a moment of her very busy schedule. Coquetta eased her current escort into the waiting arms of her political allies and swept around to guide Isabelle on a stroll through a less inhabited corner of the room.

"You look less than pleased, considering the joyous circumstances." Coquetta said.

"I am perfectly delighted by Gretl's success," Isabelle said.

"And your own, presumably," Coquetta replied. "So this must be trouble in my domain."

"Something you might tell me about," Isabelle said, but the accusation laid at Bitterlich's feet was not something she cared to repeat. "I was just accosted by Belda du Lavaudieu."

"Martyred saints," Coquetta muttered. "That hag. Let me guess; she filled your ears with that nasty business about Major Bitterlich."

Isabelle's stomach curdled. "Are you saying it's true?"

"I acknowledge the rumor exists," Coquetta said. "And its Belda's favorite pot to stir."

"So what do you know to be true?" Isabelle asked.

"Very little," Coquetta said. "You have to remember this was over a decade ago. Comtesse Eulalie was newly arrived in the capital, here to be introduced to prospective husbands. Bitterlich was young, handsome, and horny. He was warned against courting her, but that only encouraged him, and he applied himself to the project with the sort of zeal only a suicidally romantic sixteen-year-old can muster. Eulalie encouraged him because who doesn't like that attention? And then . . ." Coquetta spread her hands in a gesture of unknowing. "One morning, Bitterlich turned up in one of the water channels below Highwall Street, mostly drowned and shadowburned within an inch of his life. It took him months to recover, and he never would say what happened to him, but Eulalie was married off very quickly and without any of the usual fanfare for a wedding at that level.

"The crowd, in its collective wisdom, put these two facts together and came up with story that nicely filled in the chasm between them. Clearly the lovely Sanguinaire girl had rebuked the beastly Seelenjäger. Rejected, he became enraged and tried to force himself on her. The particulars of the story diverge from that point depending on who is telling it. The most popular version is that Eulalie's father discovers his daughter's humiliation, revenges himself on Bitterlich, and marries his daughter to the first man who will take her in haste before he finds out she's damaged goods."

"That's appalling," Isabelle said, cold and sick and outraged all at once. Bitterlich would never do such a thing. At least, not the Bitterlich she knew. How different had he been at age sixteen? She cringed to remember what a nitwit she had been when she was younger.

"Oh yes," Coquetta said. "Every word of it is horrible, and therefore delicious, and far too outlandish to ever be completely forgotten. The truth, if it were anything less interesting, could not compete with the story and would never serve to banish it."

Isabelle sought a defining flaw in the story. "If that's true, wouldn't Eulalie's father have killed Bitterlich?"

"You could make that argument," Coquetta said. "Many have, but his detractors point out that he was Grand Leon's 'special pet,' and murdering him would have been a great risk."

"But—"

Coquetta raised a forestalling hand. "Unfortunately, Capitaine, this is not a rumor you can resolve with reason. The only thing that matters is whether you trust Bitterlich more than you trust Belda."

This suggestion left Isabelle no less unsettled. Rape was not an accusation she wanted to hear leveled at her friend. "And what does Eulalie say about all this?" Isabelle asked.

"As far as I know, she's never said a word about it, and no one of any good taste would ever ask her either." Coquetta said this last bit pointedly. "In fact, getting you to bring the rumor to Eulalie's attention may be Belda's intent. If she can get you to offend la reine vis-à-vis her confidante, it might cost your commission—"

"And she could suggest a replacement," Isabelle said. *A return on her investment, indeed.*

Then Isabelle's brain caught up with what Coquetta had said. "Wait. Did you say the comtesse is here?"

"You really have had your head buried in the military minutiae, haven't you? Eulalie is a founding member of the Succoring Shadows and a primary sponsor of this teaching hospital. She'll be in the first class of students and she'll be helping Sireen dedicate the place."

Isabelle felt suddenly queasy. "Bitterlich is supposed to meet me here."

Coquetta looked thoughtful. "I can see how that would be uncomfortable, but it's not a catastrophe. There's no need for them to speak to each other, and even if they do, neither is likely to bring the matter up."

Coquetta had a point, but Isabelle still felt sick to her stomach. She saw no reason to subject Bitterlich to what was likely to be an exquisitely painful encounter, and if Eulalie was to be Gretl's student, she'd be around for years.

A fanfare of trumpets shook her from her brooding. Impératrice Sireen entered the room accompanied by her consort husband, the former roi le Duc DeStJabreaux, once known as Grand Leon.

Sireen's arrival set off a cascading series of formalities and protocols that gave Isabelle no opportunity to retreat, though she kept looking around for Bitterlich. She willed the interminable formalities to go faster so she could sneak off and await him outside.

Everyone honored l'impératrice, and then Sireen graced them all with an aria from a Vecci opera, *Il lamento dei Maximi*, her handsome voice conjuring joy and sorrow in every heart.

Isabelle did not speak Vecci per se, but the passages called up feelings from her past lives, and ghost stains from her ancestral chorus supplanted her vision and sense of place in the present world.

Isabelle found herself standing on a tall, snaggletoothed shard of sandstone, thrust up out of the pitiless Ash Wastes. The relentless sun hammered down and the wind rasped her face. Far across the drifting dunes rose a pillar of dust, the Skaladin Army on the march, the boom of their drums rolling before them like thunder before a storm of blood and steel. There would be no escaping this time. With her back to the Thornhills and the deep sky, she would make her final stand . . . at least in this lifetime.

And then the present tugged at Isabelle once more. Her breath caught, and she dabbed tears from her eyes. It was not often that such visions of the past overwhelmed her, but that song had been written about her . . . about her many-times-great-grandsire Primus Maximus. All too well it captured his despair, his lust for battle, an emotion Isabelle never would have admitted to, much less reveled in. If only he'd had the good grace to finish dying, she wouldn't be stuck with this damned muddle of memories in her head.

A royal page appeared at Isabelle's side, "Mada . . . I mean, Capitaine Isabelle, l'impératrice requests your presence."

An imperial request was as good as a command, so Isabelle made as much haste as was seemly through the crowd and was permitted into Sireen's presence. Also present was a Sanguinaire woman in an empire-waisted gown that did not manage to hide the fact that she was some months pregnant.

Isabelle bowed to l'impératrice. "How may I serve l'Empire?"

"Faithfully, I presume," Sireen said, and gestured to the other woman. "Capitaine Isabelle, be known to my friend Comtesse Eulalie. We were just talking about you, and thought it might be more pleasant to talk with you."

The comtesse was about Isabelle's age, and spritely despite her prenatal passenger. She had wide eyes, straight teeth, and a scarlet bloodshadow in which darker forms seemed to flit, like fish in a crimson lake. It was an effect Isabelle had never seen before, a reminder that not all Sanguinaire were created equal.

She was precisely the last person in this room to whom Isabelle wanted to talk, which was irrational—Isabelle had heard no rumor about any wrongdoing on her part—but an imperial command was never to be ignored. Isabelle plastered on her best courtier's smile and said, "Madame Comtesse, it is an honor to meet you. I am made to understand that we have you to thank for these renovations." Isabelle waved her spark-hand at the bright building around them.

"It is a Sanguinaire's duty to the Builder to make the world worthy to accept the Savior's coming. We guide and mold the clayborn, we improve the land, and we untangle the riddles that were left behind, but if we are to remain worthy teachers we must improve ourselves as well."

The notion that the clayborn were just things to be shaped offended every fiber of Isabelle's being, and she had long since given up on leaving such statements unchallenged. "The clayborn have more of an effect on the saintborn than we have on them. The aetherkeel, the orrery, the printing press, and almost all of the medicine you are about to learn were all clayborn discoveries and inventions."

Isabelle didn't need Belda's help to get into trouble with Sireen. She could do that on her own.

"After the saintborn primed them with proper moral guidance," Eulalie replied. "Remember they were in a state of barbarism when our ancestors emerged from the Vault of Ages. Fighting with each other for scraps like hungry dogs. It was only the saints' firm hands that saved them from devolving into beasts."

"That is what Legend says," Isabelle allowed, though her smile took on an edge. "But the bones of the elder cities were laid before the saints returned, and antiquarians have discovered aqueducts and monuments and great marketplaces that the clayborn built and grew during the Bleaktimes."

Eulalie waved this away. "Bees make combs, but that does not make them wise, and they can be improved greatly by the apiarist who provides for and protects them."

Sireen, clearly annoyed by this unexpected squabble, said, "Isabelle, Eulalie and I were discussing one of the structural problems with bloodshadow surgery, and I thought you might be able to turn your mechanical mind to it." She made a go-ahead gesture to Eulalie, who beamed as if she lived in a world devoid of ire.

"The efficacy of bloodshadow surgery greatly depends on how much of the injury we can see. As a rule, the more light we can throw on a subject, the more of their insides we can see in their shadow, but even strapping our patients into a shadowpult spotlight leaves the image murky. La reine believes you might be able to help us clarify things."

Isabelle hated bloodshadows. There was nothing so grotesque as turning a human being into a bloodhollow. Yet people were bound to use the power they possessed to whatever advantage they could, and demanding all Sanguinaire abandon the principal use of their sorcery was a fool's crusade. The only way forward was to change the principal use from harm to healing, and then to cast opprobrium on those who debased it.

For such a purpose Isabelle might be kind to the Breaker herself.

She asked, "What exactly do you see in a person's shadow?"

"It's as if the whole body has been pressed flat and made transparent," Eulalie said. "Our bloodshadows can bypass the skin and attack the ailment directly."

"Does it matter which direction the patient is facing? The shadow would be a different shape if he was sideways."

Eulalie grinned broadly. "Madame told me you were quick."

Sireen, having corrected course to her satisfaction, said, "I trust you two will cooperate."

"Yes, Madame," they said in ragged syncopation, and Sireen glided away to other duties.

The shadows in Eulalie's bloodshadow flowed in unison like a murmuration of starlings on the wing.

Isabelle asked, "Do those dark spots affect the way your bloodshadow works?"

"You mean my little phantasms?" Eulalie said, drawing her shadow up her body and along her arms until she seemed to have been dipped in blood, if blood had indistinct shadow fish swimming in it. "I've always had them."

"I'm surprised the Temple hasn't taken an interest in them," Isabelle said. The shadows looked like soul smudges to her. If the Temple had investigated Eulalie, that would at least be one thing she and Isabelle had in common.

Eulalie lifted her nose. "They wouldn't dare. My pedigree is impeccable, witnessed and notarized every generation back to the Secondborn Kings. My greatest grandfather was Saint Guyot le Sanguinaire himself, first of the unbroken line." She rubbed her mounding belly. "My blood is pure."

———

Bitterlich perched on the peak of a stone gable across from the burned-out temple. He sorrowed for the dead and their families, who had only come to hear words of wisdom from Saint Cynessus and prepare for spring after a bitter winter. He would miss the grand old building, too, with its copper dome kept polished to shine in the Solar's light. It did not take much listening to learn that the gathering had been attacked by a Seelenjäger, nor much logic to deduce that it must have been the Skaladin Hasdrubal whom Jean-Claude had been hunting. It hardly took any experience at all to realize that, being a Seelenjäger himself, it would probably not be wise to pull on his erstepelz and ask more detailed questions, even if he hadn't had other duties.

Sagax Quill stood on the blackened stone front steps, where only iron bands from the door remained, holding on to the ghosts of the wood like the shackles of Torment-bound souls. Ash swirled around his ankles, the foul air gusted around his face. He looked like he'd forgotten how to breathe.

The city, amazingly, had already begun to mitigate the damage, like a wound scabbing over. Teams of laborers shifted the debris and cranes were being erected to take down the now unstable walls. The markets up the street in either direction had sensed opportunity and set up stalls for food and drink for men likely to be working through the night.

Bitterlich half expected Quill to prostrate himself in the ash, but grand gestures were apparently not his forte. Still stricken, he stumbled across the lane to a rectory that had been turned into a hospital. A flying squad of morticians awaited outside with litters to be borne for the many who passed the Ravenous Gate.

Bitterlich dropped into an alley, became a cat, and sauntered through the doorway as if he were lord of the domain. He strolled through the sick ward. Someone had brought in several alchemical heaters to help the stricken stay warm, and the air was as warm and sticky as fresh blood. The smell of fever and rot mixed with soap. Moans and mutters drifted freely in the fog.

Quill had found Orator Marceau tending the wounded. Marceau had been a fixture at the temple as long as Bitterlich could remember, an indefatigable soul who shared the Builder's word because he delighted in it: a storyteller rather than a judge.

Bitterlich scooted under a low bench and listened to Marceau's version of Hasdrubal's attack. It was clear he'd been stunned and out of his depth as soon as the attack began.

"How did he even know about the reliquary?" Quill asked when Marceau described how Hasdrubal had taken the old box of bones and fled.

"I don't know," Marceau said. "I swear I didn't tell anyone."

Quill let out a heavy breath. "It's not your fault, and it's not the end of the world."

Bitterlich's whiskers twitched with his curiosity. There was always a relic brought out on the Feast of Saint Cynessus. Bitterlich had seen it a dozen times. What was so special about this one? Alas, the conversation did not return to it.

The city's bell tolled the hour. Gretl's gala would have started by now. Isabelle would be there. He weighed the odds of Quill doing anything else interesting, and decided to risk letting him go. Perhaps Isabelle could help him make sense of what he'd witnessed. He took wing in owl form and swooped over the darkening city. He imagined dancing with Isabelle, her hand on his shoulder and his on her hip, her big smile and her rose-and-lavender eyes flashing . . . but no. To court her would be to lead her away from the family she desired and strand her on a dead twig.

He should make his intentions clear to her. Or rather, his lack of intentions. Yes, she'd ask why, and the mere thought of that conversation left him cold—"I am not a man" were impossible words to say—but putting it off wouldn't make it easier.

He winged it to the agonesium cum medical school and drew back on his ordinary shape, startling a pair of Sanguinaire just climbing the short flight of steps from their coach. In the narrow antechamber just inside the doors was set up a gated mirror for the use of visiting Glasswalkers.

Bitterlich paused there and adjusted his cravat and the fit of his scarlet dress-uniform jacket. He was careful not to let his gaze rise above his own collar. He knew what his face looked like, covered in short, tawny fur with dark dapples and stripes, feline eyes and feline whiskers: an animal. The Célestial court had spent years reminding him that his Seelenjäger sorcery made him less than human.

But the clothes make the man. The uniform demanded respect. The rank gave authority and provided enough social elevation that his many detractors no longer dared attack him directly. They hated a target that could fight back.

Satisfied with the state of his social armor he strolled past the door wardens into the great hall, into the flow of bodies, saintborn nobles and clayborn gentry in their finery, swirling like white and red leaves in the eddies of a rill, with servants like water striders darting between them.

He scanned the room for Isabelle. Was she still here? She might have left early. Since picking up her mental stowaways, she'd been leery of crowds where there were already too many other voices.

There was Sireen in conversation with Gretl. Her husband, who would always be Grand Leon in Bitterlich's eyes, held court with a group of men who refused all evidence that he had ceded power to his wife. Bitterlich almost couldn't blame them. L'Empire had seen its share of deposed rois, but those who weren't killed outright had always been driven into exile, from whence they had a tendency to return in force. The notion of a pensioner roi was an entirely novel and welcome development in Bitterlich's opinion. L'Empire's leadership needed to be stirred up every now and again, but not at the cost of civil war.

Ah, there was Isabelle with . . . Bitterlich's heart stuttered as if he'd been slugged in the chest. Eulalie. He backed away a step and nearly tripped over a servant bearing a tray of hors d'oeuvres.

Bitterlich shrank away from the women before they spotted him. His heart beat heavy as horrid memories clawed their way out of their unquiet graves.

For an instant, he was back in Eulalie's bedchamber, naked, pinned to the wall by her father's bloodshadow, the pain unraveling the weave of his mind. Eulalie was there, equally undressed, fending off her father's bloodshadow with her own.

She pointed to Bitterlich and tried to cover herself with a sheet. "He did this, Father. He attacked me!"

Bitterlich clawed his way out of the memory, panting like he'd run an hour uphill. What in the name of all that lived was Eulalie doing here . . . aside from being a notable comtesse at a royal gala? And why was she talking to Isabelle? Saints, he wanted nothing more than to run away, but he must know what lies she was threading through Isabelle's mind.

He reknitted his ears to borrow an owl's phenomenal hearing, listening in.

Eulalie rubbed her belly in the unconscious way pregnant women often did. "The writ doesn't stop you from having children, does it?"

Isabelle, who normally would have been affronted by such a question, must have been beguiled by Eulalie's considerable charm, for she said, "Having children was the whole point, given that I was betrothed to Príncipe Julio at the time."

"But not anymore," Eulalie said.

"The political liability became too great."

"Which means you're free to make a better match."

Bitterlich shivered under his fur. Oh yes, making a proper high-enough-to-get-a-nosebleed match was very important to Eulalie. That was why she'd turned on him. Yes, he'd been a horny young lout, but she'd been wanting and willing, right up until her father walked in.

Isabelle's response was cool. "If I so choose."

"But you simply must," Eulalie said. "In you, an ancient sorcery is resurrected. What greater service could you do than pass it on?"

Bitterlich's eyes widened in anticipation of a verbal slap. A nigh-immortal fanatic had spent millennia breeding sorcerers in order to create Isabelle, who was meant to be the mother of the Savior, a fate she emphatically rejected.

Isabelle, though clearly annoyed, was dry and understated. "I've already stopped a war and foiled a coup d'état. Strange how no one ever seems to remember that. Instead it's, 'That's nice, dear, now why don't you go have children?'"

Eulalie, never one to take a hint not applied with a sledgehammer, said, "Well, of course you can do other things, too, but imagine how much easier it would be if you had a husband to stand up for you."

"If that becomes a problem in need of a solution, I'll be sure to let you know."

"Do you have anyone in mind?" Eulalie asked.

Bitterlich's heart seized up. What if Isabelle mentioned his name? What if she didn't? No good either way. He lurched through the crowd, waving his hat high, "Capitaine Isabelle!"

Isabelle and Eulalie looked up. Eulalie's eyes rounded. Isabelle started to smile, but it froze halfway there. Had Eulalie told her about their ill-fated tryst? What version of the story had she been told?

"Madame Comtesse, good evening. Capitaine Isabelle, if I may have a word alone, I have news pertaining to our mission."

He did not look at Eulalie, but kept his gaze locked on Isabelle's. Her unscarred eyebrow rose in a question. He kept on his courtier's face, the one that had served him best through a lifetime of taunts and jeers.

Isabelle said, "If you will excuse me, Madame Comtesse, duty calls."

Eulalie stepped up and Bitterlich tensed in dread. Would she denounce him again, in public this time, or would she try to apologize for her betrayal? A thousand times he had tried each scenario in his head over the years, putting different words in her mouth.

None of them were the words she actually spoke. In a delighted voice, Eulalie said, "Ewald, is that you? Oh my, what a dashing fellow you've become, and a major too! Do you know Capitaine Isabelle?"

Bitterlich's jaw nearly came unhinged. Half a lifetime ago she'd betrayed him to his very root. How could she, how *dare* she greet him like an old friend? As if what she'd done to him was nothing. As if it had never happened.

Isabelle intervened while he was still reeling. "I owe Major Bitterlich my life, and he was instrumental in stopping Lael's coup. Now he's the commander of my ship's marines."

Eulalie clasped her hands. "That's wonderful. Oh, Ewald, I knew you'd do great things."

Outrage and disbelief conspired to strangle Bitterlich's voice. Isabelle's hand clamped down on his shoulder and she steered him unresisting from the room. He staggered out into the cold night air and nearly tripped down the steps.

"Talk to me," Isabelle said. He got the feeling she'd said it several times, picking through the wreckage of his emotions, looking for signs of life. "Bitterlich, can you hear me?"

"Gah," was the first utterance, the first syllable his unknotting tongue could form. "That . . . that . . ."

"Bitch?" Isabelle suggested.

"Bitch," Bitterlich agreed. "Unbelievable, shit-tongued, bitch. Saints. Oh my saints." He rubbed his face with his hands, his pads sweaty. Isabelle guided him along the front of the building and across a pocket park to a fountain, where she sat him down and sat beside him, her one arm draped across his shoulders. It was warm and heavy, one solid, friendly human thing. He practiced breathing and tried to pull himself back together.

When at last he'd stopped shaking—when had he started shaking?—Isabelle asked, "What happened . . . back then?"

Bitterlich clenched his teeth. "What have you heard?"

"Conflicting reports," she said.

Silence stretched. Isabelle showed no sign of breaking it.

Bitterlich steeled himself. He'd never talked to anyone about this. What would have been the point? The rumor had followed him around like a badger's stink, but he would have gained nothing by bringing it up. Not even the pettiest of revenges.

Yet Isabelle changed that calculation. She needed to know. He needed to tell her.

He started slowly, "I met her at a party. I was supposed to be standing post by the door, a military decoration, as if the event might have been invaded by ruffians. People at the capital were more or less used to me by then and had taken to ignoring me whenever possible, but Eulalie was new. She'd been brought in to meet prospective suitors, it being about time to get on with the business of making heirs, but she noticed me. She was nice to me. She's nice to everyone, it turns out, but to me that was something special. I had been admired . . . by a girl."

"A very comely girl," Isabelle pointed out.

"That fact was not lost on me," Bitterlich said. "So of course I went and lost my damned mind. I courted her enthusiastically. I had it in my head that I could win her heart and get her to renounce the plans her family had for her. I was her hero and she my object of desire. Absolute romantic drivel, but she kept cheering me on."

Isabelle said, "I am reminded act three of a lovesick adolescent romance is usually a tragedy."

"Yes," Bitterlich said sick to his heart. "Not to belabor the point we made love, or at least had sex. For what it's worth, I asked her, and she pulled my pants down. Unfortunately, we had done an inadequate job of securing our perimeter."

"You were discovered."

"By her father, yes. He raged at both of us. I looked to Eulalie for support . . . but she turned on me. She claimed I had forced myself on her. I don't know if her father believed her or not, but that didn't matter so long as he could plausibly shed his family's dishonor. He shadowburned me to within a hair of my life. Only the fact that I was Grand Leon's own ward stopped him from turning me into a bloodhollow. By the time I regained my senses, she was safely married off. I went out of my way to never trouble her sight again."

"Tonight she acted like nothing ever happened," Isabelle said, her voice tight with anger. "Disgusting."

"It was a long time ago," Bitterlich said.

"It was about ten minutes ago," Isabelle said.

Bitterlich shrugged. That wasn't the whole of what Eulalie had done to him in that awful hour. Her father had demanded proof of her loyalty and she'd given it to him. To prove her virtue, her loyalty to the Sanguinaire blood, she'd cut his nerves with her bloodshadow, left him useless and numb between the legs, forever impotent. It was just one more way he was less than a man.

He couldn't give Isabelle the children she wanted. He couldn't bear the shame of admitting he'd been gelded. *Not a man.* If anyone in the world would understand, it was Isabelle, but even the thought of speaking his pain tied a knot in his tongue.

To change the subject Bitterlich said, "I still need to give you my report. I followed Quill . . ." He recounted Quill's movements through the course of the day. Speaking of business as normal helped calm his nerves; spies and intrigue were soothing, ordinary things.

"I want to know why he was talking to Pyros," Isabelle said. "As much as this will make a long night for you, I'm afraid I must ask you to go back and keep an eye on him. See if he contacts anyone else."

Bitterlich chuckled. "Better a night skulking through trash-littered alleys than going back into that party."

CHAPTER

Five

Isabelle slugged down one of Gretl's snot-flavored potions and lay back in bed, truly alone with her thoughts for the first time in days. Well, her thoughts plus the chorus, which often dulled but never entirely went silent.

You cannot deny family. Her ancestral chorus poured into her mind from the everdream.

"I decide my own destiny," Isabelle growled at them. "I did not ask for you. I do not want you. You do not get a say."

We are your duty and your destiny. It was foolish to talk to them. They weren't alive. They had no more free will than termites gnawing their way through timber, but they would never relent until they overran her mind or she shut them away completely.

Isabelle closed her eyes and turned her attention inward to the breach. When her sister had planted her vitera in Isabelle's brain, it had laid out the foundation for transforming her into a full-fledged Fenice. Isabelle had ripped the vitera out of her skull before the transformation was complete, but not before seed had been planted, and now the crop grew wild.

In a place she could only describe as the back of her mind there was a rift, a gash in her consciousness that was as real to her senses as any wound in her flesh. She could poke it and prod it, and push her mind's eye through it into the everdream.

Here was the place where all of her ancestral memories lived. By all accounts it was supposed to be like a lucid dream, where she could meet her ancestors' memories and experience their lives.

Instead, her ancestors reached for her through the fissure as if they were damned souls trying to breach the Ravenous Gate. She was put in mind of those old stories where a soul might escape Torment if only it could trick someone into taking its place.

She would not let them take her. This was her mind, not a hostel for hostile relatives. But she did have to check on the state of the breach. With the help of Gretl's potion, the wound had been shrinking. Today's hallucinations had not helped, and the edges had gone raw and ragged. She'd have to be very strict about taking her formula, but hopefully by the time the expedition was over, the breach would heal completely, and entomb the unquiet dead forever.

I cannot die as long as you live, said one voice in the center of the mob. *You are my child, my seed. Everything you are you owe to me.* Isabelle had no trouble guessing who that ancestor was, her most famous ancestor, Primus Maximus, whose boundless need for war and victory had launched the Kindly Crusade and led to the very disaster in which the flagship *Conquest* was lost. Everything about her ancestral chorus carried the taint of his madness.

Isabelle felt the drug taking hold, turning her thoughts to mush. She withdrew from from her inspection and opened her eyes to the outside world again. Tomorrow everything would be better. Tomorrow she would set sail.

—

The city bells had long struck midnight when Bitterlich caught up to Quill again, this time in the tunneled-out apartments the Temple kept for visiting guests of middling rank. Bitterlich in rat form slipped in through a crack in the wall, bypassed a rat trap that had been universally ignored by generations of rats before him, and poked his whiskered nose into a drawing room currently furnished only with a trunk and two squabbling clerics.

Quill stood next to the alchemical stove, his back turned to a larger man in the robes of a temple quaestor. Bitterlich recognized Quaestor Czensos's grating metallic voice even before he espied his clockwork hand. The man had a habit of making himself a nuisance to Impervia wherever the Temple's mandate ran afoul of imperial business.

Bitterlich scooted under a nearby table in and amongst the legs of the benches and eased in for a better listen.

"Was it not you who sent for the reliquary?" Czensos's glower was dark and disdainful.

"Why do you ask questions to which you already know the answer?" Quill asked. "The delivery was to be made in secret."

"And yet the heretic managed to steal it."

Bitterlich's ears could not have gotten more pricked if someone had starched them up. What was this? Quill had sent for the reliquary? Why?

"From the middle of a ceremony in which it should not have been involved," Quill said. "I did not ask Marceau to display it, and he should have known better."

"Fear not on that score. The orator will be punished for his part in this debacle, but his crimes are of stupidity. You, on the other hand, had contact with the Skaladin."

"Yes, I reported that to the Temple months ago, to you in fact. Now, would you care to explain to me why you think I would have conspired with Hasdrubal to steal an artifact which was due to be delivered peacefully and unobtrusively into my hands? I imagine your chain of thought will be fascinating."

"You need not have knowingly conspired with the heretic to become his pawn."

"You imagine he suborned my reason in the short half hour we spent talking about unrelated things? You assign your enemies too much power and it warps your thinking."

Czensos made a derisive snort. "You are not one to speak of warped thinking, or do you forget? I have seen your powers of reason fail in such matters before."

Quill shook his head. "I saw you mistake fear for prudence and dogma for evidence. I have seen you go out of your way to inflict pain on your victims."

"Victims?" Czensos sneered. "Victims, you say. You mean the abominations living amongst my faithful flock, tempting them to sin, corrupting their souls with false compassion. Those victims? Evil is to be destroyed, not coddled."

"Your fear corrupts you more than any abomination ever could," Quill said.

Bitterlich knew the story behind this exchange secondhand, having heard it from Isabelle. Quill had been a seeker before he became a sagax. He had come across a young man with sorcerous powers of healing. Quill had seen a miracle, but Czensos had seen an abomination. The quaestor and his carnifexes had slain the boy, his parents, his sibling, and the man whose broken bones the boy had healed, declaring the fruits of evil to be just as corrupting as evil itself.

Czensos looked ready to spend another hour berating Quill, but with an effort he gathered himself. His clockwork hand clenched and unclenched in a series of well-oiled clicks. "I expect you to remain available for further questioning should the need arise."

"I understand," Quill said, which surprised Bitterlich. Did Quill intend to ignore this command or abandon the expedition? Then again, Quill hadn't actually agreed to obey the edict.

They exchanged a few more unpleasantries, but when Czensos could not get Quill to jump for bait, he finally turned and took himself out.

Quill watched him go. His metallic footsteps echoed down the tunnel. The outer door slammed shut. Quill's body twitched as he turned to his sky trunk and began filling it with books, paper, and other instruments of scholarship. He moved with the slow deliberation of the impaired, resting when the tremors in his limbs became too great to continue, but never relenting.

He had been a seeker once, a position that demanded considerable physical and mental endurance. Had this strange palsy driven him to give up life in the rough, or had he moved to escape being under Czensos's direct supervision?

Physical infirmity or no, he struck Bitterlich as a man not to be underestimated.

—

Isabelle, her officers, and the Old Hands stood around the table in the *Thunderclap*'s chartroom, double-checking lists of stores, discussing Jean-Claude's report of the Skaladin Fleet, handing out last-minute duties, and nailing flat every other procedural board that had popped loose in the night. Everything was accounted for, down to the ship's cats. The only thing that stopped her counting rats and fleas was that she hadn't any idea how many they'd started with.

There was rap at the door. A skyman was admitted. "Capitaine, passengers aboard. Your handmaid says she wants to see you, and she's brought a child."

"Not right now," said Lieutenant Vrain, her second-in-command. He was due to be made capitaine when this voyage was over.

Beware the man who usurps your authority. The decision is yours to make, her ancestral chorus droned like a swarm of gnats inside her skull. She'd taken her draught on time last night, but her nerves before the loft made the voices stronger, or at least harder to ignore.

"Send them in immediately," Isabelle said. That was what she would have said even if the chorus hadn't interrupted, wasn't it?

Vrain looked affronted. "Capitaine, this is an officers' meeting."

Isabelle absorbed this rebuke with habitual patience. "Marie is my bodyguard, and the child is someone I need to talk to."

Vrain's gloomy mask reasserted itself. He was a man of very rigid rules, and Isabelle was far too lax on protocol for his taste.

Jean-Claude and Marie came in, guiding a girl dressed in the breeches, blouse, and vest of a ship's boy, minus the official insignia.

Marie stepped into the circle of officers, forcing the men to retreat in lieu of being collided with. She gestured to the girl. "This is Demoiselle Rebecca. She wishes to put forward her application to be your cabin girl."

Rebecca's eyes were as round as moons. She gawped at Isabelle's sparkarm, as everyone did on first seeing it, but her gaze fixed quickly on Isabelle's face.

Isabelle gave Rebecca her full attention. "Is this true, demoiselle? Do you want to be my cabin girl? I ask because I know Jean-Claude put you up to this, and he can be very convincing. Sometimes he even fools himself." She shot Jean-Claude a look that made him squirm. How hard had he pushed this idea on Rebecca? "But this must be your choice, freely made. A skyship is dangerous in the best of times and can be downright lethal in the worst. Furthermore, cabin girl is an official station on the ship, which means you must swear an official binding oath that will subject you to aeronautical law and oblige you to duties that you may not refuse."

Was Rebecca halfway mature enough to understand what was being asked of her? Cabin boys were recruited young, but just because it was tradition didn't make it decent. Even necessity couldn't make a wrong act right or excuse it from consequences.

All the blood had drained from Rebecca's face. Good. She ought to be scared, but she wasn't panicking. After a moment, she asked, "What duties?"

Isabelle said, "Broadly, to defend l'Empire from any that would do it harm. In practical terms it means doing what I tell you. In return you get an aeronaut's pay, my protection and sponsorship, a share of any spoils the ship takes, and all the education you can handle."

Rebecca scuffed her foot on the deck, weighing what personal priorities Isabelle could not guess. What had been her own great needs at that age? Avoiding her family, mostly, and caring for Marie when she'd been made a bloodhollow.

"What are your other options?" Isabelle asked, to help Rebecca work the problem rationally.

Rebecca winced as if that question had stung. "It's this or the street."

Isabelle drummed her spark-hand on the table's metal rim, sending up pink and purple embers. "A military career should never be a matter of last resort, especially for one so young. If you'd rather, I can arrange for you to be apprenticed either to a doctor or a woman of business. Both of them are highly qualified and could use the help."

"Capitaine," Vrain said, "we have important business to attend."

Isabelle gave him a disapproving look. "Signing up for the navy is a ten-year commitment. Demoiselle Rebecca is about to make a choice that will determine the course of the rest of her life. I can hardly think of a matter more worthy of due consideration."

Vrain's expression puckered, but he offered no further commentary.

Surprise flickered across Rebecca's face and her gaze at Isabelle approached wonder. Isabelle guessed she was not used to having adults defend her against other adults, or having her opinions deemed important.

Rebecca asked, "Why did you choose this?" She waved a hand to indicate the ship.

The unscarred corner of Isabelle's mouth curled up ruefully. The question was incisive, and unfortunately difficult to untangle. How might she explain the peculiar mélange of secrets, oaths, and ambition that had brought her to this point? She wasn't sure she could explain it to herself. "That's a question that could take days to answer properly. The short version is, the world has no place for me, so I made my own."

Rebecca gave this somber consideration, or at least made a believably solemn face. "I . . . Yes. I would like to be your cabin girl. If that's okay with you."

Isabelle nodded and said, "Very well, I accept your service, but we are short on time so we need to get you sworn in." There followed a brief flurry of activity as the relevant oath was discovered in the regulations. Isabelle walked Rebecca through it, though she wasn't sure which one of them was more nervous. She'd never administered an oath before, and this one was to a child who could not possibly comprehend the full depth of her commitment.

For the moment, at least, Rebecca looked stunned, as if she'd opened a long-locked trunk and found a different world within.

When the oathtaking was done, Isabelle presented her with her blue jacket and symbols of rank.

Vrain said, "Can we get back to serious work now?"

"I took that very seriously," Isabelle said.

That one must go, her chorus said. *Disrespectful and insubordinate. Make it look like an accident. Use the tragedy to cultivate the loyalty of your men.*

I am not murdering anyone, Isabelle said. It was like arguing with the wind.

Isabelle sent Marie to give Rebecca a tour of the ship and an overview of her duties, and returned to her meeting.

They were just finishing up when the ship's rhythmic bobbing stuttered and the ship lowered as if a great hand had pushed down on it. Isabelle hurried out on the quarterdeck in time to see Hailer Dok, riding a column of wind called up by his singing, descend through the rigging and alight on the capstan. He was a short, skinny man dressed in a fool's motley of yellow and black with a striped doublet that made him look like a bee. His conical hat and upturned goatee gave his profile the shape of a crescent moon. He wore a codpiece, unfortunately just at about Isabelle's eye level, in the shape of a grinning fool's face wagging an elongated tongue. No mystery what he thought of himself there. The air around him swirled in constant vortex, the blazon of his Windcaller sorcery.

Isabelle put on her most stoic face and strode to meet him.

As capitaine it was her duty to plan against ways the expedition might fail, and of the catastrophes she'd envisioned, betrayal by Dok figured in a great majority. This was problematic because, being the guide who was supposed get them through the Bittergale, he was indispensible to the operation.

"Hailer Dok," she said, "welcome aboard."

Dok drifted down from the capstan like a leaf upon the wind. "The pleasure be mine, Capitaine. Be we ready to sail?"

"Just as soon as my last obligate passenger arrives or the clock strikes noon," Isabelle said. "You'll be bunking with the guests."

"Not with you, mon capitaine?" He leered. "There's room enough in there for two."

"No," Isabelle said flatly. "And you will not make such a suggestion again, nor will you make such overtures to any of my women."

Dok laughed. "Surely ye knows a jest when ye hears one."

"I hears no jest," said a gravelly voice. Dok spun to see Jackhand Djordji's grim figure emerge from the chartroom onto the quarterdeck.

Hailer Dok's face lost several shades of color. "Friend Djordji—"

Djordji said, "Don't you 'friend' me. I sees a blackguard who hashes every chance he gets to be more than the thief the world wants him to be."

Isabelle had never seen anyone flatten Dok before. Not even Grand Leon at the height of his power had squelched the man so effectively.

Dok said, "Capitaine, no. This man be cursed. He's an ill wind."

Djordji said, "So says the man who flies false colors and claims the Black Rain Clan. Ye take upon yourself the Breaker's livery and dare call me cursed?"

"I breaks no rules," Dok said. "Besides, Capitaine knows my cause is just."

"Your stated cause is noble," Isabelle allowed dryly.

Djordji asked, "What does he say he's after?"

Dok leaned in toward Djordji as if to skewer the old man with his pointed nose. "I means to lift the anathema."

Hundreds of years ago, the Temple had declared the Gyrine anathema for betraying the Kindly Crusade to the Skaladin. Three months ago, Dok had laid out his plan to have the anathema lifted by retuning the *Conquest* treasure, lost in the Great Betrayal, to the Temple. It was a plausible enough idea, and Sireen, deducing the craton itself to be a greater prize than an uncertain amount of shipwrecked gold, had agreed to trade l'Empire's interest in the treasure for a navigable route through the Bittergale.

Djordji's eyebrows pinched together like a pair of fuzzy white caterpillars preparing to do battle. When he spoke, it was low and pointed, like a knife held to the belly. "That's not your idea."

"I presents it to the dirtborn," Dok said.

Isabelle felt another presence ghosting through the conversation, someone known to the Gyrine but not to her.

"It's not a bad plan," Djordji said. "Do you honor it?"

"Aye," Dok sounded strangled, like Djordji had a hand wrapped round his windpipe.

Djordji did not so much step back as relax in such a way that suggested that while death was still very much an option, it was not an immediate one.

"But I am disinclined to believe that Dok will see it through," Isabelle said.

Dok shot her a glare, but she continued, "You had all winter to work, which you spent laying siege to the beds of Rocher Royale instead of taking the diplomatic steps required to find out if the Temple was even open to the trade. If you think you are going to show up on the steps of the Eightfold Temple in Om and be forgiven on the spot, you are sorely mistaken."

Dok composed himself like a flustered chicken settling its feathers. "I'm not the only one who works on this."

"Then who is the other?"

Dok made a would-be airy wave. "Solo Aria goes to Om."

"Aria?" Djordji sounded surprised. "She's a clever one. How'd she get drafted into one of your daft schemes?"

"Other way around," Dok said. "She chooses me."

Djordji grunted disapprovingly, and Dok continued. "You vouches for her skills, yes? She turns the Omnifex around."

"If anyone can," Djordji said.

"Who is this Solo Aria?" Isabelle asked. "Who does she serve?"

"She's vote capitaine of the Seven Thunders Clan," Dok said.

Djordji said, "She serves the future. Long eyes she has, to see beyond the horizon. It's a fair omen if she's involved."

This explanation seemed to reassure the Old Hand, so Isabelle said, "Monsieur Djordji, shall I hand you the duty of keeping Dok on a short leash?" Jean-Claude trusted Djordji, and Marie whispered his praises as a trainer, two endorsements that meant more to Isabelle than any number of warrants or credentials.

"Aye," Djordji said. "I teaches him not to bark. One step out of line and I empty the jewels from his wrinkled purse." His sword appeared as if by magic, and sliced the tongue from the mouth of Dok's lewd codpiece.

Dok didn't exactly clench his knees, but he looked like he wanted to. "Yer point be well taken," he squeaked.

Isabelle sent the Gyrine on their way, and returned to her own preparations, which mostly consisted of double-checking things she had already triple-checked. The town bells tolled eleven and her nerves only grew worse. She wanted to be aloft, out of here, and on her way. The Craton Auroborea wasn't getting any closer. At the same time she kept scanning the quay for some sign of Bitterlich. He would not miss the loft unless some disaster befell him, but he ought to be here.

Isabelle had just stepped into her cabin to take the next dose of her potion, and to count again to make sure she had enough for a year aloft, when the ship's bell rang, and the boatswain cried, "L'Impératrice de l'Empire!"

Isabelle's heart thumped hard. What was Sireen doing here? She hurried out onto the quarterdeck, to see Sireen, or rather one of her bloodhollows, striding up the gangplank to the main deck.

Isabelle's skin shrank at the sight of the bloodhollow, its clear-as-glass skin stretched over translucent organs and stark-white bones.

Unfortunately, the making of bloodhollows was a divine prerogative, one of the few points of dogma on which l'Empire and the Temple agreed. In his time, Grand Leon had decreed that only condemned murderers were fit to be made bloodhollows, but even that crime did not deserve such a punishment.

Isabelle clamped down hard on her loathing and descended to the main deck to lead her crew in taking a knee before l'impératrice.

"Rise," Sireen said, her visage pressing out from the bloodhollow's face. "I would have a private word with you."

Isabelle led her into the chartroom and shut the door.

"How may I serve you, Madame?" Isabelle asked. What had gone wrong now?

"As you have been," Sireen said. "But given the nature and importance of your mission, I have decided to accompany you in this form."

Isabelle blanched. "Madame, I don't think that's a good idea." The last thing she needed was l'impératrice's bloodhollow on board. As ship's capitaine Isabelle was the absolute monarch of the *Thunderclap*. Her word was law and there was no court of appeal. Sireen's presence on board would undermine her authority, first by implying that la reine did not trust Isabelle enough to let her out of her sight, and second by providing an avenue of appeal to anyone who objected to Isabelle's decrees.

Sireen said, "I understand the inconvenience this imposes, and I know how much you hate bloodhollows, but I don't intend to interfere with your command."

"Then why?" Isabelle asked.

"Because I want to see the Craton Auroborea for myself. I want to set foot on it and bear witness as you plant the flag on it. I want to see the wreck of the *Conquest*."

"You want to share the adventure," Isabelle said.

"Yes," Sireen said. "Power only brings freedom to the extent that one sheds responsibility. My duties are here within l'Empire, and their chains are adamant. This gives me a way to escape, at least vicariously, for a little while."

Isabelle knew all too well how being denied a thing could increase one's desire for it, but that did not excuse the trouble she meant to inflict on Isabelle. "You could wait to send a bloodhollow along with the first colony ships. Assign one to the colonial governor."

Sireen cocked her head slightly to one side. "I want to see it first."

Isabelle gritted her teeth. "You are a passenger then."

"Cargo, if it will ease your mind. I don't expect to manifest in this body again until we make land. If anyone on your crew attempts to summon me without your permission, I will consider that an act of treason."

That was but a small concession. La reine was not to be denied, no matter how inconvenient her whim proved to be. "Would Madame be so kind as to make that royal proclamation to the crew herself?"

Sireen's translucent chin lifted as if she might consider that request impertinent, but after a moment, she conceded, "Yes, I can see why that might be necessary."

The last bell before noon had rung by the time Sagax Quill stepped from his tunnel chambers into the cold gray light of morning. A porter followed him, carrying his sky chest. Bitterlich followed him in raven form as he made his unsteady way toward the naval yard.

Bitterlich considered presenting himself as an escort for Quill sent from the *Thunderclap* to give him a chance to chat the man up on the walk, maybe find out some more about Don Pyros or the Hand of Saint Cynessus. The thing that stuck most in his mind was the fact that Quill had been expecting to receive the reliquary yesterday. That meant that unless he was planning on looking at it and giving it right back, he'd meant to bring it with him on the expedition. Why?

Yet Bitterlich held back. In his years working as one of Impervia's agents it had generally been his directive not to reveal himself to those whom he'd been sent to tail. He was to observe, gather intelligence, and report. Then he and Impervia would decide what next steps to follow. He had adopted the same habit with Isabelle so their actions might be coordinated rather than slipshod.

At least he could have a good, honest *working* relationship with Isabelle.

Bitterlich let the air currents carry him a little higher. The city looked different from on high, the cutting, curving canyons of the streets like the cracks in a desiccated oil painting. To his right rose the Rivencrag, to his left the deep sky fell away with only this thin strip of civilization between. From high above the slanting, stone-tiled rooftops he espied the *Thunderclap* still at anchor. Though only a frigate, it dominated a skyway filled with catch boats, reef hoppers, and merchanters like a hawk amongst ducks. The anticipation of her formal loft stirred his blood.

A cry of alarm on the street below him jerked his attention down. A gang of Last Men had boiled from the alleys. They'd knocked Quill and his porter to the ground and were beating them with clubs.

Bitterlich squawked in alarm, tucked his wings, and dove in the form of a peregrine. Down and down like a javelin he plummeted. Quill rolled into a ball to defend himself. The Last Men bashed him with staves and stones. One pulled a knife.

Bitterlich flattened out of his dive and changed, weaving together parts from a bear, a lion, a crackback. He exploded into the fight, twice the size of a cart horse, plowing into the knife wielder and crushing him underfoot. With claw and maw he dismembered two of the Last Men before they'd even realized what had happened, then let loose a roar that set the others to flight, their bowels giving out in terror.

Bitterlich bounded after a knot of them, plucked one off his feet, and held him dangling in a massive paw. "Who sent you?"

The Last Man squealed and tried to curl up in his own skin like a snail withdrawing into its shell.

"Who?" Bitterlich bellowed.

"Hasdrubal," the Last Man wailed. "Please, don't eat me!"

"Why?"

"Kill the sagax. Leave his body in the streets, a warning to others," said the Last Man, who had apparently decided on a life of cooperation.

"Where is Hasdrubal?" Bitterlich growled.

"I don't know," said the Last Man. "He comes to us, see." The sweat and tears pouring down his face smeared the profane symbols painted there. Apparently he wasn't enough of a true believer, or unbeliever, to commit to the full regalia of tattoos. He was likely not high enough in the ranks of the depraved to know any more than his mission.

Bitterlich considered chasing down a Last Man who might know more, but his priority had to be seeing to Quill.

Bitterlich thumped the blubbering Last Man on the head hard enough to knock him out and dropped him next to Quill, who slowly uncurled from his defensive knot. His porter had disappeared, legging it away from the mob and the monster. Bitterlich reverted to his erstepelz, wiped the blood from his mouth with a handkerchief, and checked his cravat. He could hardly bring himself to move until he felt presentable: human.

He extended a hand to Quill. "Are you badly injured, monsieur?"

Quill accepted the hand up. "Nothing broken, I think."

"It's fortunate Capitaine Isabelle sent me to look for you. Can you walk, or shall I summon a litter?"

Quill hobbled around in a circle for a moment, testing his limbs. "I had best walk. It will make things hurt less later, but my trunk . . ."

Bitterlich hoisted the heavy trunk in one hand. Even in his most human guise, he was considerably stronger than a man his size should be.

By this time, the local constabulary had showed up to survey the carnage.

Bitterlich handed the unconscious Last Man off to a guard sergeant with instructions to deliver him directly to Comtesse Impervia with Bitterlich's best regards. The sergeant bestowed Bitterlich a sort of wary look that made him wonder if he'd entirely succeeded in getting the blood off his face, but he took the Last Man away without complaint.

Bitterlich and Quill set off toward the *Thunderclap* at the best speed Quill could manage.

"Why does this Hasdrubal fellow want you dead?" Bitterlich asked.

Quill grimaced. "Because I know what he means to do, and he does not want me in a position to thwart him."

"Perhaps you should tell me what he means to do," Bitterlich said. "If for no other reason than to multiply his targets."

"If it can wait until we get on board, I plan to tell Capitaine Isabelle the whole story."

"I will hold you to that," Bitterlich said, and he would wait to see if Quill explained why he'd wanted the Hand of Saint Cynessus, or if he still had secrets he was trying to bury.

CHAPTER

Six

Lofting the ship and getting under way turned out to be the most mundane task of Isabelle's whole watch. She judged the conditions and gave the orders as she'd practiced, and the crew pulled off the maneuver without a lurch. She navigated the turbulent airs of the coastal trough and the *Thunderclap* hooked into the swift currents of the Craton Massif, whisked along until the ship climbed to the permeable ridge and passed over into more easily manageable skies.

Isabelle stood on the quarterdeck, enjoying the rolling surge of the ship and the air scrubbed clean of the fetid smells of the city. The Towering Coast carried Rocher Royale slowly away south while the *Thunderclap* set a course as near to northeast as the wind allowed. A fleet of gulls accompanied them some way out, their harsh cries an accent on the creak of the timbers and the hiss of the wind.

Having achieved free sky, Isabelle summoned Vrain, Bitterlich, and Jean-Claude to the passengers' quarters, a room she had subdivided off the great cabin. Quill had been put to bed. He'd looked absolutely wretched when

Bitterlich had brought him on board, and he looked even worse now. His bruises had expanded their reach, spreading across his face in a purple wave.

"I understand you have something to tell us. Revelations you failed to make plain to l'impératrice, or do you wish to claim infirmity?" Would he speak of Pyros, Hasdrubal, or both?

Quill winced and sat up slowly, the difficulty of his tremors compounded by the pain of his beating. "Infirmity is not a valid excuse for ignoring the Builder's work."

The rest of Isabelle's invitees crowded in. Isabelle stood, so nobody sat save Quill. His sky trunk had been secured, but not before he'd removed from it a green notebook embossed on its face with the sigil of Saint Gossamer, patron saint of gardeners.

"So you come before us in the Builder's service," Isabelle said. "Is this Temple business that you withheld from us before?"

"I serve Enlightenment in the Builder's name," Quill said. "I disagree with the Temple's ruling sect as to how Enlightenment is to be obtained, and by whom."

Quill picked up the notebook and buffed the leather face as if it had acquired a smudge. "This is Prince Lael's notebook. After Burning Night, while the rest of the city recovered from its convulsions, I did what I could to preserve the usurper's philosophical works from destruction."

"In other words, you pillaged his library," Jean-Claude said.

"'Looted,' I believe, is the correct term," Quill said. "There was no force involved on my part." He opened the book and started leafing through it. "Prince Lael was a traitor and a usurper, but before either of those things he was a scholar and a natural philosopher. Never in his quest for the power that was denied him did he fail to take notes of what he saw. His journals are quite extensive and his eye for detail quite good. His worst habit, from a scholarly point of view, was drawing conclusions from insufficient evidence and making invalid comparisons based on superficial data."

"So what did he discover that you think is so important?" Jean-Claude asked.

Quill made a sour face. "If you will let me finish."

Isabelle shook her head at Jean-Claude and he subsided.

"As I was saying, Lael was better at making observations than he was at understanding what to do with them, and being obsessed with the lore of sorcery left his education rather thin in other areas, such as botany. He was never interested in plants except as ingredients."

The book was filled with notes in a quick, slanting script. The lines of text filled in the spaces around sketches of strange plants, trees shaped like umbrellas, grasses with feathered blades, trees with an odd marbled bark. There were also pressed flowers affixed to many of the pages, blossoms of many colors and petal patterns.

"Most of these are from his earlier adventures," Quill said. "He has ghostblooms from the Ashlands and tentrumpet flowers from the slopes of the Gnarlfinger Mountains, and crystal moss from the foot of the Frostfever Falls, but on the Craton Auroborea he found this."

Quill turned over one last leaf and rotated the book to show everyone else a pressed flower. It counted amongst the least interesting of all the flowers in the book and would have been easily overlooked on any afternoon stroll. It had white petals, which indicated a night-blooming flower, if Isabelle recalled correctly, and yellow stamen and petals with gray dots on the edges of the lobes.

Isabelle's ancestral chorus stirred and muttered at the sight of the bloom, though their garbled response was no help at all in telling her what was so important about it.

"So . . ." Isabelle said. "A rare plant."

"Not just rare," Quill said. "This is a Saint's Promise flower. It grows wild nowhere on Craton Massif nor on Craton Riqueza nor on any of the skylands wandering the great gyres. Only in the Temple greenhouses in Om are any kept, and even there only with great difficulty. The first of the Temple's stock was given by Saint Gossamer herself to her daughter the Firstborn Queen Fushimo. After the Annihilation of Rüul and the death of the last Risen Saints, Fushimo passed the flower along to her children, along with the promise their grandmother made, that this bloom would guide them to the Vault of Ages, where it grew in great profusion."

Quill's words struck Isabelle like a slap of cold wind, sending a chill down her neck, for she saw the end point of Quill's deduction.

Lieutenant Vrain said, "Do you mean to suggest that the traitor Lael found the Vault of Ages?" He had a low, sad voice like a professional mourner.

Jean-Claude added skeptically, "Not only found it, but never said anything about it?"

Quill said, "Lael found a field of Saint's Promise flowers, which he wrote were 'impressive in their profusion if not their individual construction.' He didn't know what he'd found, or what it meant."

Isabelle cleared her throat and got silence. "Are you sure this is exactly that same flower. Many blooms that look quite similar come from different species."

"I am sure," Quill said. "When I first saw it amongst Lael's notes—he says he spotted an entire lakeshore covered with these blooms—I realized what it was and nearly fainted from the shock. I hardly dared believe what I saw, yet I have spent many hours in the hothouses in Om, and I know this bloom not just by its size and colors but by its scent and the sting of the oils it releases when crushed."

"And you told no one about this before now," Isabelle said.

Quill said, "As sure as I am that this is the flower spoken of in Legend, it does not by itself prove the Vault's existence."

Jean-Claude harrumphed. "You mean you wanted to get there first."

Isabelle said, "Or to prevent someone else from doing so."

Quill said, "There are sects within the Temple who would seek to interdict the Vault, to make sure they are the first to greet the Savior when he arrives."

"They want to be able to point out who all the bad guys are," Jean-Claude said. "Smite that one, monsieur, and that one called you nasty names. Perhaps give him a pest."

From the Vault of Ages comes the Savior, carrying with him the grace of the Primus Mundi, said Isabelle's chorus. *To control him, is to control the world.*

"What a trifling use for the Savior of all mortalkind," Isabelle said, at least partly to the chorus. "I'm amazed anyone who believes in the Savior thinks that such a being would be concerned with their petty rivalries."

"For people with no imagination to speak of, a petty rivalry can seem to take up the whole world and the vault of the sky," Bitterlich said. "I've seen noble houses tear each other's throats out over disputes about the pedigrees of men two centuries dead."

Isabelle could well imagine the conflict that would arise over the discovery of the Vault from whence the saints had risen and from which the Savior was destined to emerge. Every cult and sect would lay claim to being its rightful guardian. Every roi and reine would want to claim it for their own.

"So why tell us this now instead of then?" Isabelle asked.

"Because Hasdrubal knows this as well. He will do everything in his power to reach the craton and claim the Vault on behalf of the Tyrant of Skaladin."

That might very well explain the reports of the Skaladin Fleet massing near the Sundered Isles. "But if you have the journal, how did Hasdrubal know?"

"Hasdrubal was Lael's lieutenant," Quill said. "He had access to the journals before I took them. It's likely he recognized the same clues I did. He did not tell Lael because the tyrant is his true master."

Lieutenant Vrain rumbled, "Do you have any evidence to support this version of events?"

Quill's thin face pinched with pain that went beyond the physical. After a moment he said, "Yes," in the manner of a pressure vessel letting off steam. "Amongst other things, Hasdrubal stole the reliquary of the Hand of Saint Cynessus."

"I know," Jean-Claude said. "I was there. What's so important about a few old finger bones?"

Quill gave Jean-Claude a schoolmaster's look. "Really, monsieur, you should attend Temple lecture more often, or perhaps you would remember the story of Saint Cynessus."

"Every child knows that story," Jean-Claude said. "The Builder blinded Cynessus for looking back on the destruction of the Primus Mundi. Always seemed a bit shabby to me, blinding one man whilst all of the Great Work is coming unglued."

Bitterlich said, "Perhaps the Builder didn't want anyone to witness his shame."

Quill said. "Everyone remembers that part. It's the part they teach in the children's lectures. Sometimes I wonder if they teach that part in isolation so that when people get older they won't remember the bits around it."

"Do tell," Isabelle said. She had read the whole *Instructions,* of which the first book was Legend, in the Saintstongue, but that was a long time ago.

"Saint Cynessus was the gatekeeper of the Vault of Ages," Quill said. "As the last of the saints fled into the Vault, he turned to look back and see if there were any stragglers. The Builder demanded he avert his gaze, but he saw a shadow moving toward him and thought it might be another survivor. Then he was blinded and burned, but even in his agony, he managed to shut the door and seal the Vault, so that it lay safe and hidden for a thousand years, and when the saints emerged, it was he who set them free."

Isabelle was stunned. "You think the relic has the power to open the Vault." It wasn't that she didn't believe in the Builder—the evidence of his work was all around her—but the particulars of Legend had always seemed just that. Surely they were based in some truth, but they belonged to a world long lost.

Yet if the spires at Rocher Royale persisted, impervious to the passage of time, and artifacts like quondam prostheses still functioned after all these centuries, what sense would it make to assert that the Vault of Ages could not exist in fact as well as Legend.

"He means to wake the Savior," Vrain said. "To draw him into the world."

"Not exactly," Quill said. "The Skaladin are heretics. They accept the existence of the Builder, but not the divinity of the Savior. He is a sorcerer, they say, with the power to subdue all other sorcerers, to bend them to his will, and use them to remake the world in the tyrant's favor. As their book of Indictments puts it, 'And so harnessed, he will remake the world. The cullborn shall know their place and shall toil without strife, and all shall be green and growing, and each man's life will be blessed.'"

The Skaladin are blasphemers, vermin to be exterminated down to the last nit, growled Isabelle's ancestral chorus. Primus Maximus had launched a crusade against the Skaladin and had died for his sins, but his loathing lived on. She checked her timepiece to make sure she hadn't somehow missed a dose.

Bitterlich bestowed Isabelle a worried, questioning look, a silent offer of aid. She met his gaze and shook her head; she could handle this. It was just that her chorus was more sensitive to certain topics than others, like a stomach that rebelled at spicy food.

Bitterlich turned his attention to Quill. "What I want to know is what the Hand of Saint Cynessus was doing in Rocher Royale in the first place. Relics of such provenance are usually kept in the quondariums in Om."

Quill pursed his lips but then said, "I requested the reliquary be sent to me for study. It has never shown any miraculous powers and as such is not amongst the most restricted class of artifacts."

"If it has never produced a miracle, what makes you think it can open the Vault?" Isabelle asked.

Quill said, "The Prophecy says that the Savior will emerge from the Vault of Ages, but not all versions of the Prophecy are precisely the same. In the Fragments, which only sanctified clerics may read, there are mentions of the gatekeeper, the blind man by whose hand the last seal will be broken and the Savior emerge. That is all I have to go on."

Isabelle shook her head. "I am weary of men who cannot wait for the end of the world."

"The coming of the Savior is not the end of the world," Quill said. "It is the end of strife, the beginning of Paradise Everlasting."

"Show me your Paradise and I will show you my Torment," Isabelle said. "But discussions of the hereafter are a harrow without a harvest. The problem you have laid at my feet to solve is entirely of your making."

Quill hung his head. "I accept my responsibility. I have confessed it to the Builder and now to you, for I cannot solve it." He raised his gaze to meet hers. "But if I may beg the use of an imperative, we must get to the Vault first."

Isabelle said, "This was always going to be a race, and no amount of urgency will alter the wind in our favor."

"That's why we have a Windcaller," Vrain rumbled.

Isabelle shook her head. "Hailer Dok can't whisk us up there by himself. What we must do is make sure we get to the Craton Auroborea in one piece. We have the *Conquest* shard to guide us to the right spot and Dok to get us through the Bittergale. Those are advantages no one else has, which means they will be doing their best to obtain them from us. So keep your watches well. Vrain, I need you to report all of this directly to Comtesse Impervia, no intermediaries."

"Yes, Capitaine," Vrain said. "What shall we do with him?" He gestured toward Quill.

Isabelle regarded the sagax with as much capitainely gravitas as she could muster. "Is there anything else you have neglected to tell us?"

"You now know everything that I do," Quill said, in the manner of one to whom a simple "yes" or "no" was anathema.

To Vrain she said, "I want his trunk and all his stowage to be carefully examined. As for the rest, he's still a member of the expedition, and a passenger due all courtesy, but I don't think he needs to be wandering about unattended after the injuries he sustained today."

Quill's expression darkened at this command but he wisely kept his mouth shut.

"Yes, Capitaine," Vrain said.

Isabelle dismissed the audience. When everyone but Bitterlich had departed, she shut the door.

"More questions?" Quill asked.

"Just one," she said. "What do you know of Don Pyros?"

Quill's eyebrows climbed his forehead. "He is my brother."

Surprise took Isabelle aback. "You're not a Fenice."

Quill gave her a look that suggested she should know better and said, "The Fenice have their unhallowed scions too. If a child's feathers don't come in by the time they are fifteen or so, their clan assumes their sorcery is in its shell, and they give that child a vitera to try and wake the sorcery. So it was with me."

Isabelle's skin crawled. She had been drugged, limp and helpless, when her sister had placed her vitera on the back of her neck. She would never forget the pricking of her skin as the insect dragged its slimy abdominal sac to the base of her skull, or the hot-wire pain as it sank its needle proboscis into the root of her brain, or the horrid sense of dissolving into nothing when Maximus Primus and all his descendants had swallowed her whole.

Your duty is to your family, said the chorus.

I made my own family. Isabelle rubbed the back of her neck, groping for the enemy that was no longer there. It was no longer anywhere she could get at it.

She forced her hand back to her side. She had the chorus under control.

If Quill took anything away from her distracted pantomime, it didn't show on his face.

Isabelle asked, "Was this against your will?"

Quill laughed. "On the contrary, I begged for it. I wanted to join my family's proud lineage, to receive the wisdom of my ancestors. I was terrified of being gravebound."

Despite her loathing of the whole Fenice tradition, Isabelle understood the yearning for sorcery, for acceptance. For a saintborn to be unhallowed was to be condemned to a sort of living death, shunned and ignored, deliberately forgotten. For years and years, she'd prayed for her sorcery to manifest, if only to stop her father torturing her in an effort to awaken it.

Bitterlich stepped into the silence Isabelle had let grow. "But something went wrong."

Quill grimaced, the line of his mouth twisting like a snake with a cramp. "The vitera could find no place to take root in my mind even as it extended its tendrils into my body. My every nerve was aflame. My bones felt burned like dry twigs." He brought his hands up, one twitch at a time, and examined them as if they were foreign things. "This gracelessness is a reminder of my failure."

Isabelle's innards tightened with sympathy; she knew something of how that felt. "For how long did you endure this?"

"Days," he said. "I refused to yield even when the outcome was assured. How could I not be worthy? What great sin had I committed? How had I failed?" His tone was bitter. "In the end, to save my life, the vitera was removed. My parents were both horrified by what had happened to me and mortified at my failure. The pain in my body was nothing compared to the agony of the shame in their eyes. They packed me off to the Temple before I could even walk again. To their credit they secured me a comfortable sinecure. To my disappointment, they imagined I would spend the rest of my life mourning my failure and repenting whatever sins had made me unworthy to receive the Builder's gift."

"But you chose differently," Bitterlich said.

"Oh, I spent a good deal of time feeling sorry for myself, angry at the Builder, afraid of the Breaker, but eventually I discovered the freedom that comes when no one has any expectations of you. I found a passion for the truth, and I became a Temple seeker."

"How long did it take you to recover, physically?" Isabelle asked. Had he ever had voices in his head? Might he understand the everdream? Even here on her own ship at the height of her power, she dared not ask him directly. Quill might yet be here hunting evidence against Isabelle on behalf of his brother.

He held up a trembling hand. "Do you consider this recovered?"

Isabelle said, "Back to the point, your brother took the oath to hunt down the descendants of Primus Maximus. He claims he is done with the vendetta, but here you are."

"I have always opposed vendettas, or at least since I shook off the shackles of unreasoning devotion. That the Temple sanctifies vendettas in the first place is a betrayal of its entire purpose. I am not my brother's agent or his spy."

Bitterlich said, "Does he know about your other quest?"

"No," Quill said. "He would have hauled me back to Vecci to tell our father, who would then have pursued the course he deemed most advantageous for the dynasty. My opinion would have borne little weight. My family has not rejected me entirely, but they consider the unhallowed unworthy, and the gravebound of little consequence."

"One more thing," Isabelle said. "That business about Cassius's regalia."

"The story is true," Quill said. "Cassius's staff was also said to have survived the Annihilation of Rüul, if only by being absent from the city at the time of its obliteration."

Isabelle left Quill to rest, or to stew, and took herself out on the quarterdeck, where there was room to pace. Her chorus still squabbled like angry upstairs neighbors having a fight in the middle of the night, and she could not escape the feeling that she'd missed something important in Quill's testimony.

If Quill's guess was correct and the Vault of Ages was on Craton Auroborea, it would shake the world to its foundations. Even the rumor of it would launch a hundred more expeditions like this one. Actually finding it, even if it was nothing more than a cold, dead hole in the ground, would likely spark a war.

The worst possible outcome was that the Vault was everything Legend said it was; the Savior was just waiting there for some fool to come along and set him loose, to finish the work of the saints and restore the Primus Mundi, the world as it had been before Iav let the Breaker in. The saints had tried that, built the city of Rüul for that purpose, and destroyed themselves in the process.

She would never understand the allure of the mythic past, the notion that somehow the present was a mistake and the future a place to be shunned. Yet that was the scenario she had to plan for. Always prepare for a hard winter, as Jean-Claude would say.

Isabelle's timepiece chimed. It was nearly time for her next dose of medicine. She returned to her quarters. Compared to the rest of the ship, the great cabin was a spacious, sumptuous place, stretching the whole back of the ship. She'd subdivided it to make a room for her passengers but there was still enough space for a bed, a desk, and cabinets. It had space for extra hammocks to accommodate Isabelle's women.

Isabelle found Marie inside, describing her basic duties to Rebecca. A selection of Isabelle's clothes were laid out on the bed for instructional purposes.

"You must salute when your capitaine comes in," Marie said.

"You didn't," Rebecca said, eyes narrowed as if she suspected a prank.

"She's not my capitaine," Marie said. "I am not in the military."

"It's protocol," Isabelle said. "You'll get used to it. Marie, if you will demonstrate the proper form."

Marie ripped off a proper salute. Rebecca, perhaps mollified by the fact that Marie had been made to comply, mimicked the motion.

Isabelle returned the salute. "As you were." She examined Rebecca closely, wishing she could see into the girl's mind. She'd not had much experience with children, despite having been one. Somehow that experience seemed to have faded.

"Rebecca," she said, "Jean-Claude tells me you are a pickpocket."

Rebecca glowered. "Nasty tongue on that one."

Marie said, "He told the capitaine that before she agreed to take you on. She took you on anyway. What does that tell you?"

Rebecca turned her wary stare to Isabelle. "You want something picked?"

Isabelle huffed a laugh. "Not at the moment, but if I do, I'll know who to call. Speaking of which, how much have you lifted since you came aboard?"

"Nuthin'," Rebecca said unconvincingly.

"Unless you count Skyman Enzo's earring," Marie said, "which currently resides in your waist pouch amongst a collection of curios, small coin, and a phial of glimmer oil."

Rebecca rounded on Marie, but Marie's death-mask expression quelled any outburst.

A thief can be useful, but a liar is never to be trusted, Isabelle's ancestral chorus said, thicker and louder than they should have been at this hour. She prayed they would quiet down again once she found her rhythm in command.

Isabelle concentrated on Rebecca. "You managed to steal an earring. How's that done?" Someone explaining a familiar "how?" was more likely to be forthcoming than someone trying to navigate a treacherous "why?"

Rebecca shrugged. "I ask him, 'What's that bird?' His eyes go up, looking for the bird. Can't think about two things at once, so he doesn't notice when I lifts it out. Got to get the angle right, though, so it doesn't drag."

"What sort of bird was it?" Isabelle asked.

Rebecca looked perplexed. "I dunno. A gull?"

"What sort of gull?"

"A loud, greedy one," Rebecca said.

"Come with me," Isabelle said. She walked from her cabin, through the chartroom, onto the quarterdeck, and the up to the poop. The deck heaved and rolled beneath her feet. The *Thunderclap*'s great fantail swept away astern. Above, the blue sky deepened as the Solar raced toward the horizon. Far below the fetid Miasma swirled, a green mist atop the witch's brew that was the lower sky. Far beneath that lay the Galvanosphere, where lighting raced forever through bruised purple clouds. Deepest beyond the sight of mortals awaited the Gloom, the darkness that fell to the center of the world.

Rebecca stepped up beside Isabelle and peered over the rail of the ship. Marie joined them.

"I imagine you've been paying too much attention to the ship to pay attention to the sky, but what do you see out there?" Isabelle said, gesturing to the sky with her spark-hand.

"Clouds," Rebecca said with surreptitious glances that suggested she was trying to guess the right answer. "Some gulls."

"So if you were lost out here by yourself, how would you find your way home?"

Rebecca looked around again, really looked, and Isabelle could almost feel her shock as she realized for the first time that they were not in sight of land.

"Where's the city?" she asked breathlessly. She even leaned out over the rail to see if perhaps it had fallen into the Gloom.

"A difficult problem," Isabelle said, "but one Skyman Enzo might have helped you solve. You see those big gulls with the black beaks and the blue pinions? Those are grapnel gulls. They only live along the Towering Coast, so if you spot one, you know you're close to Rocher Royale. Also, it's getting on toward night, so they'll all be winging back to land."

Rebecca scanned the sky, then pointed to a flock of gulls and then at the cloud horizon. "That way."

"If you'd paid attention to what Skyman Enzo was trying to tell you, you might have learned how to find your way home in an empty sky. Instead, you pilfered his earring. Doesn't seem like the way you'd want to treat people who are doing you a favor."

Rebecca didn't do contrition very well, but she did manage to look stuffed. "I'm sorry."

"An apology isn't worth the breath it blows in on if you don't change your habits, and it doesn't get you off the gallows without penance."

Rebecca shrank away, her eyes went round, and her face grew pale. "Penance?"

Isabelle knew that look, felt it from the inside like a second skin. Isabelle's own father, may he suffer in Torment, had tortured her, shadowburned her to within a flicker of death. Someone had likewise abused Rebecca.

"Penance in this case will consist of scrubbing down the chute," Isabelle added quickly. It was a filthy job, but one somebody had to do, and it didn't involve pain or humiliation, just part of ship life.

Rebecca nodded mutely for a moment and then ventured, "What's the chute?"

Isabelle laughed, a clear laugh, she hoped, not some madwoman's cackle. "Marie will show you, and I will see to it Enzo gets his earring back."

Marie gazed down on Rebecca. "Come. You should change out of your nice new jacket and blouse before your first taste of latrine duty."

—

Isabelle hosted her first ship's dinner that night, with all her guests invited and the upper echelon of her officers included for balance. Marie directed Rebecca in serving Isabelle, which would be one of her regular duties. If all went well in that department, Isabelle would finally be able to seat Marie at the table as a proper guest, a blessing she hadn't hitherto considered.

After dinner that first night, Isabelle retired to her sleeping room with Marie and only Marie to have that chat she'd been dying for all day.

"You are tired," Marie said, helping Isabelle off with her jacket.

"Exhausted," Isabelle said. "Being a capitaine is like trying to hold the ship up by sheer force of will. Everything that happens or doesn't happen is my responsibility, whether I can do anything about it or not. And I have a whole madhouse wailing and shaking their chains at me." She tapped the side of her head.

"They are restless again?"

"It's just all the excitement stirring things up," Isabelle said. "I've taken my draughts on time. Everything will calm down once I get accustomed to the weight of command."

Marie helped Isabelle unlace her corset. "More likely you will decide you are all better, take on more load, overextend yourself, and break something nobody knows how to fix."

Isabelle was not in the mood for reprimand, no matter how gently delivered. "Speaking of unexpected burdens, Sagax Quill had a surprise for us today. He thinks he's found the Vault of Ages . . ."

When Isabelle had recounted everything Quill had revealed, Marie asked, "Do you think he's right?"

"I think he believes he is," Isabelle said. "Right now everything he said is unfalsifiable." The only rational thing to do was reserve judgment until some useful evidence presented itself.

They fell silent for a time as Marie scrubbed down Isabelle's back with a sponge and soapy water from a bucket. It was such a relief to feel clean after the grime of the day. The burn scar on her face itched almost like a scab.

Marie asked, "What would you do if the Savior really does come?"

Isabelle shook her head. "If you think about it, the whole point of the Prophecy is that once the Savior comes, what I do or you do or anyone does will cease to matter. 'He shall drive out the Breaker who Iav let into the world, and Paradise Everlasting shall be restored.' Neither Legend nor Prophecy explain what Paradise Everlasting is supposed to entail, except to say that it is the perfect place, saturated in peace and harmony by the Builder's beneficent will."

"So you hope Quill is wrong," Marie said.

Isabelle frowned, trying to put her feelings into words. "I want the world to be a better place. If someone came along and abolished slavery and ended the practice of making bloodhollows I would surely honor them, but that's not the sort of change the Savior is supposed to bring. He's meant to drive all wickedness from the world and perfect it."

"And you don't believe in perfection."

"Not exactly. In simple arithmetic, problems have a single solution: two and two sums to four. But when you start doing real mathematics, you realize that most equations don't have single solutions. In fact, most equations aren't even complete by themselves but are part of larger matrices of logic. In order to perfect the world, the Savior would have to find a solution to all the world's problems, and doing that would mean simplifying the world down to something so basic and constrained that we would have to be nothing more than ants to survive in it."

Marie helped Isabelle into her nightclothes. "Shouldn't Rebecca be handling this?"

Isabelle said, "Tomorrow. She's had enough for one day, and so have I." Her ancestral chorus kept throwing up unhelpful bits of semi-coherent babble. She'd take her next draught and escape them in sleep.

"But speaking of our latest stray; what do you think of her?" Isabelle asked.

"She's trouble," Marie said. "Too clever for her own good, impulsive, overconfident."

"So she'll get along famously with Jean-Claude," Isabelle said.

"I don't think Jean-Claude knows what to do with himself without a child to teach: You, me, now Rebecca."

"At least he's a good teacher. Speaking of which, how is your training coming along?"

Marie paused, constructing her response carefully. "Djordji says I have the potential to become a fellhand."

Isabelle's eyes rounded. "Truly?" Those were the clan champions of the Gyrine, duelists of great renown. "But isn't that a title they keep to themselves?"

"When all this is over, he means to adopt me into his clan."

"Ah," Isabelle said, trying to summon delight on Marie's behalf. Of all people, Marie deserved whatever life she wanted, but a cold thread stitched through her heart at the thought that she would be gone. "Good for you."

She plans to leave you and let you fail, her ancestral chorus said, loud and thick with resentment. Marie would abandon her. *Betrayal.*

No. Isabelle held her tongue, refused to give voice to spite. That was just her past lives talking. She would not pour poison in the well of friendship. She opened her sky chest, pulled out a draught, and choked it down, noting the time in her journal. She was a bit early, but it had been a taxing day.

"That doesn't mean I have to stay with them," Marie said. "Djordji reckons he's been away from his clan for fifty years now, but they're still his clan."

Isabelle wiped the slime from her mouth with a kerchief. She wanted to beg Marie for assurances that she would come back, but that would be too needy. "So why did he leave?" she asked by way of changing the subject.

"That's not my story to tell," Marie said.

"So, why become a fellhand?"

Marie in her affectless voice said, "Fighting . . . helps me. My emotions build up until they hurt. I can't cry. I can't smile. Even when I shout, my voice just gets louder, not more forceful. The things I feel I can't get out. Fighting lets me feel, lets me purge, lets me get empty enough to feel peace. More than that, I'm good at it. Djordji says, 'If you want to find your path, you finds the thing you'd rather fail than quit.'"

"Ah," Isabelle said. "That I understand." She was that way with mathematics. The unresolved proof was the one that called to her the most. The difference was, an unsolved equation was unlikely to get her killed.

——

After dinner, Jean-Claude found Rebecca in the capitaine's galley packing away her food like a demented squirrel on the edge of winter.

"Remind me to add table manners to your list of lessons," Jean-Claude said.

Rebecca tossed him a rude gesture and continued stuffing her face. "Nvr bn sss hngry n m lfff."

"Or at least since this morning," Jean-Claude said. "The capitaine told me about your sticky fingers today."

Outrage bloomed on Rebecca's face, "She'd no call to do that. I said I was sorry, didn't I? And I cleaned out the crap chute good and proper."

"Marie told me that with sufficient prodding you did a passable job."

When Rebecca looked like she was going to explode again, Jean-Claude said, "At this point no one is upset at you. You have a clean slate, as the aeronauts say. Do you want to keep it that way?"

Rebecca gave him a wary look. "Mebbe."

"Well then, if you're done provisioning the lower hold, come with me and I'll show you how to steal from people and make them like you for it." He'd almost forgotten how volatile children were, and Rebecca had grown up on the streets. Her expectations had been shaped in the gutter. Those wounds would take time to heal, if they ever did.

Rebecca stuffed the rest of a jam tart in her mouth and filled her pockets with bread rolls, then followed him from the room.

Jean-Claude said, "The way here is you don't steal from the ship or the crew. For one thing, it's damned foolish to steal what you can't use or sell. For another, we'll need each other's backs when the weather gets rough. This is not to say that being a pickpocket isn't a useful skill, and you have to stay in practice, but you have to do it the right way." From his belt pouch he pulled a pack of careworn playing cards. He fanned the deck before her, showing off the blue-inked backs and the colorful faces. "You see this? Forty-eight in the deck. These and nothing else are your targets, understand?"

Rebecca nodded, but her eyes were wary.

"Good." Jean-Claude led the way down past the gun deck and the keel run to the mess hall, where the larboard watch were finishing their supper. The close space was lit with lanterns and loud with talk and the clunk of wooden vessels, though more than a few men looked up in suspicion at the arrival of a passenger in their space.

Jean-Claude planted himself in the aisle and called out, "Gentlemen and the rest of you, listen up. Who here would like to earn an extra denier?"

There came a rumbling from the crew as avarice momentarily overcame hunger.

Jean-Claude held up the deck of cards. "I have here an ordinary deck of cards"—he clamped a hand on Rebecca's shoulder—"and an exceptional cutpurse . . ."

Five minutes later, forty-eight aeronauts each had one of Jean-Claude's cards and the sworn promise of a silver denier to each man if they could produce the card for him when they reached Joubert's Folly. Rebecca's gaze darted hither and yon as each man tucked the card away someplace he imagined it would be safe. Only by herding her out of the room and back to Isabelle's stateroom did Jen-Claude manage to keep her from swiping half of the cards back in that very instant.

"Your duties and lessons come first," he said. "You're here to be a cabin girl."

She looked up at him slyly. "I'm not missing out on forty-eight deniers."

"You're doing this to keep in practice," Jean-Claude said. "And to make the men respect you."

"By stealing from them?" Rebecca said.

"They know you're going to try, and the thing you're taking isn't theirs, so they'll treat it like a game. Whereas if they caught you trying to pick them—"

"They wouldn't," Rebecca said. "What you're really saying is you don't actually have forty-eight deniers."

"No," Jean-Claude admitted. "Not after I paid off your orphan indenture."

Rebecca had the good grace to wince at that reminder. "Sorry. Thankful I am."

Jean-Claude said, "Just save your cleverness for things that need it."

Seven

The morning dawned cold and clear. It was a tall sky, as the aeronauts called it. The cold air pressed the sickly green Miasma down and the thin streaming clouds up, leaving the *Thunderclap* to scud along on a fair wind.

Isabelle and Bitterlich stood shoulder to shoulder in the chartroom poring over Quill's possessions. When he smiled for her, his warmth spread through her chest, but they were here to work not chat. It occurred to her that lately he'd been a constant presence when there was work to be done, but mostly absent when there was not.

Perhaps she'd been imagining his attraction, mistaking a general affability for a deeper desire.

Yet, worrying that question wasn't productive. She and Bitterlich searched Quill's clothes and other personal paraphernalia and set them aside, which left them with a pile of notebooks and specimen boxes.

The boxes proved to contain mostly dried insects. Isabelle found husks ranging in size from a botfly to a beetle the size of a man's fist. The beetle was a cerulean blue at the front and stippled to a bright orange at the back. There were three different sorts of wasplike creatures in shades of yellow, purple, and green. There was something that looked like a dragonfly crossed with a scorpion, and something that looked like a centipede with crystal wings where legs might have been. Isabelle envisioned it undulating through the air.

According to Lael's notes, all of these had been collected from the remains of the swarm that had attacked Hailer Dok's clan on Craton Auroborea. And this was only a tiny sampling of what they could expect to encounter in the jungle there.

"Have you ever seen bugs like these?" Isabelle asked Bitterlich; he had much more knowledge of zoological empiricism than she did.

He shook his head. "All of these are foreign to me, but that's not what bothers me. Both Dok and Lael said they were attacked by a great swarm of insects of different kinds, but that doesn't make any sense. Some bugs swarm, and sometimes different types of bugs swarm at the same time, but they don't coordinate. The biggest enemy of most bugs is other bugs."

"Unless some other force is driving them," Isabelle said.

"Or maybe this is just a type of cooperation we haven't seen before," Bitterlich said. "People always underestimate insects."

"Even Seelenjägers?" Isabelle asked.

He laughed. "Especially Seelenjägers. Most of my kind aren't interested in any animal they can't take a spirit skin from, and we can't become insects."

"Why not?" She was always curious about his sorcery.

"Because insects are too simple. They don't have enough scaffolding to support a human consciousness."

"But a mouse does?" Isabelle asked.

"A mouse has a brain. It has emotions. It can think and learn at least a little. When I become a mouse, there are enough points of contact that I can hitch that wagon to my own mind."

A host of follow-on questions queued up in Isabelle's mind, but she bit her tongue on them. She turned her attention to Lael's journal, the largest book in the bunch, and flipped through several years' worth of notes until she happened upon a sketch of the *Conquest* where it came to rest, the crumbling remnants of the wooden ribs jutting up from the broken behemoth spine.

Anticipating discovery, she turned the page and scanned the headings: "Arrival," "Base Camp," "The Wreck," "Foraging" . . . It was as complete a description of Lael's exploration of Auroborea as she could have hoped for. The Gyrine had guided their clan balloon through the Bittergale. Unfortunately, the text gave no hint as to how they had done so. It was very much like Lael to completely discount the labors of others when recounting his tale. They'd sailed up a fjord into a sweltering green jungle and found the *Conquest* high up on a scarp. There followed several days of looting the wreck and repairing the clan balloon, during which time Lael himself had been primarily occupied with finding the Sanctivore, a quondam device he had then used to unleash a plague on Rocher Royale.

With better guidance, he might have succeeded, her chorus said.

Isabelle wished she could plug her mental ears, but then would she be able to hear herself think?

Only after he'd finally recovered his prize did Lael venture away from the base camp, and his description of his exploration was cursory at best. He mostly rattled on about bringing justice to his royal father.

And then the swarm had attacked, a cloud of insects that darkened the sky and drowned out the wind. The Gyrine Windcallers had fought back valiantly, summoning hurricane-force winds to blow the swarm away, but the bugs attacked from all directions, and the black swarm covered the advance of monstrous insects the size of oxen that snapped men in half with enormous pincers.

The Gyrine fled, suffering heavy losses. Isabelle ran her finger along one passage: "The Gyrine lost nearly a fifth of their number along with many officers and Windcallers, including one of the capitaines. They were also forced to leave most of the treasure behind, it being too heavy for the balloon in such poor condition."

"So Dok wasn't lying about that," Bitterlich said.

Isabelle shrugged. "The problem with good liars is that they usually tell the truth."

She turned her gaze to the ship's orrery. Along the near face of the spherical observation tank a tiny cloud of mist in the shape of the *Thunderclap* sailed northeast. To the left and behind, a similar vaporgram of the Craton Massif drifted south, its slow spin carrying Rocher Royale away. The *Thunderclap*'s return trip would be longer than its outbound one. Far to the north, at the top of the orrery, Craton Auroborea turned. It seemed more like an illusionist's prop or a huckster's promise than a real place. Just when she'd reach out to touch it, it would vanish.

Bitterlich eased up beside her. "Deep thoughts?" he asked, his voice a purr that massaged her ears just right. It was not fair that he should have such a voice when her own was so stretched and scratchy.

"Between Dok and Quill, I'm starting to wonder if there's anyone on this ship who doesn't have a hidden agenda."

"If they do, we'll have to put them on the rota. Treasonous plots will only be permitted on the larboard watch, whilst schemes to awaken sleeping deities will be restricted to the starboard watch. All spies, liars, scallywags, and layabouts will be assigned to the poisoner's mess."

Isabelle snorted. She met his gaze, deep golden eyes that greeted her like open arms, at least in her imagination. Three months ago he'd kissed her and it had felt real, and he'd hovered near her ever since, ready with a kind word or clever observation. Once, before Gretl sorted Isabelle's potion out, her ancestors had gotten loose in her mind. Bitterlich spent that whole night sitting with her in an alcove while she hallucinated her way through half her family history. He told her jokes and anecdotes, a trail of mirth that she followed back into the waking world. He was her bearer of heavy objects, lightener of dark moods, and sweetener of sour moments.

She would have sworn he was courting her, except that he always stopped short. He always showed up when she needed someone, set her back on her feet, or at least in comfortable repose, and let himself out again.

"So what is your secret ambition, oh chiefest and greatest of scoundrels?"

He assumed a very stiff posture, nose in the air, and intoned, "My dastardly plan is to forge an alliance between the ship's cats and the rats to conquer their mutual enemies, the gulls, who are known villains."

Isabelle gave him the eye roll he was looking for. "I'm sure it will be an affray to remember. But truly, what do you want?"

"To serve," he said. "I've been a man under orders since I was fifteen. I didn't have a place in the world. My family was dead. The Célestial nobility was never going to embrace me. Grand Leon gave me a place to stand. I joined the Praetorians as a dispossessed noble scion. Impervia made me one of her anti-spies, and Grand Leon assigned me to be your bodyguard."

"An order that was never rescinded," Isabelle said. That explained his near but not too near presence: duty, not desire. Yes, he was very friendly, very trustworthy. He had never offered her more than friendship. Had "more" ever even occurred to him?

Bitterlich stood all but paralyzed as Isabelle trotted out an explanation for his behavior, an excuse he could use to carry on as he had been . . . if he wanted to string her along like some abusive ass.

Of course, if carrying on like this would make him an ass, it followed logically that he'd already been an ass for the last three months. It was time to put an end to it. He owed her that.

"That order was effectively rescinded when Sireen made me a marine major."

Isabelle turned her gaze to him, searching. Her spark swarm floated about her like a swarm of exhausted fireflies, their dull pulses reflecting her mood. "That day you kissed me, I thought I knew what you wanted, but now . . ."

Bitterlich remembered that kiss. The yearning of it had never left his lips. The warmth of her affection made him feel human, wanted, equal, loved. Yet he was less than a man. Eulalie had seen to that. Some part of him was still lying in that bedroom curled into a ball while the comte said to Eulalie, "All is forgiven."

He'd already told Isabelle more about that night than he'd told anyone. The part of his mind that was still above water knew she'd understand. She'd feel sorry for him. She'd take pity on the eunuch. And with every drip of pity, respect and esteem would erode away.

And what would he give her in return for her sufferance? She wanted children someday. He could not provide those. He had no wealth to bestow her. No family to take her in. All he could do was limit her future opportunities. She deserved to be happy and fulfilled and successful beyond the dreams of annalists.

He was just in her way.

Bitterlich drew on his most pleasant and fastidious demeanor, the one that had seen him through being pelted with stones and rotten fruit and had allowed him to stand in the presence of the despicable and the mighty without flinching. He'd been polite to people who made it plain they deemed him unworthy to lick their boots. He'd been pleasant to people who smeared his reputation and called him a beast. He'd come across as genuine to men who were trying to coax him into betraying his sovereign.

Lying to Isabelle was harder. His tongue felt like it wanted to reach up and throttle his brain, but he forced it to obey his will, his choice. "That was a delightful moment, and one I shall treasure forever. Yet it was only a moment."

Isabelle lost a shade of color, as if she'd been burned by a bloodshadow, and her voice was slightly rough. "I see. Thank you for clarifying. I am sorry if I embarrassed you."

The death of hope in her eyes was a spear through his soul, but his shot was fired, the decision made beyond recall.

"The fault is entirely mine," Bitterlich said. "By your leave."

She nodded mutely, and he let himself out. He trudged to the forecastle, riding the ship through toss and tip, and stood clinging to the forward rail.

Tears as hot as molten iron welled up and he scrubbed them away. He had no business crying. This was his fault. He had hurt her. He should have known better than to let himself be attracted to Isabelle in the first place. He should have known better than to let anyone past his guard. Yet it would have been worse to let it go on to its fruitless end. Fixing his mistake hurt, like re-breaking a bone that had set badly, but it had to be done.

⸺

Isabelle sat in her cabin staring unseeing at the journal open before her. Rejection coiled around her heart and squeezed like a python, pain that robbed her of breath and bent her spine like a withered crone.

Builder and Breaker, she'd been a fool to imagine Bitterlich fancied her. She'd been a fool to imagine his flirtations anything but a friendly game, a fool to build a future on the foundation of a single kiss.

She shut the book and turned her face to the stateroom window. Her reflection in the alchemical glass stared back at her, half her face burnt and bubbled like hot tar. Who would want to stare at that every day? Who would fancy a haunted woman, possessed by fractured ghosts?

His rejection means he does not respect you. You must not allow such an insult to pass unavenged, or he will undermine and betray you, her ancestral chorus said, their anger corrupting all her good memories like acid gnawing iron. She turned her attention inward to the breach in the back of her mind. The wound had expanded again, its edges raw and inflamed. Her ancestors took full advantage of her dismay to rip off her scabs and poison her wound.

They wanted to supplant her in her own head, and they would raze the very castle they sought to keep rather than quit.

She must find her balance, put emotion away, and give Gretl's potion time to regain the upper hand. She wished she could claw her aching heart out and stick it in a jar somewhere until she needed it again, if she ever did. It would be such a relief to feel nothing.

There came a rapping at her door. She didn't want to see anyone just then, but she was capitaine, and saints only knew what new trouble required her attention.

"Who is it?" she asked.

"Marie," came the hollowed reply.

"Come," Isabelle said, putting on her diplomatic face, vaguely pleasant but unrevealing.

The door opened and Marie came in. "You look a mess. What's the matter?"

So much for her diplomatic face. "Bitterlich. I thought . . . I asked him if he wanted more than flirting."

"And he said no," Marie said, her tone as flat as still water.

Isabelle's face curdled up, and the dam behind her eyes broke. She pressed her palm to her eyes, but it was too late to stop the deluge.

"I feel so stupid."

Marie, paler than a ghost, and with about as much personal warmth, wrapped her arms around Isabelle and squeezed her tight. Isabelle sank down on the bed and wept into her hair.

Tears are a weakness you cannot afford, admonished her ancestors. Their endless nagging made her want to put an ice pick though her own temple just to make them shut up.

"I've been learning methods for killing Seelenjägers," Marie said.

Isabelle sputtered and pushed her away. "No! Marie, don't even think such a thing."

"I've also been learning methods for killing Sanguinaire, Glasswalkers, Goldentongues, Fenice, and Windcallers," Marie said. "It's part of the bodyguard training. I'm not planning on murdering anyone."

Isabelle blew out a relieved breath. "Your sense of humor has come loose. We'll need to get it bolted back on." Yet Marie's outrageous suggestion had done its work, shocking Isabelle out of her inward spiral.

"Though if anyone ever does betray you . . ." Marie let the implication hang.

"Bitterlich is innocent," she said. "I put an expectation on him that he never asked for."

"That's not how I read it," Marie said. "I would have bet l'impératrice's money he was sweet on you."

Isabelle huffed a laugh. "Sweet on my mud-slurry face, my voice like a horse's whinny, my head full of other people's voices?" She shook her head, which felt like someone had filled it with iron thistles.

Marie tilted her head, fixing Isabelle with her owllike stare. "Did he say any of that?"

"Of course not. He's far too polite."

Marie considered that a moment and said, "No one knows how best to kill a l'Étincelle, given that there's only one of you, but just now, I think I'd like to strangle you. You are smart, courageous, and compassionate. If the major can't see that, he doesn't deserve your interest."

Isabelle appreciated Marie's appraisal, even if she didn't feel it. "I suppose this does make life less complicated. I have enough to do without navigating a romance."

"Someone else will come along when the Builder wills it," Marie said.

"Is that a promise or a curse?" Isabelle asked. "I wasn't looking for anyone when Bitterlich showed up, and I don't intend to start now that he's showed himself out."

"Why not? You have plans for everything, why make an exception for *l'amour*?"

The chorus's spidery prickle crawled up the nape of her neck: *Love is an emotion. A tool. You must wield the tool, not the other way around.*

Isabelle clamped her hand on the back of her neck as if to catch and crush the insect. "For one thing, I mean to be the master of my own life. For another"—she tapped her temple—"I don't know how much of me there will be in a year and a day."

"Why a year and a day?"

"I seem to recall that's the standard length for a quest in the old tales. Sounds more dramatic than just 'next year.' The point being that if I'm going to live every day as if it were my last, it seems rather unfair to hand some poor suitor only the last page of my book."

"Not if it's pure poetry," Marie said.

"Forty-five, forty-six, forty-seven, forty-eight!" Jean-Claude declared, slapping the last of his bounty cards on the barrel. The crowd gathered on the main deck broke out in guffaws and various aeronauts turned out their pouches and secret hiding places, only to find them devoid of cards.

Rebecca, standing at Jean-Claude's side, looked as smug as a cat with feathers in her mouth. It had taken her only two days to recover the whole deck, even while maintaining a schedule of shipboard education that would have left anyone over the age of twenty completely knackered. She was learning knotwork, ship chores, reading, fisticuffs, and handmaid duties.

The aeronauts, ruffians by nature, didn't think much of girls, but Rebecca had managed to squeeze through the bars of their collective prejudice into the category of kid, just like any other boy.

"Anyone else want to have a go?" Jean-Claude asked. He peered over the tops of the aeronauts' heads to a squad of red-coated marines, Major Bitterlich amongst them. "How about you layabouts? Think you can do better than the ratings? One denier to any marine who can produce a card for me when we get to Joubert's Folly. How about you, Major?"

Jean-Claude remained unsure what to make of the Seelenjäger. He had the reserve of a diplomat and the manners of a dandy. Jean-Claude could have sworn he was courting Isabelle, but she claimed not. She hadn't invited him to the capitaine's table since their first night out, and he'd opted for a largely nocturnal existence.

Jean-Claude always made a point to weigh people by their actions, but he had to admit a handicap against Seelenjägers. He woke up in sweats dreaming about the night a Seelenjäger provisioning party had come to his village, and what they had done to his mother.

Of course, Bitterlich had nothing to do with that. He hadn't even been born. There was no doubt Bitterlich was a good man, but there remained lodged in Jean-Claude's heart the caveat, "As good as one of his kind can be."

As long as Bitterlich remained uninterested in Isabelle, that codicil remained quiet.

Major Bitterlich approached the barrel. His habitual good cheer had faded to wary politeness over the last few days. "I don't think that would quite be fair, monsieur." He selected a card from the pile on the deck and turned it over. It was the turncoat, bearing the image of a saint staring at the Ravenous Gate and a horned Torment staring into Paradise Everlasting.

He held the card up for Rebecca's inspection and said, "I cheat." His hand rippled, briefly losing all shape and twisting in directions that the human mind refused to see, and then the hand was back and the card was gone.

Rebecca's eyes grew as round as full moons. "How'd you do that? Where'd it go?"

"Same place his clothes go when he makes like a raven," Jean-Claude said.

Rebecca moved her head around like a snake, and her voice rose with excitement, "That's like stealing good teeth!"

Bitterlich tipped his hat to Jean-Claude. "I look forward to collecting my denier."

This time it was the marines' turn to laugh. Jean-Claude grunted and tapped the brim of his hat in acknowledgment.

"Anyone else?" he asked.

There was no shortage of volunteers. Rebecca hardly paid attention to any of them, her gaze following Bitterlich.

Jean-Claude tapped her on the shoulder to get her attention. "I suppose you're going to try to snatch that card from the Builder's own fingers, aren't you."

Rebecca shrugged. "Mebbe."

Jean-Claude snorted. "That would be something to see. Just make sure you get your duties done first."

CHAPTER

Eight

The *Thunderclap*'s cannons roared and the ship rocked as they pummeled an uncharted stoneberg as part of live fire drill. Gun smoke filled the air and stung Isabelle's eyes. Iron shot smacked into the tumbling rock. It chipped and cracked. Isabelle checked her timepiece. A broadside every three minutes was the accepted standard. Vrain wanted to get it down to two and a half or two.

The empirical part of Isabelle's mind bubbled up ideas to improve the cannons themselves. Given that most shots missed even at close range, improving accuracy would be more efficient than increasing rate of fire.

Those thoughts made her uncomfortable. She had never before turned her mechanical talents to designing weapons of war. Empirical philosophy should be used to understand the world and improve people's lives, not to sow death and destruction. Yet if she were forced into battle, would she not want a superior weapon?

Thankfully the question was moot for the time being. She lacked a foundry to forge new parts, and transforming anything as big as a cannon with her l'Étincelle would likely kill her.

Cowardice does not deserve command, her chorus sneered, voices rambling over one another. If she wasn't willing to kill, she had no business on a warship. Even now, with her latest potion fresh in her veins, the ghosts tugged the shadows at the periphery of her vision, making them slither along the deck and stick to her boots. She could hardly tell her ancestors' thoughts from her own. The breach to the everdream remained stubbornly open, red and raw like thoughts of revenge.

Was the potion losing its efficacy? Most likely it was the strain of command that overwhelmed the drug. She could compensate for that. She must. She would not let herself be ripped apart by ghosts like a rabbit caught by starving curs. She and Gretl had spent several weeks getting the dose strong enough to work without impairing her ability to function. Perhaps she should increase the dose or decrease the interval between doses.

One who does not wish to lead must meekly follow. That was Primus, yearning as always for control.

"No," Isabelle muttered. *This is my life. You had your chances.* She might as well be shouting at the wind.

The guns roared again. Round shot sheared off one face of the stoneberg and sent it tumbling. Two and a half minutes. The stricken rock tumbled onto a new vector. She adjusted course to keep it in range.

Something moved behind her: a looming shape that blotted the sun, a heavy tread, and the stink of fetid breath. Her pulse quickened and she turned to face the brute.

There was nothing there, not even a cloud to blot the Solar. It was just a ghost stain leaking through.

She took several deliberate breaths to calm her nerves, then returned to her observation of the stoneberg. Once more the guns spoke, spraying off more chips of stone. Two minutes twenty-five that time.

The last broadside had knocked the berg onto yet another path that the *Thunderclap* could not easily adjust to without losing way. Thank the saints.

Isabelle called off the drill, retreated to her cabin, and sucked down another draught. She was only an hour early. She noted the time in her journal and counted back all her doses to make sure she hadn't missed any. She'd been regular.

There came a rap at the door she recognized as Jean-Claude's . . . unless it was a hallucination. So far she'd only had visions of her ancestors' lives, but what if they evolved?

"Come," she said.

Jean-Claude entered, closed the door, and favored her with a worried look. "Head troubles?"

"Was it that obvious?" Isabelle asked, mortified. Nearly as terrible as going mad was being suspected of doing so. If Vrain even suspected she was losing her mind he'd be honor bound to remove her from command. After that, she'd be little more than stowage on this trip. Worse, Sireen would never trust her with any sort of authority again. Without a name, a family, or a place in the world, she'd be worse than dead, and that would drive her mad.

"Only to someone who's known you forever," Jean-Claude said. "How bad?"

"Not bad," Isabelle said, willing it to be so. "The last draught was just a little weak."

"You're a terrible liar," Jean-Claude said. "What happened?"

"A ghost stain. A minor one. A heavy shadow thumping around behind me."

"Is it getting worse?"

What would she do if Jean-Claude thought she was mad? He'd always been her partisan, no matter the odds. He'd always believed in her innocence no matter the charges leveled against her. But what would he do if he thought she couldn't handle the enemy in her head. The words she dreaded most since this ordeal began were "It's for your own good." That way lay erasure. Yet if she could not trust Jean-Claude, there was no hope in the world.

"Yes," she admitted.

"It's got you spooked."

"Yes."

"It's okay to be spooked," he said.

The potion's effect crept into Isabelle's mind like the shadow of a cloud, muffling her ancestors but washing out the colors of the world, leaving them drab and faded. The ship's creaking became more like a saw on bone than a healthy hum.

It also loosened her tongue enough to let deeper worries out. "Who will I be if I lose my mind? Will there even be a 'me'?"

Jean-Claude rubbed the back of his neck and took a long time replying. "I don't have a good answer for that."

Isabelle poured herself a cup of water and gestured Jean-Claude to the wine cabinet. Just because she couldn't drink didn't mean her friends should go dry. Besides, most of this vintage had been gifted to her by Sireen, who would be disappointed if she brought any back. "Which means you don't have an answer you think will comfort me. Tell me anyway."

Jean-Claude poured himself a cup. "My grandfather outlived his mind. Got so he didn't recognize my mother. He thought she was his wife, who'd been dead twenty years by then. Seeing him like that made her sadder than I'd ever seen her, even sadder than when my father died. At least when Papa died she could grieve a whole man. My grandfather, her father, she had to grieve in pieces, one memory at a time."

"I'm sorry." Isabelle almost wished she hadn't asked. She did not want to end up falling to pieces, the mosaic of her mind robbed away one tile at a time until nothing but broken chips of color remained, a void where a pattern should have been. Worse, she did not want to inflict that horror on her friends.

"Don't be. Mother always said that we grieve for what we've lost, but we live for what we can give. Sometimes all we can do is bear witness and hold our honor tight."

"A wise woman, your mother."

⟶

Bitterlich emerged from belowdecks to find a fight in progress. A wide ring of marines and aeronauts stamped their feet and jeered as two combatants faced off amidships. It was a mismatch for the ages. Long Thom Moreau, who had a second career as a mizzenmast, towered over small pale Marie. She held a ready stance, her pose more still than any living thing should be. Long Thom cracked his knuckles with a sound like musket fire.

To one side stood Jean-Claude and Jackhand Djordji, watching with the bored dispassion of a couple of old goats chewing their cud. The Gyrine had been training Marie in combat: guns and swordplay, but she had no weapons as equalizers here.

Bitterlich had been avoiding Isabelle's inner circle as much as possible since his rejection of her affection. He had no illusion that he would still be welcome in their company.

Even so, he was in charge of the ship's security and responsible for keeping the passengers safe. He pushed up alongside Djordji. "Monsieur, is this wise?"

"No," Djordji said, drawing on his dragonweed pipe. "No great undertaking ever is."

With a bellow like a mad bull, Long Thom grabbed for Marie. She slipped under his outstretched arm and struck at the meat of his forearms, but she might as well have been punching a timber. Long Thom kept chasing, reaching, grasping. All he had to do was make contact, but Marie twisted, bent, and flowed like water: untouchable.

Bitterlich's heart hammered with the urge to intervene. "Do you expect her to win?"

"To learn," Djordji said.

"I still need her in one piece," Jean-Claude said mildly.

"Train her yourself if you don't like my methods," Djordji said. "I trains half the fellhands in the world today. Only loses one, and that's to dysentery."

Long Thom kicked, his long leg swinging like a loose yardarm. He caught Marie midthigh with a thump like a butcher's cleaver hitting bone. Marie left the deck, flipped over, and landed in a graceless heap. She shoved up to hands and knees. Long Thom swung a fist like a block and tackle on course to take off her head.

Bitterlich reached for his sorcery and his skin rippled in anticipation of change.

Yet before he could pounce, Marie lurched to the side and Thom caught nothing but air. Never did Marie's face show pain or distress, but she came up limping, hobbling away from his blows. She couldn't slither away from him anymore, and he forced her into a corner.

"Got you!" Thom grabbed for her, hands splayed like the talons of some great eagle.

Quick as a cat, Marie ducked under his arm, seized one long finger with her whole hand and wrenched it backward. Long Thom howled in pain. Marie turned his hand over and guided him forward and down, face-first into the ship's bulwark. Pitting her whole body against his arm, she levered it up behind him and kicked him once, twice, thrice in the meaty thews of his upper arms. He heaved away and staggered to his feet, but his arm hung limp at his side.

"Saints," Bitterlich muttered. He forced his rising power back down.

Marie had been a handmaid but a few months ago, but she fought like one who had been born to battle.

"Yield," Marie demanded.

"I'll smash you flat," Long Thom growled, too angry to think straight.

Djordji's rapier appeared from nowhere and touched Thom in the chest. "Nay, lad, yer done in."

Long Thom stopped just short of impaling himself. "I'm not beat," he said, still seething. "Damn she-Torment."

"Ain't about beating. It's about learning. Yer down an arm already, you don't need to be down two. Need you for the ship, see."

Thom swung his arm limp from his shoulder, his hand twitching, and winced. "What'd she do to me?"

"Dislocated your finger and kicked you in the nerves," Marie said.

Djordji said, "You'll be able to feel your arm again, but you'll wish ye couldn't. See the sawbones and have him put that finger right."

At last, Long Thom grunted by way of acquiescence. Marie touched her temple in salute, and he grudgingly did the same with his working hand.

Djordji turned a wicked eye to Jean-Claude. "Yer turn, ye creaking barnacle."

Jean-Claude's bushy eyebrows went up. "You seem to have mistaken me for someone over whom you have authority."

Djordji's eyes narrowed. "You never is as good as you might be. Too lazy by half, and now yer nothing more than ballast."

Jean-Claude snorted. "You forget, old man, horseshit is my weapon of choice. I don't need to prove myself to you."

"You do to her." Djordji twitched his nose at Marie. The encircling crew hooted as if he'd scored some salient point.

Jean-Claude glowered at Djordji.

Marie looked back and forth between them. "You don't need to prove anything to me."

Bitterlich watched this byplay with acute curiosity. The Old Hands had known each other for longer than Bitterlich had been alive. They had levers to pull no one else could guess.

At last Jean-Claude heaved himself off the rail and divested himself of his sword belt. To the crowd he said, "Which one of you strapping young gentlemen wants to put this old dog out of his misery?"

Nobody spoke, for Jean-Claude was an Old Hand. There were a bare handful of such people in all of l'Empire, each one a living legend worthy of respect if not outright awe to common men. The aeronauts and soldiers might well all demur.

Bitterlich looked over his assembled marines and said, "Caron, you need the exercise."

The marine in question was indeed a worthy specimen, nearly as broad as he was tall. He'd been a boxer before he was pressed into the then roi's service. Caron looked startled to be called out, but nodded to Bitterlich, shed his jacket, and stepped into the ring.

Only then did Bitterlich have second thoughts about pitting him against a man clearly past his prime. Caron was apt to interpret Bitterlich's command as "Destroy that target." It was too late now to clarify, though, not without embarrassing both men, which would have been worse than any beating.

Jean-Claude gave Bitterlich a withering look and stumbled into the center of the arena, limping on his right leg. Had he reinjured it?

Bitterlich cursed his own tongue. He'd just been trying to contribute.

Mistake. It was always a mistake to join in, but it was one he couldn't stop making. Oil did not mix with water, nor Seelenjägers with Célestials.

Jean-Claude bent over as if to touch his toes and demonstrated a range of motion akin to that of a stack of bricks. Bitterlich grimaced internally. Should he be less worried about making an enemy and more worried about crippling Isabelle's adoptive father?

Marie drifted to Bitterlich's side. She had frequently been present when he spoke to Isabelle, but he'd hardly ever done more than exchange pleasantries with her outside that context.

"Mademoiselle," Bitterlich said to Marie. "How is Monsieur Jean-Claude's health?"

"He'll do well enough," Marie said. Her voice was not soft, but rather diffuse, as if it had just arrived, out of breath, from a long journey. "He could stand to bleed a little."

Just at that moment Jean-Claude was flailing his arms like a windmill in a hurricane in an apparent attempt to loosen his stiff shoulders. "It was at the Battle of the Lichfields that I got shot in my left arm, broke the long bone. Never could get it up since then. Hurts in the winter too."

Djordji called, "Stop stalling and get on with it."

Marie looked up at Bitterlich with her dead white eyes. "You hurt Isabelle. Why?"

Bitterlich had not been prepared for such a direct accusation. "It was not my intent."

He was surprised she'd bring up the matter in public, but between the noise and the spectacle, absolutely no one was paying attention to them.

"Then what was your intent?" Marie said. "I watched you two together for months. You were in love with her. She was in love with you, Breaker only knows why. She never stopped talking about you. I've never seen her so happy. You got inside her head and her heart, and then you ran away. Why?"

"I just . . . I shouldn't have let it go on as long as it did," he said, the most lame and limping words that had ever been uttered. "I was just trying to save her from disappointment."

"By becoming one? That is an interesting strategy."

Bitterlich glowered at her. "What would you have me do? I cannot hurt her less than I already have. If I am unworthy, then you should be pleased I have bowed out."

Marie refused this bait and said, "Tell me you don't love her."

Pain and shame twisted Bitterlich's heart. "I never told her I did."

"You're a coward," Marie said.

Bitterlich made no reply. He had no answer, for she was right. He had shamed himself and hurt Isabelle.

A shout, a groan of pain, and a heavy thump dragged Bitterlich's attention back to the arena. He feared to see Jean-Claude maimed and broken, but it was Private Caron sprawled facedown on the deck, moaning like a cow in labor.

Jean-Claude adjusted his hat. Master of horseshit, indeed.

"D'ye think ye can manage it without a trip to the theater?" Djordji asked.

Jean-Claude buckled his sword belt and jabbed his thumb at Bitterlich. "No encore for me. Try your luck with him, if he'll stand his ground instead of sacrificing a minion."

The marines sent up a roar of approval at this idea. "Show 'em what for, Major."

Bitterlich knew better than to make a spectacle of his prowess. A victory would show him to be a wild animal, defeat a whipped cur, either a chance to be used as evidence against him in the court of "Is he human?" So had it been since he'd first come into his sorcery.

He waved his men down. "Gentlemen, I remind you that you should never allow yourself to be baited into a fight."

"Not like Jean-Claude," Marie said, who switched back to ignoring Bitterlich as sharply as she'd interrogated him.

Jean-Claude grunted. "Has anyone ever told you sass is unbecoming in an apprentice?"

"You have," Marie said. "Twelve times in the last week. Once at breakfast on Saint Julia's Day at the Hanged Gull—"

"I didn't ask for an accounting," Jean-Claude said.

"Ahoy the deck!" came a shout from above, high up in the crow's nest. The lookout waved a bright-yellow flag toward the stern.

"Sails!" he shouted. "Sails astern!"

Bitterlich's ears pricked up. They had been expecting pursuit, and this far from the trade routes there wasn't much other reason for anyone to be here. He bounded to the quarterdeck and up to the poop, shifting his eyes to those of a gyrfalcon and sweeping the horizon.

"What do you see?" Marie scampered up beside him more readily than her elderly instructors.

"Dark sails," he said. "A sloop of war. They fly no flag. Please let Capitaine Isabelle know I've gone to have a look."

He climbed the railing to the port side of the great fantail rudder. Far below, the tips of the turvy masts swirled the upper airs of the Miasma. Bitterlich knew he could fly. He had no doubt in his abilities, but even so the sheer scale of the drop made his stomach clench. Only the ingrained habits and long practice kept him moving out past that frontier. He launched himself high, pulled on the form of a galvatross, and took wing toward the following vessel.

—

Relief filled Isabelle's breast when Bitterlich lighted on the deck, safe returned from his scouting. She resisted the urge to trot out there and greet him personally, the better to avoid any awkward silences or painful smiles. She'd hoped her absurd longing would have started to fade by now. Maybe tomorrow.

You betray yourself when you let him make a fool of you, sneered her chorus, dripping contempt into her veins. The ghosts were never far away anymore, and even when she could filter them out they rattled her skull like rain on the rooftops and the wind banging open shutters. She had learned not to jump at the noises or twitch at the candle shadows flicking at the edge of sight.

In their own strange way, the ghosts were on her side, lashing out at her enemies as they perceived them. They didn't understand Bitterlich was not to blame for her heartache, but scraping away their bitterness left her drained and weary.

Yet her mission did not care that her limbs felt like lead and her skull ached like someone was using it for an anvil. She pasted on her professional face and convened her expeditionary council to hear Bitterlich's report.

She, Vrain, Marie, Jean-Claude, and the Gyrine gathered in the chartroom in the soft green glow of the orrery. The *Thunderclap* sailed farther and farther from home. Bitterlich met Isabelle's gaze, his furry face devoid of its usual mirth. It would have been good to see him smile, even if not at her. He straightened his cuffs and then saluted, very properly. "Capitaine."

"Report," she said.

Bitterlich said. "I intercepted a sloop, the *Dame Formue*, but she disappeared into the clouds before I could close with her."

Djordji coughed into his hand, then cleared his throat and said, "I know the *Dame Formue*. Capitaine's a man named Ivar Thirdeye: professional spicer, scout, smuggler. Canny, that one. Jean-Claude knows him of old."

Isabelle turned her attention to Jean-Claude, who made dyspeptic noises and rubbed his face as if trying to rearrange it on his skull.

"You know this pirate?" Isabelle was not surprised. Jean-Claude seemed to know every crook and brigand on the craton by name.

Jean-Claude said, "I beat him in a game of thwarts once. He has not forgiven me."

"Rarely have I heard so much left out of a story," Isabelle said. "Give."

Jean-Claude shrugged. "This was before your time. I had been sent to retrieve some letters Ivar had purloined. They were very important letters, at least to the duc who'd lost them. Charges of treason would have been involved if they'd been made public. Ivar wouldn't sell, but he could never resist a bet. I bluffed my way into a game of thwarts. Ivar cheated, of course, wiped out the rest of the table, but it's called thwarts for a reason, and I kept getting between him and his winnings. That didn't bother him because once the others were sacked, he'd be free to work on me. Except that when the last other man laid a flat purse on the grid, I scooped up my share and bade Ivar good night."

"I imagine that displeased him," Isabelle said.

"He steamed up like a campfire in a drizzle. Called me the Breaker's own shit pile and a dog-humping monkey in the bargain. I said I'd play him one more round, but only if he put the letters on the grid. It was a game for the ages. We played full court. Doublets and triplets were called, pawns danced across the grid. A crowd gathered. Ivar packed his courtyard with winnings, but when the last singlet topped the pile, the pawn for the letters was still on my side of the line. The game had attracted so many spectators that he couldn't very well renege on his bet."

Bitterlich sounded doubtful. "And for that he's never forgiven you?"

Jean-Claude said. "For beating him? No. What earned me his undying enmity was the fact that all the money he won from me was drawn on forged accounts."

One corner of Isabelle's mouth turned up in spite of her headache and her capitainely sobriety. "In other words, you cheated at a higher level than he did."

Jean-Claude shrugged. "I told him he was going to lose. I just didn't say how."

Vrain said, "In the present, does he have a patron, or would he be working on his own?"

Djordji rubbed his throat and said, "He's got no hope against this ship. I'm thinking he's paid to scout. He'll sneak in and steal what prize he can if he gets the chance, a jay amongst hawks, but he won't risk his hide."

Isabelle said, "Comtesse Impervia informs me of at least three different factions after our prize. Aragoth and Brathon have an interest, not to mention the malcontents at home."

"Don't forget the Skaladin," Vrain said. "This pirate could be working for any of them."

Jean-Claude said, "Knowing Ivar, he could be working for all of them."

Dok said, "What's it matter who they works for?" He glanced at Bitterlich. "The major sneaks aboard, sets fire to the hold, burns them from the sky. No more spies."

"Never leave an enemy behind you," said Don Luggia, his gruff voice and surly demeanor at odds with the soft gray and powder blue of his crest. He stepped toward the orrery, scowling at the vaporgrams as if they might tell him. "A man who has betrayed you once will do it again."

"What if I'm counting on that?" Isabelle said, though she was not Isabelle but Primus Maximus, grand general of the Kindly Crusade, and she'd just laid a trap for her enemies.

"Beg pardon?" Vrain said.

Isabelle blinked, and Primus was gone, taking Luggia with him. Not the man, the ghost stain. Every day Isabelle lived in dread of the day that she could no longer tell the whispers of her ancestors apart from reality, and in the moment that shadow had made manifest, that fear had come true. It had only lasted for a few seconds, half a dozen racing heartbeats, but in that span she would have testified on her life to Luggia's presence.

Everyone else in the room was staring at her. What had they seen? What did they think?

"Just thinking out loud," she said, gathering her scattered wits. Had she said more than she recalled? Had she lent her voice to both parts in her hallucination?

"We aren't going to initiate hostilities," Isabelle said.

Luggia wanted to attack, but then his response to anything he didn't understand was to label it an enemy and kill it.

Except Luggia had been dead four hundred years, and she shouldn't know that much about him. But he'd been one of her lieutenants . . . that is to say Primus's lieutenants. Trusty enough when you needed someone to run down a flank, but keep him away from the wine butts.

"It's not like they'd show us any mercy," Dok said.

"I said no. We will fight to defend ourselves, but I reject the doctrine of preemptive self-defense. Killing other people on the excuse that they would surely do the same to you is nothing more than murder dressed up in a loop of braid with a tin medal."

Isabelle turned to Vrain. "Lieutenant, report the *Dame Formue* to Comtesse Impervia. If Thirdeye is working for wages, we need to find out who his paymaster is."

"I should inform the Cauldron," Vrain said. Like every Sanguinaire officer of the line he kept a bloodhollow at the naval base in Rocher Royale. This pool of tortured souls allowed the fleets to communicate with one another and with their other assets across the deep sky almost instantaneously. Isabelle hated taking advantage of such a horrific arrangement. It tainted every project it touched, but she had no other option.

"Not the Cauldron," she said. "Too many political connections." Vrain must know as well as she did that the most likely culprits for lofting fleets in competition with l'impératrice were other Célestial nobles. Nearly every officer in Fleet Command had gotten there through patronage, and they would not hesitate to warn their benefactors about inquiries into their misdeeds.

Vrain nodded curtly. "Yes, Capitaine."

Isabelle dismissed the council and sent everyone on their way, but Jean-Claude and Marie lingered. Marie closed the door.

"Your ghosts?" Jean-Claude said, his expression awash with worry.

"You looked out of your head," Marie said.

"Just for a moment," Isabelle said. "Just a hiccup."

Marie's voice was but a breath in the fog. "You just looked right through everyone, grinned a bit and said, *Cosa succede se conto su questo?*"

"It means 'What if I'm counting on that?'" Isabelle said, rubbing the base of her skull. Alas there was no more healing to be done from that end. "I pulled out of it, though. I just need to adjust my dosage again."

"What did you see?" Marie asked.

"Don Luggia," Isabelle said. "He was one of Primus Maximus's men, and he was standing right there, as plain as you are. And I knew who he was and what he wanted." She shuddered at the memory, which was as real to her as any other conversation she'd ever had.

"Your visions are getting worse," Marie said.

"It comes and goes," Isabelle hedged. "I think they were trying to give me advice. I mean, he was telling me to go along with Dok's idea of downing the *Dame Formue*."

"Advice that you did not take," Jean-Claude said.

"Would you have?" Isabelle asked. "I don't like having Thirdeye back there, but right now he's giving us more information than we're giving him. It was never a secret that we set sail for Joubert's Folly. Ivar can only report that we are doing exactly what we said we would. In the meanwhile, he gives us a thread to pull on from this end. The next time we spot him, I want to try making contact. If he's as mercenary as you say, he may sell out his current master."

"And what if he won't bite?" Jean-Claude asked.

"Then we make use of our other strategic advantages. Joubert's Folly is the Imperial Navy's supply depot, not his. Every day that goes by, he is using up supplies he can't replenish. After we are done taking on supplies, we break for the open sky. We'll put up every sail we can manage and outrun him and his allies. Since they don't know where we're going, they have the choice to chase us with low provisions or turn back."

"And if his allies attack us before we reach Joubert's Folly?"

Isabelle stared at the orrery. It was still such a long way to their fort on the Spiral Archipelago. Anything could happen.

"We run," Isabelle said. "And if that doesn't work, we fight."

CHAPTER
Nine

Curtains of lightning flashed all around the *Thunderclap,* and cold rain sheeted down, trying to scrub the decks of human life. The bruised sky boiled with clouds intent on murder.

Just when they were finally drawing close to Joubert's Folly after a month aloft, this storm had sprung up almost out of nowhere and swatted the ship around like a kitten with a bit of fluff. Saints only knew what flotsam the gale would kick up. Stonebergs and strange creatures might be heaved up from the Gloom. Capitaine Isabelle had furled every sail she didn't need to steer by and ordered extra eyes to the dark to watch for incoming hazards.

Bitterlich made an inspection of the gun deck. The ship heaved and fell, throwing the guns against their webbing. The ropes groaned in protest but did not yield, and the gun crews were all on station to make sure it stayed that way. The last thing anyone needed was a half ton of metal and wood careening around the innards of the ship.

Bitterlich floated and thumped along with the artillery. He'd experimented with several animal and hybrid forms to ascertain which was best adapted to this sort of tossing, only to discover that being picked up and slapped down like potter's clay was not a thing most animals had to contend with. Perhaps he should consider adding some reef dweller like an aethercob to his repertoire.

He took the companionway down to the middle hold and started checking the cargo lashings, but paused when a disturbance in the air twitched his whiskers. The middle hold was the stuffiest compartment in the whole ship. The air was close and heavy even in this pitching storm.

He tested the air, recognized Rebecca's scent, and followed his nose to check up on her. She'd been adapting remarkably well to ship life. He got the sense she'd been starving for new experiences, and now she was gorging herself on them.

The ship groaned, the wind whistled, the rain hammered, and the thunder crashed, but beneath it all, wending its way through the noise like a snake through a thick brush, was the thread of human voices.

"No Madame." Rebecca's voice, sounding agitated. "I'm supposed to check you for sores."

"Never mind that now. Help me dress," said a woman's voice, raspy and rough as if she had a sore throat. It must be la reine's bloodhollow, but why was it awake? Sireen had promised to stay away.

Bitterlich hurried to the locker where the bloodhollow was being kept in time to find Rebecca, wide-eyed and damp from the rain, helping the bloodhollow on with its slip. Both women looked up at Bitterlich. The bloodhollow's dead stare from its white skull, showing through its transparent flesh, made his skin crawl and the fur on his spine stand on end.

"Madame." Bitterlich made as much of a bow as he could make in such cramped quarters.

"Oh, it's you," said la reine. "Have you come to watch me get dressed?"

"No, Madame," Bitterlich said, averting his gaze. "I heard voices and came to see what was the matter. I was given to understand that you would not be joining us until we reached our destination."

Sireen said, "Plans change. I would have word with the capitaine. Fetch her."

"What shall I tell her you want to discuss?" Bitterlich asked.

"Just tell her to come and not to dawdle. Now, hurry on."

Bitterlich bowed himself out. Sireen was not usually so brusque, but perhaps this was a true emergency.

He took the companionway up to the main deck four steps at a time, and emerged into a squall. Rain lashed him through his oilskin, and he put on some otter fur to keep dry.

Isabelle stood at the rail on the quarterdeck, her spark-hand holding on to an iron ring embedded in the wood. The ship crested a pressure ridge and plummeted into the void beyond. For a moment Bitterlich floated above the deck, weightless, and then the trough bottomed out. Every man aboard slammed into the planking as if they'd dropped from the yards. Isabelle remained affixed to the deck as if nailed to it, her spark-arm holding her fast without regards to mass or momentum.

Bitterlich mounted the quarterdeck in three sodden splashing steps and gave her a salute, which she returned. She liked wild weather and might have delighted in a storm like this, dangerous as it was, but her expression was as closed as a castle gate, her skin as gray and weary as weathered stone. Even the pink and purple embers of her spark swarm seemed like the last remnants of a dying fire.

"What is it, Major?" she asked.

"It's la reine," he said. "She's awake and requires your attendance. She did not say why."

Isabelle grimaced. "Of course she does. Thank you, Major."

He followed Isabelle down into the hold. She hadn't invited him, but she didn't dismiss him either. Perhaps he could be of some use.

They found Sireen's bloodhollow in a narrow passage with crates stacked to the beams on either side. Rebecca stood stiffly to one side, doing her level best to turn invisible.

Isabelle doffed her hat and bowed. "My reine."

"Good evening, Capitaine," Sireen said, her voice still rough. "I pray the adventure is going well."

"As well as may be. How may I serve you?" Isabelle said. "I was not expecting to see you so soon."

"I know, but I can be forgiven under the circumstances." She turned her skeletal gaze to Bitterlich. "Leave us, and take the girl."

Bitterlich gestured for Rebecca and she hastily scampered to his side.

"Builder keep, Madame," he said, and she waved him on.

He led Rebecca down the passage to the stairs. They nearly trod on one of the ship's cats. It hissed at them and slunk behind the stairs in the companionway.

"That's la reine, is it," Rebecca said low enough so as not to be overheard. "Nasty mouth on her."

"What did she say?" Bitterlich asked.

"She told me standards had fallen."

"Ah," Bitterlich said. Sireen had been known to be dry and acerbic, and Rebecca was aggressively defensive when it came to being accused of things, even in jest. Still, he had an uncomfortable feeling about la reine's presence here. What did she want to tell Isabelle that she didn't want Bitterlich to know? He signaled Rebecca for silence and put on his owl ears, listening back down the corridor.

Sireen said, ". . . spymaster informs me that Hasdrubal failed his mission. He stole the reliquary from the temple, but the prize was already gone."

"How did she find that out?" Isabelle asked.

"Questioning the orator and the Last Men," Sireen said.

"Do we know who took it?" Isabelle asked.

Sireen's voice got even lower. "The only other person who knew of the relic's importance is Sagax Quill. He inspected the reliquary when it arrived in Rocher Royale before handing it off to the orator for safekeeping. He probably took the relic at that point. We suspect he took it with him on the expedition. I decided to tell you personally because I don't want this information dispersed. I charge you with collecting the relic, and above all else, keeping it safe. The Vault of Ages belongs to l'Empire."

"I understand," Isabelle said, and then there was silence.

After a moment Isabelle said, "You two can come out now."

Bitterlich exchanged a look with Rebecca. She tried to look chagrined, but couldn't quite pull it off. He sighed, stood, and adjusted his hat.

"I didn't think we made that much noise," he said, stepping into the corridor.

Isabelle stared at the now-inert bloodhollow, and it was hard to say which one looked more lifeless.

"It was the noise I didn't hear. No boots on the stairs." Isabelle finally dragged her attention away from the empty bloodhollow.

Rebecca said, "What's she talking about, the Vault of Ages?" Belatedly she saluted. "Capitaine."

Isabelle looked on Rebecca and frowned. "As your capitaine, I must swear you to secrecy. None of what you have witnessed tonight is to be shared or even hinted at with anyone else without my explicit permission. You may talk to me about it when we are alone."

"What about him?" Rebecca said.

Isabelle's gaze twitched to the side, looking at the crates . . . or focused on something that wasn't there. Her ghosts had risen. She shot Bitterlich a questioning look. He shook his head: nothing there. She squeezed her eyes shut, fighting with the vision.

Bitterlich touched Rebecca on the shoulder to divert her and said, "I've already been sworn to secrecy."

"Didn't say that," Isabelle muttered.

"Beg pardon, Capitaine," Bitterlich said, hoping his voice could guide her home.

Isabelle's gaze refocused on Bitterlich, and she took just enough of a breath to form a thought before saying, "Just thinking out loud, Major. Yes, Rebecca, you may speak to Major Bitterlich, but no one else, do you understand?"

If the adults' divergent answers perturbed Rebecca, it didn't show. "Yes, Capitaine."

"Very well. What I'm about to tell you is the absolute limit of what I may reveal. Further information will not be forthcoming, do you understand?"

Rebecca hesitated as if she thought she was being tricked, but finally answered in the affirmative.

Isabelle said, "May your vow bind your tongue. My superiors believe the Vault of Ages is on the craton where we're headed. As of yet we have no proof of that. On the small chance that it is there, it is likely to be a ruin, a spot to which people will someday make pilgrimages."

Rebecca nodded. "Good pickings on pilgrims." She was invariably pragmatic about other people's possessions. "But what if it's real? I mean, it's the Savior."

Isabelle's lips pressed into a line. Bitterlich had spent the occasional afternoon tea contemplating the divine with her. While she acknowledged the Builder as the creator of all things, she had less use for the Prophecy or the Savior it promised. If he had to guess, he'd say that the notion of trying to compress that complexity into an answer that would satisfy a child had her stymied.

He said, "The thing is, we won't know until we get there, and we don't want to start rumors. Imagine if you heard that someone had spilled a barrel of gold coins just around the corner. Everyone would rush in, looking for the gold. Fights would break out even if it turned out there was nothing there. We don't want that."

"So we don't tell anybody because we want it for ourselves," Rebecca said.

Bitterlich said, "Correct. Though our intentions are not so mercenary."

"What's 'mercenary'?" Rebecca asked.

Isabelle said, "It means done for the purpose of making money, and that will be enough questions for now. I need you to finish putting the blood-hollow away."

They left a none-too-satisfied Rebecca to her work, and mounted the stairs. His heart lifted in joyous memory of what it was like to be at her side, on the same side, in step without even trying. This was what he'd thrown away.

"We already searched Quill's belongings," he said.

"Not the clothes he was wearing," Isabelle said, her voice a growl. "Not his jewelry."

"His ring," Bitterlich said.

"That would be my first guess. It's quondam metal and it doesn't fit him."

"And it's the sort of thing a dead saint's hand might be wearing," Bitterlich said.

They arrived in the great cabin at the door to the guest quarters. Bitterlich rapped to be polite, and then opened the door for Isabelle.

Quill stood up from his cot to meet Isabelle. His hands trembled and he kept his left thumb curled to keep his ring from falling off. "Capitaine, how may I serve you this evening?"

Isabelle held out her hand as if to receive a gift. In a tone both mild and deadly she said, "Hand it over."

Quill looked taken aback. "I've already given you—"

"The key to the Vault," Isabelle said. "You can either hand it over or I can have you stripped to your shorthairs and burn every one of your possessions to ash until I find the one that does not ignite, or am I wrong to suspect that the key is made of the alloy of Legend?"

Bitterlich had seen Isabelle in battle, but he'd never seen her quite this furious before. It was the anger of someone completely out of the energy required of patience.

"You are . . . not wrong," he said, "but Capitaine, I beg you listen to reason. I—"

"You have lied to me," Isabelle said. "You lied to la reine. You lied about your purpose. You lied about the dangers we face. I am done with your lies. Hand. It. Over."

"Capitaine, I appreciate your anger, and I can't say it's unjustified, but the Vault of Ages is the Temple's jurisdiction—"

"Major," Isabelle said. "Retrieve the key."

Bitterlich stepped forward, making himself inevitable. Quill drew himself up haughtily, drawing his dignity around him like a cloak. "Violence will not be necessary." His trembling hand fumbled the ring from his thumb and passed it to Bitterlich.

Like most quondam artifacts, the ring was far heavier than it ought to be, denser even than gold. It was shaped like a signet ring, its flat face adorned with the symbol of the Builder's omnioculus. Though solid and opaque, the metal seemed to be filled with the shadows of spinning gears that one could glimpse at the edge of vision but that vanished entirely when observed directly.

Bitterlich handed it to Isabelle.

—

Isabelle took the ring and sat on a bench, braced her head with her skin hand and felt her way into the ring with her spark-hand. She lost control of her body when her consciousness left it, but with practice she'd learned to let it drift off into a light doze first, so that at least she didn't flop on the floor. Her spark fingers gripped the ring and pricked like nettles as she exerted her power. Her l'Étincelle gripped and she slid from her body into the ring, like slithering through a curtain of greasy grit.

Isabelle had experimented with inhabiting all sorts of materials, from steel to sand and stone to quicksilver, anything that had never been alive, and every substance had its own feel. In hammered steel she could feel the edges where slivers of sharp iron fitted together. Glass felt like swimming through taffy, and quicksilver was dark and heavy in her breast.

But quondam artifacts were different. The Builder and his workshops had filled their devices with gears and axles, catches and punched ribbons that turned along axes the mind could not see and filled up spaces that should have interfered with one another.

Most of the artifacts Isabelle had got her hands on were mere fragments of broken devices, machines of adamant torn apart in the Breaking of the

World. Inhabiting them was like swimming through a collapsed clock tower filled with shattered bits of nonworking machines, the purpose of which she could only speculate upon.

The key was different. All of the ratchets and springs remained intact. She flowed through their structure like the shadow of a hawk across the top of a cloud. She looped through the wheels like a rope through a series of pulleys, block and tackle designed to move not pallets of freight but spools of information. Yet though the ring hummed and thrummed with life, it slept deeply, unperturbed by her presence, and none of the gears would shift at her urging. Around and around she wound until at last she reached a gap, a space where a cog of many planes was missing. Here there were release mechanisms and flaccid springs, higher-dimensional axles that had no other end. This was the shape of the lock and the key, two halves of a whole greater than the sum of both.

She could have spent hours puzzling out the intricacy of the space, but she'd discovered what she came for. She withdrew the way she came, spooling herself back into her body until finally the last thread of her sorcery detached from the ring like pulling a burr out of a wool coat. The sensation of inhabiting her own flesh made her skin shiver. Her ancestral chorus hissed and roiled like a nest of snakes, reminding her just how blessed the silence inside the key had been. Alas that she could not trust them to remain quiescent when she was away. Ever she feared to return to her mind after an excursion to discover that it had been occupied in her absence.

She had indeed slumped over but someone, Bitterlich probably, had laid her on a cot. She rubbed her face, finding her burn scar rough under her fingers. After a moment, she stood.

"Did you learn anything interesting?" Bitterlich gave her a politely questioning look, whiskers twitching, which had the irritating knock-on effect of making her want to grin. She resisted. Mostly.

She held up the ring. "I can't prove it is the key to the Vault of Ages. But I can't prove it isn't either. It's definitely an intact artifact, alive but asleep. I can see where there's a space for it to interact with something else, but I can't tell what will happen when it does."

Quill yearned forward like a bird trapped in a tar pit, unable to escape, and his voice was strained with urgency. "Capitaine, please take warning. The Vault of Ages is not a treasure chest to be plundered. If opened at all it must be done with utmost care."

"I have no intention of cracking the Vault. My mission is to claim Craton Auroborea for l'Empire. I will keep the key safe and deliver it to l'impératrice's own hand on my return to Rocher Royale. Until then, this is the last I want to hear of it."

—

Bitterlich followed Isabelle to the chartroom. She muttered to herself all the way. Anyone unaware of her mental difficulties might have mistaken it for mere frustrated grumbling, but Bitterlich's sensitive ears picked up Isabelle's half of an argument with someone who wasn't there.

"He is a passenger, and I do not toss people overboard."

"Isabelle—" Bitterlich said gingerly.

"Capitaine," she corrected, dragging her attention away from the phantasm.

The correction stung. She had once indoctrinated him into the order of people who were encouraged to call her by her first name. He had been the one worried about propriety at the time. He'd lost that favor, but that didn't mean he'd lost his heart.

"Capitaine," he said. "Permission to speak freely."

She paused, rubbing thumb on forefinger as she did sometimes in deep thought, and then gestured him to follow her into her private cabin. The ship lurched and rain rattled. Isabelle checked her timepiece, grimaced, and then reached into her sky trunk for a potion. The bottom of the trunk was packed neatly with empty phials. She swallowed her most recent potion and placed the empty with the others.

"To answer your next question," she said, "yes, it's getting worse."

As a major sworn to la reine's service, Bitterlich ought to be most concerned about Isabelle's fitness for command. As her friend, if he could still call himself that, he worried for her well-being and ached at the thought of her suffering.

"You were talking to someone," he said.

Isabelle shook her head, but gently as if she were afraid of dislodging something. "Before it was like they were shouting at me from behind a wall, and everything they said was babble, but now there's a hole in the wall and they're getting out. They're getting into my reality, standing there as real as you are, and they're talking to me. I can't convince my brain they are false even when they make no sense."

Bitterlich had heard such descriptions before, and not from those afflicted with mental diseases. "Behind the wall? That's the everdream you've told me about, where the ancestors live?"

"Yes, except mine is broken. Or it was never fully formed. It's a void with a vortex in it, shards of memory whipping round."

Bitterlich came to stand beside her, though not so close as to make her feel crowded. "My animals don't talk to me, but they do have personalities. Some are friendlier. Some less so."

Isabelle turned her tired, curious face to him. "How do you deal with the hostile ones?"

"None of mine are actively hostile," he said. "I take care in how I select my companions. After Littlepaws, I didn't have the heart to harry an animal, fight it, drive it into submission like most of my folk do. Fear shouldn't be part of a relationship that's going to last a lifetime."

He drew himself inside out like turning a sleeve and emerged on the other side as a raven. "My raven was the oldest of the colony that lived in Rocher Royale. He was wise in the ways of ravens, but stiff and weary with the years. I offered him relief from pain, a life beyond life. He accepted the offer and came to me willingly. I have not found him weaker for that."

He shifted back into his erstepelz. "My horse was a messenger who had been wind-swift and high spirited, now old and lame. From her I learned all the roads and byways of l'Empire. My bear had ruled the Longshadow Mountains for thirty years, but would not last another winter."

"So instead of the biggest and the strongest, you curate the oldest, the wisest, and the ones most in need."

"I have never been disappointed in my choices, unlike some of my fellow Seelenjägers, who often find themselves gaolers to terrified, half-mad animals that will do anything to escape."

"Like my ghosts," Isabelle said.

"Yes." Bitterlich could have skinned himself for not grasping the similarities months ago. "Like your ghosts, they don't understand that they can't escape, but still they throw themselves against their leads, gnaw at their bindings, and claw at the gate between the Seelengewölbe and the sorcerer's seat of consciousness. In the worst cases, the caged spirits get loose and savage the sorcerer's mind, leaving him little more than a beast himself. We call that *das schwarze Biest* and it's every Seelenjäger's worst nightmare."

"How do you deal with rebellious spirits?" Isabelle asked, her expression somewhere between hopeful and desperate. "Or can you?"

"It can be mitigated. Whenever I take on a new shape, or make a chimera"—he knitted together a cat and an owl to make himself a tiny gryphon, which made her smile despite the bleakness of the moment—"I have to reach into my Seelengewölbe. When I'm ensconcing a new resident, I take my whole awareness through to set all the threads of the skein and make sure the loom receives them properly. A Seelenjäger fighting *das schwarze Biest* has to do the same thing, except the spirit is fighting back and doing everything it can to tangle and shred the loom."

Lightning flashed through the black clouds around them, too much like streaks of anger in a wounded mind, followed by the low, mournful rumble of despair.

Isabelle considered that. "So you're saying I have to go fight my ghosts in their own graveyard."

"You have to tame them, and make that place yours, or at least that's what a Seelenjäger has to do. I don't know if Fenice ancestors work the same way."

"But I don't want to keep them," Isabelle said. "They aren't mine, and I didn't choose them."

"I know," Bitterlich said. "Everyone you're related to by blood has been a lunatic or a monster. The only family who's ever cared about you is the one you picked."

She looked down at him, and her lips parted as if she were about to speak, but she thought better of it, shut her mouth, and looked away.

Bitterlich would have given his left arm to know what she'd been thinking just then. Was he part of her family? Could he still be?

There came a rap at the door, and Vrain's voice, "Capitaine Isabelle."

"Enter," she said.

Vrain stepped in, water dripping from his oilskin, his expression even more dour than usual. "Capitaine, we have a missing man."

—

Jean-Claude, still skysick from the storm, gathered with Isabelle and her officers in the tradesmen's quarters. The carpenters, gunsmiths, keel gang, and rope makers had their own space below the officers' quarters, slightly less cramped than the rest of the crew, but still dark and close.

Keelmaster Marchand spoke to Isabelle. "Keelmate Gephardt didn't show up for duty, so I came down to kick him up, begging your pardon, but he weren't here. Well, I checked around. Maybe he'd gone to the crap chute, but he wasn't there and he wasn't anywhere else I looked, and no one else has seen him either."

Isabelle frowned and said to Vrain, "All hands. Search the ship."

"Aye, Capitaine." Vrain took himself off to rouse the off watch.

Isabelle turned to Jean-Claude. "If you would find out who saw him last."

Jean-Claude was still numb about the lips, but he tipped his battered hat to her. "The capitaine's need is my pleasure." Most likely Gephardt would show up somewhere, maybe drunk and passed out in the hold, but until then Jean-Claude would search less accessible places, like other people's memories.

Just then Isabelle's gaze caught on something just over Jean-Claude's shoulder. Since there was nothing there but a bulkhead, he gave a quick shake of his head to warn her off. She squeezed her eyes shut and pinched the bridge of her nose. Giving her ghost time to fade.

Jean-Claude captured Keelmaster Marchand's attention and asked, "Tradesman, how long has this Gephardt fellow been a member of your gang?"

"Just picked him up this run," Marchand said. "Good man. Good with the valves. A bit touched, though."

"Touched in what way?" Jean-Claude asked.

"Doesn't talk much, mostly lives in his own head. Likes things just so. Some of the lads had a bit of a go with him when we set out. Kept moving his stuff around. He got flustered to tears, nearly pulled his own hair out. I put a stop to that, made sure they leave him alone."

"Not a man with many friends, then," Jean-Claude said.

"Truth be, he doesn't seem to want any," Marchand said.

"Enemies?" It didn't take much more than being a bit odd to give a man a whole world full of enemies. About half the loners he'd met enjoyed solitude. The other half just didn't want to be hurt anymore.

"Nothing private, if you take my meaning. There are always some who can't stand the odd ones, think they've got a Torment in 'em."

Jean-Claude grunted in acknowledgment. He'd been dealing with similar superstitious prejudice against Isabelle for her whole life. Since the expedition had lofted, he'd spent a considerable amount of time with the crew, telling stories of her bravery and kindness, cutting a firebreak around her reputation that had kept the crew from worrying about her mutterings and quirks.

"Monsieur Marchand, I'd like you to introduce me to the rest of your gang."

The storm ended sometime before dawn. Though the crew searched the ship down to its last bent nail, Gephardt was nowhere to be found.

As they continued not finding a living man, Jean-Claude's investigation took on greater importance. The other members of the keel gang were the most helpful in that they actually had memories of the missing man, though none of them could recall precisely when they'd last seen him. They agreed he'd been to chow because it was Saint Even's Day and nobody missed out on the lemon tarts, even if they were old and dry. They were pretty sure he'd gone back to his rack, but they weren't sure when he'd got up and left. He had a journal that he wouldn't show anyone, and sometimes he'd go wander the turvy deck, and when he wasn't doing that, he was usually in the workshop tinkering with used parts. He didn't gamble, and as far as they knew he didn't owe anybody so much as the time of day.

Jean-Claude opened Gephardt's sky trunk and inventoried the paltry findings: an extra set of clothes, books on aeromechanics, small tools, a very well-used journal. He picked up the worn leather book and flipped to the most recent page of entries.

Gephardt's handwriting was small and neat, so as to fit more words per page. The keelmate mentioned his assignment to the *Thunderclap,* noted his signing bonus, and then sketched a design for something labeled an aetheric condenser valve, beside which were scratched equations Jean-Claude was unqualified to decipher.

He closed the trunk, fastened it with his own lock, and then sought Isabelle. He found her on the quarterdeck directing the search under cerulean skies. The upper airs had been scrubbed clean and the Miasma below beaten down, leaving nothing but the coppery scent of the deep sky.

Her skin was pale with fatigue and her expression drawn. She gave him a tired smile. So far she had her ghosts under control, but he dreaded the day she looked at him without recognition. She was the child of his soul if not his seed. It was not fair that she should be afflicted by a foe he could not fight, one that attacked the very root of her being.

"Have you learned anything new?" Isabelle asked.

"Nothing useful," Jean-Claude said. "The most pervasive hypothesis is that he exited the ship by way of a turvy hatch and fell into the Gloom. The follow-up question is whether his departure was accidental, coerced, or voluntary. An odd man with no friends, he may have had cause for despair."

Isabelle grimaced. "I can understand that. Bullying is murder by subtle means."

Jean-Claude handed her Gephardt's journal. "He was working on something numerical that I can't understand."

Isabelle pulled on her *gant d'acier* to hold the book with her spark-hand while she thumbed through it with her skin hand. She got to the end, shook her head, and said, "Poor man. He was trying to work out the Maddux-Creech conjecture."

"What does that mean?" Jean-Claude said. "In terms a simple-but-honest peasant can understand."

"You were never simple. Or honest. But all it really means is Gephardt was trying to solve an unsolvable problem." She drummed her fingers on the page, and for a moment Jean-Claude could not tell if she was lost in thought or being visited by her ancestors.

"I have another responsibility for you," she said, and led him into the chartroom. A vaporgram simulacrum of the Spiral Archipelago filled the orrery, an inward curl of small skylands mostly inhabited by fisherfolk. Joubert's Folly turned in the center, a larger rock tilted like a top that was just beginning to wobble.

Isabelle drew from her pouch a quondam metal ring and held it up to the light. "This, apparently, is the key to the Vault of Ages . . ." She filled him in on her visit from Sireen and her confrontation with Sagax Quill. "And it occurs to me that Hasdrubal knows the ring is on this ship. That's why he had Quill attacked on the way to board. He didn't get the ring then, but that doesn't mean he won't try again. I am commanded by la reine herself to keep this thing safe at all costs. I am delegating that duty to you."

She handed him the ring, heavy as a deck-gun ball. He closed his fist around it.

"Safe and secret," he said, and tucked the ring in his pouch. "A secured sanctuary somewhere seriously stealthy, and several similar synonyms starting with *s*."

"Succinctly said, soldier," Isabelle said, and hugged him. "And one more thing." She opened the orrery's hyperbaric berths and extracted the *Conquest* shard with her spark-hand. The freezing mist found no purchase on her sorcerous limb. "Keep this too."

Puzzled, he took the bone needle and said, "Why?"

Isabelle's mouth worked as if she were trying to spit out ill-formed words. "Think of it as a check against my head troubles."

Jean-Claude's spirit sank. "I thought you had it under control."

Isabelle bestowed him a brittle smile. "For now. So far it's visions and voices, but what if it gets worse? What if I can't concentrate? If I lose my ability to reason, will I be able to recognize it? It's like asking, 'When does fog become opaque?' Is it when I can't see the horizon, or when I can't see the bowsprit, or when I can't see my hand in front of my face? I need someone I trust, who will let me know when it's time to let go, and who will prize my hand from the wheel if I refuse. The shard is just a little extra precaution. We won't need it again until well after Joubert's Folly. If ever it becomes necessary, you can give it to Vrain. Can you do that for me?"

Jean-Claude's heart had become lodged in his throat and he had to swallow hard to clear it so that he could breathe. He'd raised Isabelle as best he could, fostered her independence, delighted in her spirit. She was supposed to carry on being vital and brilliant long after he was gone. She was supposed to plant a sapling on his grave. He was not supposed to be the one charged with escorting her from the stage. Yet who else could she trust? Marie was growing with all the speed and persistence of snakeweed, but she deserved her freedom. Jean-Claude certainly would not trust her care to Major Seelenjäger. Thank the saints that blossom had withered.

"I will," he said, his voice heavy. "Though I pray that day never comes."

—

Aeronaut Gregor was a talented scrimshaw artist, and like all artists his work produced bits of leftover scrap. He was pleased to gift Jean-Claude with a sliver of leviathanbone, which Jean-Claude said he was going to use to make a needle.

As soon as Jean-Claude left his sight, he slipped the leviathanbone sliver into the lock box where the *Conquest* shard was supposed to be. He didn't anticipate needing to deploy the misdirection, but his life had been full of things he didn't anticipate, and it had become his habit to prepare for them anyway.

⸺

By noon it was abundantly clear that Keelmate Gephardt was gone, and the men had already started to grumble about ill omens. Isabelle summoned Quill to the chartroom.

"Learned sagax," she said, invoking the formal tone to keep her own animosity at bay. "One of the crew, Keelmate Ghephardt, has died. The crew require your spiritual guidance."

Quill adjusted his chasuble. The voluminous drapery made him look like a sail that had been taken aback. "So does the capitaine, though she is unwilling to hear it."

"I am well aware of what the Temple thinks of me. I am the Breaker's get, an unnatural creature, an exquisite, handcrafted flaw thrust into the world to corrupt the innocent and weak-minded." She'd been hearing that since she was too young to know what it meant.

Quill said, "The Temple is old and corrupt, festering with parasites living off the goodwill of ages past, protected by the common man's need for certainty and fear of the unknown. Yet there is no body, no matter how vast and bloated, that can withstand the ceaseless multiplications of maggots without rupturing."

"All the more reason to pile it on a barge, shove it out in the deep sky, and burn it."

Quill's eyebrows arched. "Assuming you could somehow disentangle the Temple from people's lives, pull it up rock and root and abolish it forever, what would you replace it with? People still want guidance. They still seek faith in the unknowable and joy in the numinous."

This was not a conversation Isabelle meant to get dragged into any further. "Is that the lecture you're going to give to the crew now that their shipmate is dead?"

Quill picked up his copy of the *Instructions* and said, "Shall I relay the Temple's orthodox doctrine: Their shipmate, whose body is lost to the Gloom, has been dragged screaming through the Ravenous Gate and condemned to Torment until the Savior comes to release him? Only their hard work and dedication to the Prophecy can help his suffering end. Or shall I provide a gentler heterodoxy, that the saints are protecting Keelmate Gephardt in Torment until the Savior comes to cast the Breaker out and release him? Or shall I tell them the truth, which is that we have no more idea what happened to Gephardt's soul than we know what happened to his body, but that we have a chance to find out?"

Anger flared like fire in Isabelle's mind, for this was a clear threat to defy her directive of secrecy about the Vault. Fortunately the solution was straightforward. "Put your staff away. You will not be delivering the lecture. I will not permit you to undermine my authority with my crew. I am confining you to quarters until we reach Joubert's Folly." And then she would put him ashore and let him make his own way back to Craton Massif.

"Be at ease," Quill said. "I have no intention of suborning your men. I will give them permission to be hurt and be frightened, to feel loss and grieve without fear of being thought cowards by their peers. As your spiritual adviser, the question I want to know is why you, who have by all accounts dedicated your life to puzzling out difficult truths, are so afraid of these. Either the Vault is there or it isn't. Either the Savior is there or not. At this point it is unthinkable that no one will find out, and then you will have to deal with the facts whatever they are. And try as you might, you cannot stand athwart the future screaming, 'No!'"

His words stung a sensitive spot Isabelle hadn't known she possessed. "Do you honestly think facts matter to those who traffic in belief? Nobody wants a Savior for all mortalkind. They instead want a judge who will decide the future in their favor. Who will vindicate their prejudices and hand them victory over their foes while asking nothing from them in return.

"While you're posing questions, ponder this one: How do you think those with vested interests in faith would react if the Savior arose from the Vault of Ages, the Builder's will incarnate, possessed of the powers of all the saints and free from corruption? She carries in her hands the ability to finish the work of the saints, to expel the Breaker from Creation, to free the souls of the clayborn dead from Torment, to restore the Primus Mundi and create Paradise Everlasting. All she requires of mortalkind is that we give up hatred, envy, greed, and fear. We must forgive our enemies, admit our sins, seek atonement, give up our wealth, and trust the stranger. Will she be beloved and obeyed or burned as an Abomination?"

Quill frowned. "Prophecy says it is the Savior who will bring such a lasting peace, which is why we seek to prepare the world for his arrival."

"Precisely." Isabelle swept her hands together asymptotically, fingertips never quite meeting. "We are supposed to improve the world. The problem with believers is that they always want the Savior to do the hard part for them."

CHAPTER

Ten

The orrery showed the *Thunderclap* had been blown several hundred kilometers off course and put them in a position trailing Joubert's Folly in its slow scud around the northern eddy of the Hoary Gyre. That would add days onto the expedition, but the mission had built in as much slack as possible to the schedule.

Isabelle ordered best speed for Joubert's Folly. With the prevailing wind, that would take the *Thunderclap* through the tail of the archipelago. There was no immediate sign of the *Dame Formue* or any other pursuit. Given that the storm that had tossed them around for two days had certainly done the same to their adversaries, Isabelle hoped to reach the fleet depot, resupply, and depart before they were espied. With luck, the *Thunderclap* might be able to avoid pursuit completely. Then all she'd have to worry about, from a military point of view, was the Skaladin Fleet.

She stood in the chartroom, listening to Lieutenant Vrain's most recent report from Fleet Command. The storm had driven l'Empire's Hoary Fleet to seek shelter in Port Verduin, closer in to Craton Massif, which put them several days out from the Spiral Archipelago.

"Is there any more news on the Skaladin Fleet?" Isabelle asked.

Vrain said, "The last time we had eyes on them they were still on course for the Lorentz Trough." There the aethercurrent and the prevailing winds could let them sweep down on imperial outposts in the Hoary Gyre so quickly that an out-of-position fleet would not be able to intercept them.

"Strike to the heart," said Capitana Falconé, gesturing at the palace walls. "The master has sneaked away to woo his mistress, and has cleared a path for his own return."

Falconé, dressed in courtesan silks, her great plume of yellow-gold crest feathers fanned, stood just to Isabelle's left. Was she supposed to be here? She'd been with Isabelle at the Sacking of Galbarron.

Isabelle held her reply. Her gaze fixed on the orrery. Falconé's reflection did not appear in the glass. She was a ghost stain, unreal. Her phantom visitors were coming closer together, even after she'd adjusted her potion schedule. If she shortened the interval again, would she have enough supply for the return trip? She tried to do the multiplication in her head and came up pottage. A month ago she could have done it without effort.

She closed her eyes until Capitana Falconé's stain faded. The visions were so very like waking up suddenly from the middle of a dream. They were more real to the mind than the evidence of her senses until they had time to fade, and then they became absurd and disjointed, hard to remember. Yet she understood the advice Falconé had been trying to give.

She said, "Suggest to Fleet Command that they might detach a squadron to threaten the Sundered Isles. The Skaladin might think twice about committing to the trough if they think the Hoary Fleet is ready to pounce on their home port."

"Yes, Capitaine," Vrain said, and his gaze became distracted as he inhabited his bloodhollow back at the Cauldron. Watching his expression go slack, it occurred to Isabelle that perhaps the reason her Sanguinaire officers had not taken much note of Isabelle's distracted fits was because it so closely resembled their own behaviors when they were visiting their bloodhollows. It never occurred to them that her moments of absence were unusual.

Isabelle withdrew from the chartroom, wondering whose advice Vrain had passed along. She never would have thought about sending a diversionary squadron if Falconé hadn't nudged her. She was not sure which terrified her more: that she had understood the suggestion, or that it seemed reasonable to threaten war with the tyrant. War was the last thing she wanted.

But her ancestors weren't helping her for her own benefit. They wanted her to be their puppet, to continue their dynasty and carry on a legacy she had not asked for. The inheritance they sought to impose was defined by war, power, lust, madness, and betrayal.

"Capitaine." Vrain stepped out of the chartroom behind her, his face as grim as a tombstone. "I've just received urgent news from the Cauldron."

Five minutes later, Isabelle and her line officers gathered around the orrery. The machine showed the *Thunderclap* on its approach to Joubert's Folly. The naval base turned at the center of the Spiral Archipelago, with the rest of the skylands trailing around it like a ribbon in the hand of a dancer.

Vrain pointed to one of the skylands on the whip end of the spiral and his low voice rumbled like an upset stomach. "Fleet headquarters informs me that a Skaladin culling fleet is ashore at Fishers Point. When last we heard, the raiders were assaulting the local garrison. Capitaine Wyatt, the garrison commander, begs us to intervene."

The news hit Isabelle like a blow to the gut. Skaladin culling fleets could strip whole skylands bare of civilization. The clayborn they killed as heretics to their twisted religion, while every saintborn would be broken and branded to be remade into a tool for the tyrant.

But Isabelle's orders were to proceed north without falter or fail, to mark the route through the Bittergale, to capture the *Conquest* and claim Craton Auroborea. She had no right to risk the *Thunderclap*.

"How long ago was this?" Isabelle asked.

"A few minutes," Vrain said. "Wyatt said Skaladin infiltrators took the shore battery by surprise just before dawn. Then they sailed into the harbor cove and landed culling parties. Everyone who could retreated to the fort."

"How many Skaladin?" Isabelle asked.

"Three ships at least," Vrain said. "Wyatt couldn't say what type, but the harbor cove isn't very big."

Isabelle's belly tightened. More than likely a culling fleet would cut ropes and run at the first sight of an imperial warship. They wanted to steal their slaves, not fight for them. Yet if they stood and fought, Isabelle would be outnumbered and maybe outgunned against more experienced capitaines, and who knew what sort of cullborn slaves to provide them with sorcerous power.

"Do we have any other ships in this area?" Isabelle asked. The best thing, the smart thing, would be to stay away and let the Hoary Fleet handle it. Let this be someone else's problem.

"No, Capitaine," Ensign Navigator Pummeroy said. "If it hadn't been for that storm, even we wouldn't be in this area. The Hoary Fleet is a week out."

By the time the Hoary Fleet arrived, the people of Fishers Point would be dead or halfway to the slave markets in Skaladin.

If the wind held, the *Thunderclap* was only half a day away. She might be able to catch the raiders ashore.

Isabelle scanned the expectant faces in the room—people waiting for her to make a decision.

"They are not left behind because they are unworthy," said Don Luggia, his eyes hard and flinty. His crest feathers flattened back in a wedge. "They are left behind to distract the enemy, while we march for the prize."

Isabelle grimaced at the callousness of that suggestion, but the advice was sound. If she allowed herself to be turned aside, it would give her foes time to catch up with her.

But it would also mean leaving defenseless people to be slaughtered or worse.

All choices were bad, but bad was not the same thing as wrong. She owed her whole life, from her first breath on, to a brave heart and a fool's chance. She would sooner cut out her own still-beating heart than abandon innocents to the culling fleets.

Isabelle checked the square of her shoulders. She glanced at Don Luggia, but he was no longer there. He had never been there. Curse this madness.

She regarded her officers and summoned her voice of command. "Helmsman, set a course for Fishers Point. We're between them and the cratonic rim. If they hope to carry their prize home, they'll have to come through us. Vrain, get back to the Cauldron and get me updates from Fishers Point. Lieutenant Simon, feed the crew, douse the cook fire, beat to quarters, and clear for battle. Rebecca, fetch me Major Bitterlich."

"Aye, Capitaine," the crowd saluted as one, and hurried to their duties.

Only when they were gone did Isabelle allow the quaking shudder that had been building in her gut to come rattling out, shaking her skeleton like a sack of sticks.

She was no stranger to violence. She'd scars both inside and out. She'd killed a man with her spark-hand once, but she'd never sought out conflict. It had always been there, waiting for her, chasing her until she finally turned and fought. This time whatever happened would be on her ledger.

"Capitaine," Bitterlich said, stepping through the door. She caught his gaze. His polite if distant expression softened a bit around the edges. He didn't seem to know what to say.

Do I look that awful? She must show strength and composure to her men.

What do his feelings matter? He is your subordinate, said her chorus.

Isabelle rubbed the nape of her neck to make the fine hairs lay flat. She needed no more advice from the dead.

"Major." She pointed to the orrery. "A culling fleet has attacked Fishers Point. We're on course to intercept. I need you to find out exactly what we're up against."

"Yes, Capitaine," Bitterlich said, saluting so primly that it seemed to pledge loyalty to fashion as well as l'Empire. "I shall come back with a complete count of their cannonballs." His brisk cheer sounded strained to her ears.

She held his gaze, golden eyes with vertical pupils and lovely amber sworls around the edges. Once he'd called her a fire under snow and she'd kissed him, and then she'd messed it up somehow.

He cleared his throat, and looked like he couldn't decide what to do with his tongue. At last he said, "Capitaine, I wish to apologize for my behavior—"

She held up a hand to stay his tongue. "I appreciate your concern, but the mistake was entirely mine." She had made too many assumptions. "Saints grant you speed. Builder keep."

His mouth hung open for a moment but finally said, "Savior come." He bowed himself out as if leaving the presence of la reine.

When the door shut behind him, she swallowed her heart. Would that it constrain itself to pumping blood and abstain from engaging in frivolous yearnings.

Passion brings only pain. Make your heart a stone, her chorus chimed in with a clawlike tapping down her spine.

"I can't disagree with that," she muttered. Some days she wished she could banish all desires, especially those of the body.

She turned her attention to the orrery and adjusted its focus to the smallest scale to keep both the ship and Fishers Point in view. She took heart from the fact that the skyland still showed up in her aetherscope, because it meant their orrery was still intact. The first and most important rule of owning a sympathetic navigational beacon was to destroy it rather than let it be captured. No enemy must be allowed access to the chartstone shards in the sympathetic matrix, lest the stolen splinters reveal the position of every ship that had the skyland charted.

Isabelle calculated the distance to the skyland, the likely average speed, the rotational period of Fishers Point. When the *Thunderclap* arrived, they'd circle to the windward side and ride the skyland's vortex around. The Skaladin would see them coming but they wouldn't have much time to loft if they didn't want to be caught ashore. It was as good a plan as she could make without more information from the site, and that would have to wait for word from Bitterlich and Vrain.

Reports started coming in from all stations. The course was set. The guns stood ready. The armory had been opened and weapons distributed. The marines were girded. The *Thunderclap* became a war falcon baring her talons, a menace on the wing, every piece of her swift and deadly.

Every piece except the capitaine. What if she froze? What if she failed? How many would die by her inexperience?

Yet those people needed her: men, women, and children. Something deeply maternal stirred in her at the thought of children being taken, something hot and sharp and made of bright-edged steel. She had always defended the weak and the helpless, often to her own great cost and the scorn of the mighty. None of those victories would she trade for more glittering prizes.

—

The whole ship boiled like a kicked ant bed. Aeronauts scurried up the rigging, everybody hustling hither and thither to make the ship ready for combat. Gun crews cleared their deck and made their weapons ready. The great cabin was broken down and stern chasers dragged into place. Everything that might topple, shatter, catch fire, or explode was lashed down and locked away. Isabelle commanded the overhaul. Djordji and Marie pitched in. Even Rebecca was kept busy with the rest of the powder monkeys, spreading sand on the decks and running gunpowder up from the magazine.

The activities left Jean-Claude, who had about as much aeronautical use as a bag of wet feathers, sitting on the quarterdeck, as out of the way as it was possible to be, with Sagax Quill and Hailer Dok, the former having no skill at ships and the latter having no use for hard work.

"Don't you fear. I sings up the winds when the need rises," Dok said, leaning back against the bulwark.

No one seemed inclined to conversation, so Jean-Claude hunkered down to the point where if he tilted the brim of his hat just right, he couldn't see the sky sloshing around. He pulled Keelmate Gephardt's journal from his pack. Not that he expected it to show him anything new, but having a dead man to talk to was better than no one at all. He put on his spectacles and opened it to the last written page.

There was an equation and a drawing of the glass spiral with the rusted wire accompanied by the words *Tested dynamic coil in proofing chamber. Twenty-five cycles. Coil degraded. Aether penetrating alchemical glass?*

Jean-Claude imagined that written on a memorial plaque. "Aether penetrating alchemical glass?" Death was a banal scriptwriter.

Jean-Claude flipped back to the previous page. There was more math, another drawing, and the words *Assembled dynamic coil. Distillate of rarefied lumin gas ~.01% impure. Try galvanic inducement. Fed Bosun Whiskers.*

There were pages and paged of similar entries. Gephardt was the sort of man who could walk into a clock shop and all the merchandise would set itself to him. Anyone who had watched his daily routine once need never do so again to know exactly where he'd be. Had someone used that knowledge to surprise him?

A whistle in the wind caught Jean-Claude's attention. A thin, cold breeze came aboard and whispered by him, carrying music heard as if from behind a closed door.

Hailer Dok stirred. His eyes rounded as the wind coiled around him, rustling his hair and tickling his ears. It was a whispering wind, the kind Windcallers used to talk to one another across the deep sky. Dok popped to his feet and hurried to the poop deck.

Jean-Claude clambered after him. Who was talking to him, and what did they have to say? Were there more Gyrine around here? The last thing Isabelle needed was more surprises.

The whispering wind danced around Dok, shimmering and singing. He listened raptly, then licked his lips and joined the music, singing a duet.

Jean-Claude did not understand the words, but the voice on the wind was female, and the song was a sweet one.

The rusty gears in Jean-Claude's head turned as understanding dawned. He watched the spiraling wind as Dok picked up the song and sang another verse after the last had ended. Tears stood in his eyes.

At last the shimmering thread of wind raced away again. Jean-Claude pulled out his compass and checked its bearing. The departing strain of music headed north.

"Who was that?" Jean-Claude asked.

Dok twitched around as if he hadn't known Jean-Claude was standing there. "That's Solo Aria."

"The one you sent to Om?" Jean-Claude asked. "That sounded a bit more passionate than your ordinary political briefing."

Dok made a snaggletoothed grin and said, "She's also me wife. Best singer in the Deep Sky."

"Truly?" Jean-Claude asked. "Funny, Djordji never pointed that out."

"That's because it's no way yer business," Dok said. "Jackhand knew that."

"That's because he thought she was in Om, talking to the Omnifex," Jean-Claude said, "but she isn't." He made a show of looking at his compass. "Your whispering wind flew off that way, which, unless the world has turned upside down, is pretty close to due north. So unless I miss my guess, she's still on the Craton Auroborea."

Dok hid for a moment behind an unconvincing smile, but at last he said, "She stays behind to fend off bugs while the rest of us escapes."

Jean-Claude was impressed by this enormous boondoggle; he would have undertaken no less for Isabelle. Yet that did not make Dok trustworthy. "If you love this woman, why have you never mentioned her before?" Did Gyrine even know how to love, or was this just part of some greater connivance?

Dok's lip curled. "Because I don't imagine yer dirtborn roi or yer reine or whatever gilt-ridden backside sits the royal stool means to keep the bargain they makes with me. Oh sure, they gets their path to the craton, but they finds a way to keep the treasure too. I has no desire to give them another cudgel to bludgeon me with."

Jean-Claude very nearly pitied the man. There was no doubt politics was a treacherous business, but Sireen was no fool, and she had more reasons for wanting to keep the bargain than to betray it.

Jean-Claude dug deeper into this vein of truth ere it petered out. "So you made up this whole idea of lifting the anathema as cover for your rescue attempt."

"Nay," Dok said. "Lifting the anathema is no lie. It be the original plan, Aria's plan. It be why we takes Lael to find the *Conquest*. We means to secure the treasure and make our offer, but the swarm cut us short, see?"

"And because it was her idea, she's the one who had to fight the rear-guard," Jean-Claude surmised.

"She's the vote captain," Dok said, which Jean-Claude supposed was a yes.

Jean-Claude scratched under his goatee. "Have you even extended an offer to the Omnifex?" If Jean-Claude had been running this scheme, he would have had that link in place early on.

"Aria does," Dok said. "She speaks to one close to Papa Justice. She just does it from Craton Auroborea. So I tells truth about that too."

"For a very loose definition of truth," Jean-Claude said dryly. "She seems like quite a woman. Visionary."

"Clear of eyes and strong of voice," Dok said. "There's none like her."

—

Isabelle and her wardroom officers gathered around the orrery in the chartroom.

Major Bitterlich said, "The culling fleet has a brig and two sloops. Maybe fifty guns between them, none as a heavy as ours. One sloop is at anchor and they've brought up guns to pound the garrison. The brig and the other sloop are standing off. There's no way we'll sneak up on them."

This is a distraction, said her ancestors. *You risk suffering losses for no gain.*

Isabelle's thoughts were heavy and slow with her potion, but still the voices intruded. *I will not leave people to be enslaved.*

"How many captives have they taken?" Isabelle asked aloud, and hoped she hadn't asked that question before. The present streamed by without forming a past.

"None or very few that I can see. The whole town is trapped in the garrison or fled into the uplands."

To Vrain, Isabelle asked, "What from the Cauldron?"

"They confirm that most of the town is within the walls, but it's not much more than a stockade. It won't stand up to a serious bombardment."

"Then we continue with the plan as set," Isabelle said to Ensign Pummeroy. "We'll ride the vortex in. Make your best course."

Outside a bell rang, and a cry went up. "Skyland ho! Sails! Sails!"

Isabelle's heart galloped along like a horse spooked at its own shadow. Fear was bad, but useless fear was worse; there were still hours before they made contact with the enemy.

"You all have your orders," Isabelle said.

She walked out on deck to see Fishers Point for herself. Even through her spyglass, the skyland was hazy against the horizon. Its upper surface was dark with woods and its lower surface hung with a forest of coral cones thrusting down toward the Miasma. Just off shore billowed the triangular sails of a Skaladin sloop.

Pummeroy said, "They've spotted us, Capitaine, and they're moving off station."

"Where's the brig?" Isabelle asked.

"Just coming around the headland," Pummeroy said. "It looks like they want to—"

A tremendous bang shook the *Thunderclap* and knocked Isabelle from her feet. Her spyglass went flying. Marie grabbed her and helped her up. The ship listed to starboard.

Pummeroy hung on to the wheel brace, his face as white as a sheet.

"Did we hit something?" Isabelle shouted. They were much too far from the Skaladin to be taking fire.

Vrain stumbled out on deck. "What happened?"

All across the deck, aeronauts picked themselves up and looked around in bewilderment. A high-pitched whistle pierced the air. The whine increased in pitch and volume until the shriek of it seemed to saw right through Isabelle's brain.

"The keel!" someone yelled. "The keel's blown!"

The ship lurched and dropped several feet as if it had hit a ridge of turbulence. Terror surged through Isabelle like ice water through a shattered dam. The whole ship would plummet into the Gloom.

"Reef the sails!" Isabelle yelled. The keel hadn't blown completely, or they'd already be in free fall. If they'd just sprung a leak, there might be a chance, but any push they got would only sink them faster.

Jean-Claude appeared at her side. "Isabelle. We have to get you off the ship."

Isabelle whirled, her heart in her throat. "No. This is *my* ship. Take the key, grab Dok, and go. Complete the mission."

"But—"

"Go!" she shouted. She yanked her gaze away from him. She stepped and slid toward the main deck. Her stomach turned and her feet found less purchase than they should. All the sails were flapping upward. The rigging screamed under the unexpected pressure. The fall accelerated.

—

Jean-Claude felt like his chest had been hollowed out as Isabelle bounded away. He could not leave her, but neither could he drag her away, nor could he serve her by staying. His course was as clear as it was horrible.

Marie sprinted across the deck and followed Isabelle down the companionway, another piece of his heart hurling itself into danger. This was not the way it was supposed to be.

With a cry like a wounded bull, he yanked his gaze away from his apprentice and child and lurched toward Hailer Dok. The Windcaller had already leapt into the air and whistled up a cyclone to keep himself aloft.

"This way," Jean-Claude shouted, jabbing his finger at la roi's cradle, a small boat kept on runners atop the poop deck, ready to be launched at a moment's notice. No ship could carry life boats enough to save every crewman in the event of disaster, but military logic demanded someone must survive if only to report what happened. So every ship appointed designated survivors. One officer selected by the capitaine and several crewmen selected by lots at the start of each watch.

Jean-Claude clambered up the stair. The ship shuddered and he fell, banging his cheek on the step. A massive hand hoisted him up. Long Thom hauled him the rest of the way onto the poop deck and shipped him into the gunwale of the escape boat. Ensign de Henault stood at the other end, his russet skin pale and sweaty, spinning the valve to charge the keel and shouting orders in sailorese. Long Thom and three more aeronauts hammered away the chocks and shoved the crib toward the rail.

The *Thunderclap* shuddered and tilted the opposite way. The crib groaned to a halt. Its aetherkeel couldn't lift it while it was still in the lee of the *Thunderclap*.

"On board, ya lubbers!" Dok shouted, alighting amidships on the launch.

He couldn't speak and fly at the same time. The aeronauts piled into the boat, and Dok sang a high, clear note. At his call, a catapult of wind kicked the launch from the ship and out into clear space.

Jean-Claude yelped, hanging on to the rail with one hand and his hat with the other. He floated, weightless, dizzy, and disoriented.

The boat leapt up and smashed him into the gunwale, knocking the breath from his body. De Henault shouted at the aeronauts and there was a great deal of scrambling about as they unshipped the sweeps—long feather-like oars that unfolded to scoop the air when pulled and folded flat to slice it when swept forward again. The boat heaved forward and rose, climbing out of the turbulence around the *Thunderclap*.

Jean-Claude managed to get himself turned right side up and turned around, just in time to see the *Thunderclap* fall, drifting downward like a leaf fallen from a tree, until the Miasma reached up to engulf it.

Eleven

"Retreat is strategy," insisted Dame Falconé, pacing Isabelle down the stair. "There's nothing to be gained here!"

"Shut up!" Isabelle didn't care if the canary-colored Fenice was real or not. This was her ship, her crew. She threw herself down the ladder, caromed off the wall, and plowed through a gang of aeronauts coming up. The keel run ran the length of the ship down the center of the lower gun deck. Its walls were thickest oak, armored outside with alchemical steel and inside with copper to keep sparks at bay. Nothing short of the destruction of the ship could crack it from the outside, which meant this catastrophe had come from within.

Marie caught up to Isabelle just as she half floated and half bounced through the doorway. The aetherkeel filled the long chamber, four bronze-and-glass tubes fitted with dozens of pressure-regulating pipes and lode coils. Every pressure chamber down the length of the shaft had been breached, the bulkheads bypassed. Hypervolatile aether sprayed and screamed from the gaps, coating the whole room in a thick layer of frost.

The keelmaster lay dead on the deck in a pool of his own blood. His throat had been cut. Down the narrow aisle one of the keelmates slumped against the wall gurgling and clutching at a hole in his chest, and beyond him a figure in plain white robes.

Shock nearly stopped Isabelle's heart at the sight of Sireen's bloodhollow walking amongst the carnage.

"Madame?" she said, bewildered.

"Close enough," said the bloodhollow, in a voice that resembled Sireen's not at all. She raised a pistol at Isabelle.

Marie shoved Isabelle aside just as the bloodhollow fired. The bullet whistled by. Marie leapt at the bloodhollow before she could retreat or re-load. The ship tilted, slamming everyone against the wall.

Isabelle lunged for the keel. It hardly mattered who the imposter was if the ship fell from the sky. She slapped her spark-hand on the shattered tube, summoned her l'Étincelle, and leapt into the metal.

Isabelle had never inhabited a machine this big before. She stretched herself through the bronze. She could feel the tin in the alloy like she'd bit-ten it with her teeth. The copper hummed like a harp in the wind. Flowing through the glass was like swimming through taffy. As she grew to fill the keel, she felt the ship's cradle strain and groan against her skin. The ship started to roll.

Isabelle felt the rips in the skin of the aether tanks like wounds in her own flesh, and in the central core of the machine the delicate reverberation helix had been cracked.

One thing at a time. She slithered to the vapor-tight bulkhead between one section and the next. The control mechanism for isolating the compart-ment had come free, but she shoved it back in its groove, slammed it shut, and sealed it. The ship could survive with just one chamber, if she could repair the rent and the coil. If the aether tanks didn't bleed out first.

She forced her attention to the jagged metal lips of the first chamber's breach. She could mold metal like clay, but even shifting tiny amounts ex-hausted her, and this was an order of magnitude greater than anything she'd ever attempted. She imagined the ragged edges to be her fingers and inter-laced them. She had no muscles to try here, no lungs to burn or heart to burst, but her mind howled with the effort just the same. Her soul burned, but the metal moved. The bronze bent, softened like butter in the sun. Oh so slowly it flowed together, and she dared force it no faster lest she thin out the surface and have it rupture. The edges of the metal touched and she willed them to join, drawing heat from every square centimeter of the skin to weld this bit in place.

Frost covered the skin of the keel even as her join heated to its blending point, each edge oozing into its mate. At last it held. She pushed the heat away. No more aether leaked. Was there any left in the tank?

The ship shook her in her cradle, slamming her against the struts. Was the descent slowing? She could not tell. Her mind grew numb and prickly around the edges. Her strength waned.

Like crawling upstream in a river of mud she oozed herself around to access the reverberation module, the thing that organized the aether and made it hyperbuoyant. She was cold, her thoughts sluggish. Like a diver too long underwater she yearned to return to the warmth of her own flesh.

Not yet. She crawled inside the reverberation helix and slithered along a spiral of alchemical glass. What was it supposed to feel like? She'd seen one before but never inhabited it.

She couldn't feel her shape anymore. Couldn't feel the ship shaking. She needed to breathe but she had no lungs.

How to make the helix work? The glass was chipped and cracked. She plucked the helix like she might a harp string.

She felt a chord, and a discord, a note gone astray. She plucked again. Followed the vibration down the shaft until it hit rough edges and sprayed away in cacophony. She drew her attention into the flaw. It was so small. She was so cold. That tiny crack. She could not remember . . . There was something she needed to do. The flaw. Fix the flaw. Stretch the glass. Weld it. Make it sing. So cold. Sing. Can't breathe. Sing. Sing . . .

⁓

Jean-Claude's soul collapsed as, in the distance, the *Thunderclap* fell from the sky.

"Isabelle!" he cried in helpless horror. All color bled away, leaving his vision gray and all his thoughts turned to smoke.

Down and down the ship fell, plunging toward the Miasma. He reached out for it, as if it were a leaf at arm's reach and not a warship far away.

Two Skaladin ships, a sloop and a brig, tacked to intercept the launch.

"Get the sail up," de Henault snapped, "unless you fancy being skinned for some Skaladin's boot leather."

The grim-faced aeronauts set to work. They, too, had lost their mates and their home, and they moved with the silent, relentless determination of bier bearers, erecting the small boat's mast, two shafts lashed together for tops and turvy, two spars for triangular sails: above and below.

"Can you get us away?" Jean-Claude asked Dok.

"A boat this size, aye," Dok said. "We runs circles around them."

"Just get us to Joubert's Folly," de Henault said.

A yowl and screech from the back of the boat made Jean-Claude jump.

"Hey," yelped Aeronaut First Class Duval, who was working the tiller. A gray blur shot past his legs and squeezed between two crates, where it remained, growling ominously.

"Breaker-be-damned cat," Duval said, hopping up and down on one foot while trying to daub at the scratches on his opposite leg with one hand and hold on to the tiller with the other.

"Ha," Thom said, "Bosun Whiskers doesn't like your steering."

"How'd he get on board?" asked Aeronaut Plonta, poking his dark, curly-haired head up through the hatch that opened up on the turvy side of the launch.

"How do cats get anywhere?" Thom said. "Probably sleeping under the tarps till Duval stepped on his tail."

"Put him in a crate then," Duval said.

"Just watch where you step," Thom said. "He'll come out when he calms down."

"And then he'll want fed," Duval said.

"He's already had a piece of you," Thom said. "Suppose you could spare a toe or two."

Jean-Claude's belly grew cold as a horrible notion took root there. "Bosun Whiskers? That's Keelmate Gephardt's cat."

"Yeah, he loved this fella. Hadn't seen him since Gephardt disappeared."

Jean-Claude's soul had been hollowed out, but his mind fished up bits of understanding from the abyss. There was only one place Jean-Claude hadn't seen Bosun Whiskers: the last page of Gephardt's journal. The man always did everything in precisely the same order, and then he wrote it down. He'd written down his business about the aetherkeel, but not about feeding the cat, which meant he must have disappeared while performing that last chore.

What if he'd gone to feed his pet and found someone else there, a Seelenjäger stealing the skin from his cat? It was something no right-thinking Seelenjäger, steeped in the tradition of Öberholz's Wild Hunt, would ever do, but there was one Seelenjäger other than Bitterlich who had not been brought up in those traditions, and who knew everything there was to know about Lael's expedition to Craton Auroborea.

Hasdrubal.

Jean-Claude drew and cocked his pistol, and shuffled awkwardly back toward the stack of crates where the stowaway was hiding. If he was wrong, he would shoot an innocent cat, but if he was right, then everything that had just happened was designed to drop the keys to the Vault of Ages into Hasdrubal's paws.

Dok sat amidships, leaning on the mast, the turvy hatch open just behind him. One good shove and he'd be safe from capture. The man could fly, after all. That would give Jean-Claude time to—

From the coil of rope beneath Dok's feet erupted an expanding, shifting form, like smoke congealing into flesh. In the blink of an eye, there stood a thing roughly in a man's shape but with the head and legs of a goat, covered in a thick green carapace. Its long whiplike tail lashed around Hailer Dok's throat and squeezed off his breath.

The aeronauts froze, staring at the monstrosity. Plonta yelped and ducked back through the turvy hatch.

Jean-Claude raised his pistol, but he had no good angle to fire, and that carapace looked bulletproof.

Hasdrubal's voice was a bray. "Surrender."

Jean-Claude locked eyes with the monster. It must have been he who had knocked Isabelle's ship from the sky. Rage like he had never known caught fire in Jean-Claude's heart.

He felt like he was moving through mud, but he reached into his bag and pulled out the chartbone case.

"You want this?" he growled, and even his words sounded underwater. "Fetch!"

Hasdrubal lunged even as Jean-Claude flung the box over the side and dodged in the opposite direction. Hasdrubal crashed into the bulwark, spun and leapt after the box, changing into bird form as he went.

Jean-Claude raced to Hailer Dok's side. He was still unconscious, but breathing. How long would it take him to wake up? Hopefully less time than it took him to plummet into the Miasma. Jean-Claude grabbed him by the tunic and trousers and tipped him through the turvy hatch.

Yet no sooner had Dok's feet disappeared than all of him came hurtling back up again, propelled by Hasdrubal, whose birdlike form grew to the size and shape of a bear with a long lizard tail as he rose from the opening with the chartbone box in his beak.

The launch rocked under his sudden weight, the small keel whistling as if in pain. Jean-Claude stumbled away. Long Thom roared and bashed the beast with a pole hook, but the stout wood bounced off Hasdrubal's scales. Plonta and de Henault piled on with knife and cutlass.

Hasdrubal lashed with his tail, which grew bony, serrated spikes on the fly and sheared Long Thom's thigh clean through. The big man gasped and fell, spraying blood, unconscious before he hit the deck and dead a heartbeat later. Duval screamed and fled to the back end.

The launch trembled as if it had hit turbulence, and the front end swerved to the left.

Jean-Claude's hand snaked into his ammo bag and came back with an alchemical glass slug packed with phlogiston wax. He crammed it down his pistol's muzzle on top of the bullet. Damned thing was likely to blow up in his face—

Hasdrubal whipped his head around and snapped Plonta's neck like a twig.

"I would have let you live!" Hasdrubal screamed in the shrill voice of a hawk. "Now see what you've done." He leapt for Jean-Claude.

Jean-Claude lunged right, raised his pistol, and squeezed the trigger. A gout of fire lanced into Hasdrubal's side. Lead might not get through to him, but the wax would keep burning even if he changed shape. The launch tilted sharply.

Hasdrubal's claws raked Jean-Claude's face.

Pain exploded through his head. The world blacked out and the flickered back to life, like a candle flame near snuffed by the breeze. He clamped his hand to his mangled face. The boat fell away from him, or he from it. Bleeding, he tumbled through empty sky.

⟶

In the form of a galvatross, Bitterlich flew toward Fishers Point. The wind lifted him and carried him along almost without effort.

One Skaladin sloop and the brig had left the skyland's vortex on a path to intercept the *Thunderclap*. They couldn't possibly be planning on engaging the frigate, could they?

A dull thump like distant gunfire caught his attention. Neither the sloop nor the brig had fired. Over the headlands he could make out the topmasts of the sloop in the cove and see the haze of cannon smoke where the raiders bombarded the garrison, but the report he'd just heard was bigger, or at least nearer.

He swiveled his head around, and his heart nearly stopped. A few kilometers behind him, the *Thunderclap* wallowed and began to sink like a deflating balloon. Her spars twisted and her sails luffed as the wind wrenched her in its grip. Smoke or steam billowed from her hatches.

"Isabelle!"

Bitterlich wheeled on a wingtip and soared toward the ship, but this form was not fast enough. He reached within himself, pulled on the form of a falcon, and threw himself into a long dive. The wind whistled through his nares, and he scanned the deck for Isabelle. Where was she?

Down and down the *Thunderclap* spiraled like a wounded leviathan seeking the depths. The haze of the Miasma enveloped it. All through the rigging, men crawled like spiders in a storm, fighting to furl the sails or cut them loose. A rope snapped and a man slipped, shrieking as he plunged.

With a twitch of his feathered tail and a tuck of his wing, Bitterlich arrowed toward the man. He reached into the thickly woven tapestry of his Seelengewölbe, looking for strength and sinew, light but strong, weaving a half dozen threads into a new and greater chimerical form. His body lengthened, and his wings stretched out in great panels of leather and feather. His talons softened into leathery fingers. He snatched the aeronaut by his arms and spread his wings to their widest as they passed beneath the lowest turvy masts.

The murk of the Miasma engulfed Bitterlich, a thick green fog that smelled of new growth and old rot. He wished that he had hunted and skinned some muck breather for his repertoire. Instead, it was like breathing cold, wet smoke that made him want to cough and gag at the same time. He twitched his bat ears into place and chirped into the haze.

Above him the *Thunderclap* descended, but more slowly now. Coughing, wheezing men in the bilge hold heaved a steady stream of crates and sacks out the back like a drunk voiding his belly in the sewer: anything to lighten the load.

Gasping for breath, Bitterlich scooped the air and swung the terrified aeronaut through the aft bilge hatch.

"Make way!" Bitterlich shouted, and got a lungful of stink for his troubles. The aeronauts at the hatch gawped in fright and scattered, spilling things they meant to be getting rid of anyway. Bitterlich tucked himself through the hole, dropping his passenger on the deck. He drew on his erstepelz as he tumbled along the gangway. He used the last of his momentum to roll to his feet, adjusting the tilt of his hat by pure reflex. The ship still shuddered, but it seemed to have stopped sinking. No telling how long that would last.

"Gentlemen," he coughed. "Where is the capitaine?"

"Don't know," gasped one man.

"Keel run," wheezed another.

"Who in Torment cares?" added a third.

One out of three wasn't bad, under the circumstances. Bitterlich scrambled up the nearest companionway. The whole ship was canted forward and to starboard, and all the angles were wrong. He considered turning into a bat, but he didn't want to spread Miasma through his Seelengewölbe any more than he already had. Saints only knew what kind of havoc it might wreak . . . or possibly just reek.

Up just one level, he nearly plowed into a slender shadow coming the other way. He dodged around the figure, heading for the keel run, but a bony hand yanked him from the ladder.

"This way, Major. Ye be needed," Jackhand Djordji said.

Bitterlich yanked away. "I have to find Isabelle."

"She's busy saving the ship. Come on." Djordji pointed into the fog murk.

A bloodcurdling shriek of terror burst from the fog. That sounded like a child. Bitterlich bolted after Djordji, through a bulkhead into the center hold. Two men lay on the floor, gasping in the tainted air. Alchemical lanterns danced from hooks in the ceiling, their light making monsters of the vapors.

Twirling in the air in the center of the chamber were Rebecca, and a ghostfire wyrm.

The beast blurred past his head flying by means that resembled neither bird nor aerofish, but rather as if it were sliding along some rail that existed only for its benefit. Its serpentine body was as big around as a man's thigh and more than thrice Bitterlich's arm span long. It glittered with shimmering scales of aquamarine, tourmaline, and topaz. A row of spines ran down each of its flanks like the serrated teeth of a saw, and it had a great dorsal mane of silvery hair. Its snakelike head had four sapphire eyes and great back-sweeping horns the color of mother-of-pearl. Threads of a cold, blue-white fire leaked from between its razor teeth.

It was by far the most glorious and terrible creature Bitterlich had ever seen, and Rebecca clung to its head like a reef kraken gripping an oyster, her arms wrapped around its snout. It rolled and thrashed, but could not dislodge her. Rebecca had grabbed it just below its great gemlike eyes, her fingers digging into its scales as if they were made of clay.

Even as Bitterlich came to grips with Rebecca's predicament, the brilliant colors of its scales ran up her arms, while her pale freckled tones flowed through it like ink in water. Her eyes turned to gemstones. Her arms sank into the creature all the way up to her elbows.

Bitterlich could not have been more shocked if he'd been hit by lightning. Rebecca was a Seelenjäger. An untrained, uninitiated Seelenjäger, and this was her first kill. She had no training, no idea what she was doing, no inkling of what she needed to do or the horrific consequences of failure. At worst, the wyrm might kill her: overpower her soul, absorb her skills and her intelligence to become a Seelenfresser, a soul eater. Or she might conquer the creature but fail to annex its shape and end up a nonviable grotesquery with not enough lungs and her heart on the outside.

Around and around girl and wyrm spun in an absurd parody of a ballroom dance.

Djordji drew sword and main gauche. "I goes for the eye."

"No," Bitterlich said. "Don't hurt it." Any wound it took, Rebecca would also receive.

"Get it off me!" Rebecca screamed. She squirmed like a hooked fish. She must not panic, but the boundary where Rebecca ended and the wyrm began was blurred beyond distinction. They were drowning in each other.

Bitterlich bolted to her side, grabbed her by the shoulders. The wyrm thrashed. Its razor-sharp spines sliced through his sleeve and into his arm.

"Help," Rebecca gasped, tears welling from her eyes and mixing with the blood on her face. "Help me." Most of her body was dissolved in the creature's greater mass.

"I'm here," he said. Drawing on years of theatrical calm, he purred, "You're going to be fine, look." From his own Seelengewölbe he produced the card he'd taken as part of her thieving practice.

The card arrested her attention even in the midst of her struggles. Her distraction stilled the wyrm, if only for a moment. Bitterlich smacked the card down on the kraken's body, and made it disappear again. He couldn't actually push the card into the beast, but perhaps the illusion would be enough.

"Reach for it," he wheezed. "Reach for the buzzing heat. It should feel like silk made of nettles, smooth and stinging."

Rebecca yearned forward and gasped. "It burns."

The wyrm shuddered and flailed ever more violently as she seized its *Seelen*.

"Pull it," he urged. "Pluck that nettle like you were picking a pocket."

Rebecca's skin turned to azure scales.

"Do you have it?" Bitterlich asked, fending off tooth and tail.

"Yes," she gasped.

"Tug," he said. "Pull. Draw it out slowly. One long thread. Can you feel it?"

"It's tight. Doesn't want to move."

"Calm it," Bitterlich coughed.

"How?" Rebecca wailed, fear rising again.

"Ask it," Bitterlich said. "Ask it what it wants. Ask it with your soul."

"It wants to eat me!" Rebecca snapped, her fear leaping to anger.

"Why did it come here?" Bitterlich whirled around with her. "It must have come in when the ship sank. Why?"

Rebecca's gaze unfocused. "I can feel it. What it feels. It's hungry. It's scared. It wants to hide."

"Show it a safe space," Bitterlich said. "Imagine a dark hole, a close space, someplace safe and sound. You will make it safe."

"Safe," she muttered.

"Pull the thread," he urged, pleading with whatever saints watched over her.

"I've got it," she said. "It's coming."

Bitterlich coughed and choked, giddy with the fumes. "Pull it to your center, but slowly, carefully. It should feel as if it is unraveling."

"Like pulling on the loose thread of a blanket," Rebecca said.

"Yes," he said. "Now you're going to unweave the whole thing."

It felt like it took an hour for Rebecca to spool the whole wyrm, though it could not have been more than a few minutes. It was exhausting work, and more than once she wanted to quit, but no one could do this for her. At Bitterlich's coaxing, she spun her thread, hooked it into her core, and wove a careful, diligent web on which many other shapes could someday be strung. The more she pulled, the more the wyrm dissolved. It was like watching fluffy wool carded out and spun into finest thread.

Bitterlich made her spin it fine and pull it tight. It was a curse of the Breaker that a Seelenjäger's greatest weaving had to be her first, for this would be her erstepelz, the skin she wore the rest of her life. Too many Seelenjägers had been betrayed by their own haste and left a tangled knot where their finest work should be. Some found themselves unable to change into their beast, or worse, unable to change back.

"The finer the thread, the smoother the cloth." He made her go slow no matter how much she cried.

At last Rebecca's hands, which had been mimicking weaving, halted with a final spasm and her awareness came back from the other space where she'd been doing her work.

"It's done," she mumbled. "Nothing left to do, anyway." She clutched at Bitterlich's shirt. "Never could find the bloody card."

"Ah," Bitterlich said producing the card. "Here you go."

She grasped it in both hands, her knees weak and watery. "Looks funny. Everything looks funny. Gonna be sick." She fell to her knees and proceeded to disgorge more than a whole stomach's worth of partially digested reef crab.

Bitterlich knelt and wrapped an arm around her shoulders. She shuddered with sheer exhaustion.

After a long moment she asked, "Did we win?"

Bitterlich looked around. The hold was no longer filled with fumes and the deck was nearly level. Sometime during her long, terrible ordeal, the ship's buoyancy had been restored. Isabelle had saved it.

"We lives," Djordji said. His face was pale and red flakes covered his sleeve from his coughing.

Rebecca stood up, only slowly becoming aware of her surroundings, trying to catch her balance in this still-cockeyed cabin. She caught sight of her hands and arms. Her skin rippled through pale blues and greens as she moved through the light. Her eyes had lost their pupils and resembled smooth-cut sapphires. Her hair had gone silver. Two mother-of-pearl horn buds had sprouted from her forehead just ahead of her temples.

What would she think of this new arrangement? Every Seelenjäger he'd ever met preferred their erstepelz to their clay skin. It marked their coming of age and was an outward symbol of their burgeoning power.

But Rebecca had not been raised as a Seelenjäger and had no such expectations. Bitterlich had her draw out the finest possible thread, which let her keep the maximum proportion of her human characteristics, not like the wild blood cult who adopted a deliberately hybrid appearance, or the ferals who lost control of the transformation and ended up in beast bodies with only a few visible vestiges of their humanity.

Rebecca looked up at him, her eyes round with astonishment. "You turned me into a snake thing!"

"Half a snake thing," Bitterlich said. "You undertook the Wild Hunt, took the spirit skin of a ghostfire wyrm, and it became part of you."

"You tricked me! You said grab the card, but there was no card, just this thread." She poked herself in the chest. Her sapphire eyes were full of a shock that seemed ready to collapse into horror or despair.

"I showed you how to turn yourself into a ghostfire wyrm," Bitterlich said. "In time, I can show you how to turn into all manner of things, a bird, a bear, a fox." Was this the right approach to take? Rebecca wasn't panicking yet.

Rebecca reached up and touched her horn buds with the same fascination as an infant touching its toes.

Bitterlich remembered that sensation himself: *This is me? This is me!*

"Strange as hen's teeth," she said.

"Wait until you actually change shape."

"Show me," Rebecca said, curiosity overriding every other emotion.

Bitterlich would have preferred that lesson for later. The first change into an actual other form of life could be nearly as traumatic as the Wild Hunt, especially if that form was particularly alien, but Rebecca was eager, and if her fascination could carry her past that obstacle, it was one less thing to dread later.

He said, "Okay, but first a few things not to be afraid of. First, the transformation will feel very odd, like dissolving, and for a moment in the middle, you might not feel like you're there anymore. When you reach that point, you just have to keep pulling your thread. Second, the wyrm is bigger than you are, so you'll have to pull really hard."

She tapped herself in the chest, "You mean that string you put inside me."

"Yes." He said, "Third—"

But Rebecca's gaze had gone unfocused and her body blurred around the edges she pulled on her wyrm shape.

"Be careful. Keep the pull steady," Bitterlich said.

"Oh bolloooxxssshhhh . . ." Rebecca's voice faded to a wheeze as her body boiled up, bubbling, churning, and expanding into the form of a ghost-fire wyrm, as thick around as a man and three times as long, all shimmering scales and razor-sharp teeth floating weightless in the aether. She squirmed in the air, grunting and snapping her jaws.

"Third," Bitterlich continued dryly, "you may not be able to talk, or hear properly." It took a great deal of practice to be able to retain those two abilities in an alternate form. Did wyrms even have ears? Despite having lived most of his life on the coast, he'd never taken a deep interest in the creatures of the sky.

Rebecca flailed around, twisting herself into a corkscrew. She snapped at a stanchion and got her teeth lodged in the wood. She thrashed even more furiously, all four eyes going wild as she sought to dislodge herself.

"Rebecca, turn back!" Bitterlich urged. He mimed pulling the string again. "Turn back!" A form as alien as this one needed a great deal of thought and planning and practice to master. "Pull the thread."

Rebecca's gaze fixed on him, her gaze perplexed.

"One thing," he said. "Concentrate on just one thing. Pull the string the other way."

Rebecca's wyrm eyes unfocused and her form roiled and settled back to her new normal. Rebecca hovered in the air for a moment, then stretched for the ground and landed on her feet. The deck had come level at last, but she swayed as if she could not decide which way was up.

"Bleeding bollocks, that were odd," she said. "Everything was gray, except it weren't, and the shadows were all wrong, and I didn't have arms or legs. It was like being rolled up in a blanket 'cept I couldn't shake loose."

Bitterlich held out his hand and she took it to steady herself.

He said, "A new form takes some getting used to. You'll be better with practice."

"Spit on that," she said. "I don't ever want to feel like that again. How do I turn back to normal?"

"Ah," Bitterlich said. There was the rub; she had thought of this as a lark, as a game. It hadn't yet occurred to her that any of this was permanent.

"There is no way back to looking like you did before," he said, the plain truth. "You are a Seelenjäger sorcerer like me, and this amazing form is your erstepelz, the blazon of your power."

"You're joking," Rebecca said, horrified. "I'm no cursed beast-man. Take it back."

"I can't," Bitterlich said. Her insult stung even if she flung it in fear. "This is you, now."

Rebecca looked down at herself again, this time in horror. "You mean I'm stuck like this?" She grabbed at her horn buds and pulled as if trying to rip them off.

"Rebecca," Bitterlich said as soothingly as he could. "Listen to me. You're fine the way you are."

"No! I am not fine. Get it off me!" Rebecca yelled. She yanked at her hair so hard a handful tore loose.

Bitterlich grabbed her by the wrists to keep her from hurting herself. "It's not on you. It's in you. It's part of your soul."

Rebecca screamed like a loosed Torment and shifted back into her wyrm form, slipping from Bitterlich's grasp. Then she yanked into her erstepelz, then to wyrm form, sawing back and forth, faster and faster until she looked like a plume of black foam with bits of girl and wyrm thrown in.

She slammed into her erstepelz, and bits of her skin were her old pale freckled flesh.

"No!" Bitterlich yelled. She was pulling at the root of her Seelengewölbe, trying to rip out the beast. She slammed back into her wyrm form and once more into her girl form, now with red hair and green eyes.

"Stop it!" he snapped. Heart hammering, he wrapped his arms around her when she appeared. "Stay, please." If she transformed again, her spines would shred him.

"Can't make me," Rebecca said, but she did not transform again, and her erstepelz reasserted itself. In a few days' time it would quicken beyond being separated.

"I am not a freak," she wailed.

"No, you're a sorcerer," Bitterlich said. "But if you rip the wyrm out, you will die. Do you understand me?" His blood hammered in his veins so loudly he could hardly hear himself.

"I don't care," Rebecca said, probably because she was twelve and not caring about things meant not having to confront them.

"So you're not interested in being an aeronaut anymore?" Bitterlich asked, trying to deflect her attention.

"No," Rebecca said, hunching away from him.

"Or the best thief ever?" Bitterlich said, releasing his hold on her. Her eyes were full of tears, but she was no longer frenzied.

That stung her. "I *am* the best thief ever."

"Hard to do if yer dead," Djordji said.

Rebecca hugged herself and looked away. She walked in circles, growling and clenching her fists. Bitterlich got the impression that these theatrics were for the benefit of the audience, and the real battle was something much harder and simpler deep inside.

The ship turned, and from the decks above thumped the sound of running feet, and the sudden roar of cannon fire.

Djordji stood up from the crate he'd inhabited and pressed his battered old hat down hard on his head. "The Skaladin arrives. Time to join the fight."

"In a moment." For now, Bitterlich's duty was right here. By the standards of Öberholz, Rebecca had made an excellent and noteworthy first kill, a powerful and dangerous predator in a forbidding location. It was the sort of thing from which one could coin a new surname: Rebecca Ghostfire. Yet none of that would matter if she couldn't accept the transformation.

"How"—Rebecca shook her hands as if trying to get water off them— "How am I supposed to do anything like this?"

"The same way you always have," Bitterlich said, allowing his own tension to unwind; those words were of someone who meant to live. "Only with more panache."

A tremendous blast jolted Isabelle awake, not from sleep but from some greater absence. That was a cannon shot. It wasn't the first blast she'd heard or felt, just the first one she could give a shape and a name to. She had been far away. The world shook and smoke filled the space around her.

"Where am I?" she croaked. Her head felt stuffed with hot coals.

Marie hovered over her. "Bilge hold. Somebody blew holes in the keel. You jumped into the machine and healed one of the chambers."

"I did?" Isabelle tried to call up this memory, but nothing came. The last thing she remembered was Sireen. "La reine?"

"I think somebody took over her bloodhollow, killed the keelmaster and his mate, and set charges on the keel."

Isabelle sat up on the cot where Marie had apparently laid her. The movement threatened to shatter her skull. "You can't hijack a bloodhollow."

"You can't bring someone back from being a bloodhollow either," Marie said, "but you did it for me. Besides, either someone stole la reine's bloodhollow, or Sireen just tried to kill us all. Which do you think is more likely?"

"Where is she?" Isabelle asked.

"Dead," Marie said. "I had her pinned. She knew she was beaten. She said, 'It would actually be simpler for everyone if you started a fire and burned the ship out of the sky. It's not as if you dare return home after losing your precious cargo.' She withdrew from the bloodhollow and killed it on her way out."

Cargo? Isabelle's heart near seized as the full import of what the blood-hollow had said struck home. This whole scenario, the Skaladin slavers and all of it, had been nothing but a ploy to expose and steal the key to the Vault of Ages, and Isabelle had fallen for it.

"Where's Jean-Claude?"

"He took la reine's cradle," Marie said. "Him and Dok."

"We've got to get him back," Isabelle said. She'd sent him into danger without warning. Saints, but she was ever so much worse than a fool. She was a dupe. The hollowjacker not only meant to steal the key but also the navigator and navigation tool and to conceal their crime with the destruction of the *Thunderclap*. If the ship went down, no one would even know to look for them.

"We're in the middle of a battle," Marie said as another thunderous blast shook the ship, the smell of gun smoke finally penetrating Isabelle's murky awareness. "After you healed the keel, we regained buoyancy, but we've got no margin. When we came back up we surprised the Skaladin brig. Vrain's been trying to run it down."

Isabelle said, "It's a decoy. The Skaladin are after the key. I need to get topside."

She stood and felt woozy. A ghost stain spread across her vision. She stood in the vestibule in the Temple on Hadon Hill outside of Om. She knew that the vestal standing before her was Marie and the sound of men chanting was actually the shouts of battle, but that knowledge eroded like a sand castle in the rain under the onslaught of hallucination.

Isabelle closed her eyes, but the visions inside her head were no better, because her head was no longer entirely Isabelle. The fire in her skull grew hotter, spreading like a fire that had leapt its hearth and caught on the rug. She turned her attention inward to the breach and found it crumbling and fraying like ancient cloth.

Escape is called—seize the advantage while—traitors in your ranks . . . Her ancestral chorus shouted over one another as they whirled by in the current of the everdream.

"Make sense, curse you." It was as if all of her past lives had something to tell her but could not agree on how to say it.

Vestal Marie put a hand on Isabelle's shoulder. "You need to stay here."

"I have to tell Vrain," Isabelle said.

"I'll tell him," Marie said. "You're in no shape to lead."

"I'll manage." Isabelle opened her pouch to retrieve a potion. She just needed a little space in her head. She ought to still have plenty of time left on her current dose of medicine, but perhaps overextending her sorcery had burned through it faster than normal.

Her fingers found no phials. She opened her eyes and spread the mouth of the pouch. Empty. Fear howled like winter through her chest. "Where's the medicine?"

"I used it up." Marie said. She was a silk-clad dancer, out of place in this dank tunnel. "When you jumped into the keel, it was like that thing in your head got loose. You started babbling, by the time I got you down here you were raving, trying to fight me. I didn't know what to do, so I started pouring potions down your throat. It took everything you had in your pouch to drown the rat."

"All of it?" That should have rendered Isabelle comatose for at least a day.

"I'm not a mathlogician, but I can count to three." Marie held up three empty bottles. "And you're still seeing things." As she moved, her body seemed to break up, like a deck of cards being shuffled into a new configuration.

Isabelle's heart ached almost as much as her head. Minute by minute the world became more scrambled, past getting tangled with present, other lives with her own, until the potion beat it back again. If the medicine stopped working, her consciousness would dissolve, her identity melting into formless sludge without even a name to give it shape.

Let go, rumbled the chorus. *There is no dishonor in putting away pride and accepting your place in the grand lineage.*

"I will not bring up the rear of your parade," Isabelle said. They all wanted a bite of her, to attach themselves to her identity so that her notion of "me" included them, along with all their grudges, ambitions, and the blood on their hands.

Marie said, "I'll tell Vrain about the key."

"He won't listen to you," Isabelle said. "I need to speak to him."

Marie put a hand on her sleeve. "The only thing you should be doing right now is figuring out how to get this thing out of your head."

"I'm the capitaine," Isabelle said.

"But should you be?" Marie asked.

Marie's words punched like a musket ball through Isabelle's heart. Had she not asked Jean-Claude to tell her when it was time to step down? Did she not owe Marie the same respect?

Isabelle's vision shifted again and she found herself on the floor of the senate in Om. A consul with great blue crest feathers and a flowing red toga was dragged before her in chains.

He glowered up at Isabelle. "This is an outrage. If my legion is lost, it is only because I followed the orders you gave me."

"Your obedience is laudable. It has cost you all your support in the senate and given me just cause to have you executed," Isabelle replied, but she was not Isabelle but rather someone older, stronger. This was the voice of Primus Maximus, her first ancestor.

"I am loyal to the republic!" shouted the consul.

"Loyal is not the same as useful," Isabelle said.

Marie gave her a shake. "Isabelle, you're raving. You have to stand down."

Isabelle's vision faded, but Primus's message was clear and undeniable. She lived only because she proved useful to la reine.

"And then what?" Isabelle's words were hot and bitter. "I am de rien, remember: of nothing. No family. No power. No name. Capitaine is all I have. I can do this. I have to do this."

She spun, wrenching free of Marie's grip, and climbed the companionway to the gun deck. Powder monkeys raced up and down the ladder from the magazine carrying buckets of charges for the cannon. The gun smoke burned Isabelle's eyes. A blue-scaled dragon girl sped by. Another hallucination. Up and up she climbed to the main deck, with Marie close behind.

A cold wind slapped her face as she oriented herself in the battle. The *Thunderclap* sailed one pistol shot to starboard of the Skaladin brig and half a mast below. Ballast barrels in the *Thunderclap*'s bilge hold had been rolled to larboard, tilting the ship just that extra bit so the elevated guns could gouge the brig from below, like a great cat disemboweling its prey.

"Capitaine on deck!" shouted the boatswain, though how he'd even noticed her in the chaos remained a mystery. Blood clotted the sand on the deck, holes pierced the bulwarks, and several sails were shredded. One of the ship's shadowpults had been smashed, its shattered mirror smeared with the blood of the Sanguinaire who had been trapped within.

Aeronauts swarmed in the rigging, braving a fearful hail of enemy fire to cut down ruined sails and replace severed stays, repairing the ship almost as fast as it was damaged.

A volley from the brig rained down, ball and shot whizzing through the tops. Most of it missed entirely, but one cannonball struck the deck close enough to Isabelle that her bowels near turned to water.

She clambered to the quarterdeck and joined Vrain in the dubious shelter of a sniper's bastion and said, "Report."

Vrain saluted and said, "They came after us when we were floundering, didn't know we'd recovered. We sent up surrender flags, then pounced when they got into spitting range. If we'd had a bit more lift, we might have boarded, but she climbs faster than we do. Even so, we've just about got her sticks off."

"Good," Isabelle said, glad that the situation was well in hand, even though it made her redundant to needs. "But we have another problem. The brig is a decoy. Their real target is la reine's cradle. Also, someone hijacked la reine's bloodhollow and used it to gas our keel."

Vrain's sweaty, smoke-smudged face betrayed emotions at roughly half the speed and intensity as other men, so the pallor that washed across his visage must indicate an existential dread. "Compromising a bloodhollow isn't possible."

"So I've been told, but either someone else was riding that bloodhollow or la reine wanted us dead," Isabelle said repeating Marie's logic. "I need you to get back to Rocher Royale and inform l'impératrice personally."

"Yes, Capitaine." Vrain saluted, then hurried below, out of the direct sight of the enemy guns so he could concentrate on casting his presence all the way back to Rocher Royale. Isabelle pulled out her spyglass and focused on the brig. Defeating the brig was vastly less important than retrieving Dok, the key, and Jean-Claude, but she didn't want to break off and leave the enemy in any condition to harass the *Thunderclap* either.

—

The forward turvy mast of the Skaladin brig creaked and shrieked and finally shivered, falling away from the bottom of the ship in a great clot of tangling rope and collapsing sails. It was like watching a man being hanged, only much more slowly.

Bitterlich darted through the web in the form of a falcon, changed shape, and slammed into the main spar of the aft mast as a massive flying ram. The yard swung around, snapping ropes as it went. Skaladin turvymen plunged, screaming, into the deep sky.

Sharpshooters in the brig's lower hold fired at him through their murder holes. Bullets whizzed by on all sides. He ducked into the form of a bat and darted out of the way just as the *Thunderclap* fired. Cannonballs flashed by. One clipped the weakened aft turvy mast, sending cracks along its length. Bitterlich looped around, got up a quick burst of speed, and then transformed into a great gray-backed mountain bear. He crashed into the damaged mast and snapped it in two. It joined the foremast in its fall.

The brig, now top heavy and with wind still in its sails, rolled like a pig in muck. More raiders fell from the rigging and tumbled shrieking into the Gloom.

For the first time in an hour, the cannonade stopped, leaving nothing but the creak of wood and the screams of wounded men to compete with the rush of the wind.

Wheezing and panting from his long exertion, Bitterlich switched back into bat form and swooped around the ship as it finished capsizing. He landed on its side as a furry lizard and peeked in the gunports. Within was the sort of carnage bloody-minded poets and propagandists dreamed of: crushed bodies and blood from stem to stern. As saturated as he was in the humors of battle, Bitterlich could find no pity for them; they had attacked l'Empire. They had attacked Isabelle. There would be survivors—there always were—but they would rue the day they had attacked Bitterlich's people.

Bitterlich scampered along the outside of the ship until he reached the cabins, then he bounded into the chartroom. With the whole ship flipped sideways, everything that hadn't been secured, including the navigator, had slid to the lower wall. The officer had been crushed by sliding debris.

Bitterlich perched on the orrery's pedestal, now sticking out horizontally from the floor. It was an older design, without a vaporgram tank or an anisometric pressure array, the sort of thing that had stopped being built in l'Empire half a century ago. The whole ship was aged, and while it was true that some ships stayed in service for a century or more, it was only due to constant care. This brig plainly hadn't seen a refit in quite some time. Its boards were warped and infested with puff worms. Perhaps slaving was not good business in Skaladin these days.

The orrery had been depressurized, and Bitterlich was not surprised to find that the hyperbaric sympathy berths had been emptied, the chart-stones taken to prevent precisely the sort of looting Bitterlich had in mind. Bad luck if they'd been destroyed.

He dropped down to the smashed navigator, who presumably had been in charge of disposing of the chartstones, and hoisted the bloody beam off his chest. A search of his person turned up no chartstones there, either. Whatever had happened to them, they were out of Bitterlich's reach now.

Bitterlich flew back to the *Thunderclap*. Despite the horror and the gore that painted their legs to the ankles, the aeronauts on deck whooped and hollered with the joy of their victory. Bitterlich's heart lifted to see Isabelle prowling the quarterdeck, shouting orders, surrounded by her firefly escort of pink and purple sparks, Marie at her side. She'd lost her wig somewhere, but her voice was clear and strong. He floated in on spread wings and pulled on his erstepelz as he lit beside her.

"Capitaine," he said, ripping off his crispest salute. "I'm glad to see you up and about." When he'd heard she'd felled herself saving the ship, he'd been all but beside himself, but there was nothing he could do except take out his dread on the Skaladin.

"Major," she said, blessing him with a smile. Her skin was flushed and sweaty under the soot and her eyes looked weary beyond words. She did not look steady on her feet.

"Well fought," she said. "What's the condition of the enemy crew?"

"They're done in," Bitterlich said. "We should be able to obtain a surrender and take her as a prize. I went after the chartstones, but they'd already been removed."

Isabelle nodded and pursed her lips. Her gaze kept darting about as if drawn to things Bitterlich could not perceive.

More quietly he asked, "Is your stowaway acting up?" Her symptoms worsened when she was under pressure.

"Stowaway," she said, blinking. "How did you know . . . oh you mean here." She rubbed her temple over her scar, smearing soot.

"Was there another stowaway?" Bitterlich said.

"Someone took over la reine's bloodhollow. I don't know how. Vrain is looking into it, but we have another problem. Jean-Claude . . . I mean, the launch. This whole battle was a setup. They're trying to steal the key. Jean-Claude has it. I need you to find the launch. Bring them back. Dok, too, and the *Conquest* shard. Bastards. One basket. All the eggs. Find them. I need you." Her spark-hand and her skin hand worked as if she were physically placing her words in order. Her firefly nimbus throbbed like an old wound.

Cold dismay spread through Bitterlich's arteries like hoarfrost on leafless branches at the end of the year. Isabelle was decaying. He shot a questioning look at Marie.

Marie said, "I'll take care of her."

Bitterlich looked back and forth between the women. He couldn't leave Isabelle like this, but what could he do if he stayed? Whatever she needed, he would give, even if it was the wrong thing and too little by half. Rarely had he felt so powerless or useless.

"Find Jean-Claude," Isabelle said.

"Yes, Isa . . . Capitaine," he said. "Don't . . . don't leave. Please." He wanted to take back his lie to her, but now was not the time to burden her with confession or confusion.

A pained smile creased her face. "Builder keep."

"Savior come," he replied, and made himself as neat as he could. The mission called. Her mission. He mounted the bulwark and leapt into space without giving himself time for second thoughts. He transformed into a galvatross. Lightning rippled along his wings. He rode a warm spiral up and around the ship. Only then did it occur to him that he'd forgotten to tell Isabelle about Rebecca. No time for that either.

He oriented himself on Fishers Point and set off in the direction from which the *Thunderclap* had come. With any luck, he'd find Jean-Claude and Dok quickly; perhaps that would bring Isabelle some relief.

——

Isabelle's gaze lingered on Bitterlich as he flew away, and she entertained thoughts of what might have been in some more peaceful life. She wished . . . but wishing had never solved a single problem.

She turned away. It was getting harder to think, as if she'd been awake for a week. Yet sleep could not save her.

"Capitaine," said another voice. It took her a moment to recognize Vrain. Where had he been? Rocher Royale. The Cauldron.

"Report," Isabelle said. Her mind felt like a watch with all the axles removed. Everything lined up neatly, but when one bit tried to turn it knocked the others askew until she put them all back together again.

Vrain said, "I reported the bloodhollow sabotage to la reine. She claims that she felt that bloodhollow die, and requires your full report when the battle is over."

"Of course," Isabelle said. "Meanwhile, secure the brig." She had to keep giving orders, stay on top of the tiger. "Find the chartstones." If one of the other ships had already captured Jean-Claude, the brig's chartstone would help them locate it.

Isabelle retreated to her cabin, or tried to; the space wasn't enclosed, as the cannon were still emplaced. Marie guided her down the ladders to the middle hold.

. . . the skin shrivels and rots in the soil revealing the seed, roots gasp in the air, begging mercy . . . the ancestral chorus shouted.

The senseless words snared her mind like a burr in matted felt; there must be shape and meaning in them, but her ancestors were broken in pieces and mixed up, trying to talk to her but talking over one another, impossible to tell if it was one message or many.

Marie hauled Isabelle's sky trunk out of a locker and rooted through it, coming up with more phials of borrowed sanity.

"Drink," Marie commanded in her toneless voice.

Isabelle downed two phials in rapid succession. A dullness approaching numbness spread through her veins. She paced in circles in the cramped space, waiting for the medicine to work. If it worked. For how long?

Where was Jean-Claude? As capitaine she ought to be more concerned about her ship, her crew, and her mission, but Jean-Claude was her lighthouse, a fixed point in an ever-shifting sky. He'd always been there for her, always been home and safe even in the midst of chaos. It would destroy him if he came back and found her gone, lost inside her skull.

All gravebound die. They are tools, the ancestral voices blurred to a mumble. The hull and the bulkheads stopped trying to be made of brick and stone and remained solidly wooden.

"Capitaine?" asked a voice, nearer to hand and yet farther away. "Capitaine?"

Isabelle turned and gasped, for what stood before her was a girl with a skin of iridescent scales, a spiky mane of white hair, and tiny silver horn buds.

"Rebecca?" Isabelle asked when she could draw breath again. "What happened to you?" Or was this another hallucination? The potion seemed to be working, for now, though all her perceptions seemed underwater. She glanced at Marie, who returned a hand sign of "Seelenjäger."

"I fought a flying snake thing," Rebecca said. "I won. I think."

Isabelle examined her cabin girl more closely, all glittering scales in pale greens and blues. She must be some noble's by-blow abandoned in Rocher Royale's gutters.

"So tell me how you defeated this snake thing," Isabelle said.

Rebecca looked at her hands as if just reminded of their existence. "I was down in the hold when the keel blew, and the whole thing fell out of the sky . . ."

Isabelle listened intently to her account of the disaster, how she'd hung on to the stanchions while the ship fell. How she'd just about choked to death in the Miasma, how she'd been helping shift weight overboard when the ghostfire wyrm—Rebecca finally recalled the name—slithered through the turvy hatch and attacked her. Her excitement grew as she recounted her epic battle with the beast, and how Bitterlich had shown her how to beat it.

". . . and finally I got to the end of the string and it was gone," she said breathlessly, "and here I am." She tapped the blunt tips of her horn buds and grimaced. "Like this, and Bitterlich says I can't ever turn back." This last came out as a plea.

Isabelle felt Rebecca's pain all the more keenly because there was no antidote for it. There was only the truth, which, like small doses of poison, might help her build up a tolerance for her new reality.

To her surprise it was Marie who spoke. "Djordji tells me you are the best thief he's ever seen, and I bow to his wisdom. You are even more amazing now. The fear you feel is the fear of the unknown. You were living in the present when the future ambushed you and caught you unawares. It is natural to retreat, assess the situation, then learn and grow from it."

Rebecca's expression betrayed a certain amount of doubt about this prospect.

Isabelle said, "You know what I'm going to say, yes?"

This earned a twelve-year-old's eye roll. "Break it down logically. But it's sorcery."

"So it is," Isabelle allowed. "But that's not quite what I meant. Tell me what precisely you are afraid of."

Rebecca opened her palms, which sent a shimmer of color running every which way across her skin, displaying the answer in its most obvious form.

The drumbeat of her own troubles tested Isabelle's patience, but Rebecca needed her here and now.

"Are you afraid you're going to hurt someone?" Isabelle asked.

Judging from the bewildered look on Rebecca's face, the thought of being a threat to anyone hadn't even crossed her mind. "Do you think I will?"

"You're strong enough that you could," Isabelle said. "Do you want to be a menace?"

"No," Rebecca said. "Well, not to everyone," she amended.

Isabelle moved on from this before she could turn her mind to her personal rivals. "Are you afraid of other people hurting you?"

"Well, no, but . . ." She struggled to give form to her fears. "I mean I don't . . . I'm not . . ."

"Yourself," Isabelle suggested. "Like you're not the same person you were before?"

Rebecca relaxed a little. "Yeah."

Isabelle sat on a crate and gestured Rebecca to sit beside her. "Being a Seelenjäger doesn't change who you are, it just means you're a sorcerer and a noblewoman."

Rebecca squirmed. "Does that mean I have to wear frilly dresses and talk like I have my thumb up my arse?"

"Sometimes the dresses are fun," Isabelle said, "but you don't have to wear them all the time. They're a tool, a disguise for special occasions. And being a noble is just another skill you'll have to learn, like tying knots, or picking pockets. It's something you do, not who you are. Marie, Major Bitterlich, and Jean-Claude will show you."

"What about you?" Rebecca asked.

And what should Isabelle tell her? Marie, Jean-Claude, and Bitterlich had been privy to Isabelle's secret since the beginning. They'd made up their own minds that she was going to be well, that she would beat this corruption like she'd overthrown every other foe.

"I'll help you as long as I can," Isabelle said. She could promise no more.

Even now with her medication in full effect, the headache squeezed her head in a vise, and her chorus of ancestors was banging on her skull like inmates at the agonesium. She couldn't stop, wouldn't stop, fighting until there wasn't any Isabelle left to fight with, but the thing about last stands, even famous last stands, was that they were, in fact, last. Isabelle was coming to an end. Her body would live on for a while, she supposed, but whatever strange residue remained once her identity had been annihilated wouldn't be her. It would be up to other people to remember her.

"You mean you're dying," Rebecca said. It took a child to say what no one else had been willing to, but Rebecca had grown up on the streets, with death all around her. Rebecca looked back and forth between Isabelle and Marie. Isabelle filled in the unspoken *What about me?*

"Marie will take care of you," Isabelle said. "She gets cranky if she doesn't have someone to look after."

"I do not," Marie denied. "But that is beside the point. You're not allowed to die."

"Alas the Breaker's fetch does not ask your permission," Isabelle said. She forced some cheer into her voice before the morbid conversation cracked her resolute façade. "Also, impending death does not duty discharge. Rebecca, make us some tea. Marie, I'll need my writing desk." She must explain the bloodhollow and the key to Sireen.

With habits nearly as old as she was, she trimmed her quill, dipped it in ink, and turned her paper to accommodate her left-handed grip. Gathering words from the fringes of a drying well of eloquence, she began formally:

I am Isabelle, Capitaine of the Célestial frigate Thunderclap, *and this is my testimony.*

Isabelle's blood felt as thick as mud. She detailed how the bloodhollow had deceived her, how she had obtained the key to the Vault of Ages, and how she had sent Jean-Claude away. She prayed he would read this and understand.

She had just finished detailing, with the help of Marie's perfect memory, what the bloodhollow had said in the keel run, when Rebecca returned.

"Capitaine," she said, "Lieutenant Vrain reports they have captured the slaver capitaine."

Isabelle blinked at her, recalled from the turgid flow of her narration. The Skaladin capitaine must have been part of the plot to steal the key. He might know where it had been taken.

"I need to question him," Isabelle said. "Tell Vrain."

Rebecca saluted and departed. Isabelle put aside her writing to let the ink dry.

Marie said, "You don't have to do this. Let Vrain handle the interrogation."

"He doesn't have the right questions," Isabelle said. She checked her watch and counted the numbers carefully. One hour. She should still have time to find out what the Skaladin capitaine knew, to find a way to thwart the thieves and recover her failure.

Marie said, "Pushing yourself is only making it worse."

"Too late for rest," Isabelle said. "Would be like going to bed in a burning house. Help me dress."

Marie hesitated then helped Isabelle into her coat and fitted her recovered wig in place. Her fingers brushed Isabelle's forehead.

"You're burning up," she said. "And you've got goose pimples all over."

"I'm the capitaine," Isabelle said, as if that answered Marie's concerns. "This duty was given to me. I won't fail." Her head pounded like someone was using it for a gun deck, and she was weary beyond all reason, but she'd been near death before and that had not stopped her from saving two kingdoms.

"And I'm your bodyguard. My job is to keep you alive, which I can't do if you commit suicide by sheer stubbornness."

"Help me up the ladder," Isabelle said. She composed her questions as she climbed, putting them carefully in order so that she did not have to invent anything in the moment. She must find out who was behind the conspiracy and what they meant to do next.

She ascended to the great cabin, where Vrain, Rebecca, and her other line officers waited. The cannons had been cleared out, though the reek of gun smoke lingered like the last unwanted guest at a party. A heavy chair had been installed. Isabelle received and returned salutes, then took her place in the chair.

Two marines marched in with the Skaladin capitaine.

She was a woman. Isabelle had not expected that. Her graying hair was tied back in a queue, and her eyes were as dark and hard as flint. She'd been stripped of her weapons and stood before Isabelle in bare feet, striped breeches, and a green blouse that had seen better days. Her hands were manacled behind her back.

The marines forced her to her knees. She grimaced with pain, fear, and fury.

"Identify yourself," Isabelle said.

The Skaladin returned a string of what was undoubtedly invective in her own language. The shadows in the corner bubbled like a kettle on the boil.

Isabelle cast a questioning glance at Vrain who said, "She does not think kindly of your ancestors."

"Neither do I," Isabelle said. "Does she speak la Langue?"

The Skaladin growled, "Even a child could speak your language."

Isabelle resisted the urge to trade insults. "So, do you mean to make yourself useful to me, and be treated as a prisoner of war, or do you wish to be treated as a pirate?" The penalty for piracy was summary execution. It was not a threat she wanted to carry out, no matter how warranted it was. She prayed the Skaladin would not put her to the test.

The Skaladin considered that. "What do you want?"

"To begin with, your name."

She lifted her chin. "I am Similce, capitaine of the *Saint Asne*, sister of Exarch General Ptoleus, cousin to Tyrant Hanilcar. If you are fool enough to slay me, my death will not go unavenged."

Isabelle shook her head. "Neither the exarch general, the cousin of a tyrant, or anyone in good standing would send their sister to cull Célestial slaves from a deep sky eddy in an eighty-year-old, top-heavy tub with a puffworm infestation. No one will ransom you, and no one will complain if you disappear."

This was a guess, but only just. Isabelle had seen the dilapidated condition of the brig during the battle, and Similce's secondhand clothes and sunburned feet spoke of a poverty rarely seen in ship capitaines.

The corners of Similce's mouth tightened ever so slightly. A ghost stain spread through Isabelle's vision. Between one thought and the next, Similce became a pale-skinned slave girl kneeling on the auction block and the cabin became a flesh market.

Isabelle's heart raced. This should not be happening. No so soon.

Slave girl Similce said, "And yet I have something you want, or I'd already be in the gullet of the Gloom. What is it you want for my life and the life of my crew?"

Vrain in the guise of a fleshmonger leaned over to whisper in Isabelle's ear, "Capitaine, we owe these pirates nothing."

Isabelle interlaced her fingers, being sure not to let her spark-hand pass though her skin hand, and pretended nothing was wrong. On top of everything else, she was all too aware that she now stood poised to make exactly the same sort Breaker's bargain she had always railed against. The raid on Fishers Point and the attack on the *Thunderclap* both demanded justice for the dead. Yet Isabelle had no love of killing, no matter how well justified. It was always a victory for the Breaker.

Isabelle said, "Two things, for your life and the life of your crew. Thing one: all you know of the conspiracy that included your ill-considered attack on my ship, including the names of the other conspirators." The smell of the slave market enfolded her, dust and the stink of sour sweat and the perfumes meant to cover it up. The market always boiled this time of year, and there was no water for bathing.

Similce considered Isabelle's demand. "What is the second thing?"

"One thing at a time," Isabelle said, ignoring the lurching of the crowd around her, the shouts of the auctioneer. It was not real.

"What guarantee do I have that you will keep your word?"

"My word is good enough for la Reine de Tonner; it should be good enough for you." Alas that she was trading on debased coin, there. Sireen had trusted her with this mission, but Isabelle had not told her of her voices and visions. She had wanted to prove herself, and she had proven herself a fool.

Similce growled helplessly, but finally said, "I don't know the Célestial witch's name. The beast rider is called Hasdrubal."

Isabelle rubbed at her neck. The slave's words bothered her. She'd been so wrapped up in other worries that it hadn't occurred to her that the hollowjacker must have been a Sanguinaire. This conspiracy had roots in the Célestial court as well as in Skaladin.

"What is Hasdrubal's plan?" Isabelle said, a dullard's question, but her fever had grown worse. Her whole skin felt baked and ready to blister. The dry air of the desert got under her collar, and sweat made mud of the grit on her face.

"They didn't tell me their whole plan," the slave said. "I was to bring my fleet to this place and wait for their signal to attack the town. The witch brought our orders. I sent one ship to fetch Hasdrubal and brought the *Saint Asne* to rescue any survivors from this ship, which I saw fall out of the sky. Rescuing wreck survivors is the law of the sky, yes?"

The slave was bringing her fleet? What sense did that make? No. She wasn't a slave, just a captive. She needed to get done with this auction . . . interrogation. She reached for her flask, her phial, to slake her thirst and drive the ghost stain away, but it was not on her hip. She looked around for Marie, but the girl was gone.

No. She was just hiding in the crowd. This wasn't real. Isabelle was capitaine of the *Thunderclap,* not a meat merchant.

Isabelle dragged her attention back to the slave girl. She had questions to ask. All lined up. "You came to ensure that the *Thunderclap* went down. What were you supposed to do after you'd made sure of our demise?"

"We were to rendezvous with Hasdrubal and receive further instructions."

Isabelle's mind felt bloated and swollen like an impacted bowel. Sweat rolled down the line of her jaw to dangle from her chin. The sky roiled, brown turning to black as a dust storm approached. It would bury the market.

"Thing two," Isabelle said. "I want your chartstones." More precious than gold were such stones, and she could not begin to guess how a slave had come to possess them.

The slave stiffened. "But . . . I can't give you what I don't have."

"Lies," she said, rising from the barrel where she'd been watching the auction. It was the pale girl's turn to be bid on. That wouldn't usually be a problem, but Forenzio's buyer was here, and she was just his kind of meat. Isabelle couldn't let her go or the stones would fall into Forenzio's clutches. Unfortunately, Isabelle couldn't hope to outbid Forenzio's buyer, but killing the slave before she was bought only meant paying a fine to the previous owner at slaughterhouse prices.

She pulled her maidenblade—the razor edge was made for cutting throats—and stepped forward quickly before either of the burly slaveholders had time to react.

She grabbed the girl by her tawny hair. "This won't hurt much."

Like a kick from a mule, a fishwife barreled into Isabelle and bore her to the deck.

"Isabelle," she said in a voice too flat for such a heavy blow. "Look at me."

"I'll see you in Torment," she snarled, and stabbed, but the other woman twisted her wrist and took the blade away.

The rest of the market erupted with shouts. Men rushed in from all sides, to grasp and pin.

"Look at me!" said the wench. She had eyes the color of moons in a face whiter than pearl.

"Marie," Isabelle choked, grasping for a thread of the present. She couldn't see the *Thunderclap*, couldn't make out the cabin. Even Marie's face refused to stick.

"Help," she whispered.

We live! her ancestors howled. The breach had fallen, the last of its containment crumbled. Her ancestors' memories spilled into her waking mind and forced her from the seat of power. Her body moved without her will, struggling against Marie.

Isabelle had sworn never to give in to the temptation of the everdream, never to crawl the path her past lives chose for her. This life was hers, not theirs . . . except it wasn't anymore.

As the outside world fell to pieces, she turned inward toward the everdream. As Bitterlich said, if she could not escape her progenitors, she must master them, not here but on their own ground.

As the crew of the *Thunderclap* pinned her down and bound her fast, Isabelle let go her flesh and leapt into the everdream.

CHAPTER

Thirteen

Jean-Claude crashed through twisted, thorny branches, smashed his arm against a stout limb, and whacked his head on something solid.

He must have blacked out, for he woke to find a gull jabbing at his face with its sharp beak, trying to pluck his right eye from its socket. The left side of his face was a boiling cauldron of pain and he could not see out of that side. Jean-Claude raised his hand to swat the bird, only to feel his weight shift and slide. He hung from a twistthorn tree, caught like a bit of wool on a thistle. Thorns poked through his coat and skewered his flesh, the chin strap of his hat tried to choke him. The twistthorn itself clung to the side of a tiny skyland, one of the reef-rocks surrounding a larger atoll.

He reached for the branch above his head, but that shift made the tree adjust its grip, and he slid a few more inches along, stripping off several of the long pointed thorns that held him in place. The wind whisked the fallen spines away.

The gull came back, with friends, determined to strip all the usable flesh from his bones before he finished his plunge into the Gloom.

Jean-Claude had lost his rapier and his pistol, but managed to draw his main gauche. Feeble and half-blind, he slashed and poked at the swelling flock of scavengers. Their indignant shrieks berated him for fighting back. Didn't he realize he was wasting good meat?

"Bugger off," he wheezed. Blackness swallowed his vision and then vomited him up again. The birds opened up more wounds in him.

Where was Isabelle? In his moments of greatest lucidity, he turned his head as far as agony would allow, but saw no sign of the *Thunderclap*. Had she rode the ship down to the Gloom?

Stab and swat, fade and recover. Each waking moment was slower to mature than the last. The haze of pain and exhaustion closed over him, like a drowning man sinking ever deeper beneath the breathing world's shimmering surface. Jean-Claude could not say whether he'd dangled for hours or years, only that he could find no way off this gibbet that didn't involve an endless drop . . . but that was preferable to being eaten alive by gulls.

Shouts reached his fading hearing. The shouts of men. He opened his working eye and turned his head. A shadow moved down there. The branch creaked, and he slipped a handspan closer to Torment.

"Get the boat under him," someone commanded, and there was much cursing and thumping about.

"He's dead," somebody said.

"Doesn't matter as long as he's got the quaestor's relic," said another voice.

"He's not dead yet," said another voice deep and rumbling like a millstone. "He's coming down on your side, Jake. Now."

The last spiny finger of the twistthorn lost its grip. Jean-Claude fell, croaking in dismay. He landed on or was caught by several strong men who dragged him aboard a launch and laid him out on the bottom bit.

The pain of even this controlled impact blotted out his mind again, and when he once more dragged himself to the surface he found his lopsided vision filled with a grinning visage of a man with one blazing blue eye and a bristling blond beard that looked like a colony of hedgehogs had taken up residence under his chin. Around him flickered a dozen other images of himself, like refractions seen in bits of spinning crystal, there and gone again. As addled as he was, Jean-Claude recognized the man, a phantasm from his distant past: pirate, gambler, sorcerer, and adversary.

"Ivar Thirdeye," Jean-Claude mumbled.

Ivar gave a booming laugh. "Look what the sky serves us up today. If it isn't the mighty Jean-Claude, and he still remembers his old mates."

At least Fortune and Fate were being prompt with their judgments today.

"You're too late. Relic's gone overboard," he said, flopping his hand toward the side of the boat. Isabelle had charged him to keep the key safe. But the other pirate had called it the quaestor's relic. Has Czensos hired Thirdeye?

"We'll see about that," said Ivar. "And afterward, you've a debt to pay."

Someone tipped a shot of liquid into Jean-Claude's mouth. Parched, he swallowed it before even realizing it was poppy milk. The pain dissolved like honey in hot tea and flowed away, taking consciousness with it.

—

Bitterlich's nerves stretched tight and worry scratched at his mind as he soared in the form of a galvatross above the jagged shoreline of the thorn-scrub skyland where the *Thunderclap*'s ill-fated launch had crashed. Its aetherkeel was cracked in half, and two bloody corpses lay within. Black, bloated flies swarmed all around. Gulls tore at the carcasses.

Bitterlich landed in the center of the mass and set loose a galvanic charge that sent the gulls flapping away, screeching their avian indignation. Dozens of crispy flies rained from the sky like tiny hailstones. The rest of their mindless ilk buzzed on, undeterred.

Bitterlich recognized what was left of Long Thom and Skyman Plonta. Of Jean-Claude, Hailer Dok, and the other aeronauts, there was no sign.

He pulled on his erstepelz and, standing upwind from the reek, quickly gave the dead men the rites of last watch. Then he waded into the cloud of insects, hefted a body in each hand, and hurled them off the sky cliff. It was not a proper send-off, but it was better than being food for the gulls.

Someone had survived the crash, for the bracken around the wreckage had been stomped down, and a path cleared to a more hospitable spot on the skyland's rim. Bitterlich turned into a dire wolf and sniffed along the path. He smelled Dok, several other people, and the stink of burned flesh. Of Jean-Claude there was not an iota of scent. Dread for the Old Hand grew like a canker in Bitterlich's heart. Jean-Claude had never had much use for Bitterlich, but Isabelle loved him as her father.

Bitterlich picked up a trace of another smell, an odor not entirely of this world, a volatile oily musk tinged with an accent he could only call the vault-reek. It was the scent that leaked out of a Seelengewölbe when a Seelenjäger shifted shape.

He followed the scent parade along the rim of the skyland to an inlet. There he found scrape marks where another boat had been dragged ashore. Dok and the Seelenjäger had been picked up by another ship, probably one of the Skaladin sloops.

Bitterlich transformed into a galvatross and rode a thermal up, looking for some sign of his quarry. The skyland was surrounded by a reef of unincorporated stonebergs and aethercorals, but they were likewise unoccupied by anyone living or dead.

Bitterlich's worry grew heavier the harder he looked. If Jean-Claude had fallen into the Gloom, there would never be anything to find. He shuddered to imagine facing Isabelle with such news. It would shatter her in ways no physical wound ever could.

He circled several times, adjusting his eyes to scour the skies, but the Solar dipped toward the horizon and the clouds thickened toward opacity. He could barely see the *Thunderclap*, even with his best vision, and no sign of the Skaladin at all. He hated returning with nothing to show for his efforts, but there was nothing more to be learned out here, and this wreck must be reported.

With a twitch of his tail feathers he turned and made the long slow glide to the *Thunderclap*. This mission must go on, which meant they must find Dok and the key, but plucking them out of the deep sky would take a miracle, and Bitterlich knew better than to wish for divine aid.

By the time he returned, the *Thunderclap* had transferred a prize crew to the Skaladin brig and gotten it turned upright. The ship would be turned over to the prize board, who would assay its worth.

Bitterlich swooped in, pulling on his erstepelz and landing lightly on the *Thunderclap*'s deck amidst the startled crew. Two of his marines stood guard by the capitaine's cabin. They saluted at his approach.

"Major," said Louis, his face drawn. "Capitaine Vrain requires you to report as soon as you return."

Bitterlich's heart fell out of his ribs and didn't hit bottom. "What happened to Capitaine Isabelle?" Had there been some sort of coup? Vrain was the stick to which others were compared for stiffness, but he was no mutineer.

"She . . . had a fit, sir," Louis said. "She's been relieved."

Dismay sucked all the heat from Bitterlich's body. Isabelle's head troubles must have gotten out of their cage, as she had feared all along. He yearned to go to her, right now, even if there was nothing he could do for her.

But protocol must be followed. He had a duty to report to his commanding officer. Also, Vrain would know exactly what form Isabelle's removal had taken.

He stepped into the capitaine's cabin to find Vrain dispatching orders to the other officers. ". . . and make sure Joubert's Folly knows to expect us."

"Aye, Capitaine," said a lieutenant.

Vrain took note of Bitterlich, who saluted.

"Major Bitterlich," Vrain said. "Report."

Bitterlich said, "I found the wreck of la reine's crib on the barrier reef of a skyland north of here. There had clearly been some sort of struggle. I found Long Thom and Plonta's corpses, but everyone else was gone when I got there. The passengers had been picked up by another launch and carried away. I did not see any other ships, nor did I find Hailer Dok. I did, however, smell another Seelenjäger."

Vrain nodded. "Very well. Dismissed."

Bitterlich hesitated, flummoxed by his brevity. "Yes, Capitaine. Will there be a council to discuss strategy?" Vrain was the most taciturn man Bitterlich had ever met, but surely he had some information to give in return, some notion of a plan to share.

Vrain's craggy eyebrows inched down, like a ridge line contemplating an avalanche. "Committees make poor capitaines, Major."

Bitterlich only winced on the inside. "Grand Leon always said active collaboration makes for better coordination in any complex endeavor."

"Grand Leon ruled by inspiring his nobles to fight each other instead of him. A warship cannot afford such chaos. I expect my officers to know their duties. When given orders, they will carry them out. Do you object?"

"No, sir," Bitterlich said, though he dreaded the future this portended. There was no one in the world more misguided than a man who heeded only his own advice. "May I inquire what prompted this change of command?"

Vrain's expression became even harder, moving from marble to granite. "Capitaine Isabelle became incapacitated."

"Thank you, Capitaine," Bitterlich said. He did not add, *Your answer, while concise and probably accurate, was also entirely unhelpful.* He slipped out of the cabin and was ever so grateful to breathe in air that Vrain was not personally oppressing.

He found Isabelle in the infirmary in a curtained-off nook. She appeared asleep, buried under blankets. Her face was flushed with heat but without sweat. Her spark swarm had diminished down to a few stray pinpricks of light, like dying fireflies forlornly winking out calls to mates that would never come.

Marie sat on a stool by the hammock, holding Isabelle's hand.

Bitterlich doffed his hat. "Mademoiselle, may I come in?"

"Are you sure you want to?" Marie said without looking up. Her toneless voice seemed to bleach hope from the room.

He looked around to see if there was anyone who might be listening in. Seeing no one, he approached the hammock and said, "Hallucinations?"

"Hallucinations, delusions, garbled speech. I poured a quart of potion down her throat and it didn't help. It took poppy milk to get her to sleep. Builder only knows if she'll wake up again, or whether that would be a blessing or a curse."

Bitterlich's heart shriveled like a raisin, and words failed him completely. After a moment, he collected another stool and sat down. He couldn't feel his own heartbeat. Why in all the world did this have to happen to her? Why did it have to be a foe no one could fight?

"You don't have to stay," Marie said. Her voice had no tone, but it did have a rhythm that suggested he was not wanted.

Bitterlich was used to not being wanted, though. "If I could trade places with her, I would." But he couldn't, and that was the damned hopeless truth of it. He wouldn't inflict himself on Marie, though, who had been Isabelle's faithful companion long before she'd ever met Bitterlich. "I have news for her when she wakes."

"You didn't find Jean-Claude," Marie said. At Bitterlich's surprised expression, she added, "If you had, he would have come here straightaway."

Her assessment assumed Jean-Claude would be found alive, a possibility that seemed less likely with every passing hour. Yet he would not disabuse her of that hope. "The launch crashed, but the survivors were picked up by someone else before I got there. They had a Seelenjäger with them."

"Hasdrubal," Marie said. "Isabelle learned that from the Skaladin capitaine."

The strategic part of his mind extrapolated from that news. "He'll be running straight back to the tyrant. Did Isabelle find out anything else?" Was there anything at all that was not too broken or too late for him to act on?

"No. Isabelle believed the capitaine hid away her chartstones, but she had her fit before she could find out where."

"I'll find out," Bitterlich said. His gaze lingered on Isabelle. She seemed so much smaller now without the boundless force of her personality. Marie was right about his cowardice. He owed Isabelle an explanation and an apology . . . and penance for his sins. He prayed he would get the chance to offer them.

At last he said, "Builder keep you and Isabelle safe from harm."

"Until the Savior comes to take you home," Marie said.

Bitterlich slipped away. He wanted to talk to the Skaladin capitaine, but not just yet. He was tired from fight and flight, weary with dread and shame, and hungry enough to eat a spineback, barbs and all. Plus it was always a bad idea to try to question someone without at least a few solid facts to use as leverage.

He took the time to eat, with fork and knife and manners, never ever wolfing his food. It would not do to look like an animal. The ritual of the meal also gave him time to think.

What was Hasdrubal's plan? He had the *Conquest* shard, Dok, and the key, but he couldn't expect to pierce the Bittergale with the motley fleet he'd used at Fishers Point. Likely he'd be running for a friendly port to deliver the shard to the tyrant, or to rendezvous with a stronger fleet somewhere between here and the Craton Auroborea.

Bitterlich finished his meal and found his lieutenant, a Sanguinaire named Malgiers, reading a book in the curtained-off alcove that counted as officers' quarters for the marines. He was the fourth son of lesser gentry, a man with no prospects of social elevation and no outlet for whatever useful talents he might have developed, nobles being discouraged from meaningful work. His parents had purchased his commission in the hopes that he would make something of himself, or at least be cleansed of his poetic inclinations in the fires of battle. So far there had been little cleansing, though there had been more than a few sonnets, a handful of short stories, and at least one new sky chanty.

Malgiers was off duty and as out of uniform as one ever got on a warship, his white overcoat, waistcoat, and hat hung up on a hook.

He came to attention at Bitterlich's approach. "Sir."

Bitterlich returned the salute. "I understand we have taken some captives."

Malgiers said, "Yes, sir. The Skaladin capitaine is being held below-decks. I've posted two men to keep watch. We ended up with forty-three captives on the brig, including the wounded, and I have a squad there, keeping watch."

"Has anyone questioned them yet?" Bitterlich asked.

"Vrain interrogated the capitaine. I don't know that anyone has questioned the crew."

"Do you know if Vrain learned anything about the Skaladin mission?"

"If he did, he didn't tell me."

Bitterlich cursed Vrain's secretiveness. He didn't want to step on the new capitaine's tender toes, but Bitterlich's job was to protect the ship and he couldn't do that without good intelligence. Fortunately he had access to some of the best intelligence in the Risen Kingdoms.

Bitterlich said, "I need you to contact Comtesse Impervia in my name." He absolutely hated using bloodhollows, but there was no practical alternative.

Malgiers turned green, and his voice carried a note of dread. "You mean the spymaster."

At least Impervia hadn't lost her frightful reputation as l'impératrice's all-seeing shadow. "Yes. Tell her that I'm on Hasdrubal's trail, and I need to know if she's learned anything else about him since last we spoke."

Malgiers's expression betrayed the sort of dread that suggested a man being volunteered for a suicide mission; no one in their right mind just walked up to the wicked spymaster and asked her a question. It probably would have broken his mind to know that Bitterlich had witnessed Impervia grinning like a loon whilst playing peekaboo with her grandchildren.

"Yes. Sir," Malgiers said, as if each monosyllable were made of poison.

Contacting Impervia would take some time. Bitterlich left Malgiers to it, donned his bat skin, and flew across to the brig. The repairs, now well under way, only served to highlight the vessel's overall decrepitude.

Bitterlich pulled on his erstepelz and descended to the gun deck. One end had been partitioned off into cells to hold the remaining Skaladin. Bitterlich inspected his men and their prisoners and found their precautions satisfactory. If Fleet Command and the Célestial ambassador to Skaladin concluded the aeronauts belonged to the tyrant, they would be treated as prisoners of war; otherwise they would be executed as pirates.

There was nothing about the bedraggled crew or their run-down ship that suggested to Bitterlich that anyone in Skaladin would want to claim them. Most were older than the average aeronaut, grizzled and spare. Their green-and-black uniforms were patched and worn, those who even had uniforms. Interspersed amongst the captives were younger men in Célestial garb with clean-shaven chins and tattoos such as the Skaladin never wore.

Why would Hasdrubal need to employ pirates and riffraff in the first place? As an agent of the Maze of Eyes, he ought to have all the resources of the tyranny at his disposal. He could have called upon a crack raiding squadron instead of this motley lot.

Bitterlich strolled to one of the cells. Most of the Skaladin gazed on him with a sullen anger, and many made signs against evil. They could not abide sorcerers as anything but slaves.

The foreigners amongst them were more fearful than furious. How had they had fallen in with the pirates? They might have been criminals or fortune-seekers or just drunk in the wrong alley at the wrong time, but they were much less likely to be loyal to the collective than the Skaladin.

"Bring me that one," Bitterlich said, pointing to one of the Célestials, a man with a pox-pitted face and many small scars on his work-hardened arms.

A marine hauled the man up. Bitterlich led them to the chartroom. The pirate looked around like a caged beast introduced to a new environment. He might not have liked the cage he'd left, but he did not trust the one he was in.

"Do you have a name?" Bitterlich asked.

"Sinclair," he said. "Please. I'm not part of this." He gestured at the ship with his hands still bound. "Didn't ask for this. Got pressed, see?"

"So, you fell into a barrel of beer, and woke up on a pirate ship," Bitterlich said.

"Yeah," Sinclair said. "Not my fault."

"Then you'll agree to testify against your kidnappers," Bitterlich said.

"Will you let me go?" Sinclair said.

"That depends on how truthful your testimony turns out to be," Bitterlich said. It was not technically up to Bitterlich to decide what happened to these men, a but a judge was unlikely to deny Bitterlich if he asked for clemency.

"How long has it been since you were abducted?" Bitterlich asked.

Sinclair shook his head slowly. "Little more than a turn. Took me on as a carpenter, see. The ship was a mess. Worse'n now."

One turn was a rotation of the Craton Massif, a little more than a third of a year. That would be just about the time that Lael had arrived in Rocher Royale to make his play for the throne and brought Hasdrubal with him.

"And where were you before that?" Bitterlich asked. It was generally harder for people to stick to a lie if they had to present the bits out of order.

"In Malbis," he said. "I was a journeyman shipwright."

The shipyards at Malbis were not the biggest in l'Empire, but they were the most convenient to Rocher Royale, being just a hundred kilometers up the coast.

"And what happened after you were kidnapped?" Bitterlich said.

"Worked on the ship," he said. "Ribs were broken, staves needed replacing. It was hard work, see. I never got paid."

"Did the Skaladin ever say how the ship got to be in such bad shape?"

Sinclair shook his head as if shuffling his thoughts. "It's not easy to understand their chattering," he said. "But I think they lost a war."

The answer stirred Bitterlich's thoughts. One of the reasons the Tyranny of Skaladin was not more of a threat to the Risen Kingdoms was that they spent so much time fighting amongst themselves. A goodly number of the bandit armies, pirate fleets, and smugglers that troubled the civilized world were outcasts, refugees from those internecine struggles.

Bitterlich applied this logic to Hasdrubal. If there were outcast warships, there might also be outcast spies. Perhaps Hasdrubal had suddenly found himself out in the cold. That would explain why he had been reduced to recruiting these slavers. Perhaps the Skaladin capitaine could be inspired to provide a more definitive version of events.

"Where was the ship when you were making these repairs?" Bitterlich asked.

"She were laid up at l'Île Tromelin," Sinclair said. "Least that's what the bloodhollow called it. Bare rock, really, nothing more there than a flock of hook gulls."

"There was a bloodhollow on board? Whose?"

Sinclair shivered. "Don't know. I don't want nothing to do with glass ghosts. Don't want 'em to make me one."

"An understandable fear," Bitterlich said. The bloodhollow certainly wasn't aboard now. "What about when the ship left l'Île Tromelin? What was their plan?"

"The capitaine said we were going to finish the mission. Don't know what mission. Kept my head down and just worked on the ship."

"Where did you get supplies to work on the ship?" Bitterlich asked. It sounded as if they'd been laid up for a long time in the middle of nowhere.

"There was a barge that came in every week or so out of Malbis. Shore smuggler. He brought supplies. 'Compliments of the comte,' he said."

"He didn't happen to say which comte?" Bitterlich asked as casually as he could. He should have known that somehow this whole plot would work its way back to Célestial intrigue. Somehow they always did.

"He never said," Sinclair said.

Bitterlich repeated his questions in a different order, but Sinclair's answers remained consistent. On the whole, Bitterlich believed his story. He didn't know enough about what Bitterlich really wanted to lie about it.

Bitterlich told the marine standing guard, "Hold him separately from the others. They'll probably kill him if you put him back in with them."

Sinclair went pale, and the marine hauled him away.

Bitterlich descended to the hold and found it exceptionally well stocked for a pirate ship. He found sacks of beans and crates of lemons and barrels of brandy with a Célestial maker's mark and the stamp of the Imperial Treasury that indicated its tax had been paid.

He hurried through the stacks of provender until he found the crates of hardtack and flipped the top from one that had already been opened. Inside were stacks and more stacks of ship's biscuit, the most despised foodstuff in the history of digestion. Into each brown, tooth-cracking, weapons-grade wafer was stamped the imperial seal.

Bitterlich took one biscuit for evidence and closed the lid. The making of hardtack was a regulated enterprise. They were created in imperial bakeries, stored in imperial warehouses, and shipped exclusively with the Imperial

Army and Navy. This whole ship had been supplied with embezzled military rations.

Bitterlich tapped the biscuit against his palm. When Lael had fallen, Hasdrubal disappeared into the capital. No one had been able to find him. Perhaps he'd managed to find aid and succor in one of the high houses, someone especially displeased with Sireen's ascension to the throne. It was not a stretch to imagine that he'd made an alliance with his benefactor and persuaded them to supply his mission.

These stolen supplies might help Impervia track down which noble had turned traitor. Perhaps she could unravel the plot from that end. Yet that would take time. The *Thunderclap* couldn't wait for answers to come from elsewhere before making pursuit. They must find Dok and the shard. The Skaladin capitaine must know where they were going.

Bitterlich returned to the *Thunderclap*. The marines assigned to guard the prisoner saluted at Bitterlich's approach.

"I need to speak to the captive," Bitterlich said.

The marines exchanged a look that suggested each was willing the other to be the bearer of bad news. The senior man, Paul, said, "Yes sir, but it may not do you any good. Vrain was . . . hard on her."

Bitterlich scowled, but cursed only on the inside. Paul opened the door and lifted a lantern so Bitterlich could see properly.

The Skaladin capitaine was chained to a wall, but it was only for show. All the color had been drained from her body, leaving her as gray and washed out as a tombstone in the rain. Her eyes were vacant and staring, her breath shallow and weak. Vrain had shadowburned her within a breath of death.

Bitterlich's gut curdled and he had to breathe carefully to keep down his bile. He had been burned that way before. The sight of her brought it back to him: agony beyond the reach of comprehension, every nerve aflame and every thought burned in acid.

"That idiot!" Bitterlich growled.

"Sir," Paul's voice rose in fright.

Bitterlich closed his eyes and unclenched his fists. "Lieutenant, get that woman a blanket. Make her warm. Keep a light on in there. If you can get some soup down her, do that."

He left the marines to their job and stumbled into the hold. Saints, but Vrain was a fool. Not everyone recovered from being shadowburned. As an imperial officer Vrain might not be allowed to torture a prisoner, but as a Sanguinaire he could turn any clayborn he liked into a bloodhollow or reduce them to a soul smudge. Such was the divine warrant of sorcery.

The fact that Vrain had also fouled up Bitterlich's best hope of figuring out where they might catch up with Hasdrubal was a bitter wound on top of the loathsome cruelty.

A soft sigh and a snuffle reached his ears. He followed the sound to a bay. There on Isabelle's sky trunk sat Rebecca, her jacket across her lap, her face in her hands, sobbing.

"Rebecca," Bitterlich said. What had brought this on . . . aside from the business of being transformed into a Seelenjäger right in the middle of a harrowing sky battle and then being promptly abandoned by every adult who had more important things to do.

Rebecca started and stared at him. Her pupil-less eyes were bloodshot and her nose snotty. He extended his handkerchief. She stared at it mutely for a moment, then took it and emptied her face into it.

"May I sit down?" he asked.

"Don't care," she mumbled, but she scooted over when he planted his posterior on the chest beside her. She handed him back his handkerchief, which was going to need laundering before it went anywhere near his pocket.

"What happened?" he asked, bracing to be blamed for her sudden acquisition of scales and horns and obligate nobility.

"I don't know," she wailed. "I just . . . I was trying to fix this stupid jacket." She shook the offending garment like a terrier shaking a rat and threw it on the deck. "I can't do this. I don't want to. I don't know how." She wasn't talking about sewing up a rent.

Bitterlich resisted the urge to try to buck up her spirits. "Yes. It's really hard. It feels like you've tripped in the dark and you're falling and you don't know where the ground is."

Rebecca bobbed her head morosely. "Something like that."

Bitterlich exercised patience. She didn't need judgment or advice or wisdom, just simple understanding and acceptance.

At length she sniffed and wiped her nose on her sleeve. "What happens now?"

"You breathe," he said. "And your heart beats, and you pick yourself up, and you keep going. That's really all there is to it."

"But where am I going to?" she asked, a trace of the panic echoing in the back of her voice. It was the future that had come unstuck in her mind.

"Nobody really knows," Bitterlich said. "When I was your age I thought I was going to inherit my father's lands and become Herr Bitterlich. That didn't happen. Neither did anything else ever turn out like I expected. Last year I was serving as a spy for Comtesse Impervia. I never dreamed I'd be a marine major on a ship hunting for treasure on a craton nobody even knew existed. Three months ago it probably never occurred to you you'd be Capitaine Isabelle's cabin girl. Yesterday, you didn't know you were a Seelenjäger. Tomorrow will bring its own surprises."

Rebecca fell silent again, working all that out. He remembered Monsieur Belleaux saying, "A young person's mind is like a wine cask. Clearly something is going on in there even if nobody understands it."

"So," she said, "why did all my buttons pop off, and my belt buckle?"

"Ah," Bitterlich said. He imagined she'd circled back to the otherwise trivial question that had started her emotional avalanche. "They're made of metal. You can bring a small amount of extra material into your Seelengewölbe, but it has to be something that was once alive, like wool, linen, or leather."

"Your buttons go with you," Rebecca said.

"Mine are made of bone," Bitterlich said. "It's a problem all Seelenjägers deal with."

"Oh," Rebecca said, holding her buttons. "So sewing these back on isn't going to work."

"Not even a little." He stood. "Come. I'll give you some of my spares."

CHAPTER

Fourteen

Jean-Claude wobbled back into consciousness, a condition complicated by the looking-at-the-world-through-a-greasy-windowpane feeling of a poppy-milk hangover. Pain waited for him like a ring of torch-and-pitchfork-wielding peasants, and his limbs seemed to have gone off on pilgrimage for all that he could feel them.

His vision was blurry in his left eye, and every inch of him was cross-hatched with scratches and punctuated with punctures.

He lay under an open porthole that let in the coppery tang of the deep sky. At least he still had both eyes, and there were no damned gulls trying to peck them out.

Where was Isabelle? The question hounded him into restless dreams and then chased him back out again. Only on waking did he remember what he'd lost. He'd seen the *Thunderclap* fall from the sky with Isabelle, Marie, and Rebecca aboard. They were all so young. Even all grown-up, there was a part of Isabelle who would always be a newborn, a child in his heart.

He'd counted Isabelle amongst the dead once before only to have her turn up days later and half a sky away, but this time he'd seen the ship go down. That memory hurt more than every pain in his body. No matter how he tried to guide his mind to other things, like where in all the sky he was, he kept circling back to a vision of the great ship plummeting.

The corner of the cabin where he'd been laid out had been partitioned off from the rest of the ship by a heavy curtain. He briefly considered getting up to look around, but any motion more ambitious than blinking brought reprisals in the form of pain like someone splitting his skull with a chisel.

A gull screamed somewhere in the distance. If Jean-Claude never heard that noise again it would be too soon. His wounds burned and itched madly, though they had neither the heat nor stink of infection.

"Ahoy," he croaked through parched lips. He felt the aeronautical term was a nice touch, not that it elicited a response.

He sucked on his tongue for a few minutes trying to work up some spit, and tried again. "Hello, the ship. Can anybody hear me?" His own desiccated voice rasped against his ears.

In due course, the curtain brushed aside and the ship's surgeon came in. He was so covered in scars that Jean-Claude wondered if he practiced his stitchery on himself. He wore a bloodstained apron and held a short clay pipe clenched in his teeth.

"Well, there's a surprise," the surgeon said, pulling aside the sheet that covered Jean-Claude's chest and prodding at the many wounds thereon. "Figured you for a dead man."

Jean-Claude winced at his touch. "Keep that up and I will be."

"Always knew you lemon eaters were damned babies. No heat. No rot." He pulled the sheet back up and waggled his fingers by the left side of Jean-Claude's face. "See this?"

"It's a blur," he said.

"Good enough," said the surgeon, and went on to examining Jean-Claude's lacerated and broken arm with all the care and delicacy of a man digging a trench.

"Nnngh." Jean-Claude clenched his teeth, which made his eye socket feel like someone had shoved a galvanized icicle in there.

When the pain at last faded to the point where he could open his mouth without screaming, he said, "My ship. What happened to the *Thunderclap*?"

"Fell like a stone," said the surgeon.

Jean-Claude's heart felt like it imploded, leaving a gaping hole in his chest that no suture could close. Isabelle had fallen into the Gloom.

"Damned thing was that it fell right back up again. Popped up like a cork in water. Never seen the like."

Jean-Claude breathed again. His rigid muscles all relaxed, and he could have kissed the surgeon for all his ham-handed prodding. If the *Thunderclap* survived, Isabelle lived, and Marie and Rebecca. With their lives came hope and a calm that did more to ease his aches than a whole tub of poppy milk.

Moreover, this news allowed his mind to unclench and focus on other things. He had been stripped to the skin, so the key was gone, as was the *Conquest* shard. But what had happened to Hailer Dok? Without him, the mission could not penetrate the Bittergale.

"When I fell," Jean-Claude said, "what happened to the launch?"

"No idea," the surgeon said.

Jean-Claude's humors roiled and he felt sick to his gut. Hasdrubal had escaped with Dok, the only man who knew the way through the Bittergale.

The surgeon said, "Give it another day. If you haven't gone septic by then, you'll probably live."

"I need to speak to the capitaine," Jean-Claude said. He must recover the key and the shard and find a way to retrieve Dok.

The surgeon grunted, leaned out the door, and shouted, "Hey, Cap'n. Your meat sack woke up and learned to talk."

The surgeon stepped aside and Ivar Thirdeye arrived by stages. Like a brazier aflame with colorless fire, Ivar sent off flickering alternate images of himself in all directions. In some he strode through the open doorway, in others he paused on the threshold, in others he had more swagger or dignity. Each image lasted only the blink of an eye before vanishing without smoke or spark. Each flicker represented an alternate possibility, a path not chosen, for such was the power of Tidsskygge sorcery. They could see many possible futures stretching out before them and pick the one that suited their needs. Most could prophesy only a few seconds into the future, but the best could push their foresight out to a minute or so. Between that and the ability to dam up or unleash the flow of time to their benefit, they were the slipperiest of sorcerers.

This particular Tidsskygge was broad and square, as if he'd been raised to adulthood inside a shipping crate. He wore a fine leather long coat decorated with stitched-in scenes of hunting and fighting. He'd also acquired an eye patch somewhere along the way. A smuggler, mercenary, and an all-around scoundrel, he was wanted by half the Risen Kingdoms on any given day and employed by the other half on any given night.

Just behind him, clicking and clanking, came Quaestor Czensos, but not as Jean-Claude had seen him before. He bore a staff of quondam metal in his mechanical hand. It was as black and gritty as wrought iron, and the mere sight of it made Jean-Claude's skull throb. Even more alarming, the symbols of his office had all been desecrated, his mantel torn and his omnioculus medallion punctured and blinded. He'd shaved his head and wore a crown of new tattoos, blasphemous symbols braided together in an embrace of the Breaker.

He'd become a Last Man, or more likely he'd been a mole, working within the Temple to guarantee its downfall. He must be in league with Hasdrubal, but where did that leave Ivar? Was he part of their scheme, or was he just hired help?

"Awake at last, Monsieur Jean-Claude," said Ivar in a rumbling yet charming bass. "Welcome aboard *Dame Formue*."

"Ivar." Jean-Claude tried to sit, but a sharp pain in his face slapped him back down. He grunted and continued, "On behalf of l'Empire Céleste and her Majesty La Reine de Tonner, Sireen the First, I thank you for rescuing me from the deep sky. A substantial award awaits you for returning me to any imperial port of call."

Ivar laughed. "Do you remember Puerto Mal Aterrizaje? Thirty years ago?"

"That's not a Célestial port," Jean-Claude pointed out.

"That's where you cheated me out of a fortune, a crime for which no justice was ever procured. No restitution. No punishment. It was as if the Builder had forgotten his most faithful son." Ivar put his hand on his chest. "But a long season brings a great harvest, or so they say, and now here you are, a dead man rescued from the gibbet by my own hand."

"For which you will be richly rewarded," Jean-Claude said.

Ivar's grin grew so wide it was in danger of bisecting his head. "Oh, I'll take my due, sure enough, not by some fickle reine's charity."

"Did I mention the reward was very large?" Jean-Claude said. "I'm sure l'impératrice can more than double what Czensos is paying you. Speaking of whom, bonjour, Quaestor. I see you lost a fight with an angry but artistic kraken. My condolences."

"Save your prattle," Czensos said. "You are alive now only because I have use for you."

Jean-Claude found that oddly comforting; he could find many ways to make himself useful, and people who needed something were almost always willing to give something in return, even if it was trivial. The trick was to make trivial concessions add up.

To Ivar he said, "Is that true? He's the capitaine of this tub now, to make decisions of life and death?"

Ivar scowled, and his various time shadows flickered around his face as he tried out different statements and possible responses. It made Jean-Claude's skin crawl to think that Ivar could interrogate a dozen versions of him and then follow the line of inquiry that seemed most fruitful. It was like playing thwarts with a marked deck and a loyal dealer.

"Monsieur Czensos paid for a fishing trip, and you're the fish. What he catches is up to him to keep or throw away, but even a kept fish gets gutted."

Jean-Claude said, "So no revenge for you unless he says so."

Czensos said, "Rest assured, Capitaine, that if this man's suffering pleases you, le Comte Travers shall provide it in buckets. The Old Hand was part of *Thunderclap*'s inner circle, and le Comte Travers will skin him and scrape his hide to find out what he knew about their mission."

Jean-Claude knew Travers's name. They were an old family, rich in history and undiluted wealth. Members of a purity cult, they only sowed their seed in the family fields. Thus they counted amongst their numbers some of the weakest chins, most twisted limbs, daftest madmen, and most fragile constitutions in all the Risen Kingdoms.

The last thing Jean-Claude wanted was to be handed over in secret to a demented Sanguinaire who considered himself superior to all persons whose family trees had more than one branch.

Jean-Claude said, "Strange that you would ally yourself with Travers and his sister-humping ilk. The whole point of their project is the notion that the Savior will choose one of them as his vessel, whereas the Last Men preach the Savior is already dead."

"We didn't recruit him for his theological opinions," Czensos said, "but for his ships. The Bittergale will not yield without a struggle."

"So you need him, but what does he need you for?" Jean-Claude asked.

"He badly wants an introduction to the Savior, which is why he'll gladly dismantle you to find the *Conquest*'s keel shard."

"I don't have it," Jean-Claude said honestly.

Czensos said, "Then he will find that out, along with every other secret you hold dear."

"And after that, the Vault of Ages," Jean-Claude said. "To undo all the Breaker wrought."

Czensos clasped his flesh hand around his headache-inducing staff, ever so casually displaying Saint Cynessus's ring in the process. "This broken world was born when Saint Iav betrayed the Builder and let the Breaker in. It has only become more vile and wicked with every passing generation as she weaves herself into every thought, every action, every dream. We live in a wretched age. There is nothing left but scraps of the Builder's designs. We must cast the Breaker out now, before the last light of reason fades, or consign the world to darkness everlasting. If you were truly a man of faith, you would understand that."

"Faith doesn't feed chickens, as my mother used to say," Jean-Claude said. "The Builder made the world, but it's up to us to live in it."

"Not for much longer," Czensos said, and took himself out.

Jean-Claude cast a questioning glance at Ivar. "And you go along with this madness?"

Ivar rubbed his cheek below his eye patch. "He's not the first zealot I've ever shipped. He won't be the last. The wonderful thing about them with the Builder on the brain is they don't care much about money. A madman will always think you're trying to cheat him, but a fanatic doesn't care. He'll give you everything he owns to get to the end of the world because he knows he's not coming back."

"But what if he's right?" Jean-Claude asked. "What if he finds the Vault of Ages and opens it."

"All the better," Ivar said. "What would it be, save a broken old ruin, and who knows what treasures lie within, ripe for the taking."

"Except that, from the sound of it, you're going to be on this side of the Bittergale," Jean-Claude pointed out.

"Haven't you been paying attention?" Ivar asked. "There's more money in selling people shovels than there is in digging for gold. I've got backers lined up looking for a path through the Bittergale. Once Travers shows me the way through, that's gold in the sack. Of course, it'd save me a bit of trouble if you'd give me the keel splinter."

"I don't know where it is," Jean-Claude said, a fact that distressed him mightily. "But what makes you think Travers will actually show you the way through the Bittergale?"

Ivar smiled, and his teeth looked like weathered gravestones. "You'll see."

CHAPTER

Fifteen

Night had pulled a heavy cloak over the sky, and the stars struggled to make themselves seen through a layer of high clouds. Bitterlich stood on the forecastle, scanning the sky ahead for hazards and picking at the tangle of his circumstances. He had not meant to acquire Rebecca as his apprentice. He had no experience with children, or with being a teacher, but she needed guidance that only he on this ship could give.

Yet at least that was something he could give. For Isabelle he could do nothing.

"Major," said Lieutenant Malgiers, mounting the deck behind him.

Bitterlich received his salute. "Lieutenant."

Malgiers, looking slightly stuffed, said, "Sir, I contacted Comtesse Impervia as you directed."

This introduction should have been followed with a revelation of the information exchanged, but Malgiers wore an expression that spoke of a reluctance on the order of a three-day bowel blockage.

Bitterlich waited. Malgiers turned steadily more crimson.

At last Malgiers said, "Sir, I am commanded to quote the comtesse . . . her words, sir, 'You tell that flea-bitten, mange-ridden, curtain scratcher to pull his fuzzy head out of his bunghole and write me a proper report, or I swear I will rip his whiskers out and use them to tattoo the instruction on his eyeballs.'"

Bitterlich very nearly chortled. This was not the first time Impervia berated him for neglecting to provide her with context for his information requests. Possibly only the fact that he was using poor Malgiers as an intermediary kept her invective from getting really creative.

"Noted," he said. "Was that the entirety of her response?"

Malgiers relaxed slightly. "No, sir. She said at least now they know why they weren't having any luck finding Hasdrubal in Rocher Royale. She says something stirred up the Skaladin spies in the city just after the *Thunderclap* left, but so far nothing seems to have come of it. Also, she said you needed to know there's been a great uproar about Capitaine Isabelle. There's a rumor that she's gone mad, and now that she's been incapacitated there's a petition before the Crown to recall her. Comtesse Impervia wants a report and a recommendation from you."

A chill trickled down Bitterlich's spine. It was inevitable that news of Isabelle's breakdown would be transmitted to Rocher Royale, if only to explain to Fleet Command why Vrain had taken command. Unfortunately, nothing about Fleet Command was apolitical. Isabelle had not been a popular choice for capitaine, even amongst Sireen's partisans, who defended her spreading branches only because that's where the fruits of empire hung. The fact that a coveted plum had been given to a no-account woman who had been stripped of rank and title, and who wasn't even a Sanguinaire, was an offense to their finely honed and delicately balanced sense of entitlement.

If Isabelle were recalled, if she even survived her coma, it would mean not only the end of her mission but of her career. Having been stripped of all other status, even her family name, she would become, in effect, a nonperson devoid of rights and privileges.

It was against that future that Bitterlich must raise a palisade, and he must do it with nothing more than the words from his ungifted tongue.

"Thank you, Lieutenant," Bitterlich said, and dismissed Malgiers. He would write that report, but first he had to deliver this news to Marie. Perhaps Isabelle would be awake, not that he wanted to greet her return to consciousness with such vile news.

Yet even as Bitterlich approached Isabelle's nook in the sick bay, Sagax

Quill emerged carrying an armload of Lael's notebooks. Anger flashed through Bitterlich's mind at the idea of this theft, only to be doused by grief. Those were the books Isabelle had borrowed from Quill, and of course he wanted them back. The *Thunderclap* must sail as soon as it was provisioned if it were to have any hope of catching Hasdrubal and making its way to the Craton Auroborea. Lael's ledgers were vital to that effort.

Bitterlich arrived at Isabelle's nook to find her situation unchanged. Marie, seated by Isabelle's head, looked desperately tired. She was doing her best to ignore Jackhand Djordji's cajoling.

"You need rest," Djordji said to Marie. "Gets some sleep when you can or you fails when she needs you sharp."

"I am fine," Marie said, in defiance of the obvious. Stone-cold her expression might be, but her eyelids hung like lead curtains.

"I'll take a shift," Bitterlich said.

Marie swiveled to face him. "Why should I trust you?"

Her palpable distrust stung like a slap to the face, but he did not flinch. He opened his hand toward Isabelle. "Because she would."

"Not fair," Marie said. "She trusts too much, forgives too much. Look where it's got her."

"And would you change anything about her?" Bitterlich said.

Marie grimaced.

Djordji said, "I'll watch her too."

Grumbling, Marie allowed herself to be displaced from her seat. "Make sure she gets water and stays warm."

Djordji led Marie out. Bitterlich would tell her about Isabelle's potential recall after she'd rested and had enough energy to be properly outraged.

Isabelle's skin had wrinkled as if she'd aged thirty years overnight, and her halo of sparks was down to a few intermittent flickers like stars peeking through a heavy fog. Her breathing was dry and shallow.

Bitterlich sat at her bedside. His heart felt empty and heavy at the same time. She should be up and about, turning the world on its ear, not laid out like a corpse on a bier.

He took up the cloth Marie had been using to drip water into Isabelle's mouth, and squeezed a few drips past her lips. He'd never dared touch her face while she was awake. It felt intrusive doing so now, even if wholly necessary.

Her eyes showed no sign of fluttering open. She displayed no reflex at all.

He imagined what he would say if she woke, if he could form the words.

He would say, *I'm sorry I lied to you,* or, *I'm sorry I hurt you,* or, *I'm sorry I'm not the hero you deserve.* The "I'm sorry" seemed to be the important part.

Yet an apology was nothing without penance and restitution.

And what if she never woke up? How then would the world keep turning? Undoubtedly the Solar would rise, the cratons would spin, and Ciel itself would continue its Builder-ordained circuit through the icy, dark void in which the stars were hung. Yet it would be a lesser place. It wasn't just that Isabelle looked at him as a person; she looked at everyone that way. It was also that she had been betrayed, but she still trusted. She had been hurt, but she was still brave.

"Wake up," he said. "Please." But no miracle was forthcoming.

He squeezed more water into her mouth. She still seemed able to swallow by reflex, which was something.

Bitterlich stepped out of the nook long enough to corral a ship's boy and send him to fetch Bitterlich's writing kit. There was no reason he couldn't compose his report while sitting watch, and he served Isabelle better by defending her against her sleepless foes than by moping over her unconscious body.

—

Night had fallen, the ship's watch had changed, and Jean-Claude sat on the edge of his cot. Normally he would not have counted this as much of an accomplishment, but he was working with more of a handicap than usual. He might have owned some span of skin that wasn't cut or bruised, some organ that didn't ache, but if so he was just as aware of them as he might be of a quiet figure amongst a shouting mob.

He wrapped the thin blanket around his waist and considered his approach to standing. If he could get hold of the stanchion he could pull himself up, and hopefully not fall right over again. As much as he didn't want to move anymore, he needed to talk to Ivar and Czensos, preferably not at the same time.

"Don't bother to get up on my account," said a familiar drawling voice.

A magnificent dwarf leaned against the doorpost. He was as dashing and clever a fellow as could be imagined, with golden curls, glittering eyes, and a smile full of teeth that outshone pearls. He wore an embroidered waistcoat over a fine linen shirt and porkpie hat with the iridescent feathers of some rare bird curling over top of it. In his presence, even the weather-worn doorposts gleamed with a new coat of paint. A gold coin tumbled through his fingers in an endless loop, every now and then leaping up like a fish from a lake to land in his opposite palm and take up its gymnastic course in the other direction.

Jean-Claude winced at the extravagant vision. "Sedgwick, or should I say Lord Mistwaithe." He was a Goldentongue from Brathon, a master of illusions and a go-between for rich folk who liked their improprieties freshly laundered. This vision of perfection was his gloriole, the blazon of his sorcery. When Jean-Claude shifted his gaze away, he caught a glimpse of Sedgwick's true appearance, a slightly shabby little man with a lopsided face. The coin, however, still spun in the greasy vision of Jean-Claude's wounded eye.

"Sedgwick will do for now," he said. "Though if I am ever hanged, let it be under my family's name so they may enjoy the embarrassment of it."

Jean-Claude said, "I never pictured you as a pirate."

"I never pictured you as a pincushion, but here we both are."

"I put you on a ship to Brathon; how'd you end up here?" Jean-Claude asked. How deeply was he involved with Czensos's scheme? The last time Jean-Claude had seen him, he'd been grieving the death of his lover, but grief could take a person in strange directions. Jean-Claude had seen people walk away from house and hold rather than endure a profound emptiness.

"I made it about halfway to Brathon before my ship was waylaid by pirates." He made a sweeping gesture to indicate the *Dame Formue*. "Being short on coin for ransom and in need of gainful employment, I signed up. He pays me to keep the ship hidden."

"I didn't think you could hide yourself with glamour," Jean-Claude said.

"All I have to do is stay inside and make the ship look like a galvatross," Sedgwick said. "And then it turned out our old friend Lael discovered the *Conquest,* and Capitaine Thirdeye had a plan for getting a share of that treasure without putting our necks out."

"Nothing about Czensos is safe," Jean-Claude said. "Or are you not aware of his plan?"

Sedgwick's glamorous eyebrows arched elegantly. "I'm sure you're dying to tell me."

Jean-Claude desperately wanted someone to be on his side, but that very need must make him wary. Sedgwick was not a particularly evil man, but whatever nobility he might have once possessed had been blunted by rejection and corroded by cynicism. He might be concealing Ivar and Czensos behind a veil of illusion at that moment, and Jean-Claude would never be able to tell.

"The *Conquest* wasn't the only thing Lael found up there. He also found the Vault of Ages, or at least Czensos and Hasdrubal think he did."

"Hasdrubal?" Sedgwick asked.

"He was Lael's lieutenant, a Skaladin Seelenjäger agent provocateur. After Lael died, Hasdrubal took up with the Last Men, which I would guess is how he met Czensos. That ring Czensos is wearing is a relic of Saint Cynessus. It's supposed to be the key to the Vault. Hasdrubal plans on opening it and heralding in the end of the world."

Sedgwick frowned. "You mean the actual end of the world."

"Waking the Savior, or killing him, or just tipping him out in the street. It's turned into a game of theological find-the-red-queen."

"The Savior's coming is supposed to be a good thing," Sedgwick said.

"If that's so, why are all the people looking forward to it the sort you wouldn't trust with a wooden spoon?"

Sedgwick considered that for a moment, and his eyes darkened with doubt. "Are we getting to the part of the conversation where you ask me to risk my neck for your benefit?"

"No, but if you have some interest in doing me a favor, returning my clothes would be nice." Sedgwick might not be a coward to the bone, but it was definitely tattooed into his skin; best to ask him for small things first.

Sedgwick stepped out of the partitioned-off area, looked around, and then disappeared for a moment before returning with Jean-Claude's things. In his hands they looked like a stack of freshly folded laundry, but when he set them on the cot, the glamour drained away, revealing a bloodstained wad of fabric.

What was left of Jean-Claude's clothes would have been wasted on a bird scare. He only got his drawers on with help, and he couldn't manage the buttons on his doublet. The pirates had, of course, taken his weapons, his bag of tricks, and his coin purse. They had left the wallet with his passport in it. He looped its cord around his neck.

"It's probably not even real, is it?" Sedgwick said. "The Vault, that is. I mean, people are always coming in from the wild with stories of finding the Vault of Ages, or the lost city of Rüul, and it always turns out to be either a mistake or madness or some kind of shell game."

Jean-Claude worked his swollen feet into blood-crusted boots. "That's true."

"But you don't believe it, or rather you do believe they've actually found it."

Jean-Claude had given some thought to the evidence he'd seen, but had come to no conclusion. "I believe seeking the divine is more important than finding it."

"How do you figure?"

"If the Vault of Ages is nothing more than one place with one key that can be opened by one person, then every other seeker has truly searched in vain." Jean-Claude got his belt snugged on. "And even if the Vault is nothing more than a fancied-up ice house, do you imagine a loose bowel like Czensos ought to be the one to crack the seal?"

Sedgwick's expression puckered. "He wouldn't be my first choice."

"That's why I'm going to stop him, but I would beg a favor from you."

Sedgwick withdrew half a pace. "Your need for help doesn't translate into any need on my part to help you."

"No, but I helped you once," Jean-Claude said. "I couldn't save your partner, but I found out what happened to him, and I helped bring down his killer."

Sedgwick's coin stopped dancing. When he answered, his voice was a bit strangled. "Am I supposed to be happy to be reminded?"

"No, but right now Capitaine Isabelle, who is the closest thing I have to a daughter, is in much the same fix as you were in. She doesn't know what happened to me. She probably thinks I'm dead. All I want is for you to let her know I'm alive. Surely that's not too much."

Sedgwick's mouth tightened just enough to let Jean-Claude know he'd found a soft spot.

"What's to stop your Isabelle from coming after me, looking for you?"

"Tell her I've gone hunting the missing trinket," Jean-Claude said. "If Travers wants it, he's going to have to help me find it."

A look of disbelief washed over Sedgwick's face. "You think you're going to use le Comte de Travers? I would almost pay to see that. Almost."

"Please? I can't stand to leave Isabelle wondering if I'm alive or dead."

Sedgwick frowned and rubbed his palms together. At last he said, "Aye. I'll get word to her, not that she's required to believe me, mind."

Jean-Claude handed over his much-battered and abused hat. "Give her this. She'll recognize it."

Sedgwick took the hapless headgear and rolled it over in his hands. "You have my word."

Sixteen

Joubert's Folly was as ugly a hunk of rock as had ever been hung in the sky. The skyland was the shape of a crescent, and wobbled like a vast coin just spinning to a stop. Its two curved arms, tipped with sturdy forts, embraced a sizable harbor.

The base ran out a harbor pilot to bring the *Thunderclap* in. Dockworkers tied it off to a short flexible pier so it could remain steady and level throughout the skyland's precession.

The depot was laid out in a ring around the sky harbor. All the wood-framed buildings had canted walls and, as it turned out, a nearly tubular inner construction to keep them stable on the ever-tilting surface. It was a place where an unlucky pedestrian really might end up walking uphill both ways.

Bitterlich had given his report to Malgiers to read to Impervia and briefed Vrain on what he'd learned from his search of the sloop and interrogation of its crew. Then he oversaw the provisioning of the prisoners. He separated out the native Skaladin from their foreign replacements and held them in separate groups. He let none of them see what had become of their capitaine as he installed her, under guard, in the base's stockade.

He wanted to see Isabelle, who had been taken to the officers' ward, but he also had a duty to train Rebecca to use her sorcery. He led her to the courtyard between the headquarters, the barracks wing, and the warehouses. Someone had gone to the effort to plant a garden, really not much more than a square hedge with a fountain in the center. The fountain itself was a work of greater mechanical ingenuity than artistic merit. The basin was taller than ordinary and filled only half-full to keep the water from sloshing out. The spigot was on a weighted gimbal that kept it pointed vertically. Even so, the brisk cold wind carried most of the spray away.

Bitterlich ascended the sloping flagstones and sat on one of the tilted benches, gesturing Rebecca to sit beside him. It helped avoid the sensation of conflict if two people were facing the same direction, shoulder to shoulder.

Rebecca regarded this move with due skepticism. She was rightly wary of adults trying to take advantage of her. It was a minor miracle that she gave them any slack at all.

At last, she yielded to his superior patience and plopped down beside him, but in an attitude that suggested being spring-loaded.

"I need you to help me figure out the extent of your powers," Bitterlich said.

Rebecca regarded him mulishly, arms crossed. "I don't like changing. It feels strange."

"Strange how?" Bitterlich asked. "Does it hurt or burn or itch?" Those could be signs of something seriously wrong with her sorcery.

"No," Rebecca said. "It's more like being wrapped up in a blanket." She held out her hands. "I don't have arms or hands or legs and I can't talk."

"Ah," Bitterlich said. "That makes sense."

Rebecca scrutinized his expression for any sign that she was being wound up. "It does?"

"Yes. When I turn into a cat"—Bitterlich did so, pulling on Littlepaws's form—"at least I have four limbs, and paws make pretty good hands. I can walk and manipulate things. I can see how it would be disconcerting not to be able to do all those things at once."

"And you can talk," Rebecca said.

"So can you, with practice. With a lot of practice you can probably learn to keep your arms even while in wyrm form. And just think of everything else you'll be able to do. You'll be able to fly and breathe fire." That was, alas, the extent of his knowledge of ghostfire wyrms.

"Fly?" Rebecca said, her eyes growing round.

"You were doing it on the ship when you first transformed. You were just too panicked to remember."

Rebecca considered that for a moment. "And you can teach me to talk."

"Yes, though it will probably take several weeks. The first thing to practice, if you want to be good at it, is switching back and forth between your wyrm form and your erstepelz. Once you can do that as easily as putting on a hat, then we can talk about voice lessons."

Rebecca puffed out her cheeks and stood up. "So all I have to do is pull the thread."

"Before you start," Bitterlich said, holding up a paw, "the thing to practice is making sure you don't tangle your erstepelz as you unravel it. You should be able to loop it like holding a coil of rope. Also, if you do get tangled, which happens to everybody at some point, you'll get stuck halfway between one form and another. It will be the scariest thing that's ever happened to you, but don't panic. You can always tease out the knot and try again."

"Chop my own hands off and be done with it," Rebecca muttered.

"Pull and coil," Bitterlich said. Rebecca seemed less inclined to dispute his instructions when he was a cat rather than an adult, a fact that he tucked away for later.

With the set face and the squinted eyes of theatrical concentration, Rebecca tugged on her soul skin. Her body elongated, becoming snakelike, with rows of spikes down her flanks. There was a moment of fish-flopping panic as her arms and legs blended into her body. Then, between one heartbeat and the next, she'd grown into a huge floating blue-and-green serpent with mother-of-pearl horns and four eyes of aquamarine. She twisted her head this way and that to get a good look at herself and pulled her serpentine body into a gliding helix.

"And there you are," Bitterlich said, letting go his held breath. "Flying." In general only things with wings could fly above the land, but the ghostfire wyrm was a weirdling and played by its own rules.

Bitterlich donned his raven guise, hopped into the air, and squawked, "Follow me!"

Startled, Rebecca twitched through the air. She flew awkwardly at first, but soon took up an undulating rhythm, slithering along the wind. Up over the rooftops of the warehouses and spiraling around the lighthouse they went, up higher than the masts of the ship at anchorage.

Only when they reached the top of the lighthouse and looked down did Rebecca have a hiccup of fear, scrunching up into a ball at the sudden vertiginous sensation of height.

"This way!" Bitterlich cawed. He swooped to the walkway around the lighthouse's main reflector and landed in his erstepelz.

Rebecca followed closely, her long body hugging up against the walkway's inner wall.

"Now come back to yourself," Bitterlich said. "Reel in your erstepelz and coil the wyrm."

With a sound like rope whizzing around a turnbuckle, Rebecca returned to herself, shaking out her hands and wagging her tongue. "Pox and blisters. I was flying!"

"You still are," he said. Even after returning to her erstepelz, she hovered about knee-high above the platform.

Rebecca looked down, gasped, and promptly fell out of the air, landing in a heap on the walkway. "What! How?" She scrambled to her feet.

"You can fly," Bitterlich said, amazed.

"So can you," she said, dusting herself off. Her clothes had come back crooked and disheveled, as if she'd been in a fight with a mad laundress.

"You can fly without transforming. It's incredible. I've certainly never seen anything like it. Every Seelenjäger gets certain gifts from their first soul skin. They're Seelengeschenke—abilities the creature has that you can use without changing shape. Flying is so intrinsic to being a ghostfire wyrm that you kept that gift even in your erstepelz."

Rebecca looked at her feet still firmly stuck to the planks. "Are you sure? The minute I realized I was doing it, it stopped working."

"Because you told it to stop," Bitterlich said. "Now we have to figure out how to tell it to start again. What did it feel like to fly as a wyrm?"

"I dunno," Rebecca said. "I just . . . you know how you can feel which direction is down, which way your weight is pointed. I could just sort of turn it around to point the direction I wanted to go."

"Can you do that now? Don't think about flying, just think about that sensation."

Rebecca closed her eyes. "It's just like falling . . ." Slowly she lifted from the walkway and drifted skyward.

"Perfect," Bitterlich said.

Rebecca opened her eyes and looked around. "Sodding saints!" She wobbled a bit and then caught herself. "We're so high!"

"So?" Bitterlich said, hopping up on the guardrail, balancing despite the persistent breeze. "It doesn't matter how far away the ground is if you can get there at your own speed. Follow me."

Once more he took on wings. "Come on!"

Rebecca followed Bitterlich as he spiraled away from the tower, swooping up and diving, rolling and twisting. Within five minutes they were chasing each other across the docks in a game of aerial tag. Rebecca forgot her worries and cackled gleefully as they shot through a warehouse that was open at both ends, startling the workers. Bewildered, angry shouts followed them around the depot's perimeter.

At last Bitterlich brought her back to the courtyard where they'd started. Both of them were huffing and blowing with exertion, but Rebecca was grinning so hard he feared her face might split.

"Did you see that?" she said. "Whoosh, right through the building! And you can see everything from up there! And everyone looks so small! I can go anywhere!"

"Yes. You did very well." Bitterlich said, basking in her glee. "But you still need to practice changing forms."

"What about breathing fire?" she asked excitedly.

He arched an eyebrow at her. "I thought you didn't want to be a Seelenjäger."

"I want to breathe fire," she said, flicking her fingers out in front of her face.

A bell tolled the quarter hour. Bitterlich turned his attention to the depot. "Time to go."

"But what about—" Rebecca said.

"We'll practice more after the staff meeting, assuming I have time. Right now I need you to go eat, replenish what you used. Then take a nap."

Rebecca rolled her gemlike eyes. "I don't need a nap."

"You will after you eat," he said.

Bitterlich left her at the mess hall and arrived at headquarters with several minutes to spare. He checked his uniform and straightened his cravat.

It would never do to be late or disheveled. The Sanguinaire might not give him any credit for doing things properly, but he'd never hear the end of it if he did things improperly.

The war room was a flattened sphere. The whole floor was a raised platform that rested on a weighted gimbal that kept the surface level as the skyland tilted around it. In the center was the requisite table, round and carved of some heavy wood. To one side stood Capitaine Vrain, looking every bit as wooden as the table, and the base commander, Commandant Turenne, a big beefy Sanguinaire with a wind-burned face, and the sort of aggressive cheerfulness of a man who considered a twenty-kilometer hike before breakfast invigorating and declared ice baths a bracing restorative.

Bitterlich imagined all such men would die alone, their enthusiasm for healthy living proving fatal to everyone around them.

Bitterlich presented his salute, which Vrain returned.

Commandant Turenne looked Bitterlich up and down. "So you're the pelter I've heard so much about. Counteragent and hero of the coup, my brother tells me. Damn strange world we live in, but I suppose it makes sense that the spymistress would employ an actual weasel."

He laughed at his own joke.

Bitterlich did not react to the insult, the implication that his kind made good pelts, nor to the joke, though both made his blood boil.

"I am but a servant of l'Empire," Bitterlich said.

"It's good you're here early, Major," Vrain said. "We have business to discuss. We have received a directive from Madame. In light of Capitaine Isabelle's apparent breakdown, she is to be recalled to Rocher Royale, assuming she regains consciousness."

Bitterlich had known the news was coming, but it still hit him like a blow to the solar plexus. Being recalled was not, in and of itself, a legal penalty, but it was understood by anyone with even the most cursory knowledge of royal politics that someone who was recalled was also expected to resign. That would cut Isabelle's last lifeline to society and make her an outcast in the very kingdom she had saved from war and coup.

Vrain showed no relish as he produced the official summons, and Bitterlich could almost believe he had some sympathy for Isabelle, but it was equally true that he would not let such a paltry emotion stand in the way of his own elevation. Vrain had been lured into this mission on the promise of being made a capitaine when it was done. Isabelle's fall merely accelerated his rise, like dropping ballast.

Bitterlich read the summons, which was as short and to the point as legal phrasing and diplomatic flourishes would allow. It was stamped with the imperial seal.

It was not possible for an actual letter to have been delivered from the capital in the last day or so, but Joubert's Folly kept an imperial transcriptionist on retainer. He or she would be a Sanguinaire with a bloodhollow in the capital who could duplicate an official document and apply a copy of the seal to it.

Bitterlich returned the document. "I see, sir."

Vrain said, "As the new capitaine of the *Thunderclap*, I am detailing you to ensure Capitaine Isabelle reaches Rocher Royale safely."

All the fur on Bitterlich's spine stood up in anger, for this move was as cowardly as it was cynical. Vrain was removing him because he was Isabelle's ally and possibly because he was a Seelenjäger. Yet it was a command well within his authority to give.

"Yes, sir," Bitterlich said. As furious as the dismissal made him, Isabelle was the reason he'd signed up for this adventure. Given the choice, he would have volunteered to stay with her. Yet having it done this way was like being handed a plum after it had been smashed in the dirt.

Turenne said, "There's a regular tender that arrives in a week. I'll have a berth made for you on its return trip."

"Very good, Commandant," Bitterlich said. One of the beauties of military communication was that it could conceal a great deal of outrage under brief formalities.

The other officers began to arrive in pairs and triples. Out of pure counteragent reflex Bitterlich faded into the background, watching and listening even while he fumed.

Vrain said, "One of our allied scouts has spotted Hasdrubal's sloop making speed toward the City of Gears. We've also received word via the Cauldron that the tyrant's own fleet is massing off the Sundered Isles. Intelligence suggests they mean to rendezvous with Hasdrubal. Our best chance of recovering Windcaller Dok, the relic, and the *Conquest* shard is to catch Hasdrubal before the Skaladin can join forces. The Hoary Fleet has already sailed into the outer vortex to try and cut off Hasdrubal's escape route. As soon as we are resupplied, the *Thunderclap* will give chase and put the pressure of the hound on him."

Several of the other officers asked questions generally pertaining to the execution of the mission, but one element seemed to be missing from the discussion as a whole. While just now he wanted to invite Vrain to stick his head up a cow's bung, this was still a Célestial mission. Pardons and forgiveness would be easier to obtain for those he cared about if Dok and the shard were recovered and the Craton Auroborea reached than if they lost both to the Skaladin. Isabelle needed Vrain to succeed.

Bitterlich left as soon as the meeting broke up and flew to the *Thunderclap*. If he was to be dispatched, he would do so on his own terms as much as possible, which meant taking with him Malgiers, a squad of marines, and Rebecca.

⟶

Isabelle glided into the gyre of the everdream. Ghost shards whirled by on an intangible wind, each illuminating only itself. Even here, her fever burned, and she felt like nothing more than a sack of skin filled with stinging nettles.

Isabelle wafted alongside her past lives. From each jagged pane came a different voice, the various members of her ancestral chorus. Her confusion and fear drew them like moths to a flame, and they had answered her mood if not her questions. Long had she resisted facing them, integrating them, but now she had no choice.

Any full-blooded Fenice would have dived into her everdream as a first reflex, to interrogate her past lives, embracing them as chapters of her own life.

Has this ever happened to me before?

The ghost shards flocked toward her question. The smaller, lighter ones came first and fastest, twisting and tumbling until they joined her in her orbit far from the center of the gyre. Like so many excited dogs they danced about her, each yammering their own fragmented answer, bewildering taken together.

A great need emanated from them, a hunger to partake in the "I" of identity, to perceive the world through her, to sense themselves and one another as part of a whole.

I am whole! Isabelle insisted, and the eager pack scattered, still orbiting but at a safe distance. *I am complete.* Adding more minds to the mix could not make her any more herself than adding more water to an overflowing cup could make it more full.

Yet her head pounded as if a pack of amateur stonemasons were using it for practice. Her teeth were hot coals sunk in their sockets. Was it better to die whole and herself, or to be possessed by the ghosts of murderers, thieves, traitors to kings and causes long extinct? If she took this path, she lost Isabelle.

If she died, she lost everything.

"Having a place in the world isn't about what you get, it's about what you serve." Jean-Claude had said that to her once, words that had lain cold and forgotten until fear and need stirred them up. The world had stripped her down to the nub. The powers that be feared her, not for anything she had done, or even for her strange forgotten sorcery. They feared her because they looked at her and saw instead what they would do in her place, how they would reach for power and seek revenge.

Yet power and vengeance were not the principles Isabelle served. She followed her curiosity wherever it led. She served peace. She practiced mercy. She could not be empty while she still had strength to give.

If she let her ancestors in, she might lose her singularity, but as long as she stood by her purpose, she might at least salvage a functional human being from the wreckage. It would be a sin not to try, not while she possessed the strength to act.

But deciding to act was not the same as knowing how. When before she had chanced to touch the ghost shards, they latched onto her like ticks and tried to empty her to fill themselves. Always she tore them off before they could drain her. Always they carried bits of her away, leaving holes in her thoughts, like words she ought to know but could only almost remember.

If she could not remain separate from her past lives, her only option was to draw them in. Bitterlich said absorbing new soul skins was like taming the beasts and giving them a new home. Rebecca had described in detail what it felt like to absorb the ghostfire wyrm, how she drew it into a thread and wove it onto a loom, a structure that she had discovered and developed deep in her own mind.

Fenice sorcery was not the same as Seelenjäger sorcery, but both were gifts of the Builder. They were deliberate constructs of divine power, just like the great ruins of the Primus Mundi or any of the quondam artifacts that survived the Breaking of the World. Designed and bestowed by the same hand, might these sorceries work the same way?

Isabelle gathered herself for a great leap. Her body's fever burned hotter with every second. There would never be a better moment than now.

Come, Isabelle commanded the circling fragments.

Like a cloud of many-colored insects they swarmed toward her. She reached for the smallest one. Her fingers brushed its edge.

It melted and flowed into her fingers and up into her awareness. She found herself male, and young, kneeling on a high plateau overlooking a burning city. In this life, his name was Galleni Sigsimondo. He cradled his dead son in his arms, and howled in anguish. "Mateo!"

He wept and moaned, stroking Mateo's downy head. Grief like molten iron coursed through his veins.

Isabelle recoiled from this sudden agony. She jerked away from Sigsimondo. Her spirit self, half merged with his, rent and tore, like peeling off tar that had burned onto her skin.

No. She must not panic. Grief must not be shunned. It must be answered with compassion.

She reclaimed her grieving ancestor before his ghost shard slipped away. He needed what she had always claimed to give.

Mercy, she said and reached out again. *You pain is my pain. Tell me of your son.*

"My boy," he wailed. "My beautiful son. He was quick and wise, a butterfly child. If only his feathers had come in. Damn those who did this to him."

Isabelle took in his grief and his rage. It hurt like burning a hole through her heart. Yet as his pain resolved she found she could grip the memory's substance, shape and pull and untangle it. She drew the ghost out, not as a wire, but as a many-colored pigment.

The joy of discovery kindled in Isabelle's heart. Too long had it been since she had felt that particular elation, but pigment she knew what to do with. She drew it inward like inviting a guest into her home, into the center of her being. Behind the façade of the outward-looking present, above the neat but crowded workshop of logic and reason lay the studio of her memory, a canvas with no edges and immense depth. Like a great slow river the hues and shadows of her life flowed and mixed, the paint never quite drying, the past never quite settled.

Into this living stream she guided her grieving ancestor, blending him into the edges of her life. It was like sculpting with color, emotion, and belief. Bitterlich had admonished Rebecca to take her time drawing in the ghostfire wyrm lest she be saddled with some aberration of her powers, and Isabelle took that advice to heart.

As she developed her study, she was Sigsimondo, administrator of the Leccisi District, and father of Mateo, his poor lost child. It took some time to figure out how to work Sigsimondo's grief into Isabelle's life, but it turned out that it belonged with her own memory of the moment her father had turned Marie into a bloodhollow. Sigsimondo's love of his child was reflected in Jean-Claude's love of Isabelle. Such pride. Such joy. Such terror. She knew Jean-Claude cared for her, but she had never been able to imagine precisely how that felt until now.

She brushed in Sigsimondo's knowledge of administration, some techniques that would help her friend Valérie's business, and his language . . . she realized she was thinking in the Vecci tongue.

A thrill of anticipation rippled through her. What other languages might she gain access to? If some of her incarnations were very old they might remember the Saintstongue as it used to be. They might even know scraps of the Builder's tongue that had been lost with the Annihilation of Rüul.

She could not tell where Isabelle ended and Sigsimondo began. She had been a father. She had lost a son. Yet Sigsimondo remained in the past, like the child she had once been. She owned his pain and his anger and his mistakes, his bloody-handed revenge. Yet that rage was like the stink of ash after a fire, bitter and cold.

We are Isabelle. She trembled with exhaustion, but Sigsimondo could not tell her about her fever or her hallucinations; not much of him had remained. She had a horrible feeling she was going to be stuck not with the memories her ancestors chose to keep, but all of the anger and trauma they could not forget.

While she had worked, the ache in Isabelle's head intensified, as if someone were squeezing her skull in a vise. Her fever was hot enough to raise blisters. Breathing hurt.

She turned her weary attention to the rest of the circling ancestors. There must be a hundred at least, not that many generations, but aunts and uncles and siblings, all of whom had traded vitera and shared memories. There was no way she could absorb them all, not in her current state. She had to find one who might rescue her from fever and hallucination.

She posed the question to Sigsimondo. He might not know anything himself, but he had shared a mind with all her other selves and might point someone out to her.

With a nudge on the edge of her attention, Sigsimondo shifted her gaze to a black fragment that was only visible by a bruised, throbbing light that clung to its edges. Unlike all the others it made no response to her call, but tumbled in its orbit as lifeless as a moon.

Isabelle's stomach tightened with dread, for she knew who that must be. *Brunela* was Isabelle's half sister. She had been a doctor. She had also been tortured so severely that her mind had withdrawn and shut down, seeking oblivion as the only refuge from pain. Worse, Isabelle knew how she had been tortured, a ritual so hideous that the mere thought of it made her want to vomit. She'd been eaten alive by flensing worms. Her Fenice sorcery had saved her, but at the cost of turning her into a bone queen, a husk as dry as the parchwinds and barren as the Ashlands.

Sigsimondo's natural grief had nearly whelmed Isabelle's mind, but now she must pry poor Brunela from her crypt, endure her pain, and make it part of her.

She drifted over to the sullen shard, an unmarked gravestone. It was not a color, not even black, but more like a hole in the everdream, an exit into nothing.

In the oldest tales, the ones etched into the bones of every story that followed them, there came a moment when the hero stood before the Ravenous Gate and heard the screams of those condemned to Torment. Isabelle had seen many depictions of the portal to the Breaker's Torment. All fell short of this awful absence. The repulsive menace of its obliterating silence shriveled her spirit. Every instinct urged her to flee.

In all the old tales, the hero stepped through the gate.

But I am not a hero. Heroes didn't feel like wetting themselves. Besides, most of those heroes never came back out.

Yet beyond this hole into agony was a soul, a human being who needed her help.

Isabelle swallowed her lurching heart, and reached for Brunela. Cold rushed through her as she made contact, the chill of a thousand winters numbing her mind. Far from trying to absorb her like the other fragments, it solidified against her and pushed her away. She took hold of its substance and pulled. It was like trying to shape frozen clay, stiff and unyielding.

Isabelle's fever flared and she faltered. She could not win by pitting her will against Brunela's anguish.

But then the point was not to win. She did not want to conquer her sister, beat her, or break her. She wanted to help and be helped.

Brunela, she said. *My name is Isabelle. I am your sister. I could not save you from our father, but I can help you now. I can give you a place to be. A place where no one can hurt you.*

The void remained thick and cold. Isabelle wrapped herself around it, like hugging a glacier whose cold sucked the life from her soul instead of her limbs. She let go her heat, let it flow into the tombstone and through the gate. Please let Brunela feel the warmth of her comfort.

I need you, she said. *I know it hurts. I know it's hard to look up from the misery, but you still have much to give, and many who will be thankful for it. Please, sister. If you ever begged as I do, I need your help.*

The chill quivered and a needle of pain stabbed Isabelle through the center of her being.

She screamed. Many times had she been shadowburned, she'd been shocked with galvanic fluid, had her arm amputated, and been set on fire. This was worse than all of those at once. Nothing human could have withstood it. Isabelle's heart and breath both stuttered and nearly stopped.

She couldn't absorb this. There was no way. She tried to clutch the pain, to direct it, but nothing responded to her will.

Help!

Sigsimondo reached into the fountain of pain and diverted some of the agony into himself.

It was not much, but it was enough.

Isabelle grasped the flow, teased it into the studio, and began to work it into her identity, but where to put it?

She immersed herself in the stream to find its source and nature. It felt as if every inch of skin had been flayed from her body, her muscles and innards scraped from her bones. She was pinned to a table with a steel spike, like an insect in a specimen box, while the flensing worms consumed her flesh.

228 — CURTIS CRADDOCK

But the worst of the pain was not physical. Standing in the gallery, their faces shadowed by harsh alchemical lights on the domed ceiling above, were her mother and father, her brother and her grandfather, the patriarch of the clan. Each had their *piume* on full display, their crest feathers flared out in great fans around their heads.

"Why?" Brunela sobbed, her voice a husk from shrieking. "Why are you doing this to me?" What had she done wrong? What had she done? She'd always been a good daughter. She loved them. Why?

Abandonment, loneliness, betrayal: Isabelle's soul swelled to take them in, for these were emotions she knew well. She painted them into the history of her own father, le Comte des Zephyrs, who had always despised her. It might not be possible to explain anything to the dead, but Isabelle painted Brunela into her understanding of her family's treachery. Her family had been trying to avoid being targeted in a four-hundred-year-old vendetta, and sacrificing Brunela had been the only way. Not that it excused their cowardice.

Brunela's soul stuff burned like acid, but stroke by sizzling stroke, Isabelle smoothed Brunela into her memory until the frontiers between them disappeared. The physical pain lessened to an ache like the last days of a bad flu. The pain of betrayal burned on like a coal fire in a collapsed mine.

Isabelle's own fever made it hard to concentrate, which slowed her laborious progress even further. She had no idea how much time had passed in the outside world, or if any had passed at all.

At last she looked up and found her task complete. She had no more ghost pigment left, and the Ravenous Gate had disappeared. Sigsimondo was there with her, and another silent presence: Brunela, a ghost bled down to a wisp, without color but not without form.

Isabelle was almost too exhausted to ask the question, but she sorted herself out and reached out to the misty memory. *Have you seen a fever such as this before?*

The apparition that was Brunela took Isabelle's hand. Between one heartbeat and the next she found herself in a low room with stone walls. Thick arches held up a barrel-vaulted ceiling. Round windows high up let in streams of warm golden light that strained against the subterranean chill. A young man lay on a small bed between two of the pillars. His arms and legs were tied to the bedposts with silken cords. His glassy eyes rolled in their sockets, and he raved, alternately sobbing and shouting gibberish.

Brunela's voice was a heavy whisper suffused with pain: "He was a late bloomer, like you. He had been gifted with the vitera of his grandfather, the patriarch of the clan. His elder cousin, enraged at having been passed over for this honor, broke into his room at night and tore the symbiote from his head, perhaps thinking to take it for himself."

"But it doesn't work that way," Isabelle surmised.

"The symbiote had already bonded with this boy, and the Fenice trans-formation, once begun, cannot stop until it is finished. Without the vitera, there was not enough of the vital reagent to complete the process. It's like burning charcoal in a closed bottle; the reaction continues until it runs out of lumin vapor and then stops."

Isabelle's chest felt hollow. She'd ripped Immacolata's vitera out of her own head rather than be possessed by her.

"What happened to him?" Isabelle whispered.

Brunela said, "At first he heard the voices of his ancestors gibbering at him, and then he began to see things. Within a few weeks he began to break with reality. He could no longer understand speech or recognize the people around him. He took a fever from no apparent source. His skin turned to gooseflesh and blistered in every follicle where a feather might have come in. For the last week he lay raving, covered in suppurating sores, restrained to his cot so that he would not claw at his crumbling skin."

The scene shifted slightly, the beams of light on the wall coming in at a different angle. Other ghosts occupied the room now: the boy's family. Brunela had paid them no heed and remembered them only as solid shad-ows.

The boy had changed too. Through the lens of Brunela's memory, Isa-belle witnessed the young man's final hours. His skin sloughed off and what lay underneath resembled little more than a chick that had failed to hatch from its egg: downy feathers, stringy flesh, serum, and blood.

Isabelle's spirit sank as if into an icy marsh. "Is there nothing that can be done?" Or was she condemned to the same horrific fate?

Brunela's hesitation spoke volumes. At last she said, "It is such a rare occurrence. The metamorphosis needs the right kind of fuel."

"And air to breathe," Isabelle said, a glimmer of hope lighting in her breast. A fool's hope, to be sure—fire in a bottle was only a metaphor—but desperate hope was better than none.

"Thank you," she said. "I'm still not sure how all this works"—she gestured to the everdream—"but if I am to see you in the next life, I look forward to getting to know you."

"If there is time," Brunela said sadly.

Isabelle turned her attentions away from the everdream. Leaving that Builder-blessed space was like stepping into a furnace. Her bones felt like sap-filled twigs in a bonfire ready to crack and split. Opening her eyes felt like peeling off scabs.

Her vision was fuzzy, but there could be no doubt that the pale figure asleep in the chair beside Isabelle's cot was Marie.

"Marie," Isabelle said, and her voice sounded like someone crushing dried leaves. She reached toward her friend and found her hand bound up in a soft mitten. Had she been scratching herself? Was she too far gone?

She bumped Marie's arm.

Marie jerked awake and spun. "Isabelle? Are you there?"

"For now," Isabelle whispered. "How long was I gone?"

"Two days. I feared . . ." She paused, gathering her wits. "The main points are: We're on Joubert's Folly, the *Thunderclap* is resupplying, and you've been relieved of command."

This stabbed Isabelle's heart, for it was another place she did not fit in the world, but truly it was far down her list of concerns just now.

"Where's Jean-Claude?" she asked. Had he been found? Surely he would be here.

"He hasn't come back," Marie said. "Once Vrain took command, he cut all your guests out of military communications."

Isabelle's soul keened for Jean-Claude, yet she had no time to worry or mourn. And if he was not here, she still needed his cunning and his way of thinking. She took in the room, a stone quadrangle barely bigger than the bed. On a small table stood bottles of medicine and an alchemical lantern. At the far end of the room was a heavy door.

"Where are we exactly?" Isabelle asked.

"Officers' infirmary," Marie said. "There's a guard outside, but he's bored stupid."

"Guard?"

"You're not exactly under arrest, but you're not exactly not under arrest either."

"Can you come and go?" Isabelle asked.

"Yes," Marie said. "As far as anyone is concerned, I'm just your nurse."

Isabelle cracked a painful smile. "You're much more than that. I need you to fetch a few things from my trunk."

"It's under the cot," Marie said.

"Good," Isabelle said. "I also need you to fetch Quill for me."

"Have I started hearing things, or are you babbling again? Did Isabelle the unsanctified actually ask me to descend on her with clergy in tow?"

"Yes," Isabelle said. "But keep it quiet. If anyone asks, tell them you think I need last rites. For now, everyone is to think I'm still unconscious."

"Of course, but what are you up to?"

"Human sacrifice," Isabelle said, and sank down into her pillow.

"You're even less funny when you're sick," Marie said, but she lifted a cup of water to Isabelle's lips. She was so parched it seemed to seep right into her flesh without ever making it down her throat. She followed water with a full bowl of hot broth. Then she smoothed away the matted hair from Isabelle's forehead and stroked her cheek with her thumb before turning away.

Marie knocked on the door and the guard opened it a crack.

"I heard voices," the guard said.

"She's been raving for two days," Marie said, her tone flat enough to slide under the door. "Do you want to come in and listen for a while?"

The guard grumbled and then let her out, shutting the door and leaving Isabelle alone with her aches and her fevers, and the memories of other lives leaking once more into her perceptions. She was tempted to slip back into the everdream—the constructed space must exist at least partially outside her own flesh, for it didn't hurt so bad—but there was no guarantee Marie would be able to pull her back out.

Instead she lay and worried about Jean-Claude. If something had happened to him . . . if the worst had happened, the deep sky would yield no clues.

The gravebound betray, said her chorus. *Only family matters.* She could almost pick out the individual voices. None of them sounded like Sigsimondo or Brunela. Ghost stains spread across her senses. The bare stone walls of the infirmary wavered in her vision and she found herself in a dark tunnel. The mine had collapsed and the dust smeared the light of her lantern into an impenetrable haze. She closed her eyes against the hallucination but could not convince her mind's eye that it wasn't real. Would these visions go away once she assimilated her memorial menagerie? She could not endure this forever.

It seemed like hours before voices filtered in from the hall. Isabelle lay as still as death when the door opened.

"If she's dying, Commandant Turenne will want to know," said the guard.

"Does he want to watch?" Marie asked. "I didn't think he had a taste for the macabre."

Quill's shaky voice said, "You may tell the commandant that I am ministering to a sick woman, if you wish."

Isabelle took note how Quill evoked an air of authority he did not possess to give the guard permission not to do his duty.

The door shut, and Quill said to Marie, "I am surprised you requested these rites of me."

"She didn't." Isabelle croaked. "I wanted a private and very quiet word."

She opened her eyes. The collapsed mine was gone, fortunately. Quill hovered above her, shock rippling across his face. He wore his full ceremonial regalia, a mustard chasuble and a russet stole.

"And have you chosen to repent your sins at last and accept the Builder's direction?" Quill asked in a whisper, curiosity rather than condemnation in his voice.

"If I were to give up all the Temple deems sinful, there would not be enough of me left for the Builder to direct," Isabelle said.

"Then what do you want?" Quill said, leaning on his staff.

"Your help. I need you to humor me, so to speak."

Quill looked to Marie. "Is she babbling again?"

"No, she just thinks she's being clever, but her brain's too fried to know she's missed the mark." Marie turned to Isabelle. "Get to the point."

Isabelle said, "I need a transfusion. As much blood as Quill can safely spare."

Quill looked taken aback. "Why?"

"Because you are a full-blooded Fenice."

Quill's expression puckered as sour as vinegar. "A failed Fenice, unhallowed."

"The question is why your sorcery refused to manifest," Isabelle said. "We have long known each sorcery is born in a different organ of the body: the eyes of a Glasswalker, the skin of a Sanguinaire, and so on, but it was lately discovered that there is a second necessary component, a sub-organ in the brain we call the Builder's node that controls the sorcery."

Quill leaned forward attentively, though his head still twitched as if it couldn't quite decide where it attached to his neck. "I heard rumors that unhallowed sorcerers had been vivisected."

"The one who did it is dead," Isabelle said, still speaking low. "But facts are facts no matter how they are obtained. To the point: you and I were each given a vitera, and we both had them removed, but with vastly different results. I began to transform into a Fenice. You did not."

Quill withdrew from this simple statement as if from a bad smell.

Isabelle moved on quickly. "I am reliably informed that once a transformation begins, it cannot be stopped short of completion or death, and here I am. My body lacks the reagent it needs to complete the transformation. Conversely your vitera was removed but your transformation never started. Most likely your Builder's node is stillborn. It is possible that between us we have enough pieces to complete a single transformation. My brain, your blood."

"This is speculation, the worst sort of wishful thinking," Quill said, clutching one quivering hand to his chest.

"Some of it I can test," Isabelle said. "Marie. The blood ciphers."

Marie dragged Isabelle's trunk from under the bed and from its depths extracted a quondam metal cylinder about the size of a man's thumb. Bronze in color with a purple patina, it bulged around its waist, with a spherical head at one end and a semicircular stirrup at the other.

She presented it to Quill, whose eyes went round at the sight of it.

"Where did you get this?" he asked.

"I took it from the corpse of the first man who tried to kill me," Isabelle said.

"Just press the round end against your skin," Marie said. "Be careful. It stings."

Quill examined the cipher closely and carefully, an antiquarian in sudden possession of the rarest of finds: a working quondam artifact perhaps touched by the Builder's own hands. Quite reverently he pushed it into the pad of his finger. It snapped, the needle stabbed and drew blood. He winced and sucked his finger, handing the cipher to Isabelle.

Isabelle's muscles ached, but she twisted the head to activate the cipher's analytical function and the word "Fenice" appeared in raised letters along the barrel above a series of strange glyphs Isabelle had yet to interpret. Isabelle twiddled the now-evident dials on the barrel and entered Quill's name above his sorcery. It never ceased to amaze her how the cipher could be seamless one minute then display grooves that ran latitudinally around the barrel in its diagnostic configuration, then sprout longitudinal legs when activated as part of its swarm. Yet it never seemed to be of more than one piece.

"According to this, your body at least is Fenice," Isabelle said.

Quill sagged as if shedding a heavy weight he hadn't known he'd been carrying. He looked down at his hands as if imagining them sheathed in feathers and equipped with talons. He turned his gaze to her, his expression clouded with loss and resentment. "First you steal from me the key to the Vault of Ages and manage to lose it, and now you want me to give you the power that should have been mine. Is there anything I possess you do not covet?"

Isabelle grimaced. "I understand what it is like to have something taken from you. I have lost my arm, my title, my rank, and my name. All were taken from me against my will, and some by those whom I had helped lift into power. The betrayal hurts worst of all. I will not hold it against you if you deny my request, but I will tell you this. No matter how much I have lost, I have never once felt bad about helping another person, even those who might not deserve it."

Quill looked away. His mouth flattened into a line and he quivered as if he wanted to unleash a tirade.

Instead he asked, "What happens if the transfusion doesn't work?"

"Then I'm dead anyway." Isabelle's tone was lighter than her heart. "But at least you will have tried, and for that I will thank you."

Quill stared at the door for a minute, his gaze far away. His hands clenched and unclenched in a way that was not strictly spasmodic.

"I will help," Quill said at last. "Shall I fetch the doctor?"

"I'd rather do this as discreetly as possible," Isabelle said. Her letter of recall would not be delivered as long as Vrain believed her mentally incapacitated. "I have my own rig."

Marie dove into Isabelle's trunk again and surfaced with a case containing tubes, needles, bottles, and a pump.

Quill gave Isabelle a wary look. "Do you do transfusions often?"

"This will be my first," Isabelle said. "I salvaged this gear from the man who rescued Marie from being a bloodhollow. I had hoped to analyze the residue left behind in the equipment to figure out how he'd done it. Unfortunately, there was not enough of his serum left for me to puzzle it out."

"And asking him was out of the question?"

"He was dead by then, and his records did not describe the process."

Marie set up the rig and, after some inexpert prodding, managed to get a needle in Quill's arm. She worked the pump until a drip of red appeared at the opposite needle, which she then inserted in Isabelle's vein.

Isabelle did not know what to expect, and was therefore not surprised to feel nothing at all except the pain of the needle wound.

"How much do you need?" Quill asked.

"I have no idea," Isabelle said. Her ghost stains bloomed again. She knew Marie was working the pump, but her mind insisted on identifying her as the nurse she'd met outside the walls at the Siege of Grimhold three centuries ago.

Marie said, "A third of a liter is safe to give."

"That much?" Quill asked. To Isabelle's confused perception, he had become the quivering prophet from the divine well below Gnossos, one of the supposed locations of the Ravenous Gate.

"I'm seeing things again," Isabelle said. It was hard to hold on to what she knew to be true in the face of contrary experience. The real world slipped through her grasp. "I must retreat."

"Go," Marie said.

Isabelle turned from the light and dove once more into the everdream to put as many of her ancestors in order as she could. She prayed completing the transformation would silence them for good, or at least teach them to tug her sleeve before whispering in her ear.

If she survived.

If.

CHAPTER

Seventeen

A commotion from the main deck caught Jean-Claude's attention and compelled him to his feet. Had the *Dame Formue* caught up with Travers? He lurched to the front of his enclosure, which was as far as he'd been permitted to go, and indeed, the pirate on guard growled quite menacingly at him.

The Solar had risen, though its winter light was thin and the shadows deep and disturbing to Jean-Claude's wounded eye. Over the pirate's shoulder and through the open door, he caught the moment of transformation as a winging gull erupted into Hasdrubal's goat-man shape.

Ivar and Czensos met him, and began a discussion Jean-Claude could not hear. That wouldn't do.

He cupped his hands around his mouth and shouted, "Ahoy Hasdrubal, you great goat-humping bastard. You missed me!" There was naturally a danger in getting his attention, but he'd learn little watching from afar. Besides, Czensos had plans for him that precluded him being prematurely killed.

Hasdrubal's ear twitched around and his gaze fell on Jean-Claude. He let off talking to Ivar and stalked toward Jean-Claude, brushing Czensos aside. As he drew near, Jean-Claude was happy to note a long patch of burned skin along his neck; the phlogiston wax had given him a wound he could not easily shift away.

"Heretic," Hasdrubal brayed, his horizontal pupils narrowed to slits. His right hand blurred and grew talons the size of poniards. "Consider yourself blessed beyond measure that you will be slain by the hand of Hasdrubal himself. I will feed your soul to the Breaker so that she may carry it with her into oblivion when I cast her out of Creation."

Czensos hooked his arm with his wicked staff, the quondam prosthesis holding back sorcerous strength. "Hasdrubal, stop, we need him alive. Travers will extract the location of the bonekeel shard from him."

Hasdrubal withdrew his hand but did not put his talons away. "The shard is redundant so long as we have the Windcaller."

Ivar said, "Aye, but Travers doesn't know that, and giving him Jean-Claude to play with will make him think he has more leverage than he does."

"We have the key," Czensos said, removing the ring from his finger and presenting it to Hasdrubal.

Hasdrubal growled but subsided, returning his hand to its normal blunt-fingered shape before accepting the ring.

Jean-Claude said, "You really think you're going to fulfill the Prophecy?"

Hasdrubal peered at Jean-Claude through the loop of the ring. "The Prophecy is the Breaker's greatest lie. I was raised and trained to believe the Savior will come and finish the task the saints began. He will restore the Primus Mundi, but only once we have prepared the way. My belief in the Prophecy was absolute, but so was that of every other fanatic. Thus every sect and cult seeks to impose their will upon the world, believing that only their truth can save it. Yet with every passing decade, the number of sects grows. The number of heresies multiplies with each new schism, perfection recedes into confusion, and the soul of the world rots. With so many truths to choose from it becomes clear that all roads are false, and the quest itself a delusion. Mortals do not die into Torment, we are born into it, and it is time to bring our suffering to an end."

Hasdrubal's cold determination put a chill in Jean-Claude's bones.

Ivar's time shadows skirled about like leaves on an invisible wind. What he saw in those might-be moments Jean-Claude could not guess, but to Hasdrubal he said, "You have what you came for."

Czensos herded Hasdrubal out the door, the two of them speaking in low tones.

Jean-Claude said to Ivar, "Are you sure this is what you have signed up for? Madmen and the end of the world?"

Ivar rubbed under his eye patch. "Most likely they'll turn on each other before they even get where they think they're going, and by then they'll have showed me where the *Conquest* lies. Leaves the way clear, and the wonderful thing about gold is that it doesn't go mad."

⸺

"Watch this!" Rebecca cried as she leapt into the air, did a backflip, and snapped into her wyrm form like the crack of a whip.

Bitterlich was tempted to make a comment about famous last words, but Rebecca was clearly beside herself with glee, a welcome reprieve from the general gloom of the last few days, and it warmed his heart that he was the one she'd come running to with her very important yet secret discovery.

She'd brought him out past the edges of the current depot to the remains of a previous settlement, evidence that it had taken the navy several tries to figure out how to build on an ever-tilting surface.

She circled around a section of an old stone fence that had mostly fallen over or been robbed away. She gave a preparatory wriggle, curled into an *s* shape, and spat. A lance of flame shot from her mouth. Blue white at the center, fading to pale green at the edges, it lit up the lowering sky. The strange flames crackled in the air, and galvanic tingles stood all of Bitterlich's fur on end. The fire splashed on the surface of the stone, which caught fire and glowed from within like aquamarine charcoal. After a moment or two, the flame erupted from the far side of the wall. The fire guttered and died, but it had left the stone translucent.

Rebecca did a loop in the air almost tight enough to bite her own tail, and dove through the ghostly stone in a long liquid swoop, transforming back into her erstepelz on the far side. "Ghostfire!" She stuck her arm through the phantasmal stone.

"That's . . . astounding," Bitterlich said. He held his hand near the soft spot but the stone was not hot. "How did you figure that out?"

"I asked her." She pointed to her chest. "Or more like I listened to her. She dreamed about hunting, and it was like was swimming through stone, and she'd find a crackback hiding in a stoneberg and then smack!" She brought her hands together like jaws snapping.

"Well done," Bitterlich said. "Our soul companions have a lot to teach us. A note of caution, though. Your wyrm may have urges—"

"Thrasher," Rebecca said. "That's her name."

"Right," Bitterlich said, and why not. Littlepaws had a name, after all. "As I was saying, Thrasher may have urges, but she doesn't get to be in control, not even a little."

"Why?"

"Because while Thrasher will happily take control, she may not happily give it back. The longer you have her, the tamer she will become, until you hardly have to think about it. Until then it's a bad idea to sleep or especially to eat in your animal form. Thrasher must be trained to understand that it is through your mouth that hunger is satisfied and your sleep through which weariness is dispelled."

"So what happens if she gets loose?"

"You could end up a prisoner in her mind, without any say in your own life."

Rebecca's face scrunched. "You mean I could end up like the capitaine."

"Something like that," Bitterlich said, pleased at her understanding but stung by the thought of Isabelle.

"She said she was going to die," Rebecca said.

"She might," Bitterlich said. Marie said she'd woken up briefly, but that was a full day ago. She was still there inside her head, still fighting. She'd gathered the resources she needed and marched into the everdream, to grapple with her Torments. Bitterlich wished he could join her in battle and fight by her side.

"Then what?" Rebecca asked. "I mean, the ship left without us." They had stood on the lighthouse and watched the *Thunderclap* sail into the distance, taking with it what little hope remained for the expedition. What had started with such promise had ended not with success or even failure, but with the disintegration of purpose.

What if Isabelle lived? What if she died? The options in either event were distressingly similar.

He said, "We carry on. A ship will be along in a few days to take us back to Rocher Royale. I will take you on as my apprentice; teach you how to be a Seelenjäger, unless you want to find a different teacher." He didn't have much to offer her except training. Other Seelenjägers with better connections could offer her contacts and court positions, things she would need to thrive.

"No," Rebecca said. "I'm happy with you."

"You say that now," he said. "But we have a lot of work to do."

"More powers?" Rebecca asked, lifting off the ground to sit cross-legged in the air.

"After you practice reading and math."

Rebecca rolled her eyes so hard she flipped upside down. "Unngh!"

"There's a time and a place for everything," Bitterlich said. "The time for setting rocks on fire is after reading lessons."

They settled in his office in the barracks, it being one of the few rooms in the place with a gimbaled floor. Rebecca brought in her sky bag and rooted through it. Tossing books up on the table. From the look of it, Isabelle, in her enthusiasm for reading, had gone quite overboard in supplying printed material for her cabin girl. Alas that all of it seemed to be histories and philosophical treatises . . . probably because that was what Isabelle actually had on hand.

Bitterlich flipped open a book full of closely printed text about the historical context of a rebellion in the St. Germain Province two hundred years ago. Another book opened to a description of the various minutiae of distilling naval-grade lift-volume aether from crushed aethercoral.

He cocked an eyebrow at Rebecca. "Did the capitaine actually have you read this stuff?"

Rebecca leaned her elbows on the table, contemplating the books with the same level of enthusiasm as she might look at piles of rotten meat. "Bits of it. She tried to find stuff that wasn't too hard. That's why there's so much of it."

"Well, that won't do," Bitterlich said. He leaned out the door and shouted, "Malgiers!"

The lieutenant appeared with all due alacrity. "Yes, sir."

"I have a new mission for you, one that requires your particular skills. It will also require the utmost in delicacy and dedication. There is no one else I can entrust with this task. Do you understand?"

Malgiers looked both flattered and terrified. "Yes, sir."

"Good. Then fetch your books of poetry, song, and fantastical tales. You're going to help me teach Rebecca to read."

"Sir?" Malgiers went from frightened to perplexed without passing through any intervening steps.

"Poetry," Bitterlich repeated. "Songs. Tall tales. Things that a new reader might actually be interested in. Education is important. An enthusiasm for learning is even more important."

"Yes, sir." Malgiers disappeared to collect his books. Much of the poetry would be too advanced for Rebecca, but the songs and the stories might at least hold her attention.

Bitterlich returned to the table and gestured to the tomes thereon. "You can put those away."

Malgiers returned bearing a pair of books and looking very pleased with himself. "This is a book of stories I've had so long I just about wore it out. Before we left Rocher Royale I found this other collection with most of the same stories in it. We'll be able to read side by side." He sat down next to Rebecca and opened the book. "When I was young, my governess used to read to me, so that's where we'll start . . ."

Bitterlich observed the process for a few minutes. Fortunately, it didn't take long for Rebecca to get drawn into a story about a rampaging giant and a forest witch.

If only Bitterlich could be so easily distracted.

CHAPTER
Eighteen

Le Comte de Travers's ship *Potencia* was a galleon of the previous generation, bigger and bulkier than the *Thunderclap,* but less imposing than a ship of the line. Its sides were painted with a mural in the style of a liturgical procession: Saint Guyot le Sanguinaire, from whom the sorcery took its name, led an unbroken line of Sanguinaire saints from the Vault of Ages. The line of descendants, each in a different period costume, filed down through the eras of the broken world. They marched through the Bleak-times, through the saintly city of Rüul and its destruction, through the age of conquest, the time of reckoning, and the era of discovery toward the figure of the Savior, portrayed as the scarlet silhouette of a man surrounded by a nimbus of white light and emblazoned with a golden omnioculus. Subtle it was not.

Jean-Claude sat shackled aboard a launch from the *Dame Formue.* Ivar stood in the gunwale, guiding the craft through the ethereal eddies alongside the larger vessel. The launch was captured by the *Potencia*'s boom, gently reeled in, and moored to her side. Several aeronauts hoisted Jean-Claude aboard and frog-marched him to the great cabin. Every chain-clanking step reminded Jean-Claude of his wounds and the rough stitches holding them together.

With Hasdrubal flown off with the ring, this was not the ship Jean-Claude wanted to be on. Yet the goat-faced bastard had to rendezvous with Travers eventually if le comte was supposed to get him through the Bittergale.

He kept his gaze on the move, trying to track everyone out of his one good eye. His vision had improved such that his left eye could tell blurs apart, but faces still looked like mud. He supposed he should count himself lucky Hasdrubal's swipe hadn't taken his head off.

An aeronaut in Travers's brown-and-black livery opened a cabin door. Ivar stepped through, and Jean-Claude was compelled to follow.

Le Comte de Travers stood poised, an ivory-tipped cane in each spidery hand, in the center of the wide cabin. He was tall and skinny, as if a scrawny youth had been stretched into an adult without any adding any extra mass. Like most Sanguinaires, he dressed in white, with accents of bone and silver the better to show off his bloodshadow. He wore a white domino mask such as had not been in fashion for a generation and sported buckteeth that gave him more than a passing resemblance to a rabbit.

"Let us see your wares, merchant," he said in a voice so nasal that there was a notable echo from the recesses of his sinuses.

Ivar ignored the slight to his station, and gestured Jean-Claude forward. "As promised, monsieur. His name is Jean-Claude, formerly of the—"

"His kind do not have names," Travers snapped. "A dog does not possess a name, but merely learns to respond to a noise its master makes. The clayborn must be treated the same way. Remember, the Breaker made the clayborn in mockery of the saintborn. It is only by the Builder's boundless generosity that they are given the chance to serve us and thereby earn their souls. Even then, their primal and irresistible instinct is to challenge and corrupt, and claim for themselves the trappings of personhood. This must never be permitted."

Jean-Claude looked at Ivar. "Are you telling me this inbred mole rat is the best—"

Travers's bloodshadow stabbed through Jean-Claude's shadow. Pain crashed through him as if every nerve were drenched in acid. He would have screamed and collapsed with the agony except that the bloodshadow also held him paralyzed. With no place else to retreat his consciousness collapsed in on itself and the world went dark around the edges.

As if from a great distance, Ivar said, "I would appreciate it if you don't kill him until after you've paid for him."

Travers sniffed and his bloodshadow withdrew. Jean-Claude collapsed like a rag doll, too enervated to even catch himself when his face hit the floor.

One of Travers's men approached Ivar with a clinking sack. Ivar glowered at him and snapped his fingers. One of the pirates who'd dragged Jean-Claude in stepped forward, snatched the sack, and began counting the coin inside.

"You had best be going," Travers said while the pirate was still counting.

Ivar didn't budge, though his time shadows flickered to different parts of the room, such that Travers's men got twitchy trying to follow their movements.

The counting pirate gave Ivar a nod. He poured the coins into the bag and departed with his companion.

Ivar said to Travers, "Your conspirators have requested that I inform you that the *Thunderclap* has departed from Joubert's Folly and is sailing to join the Hoary Fleet. They direct you to set you course for the Bittergale, and they will meet you on the way."

"You tell Sagax Czensos I will not be—" Travers began, but Ivar disappeared between one eyeblink and the next, dumping stored-up time to move faster than the human eye could see.

This conspiracy was not long for this world, if Jean-Claude was any judge.

"You won't need those chains," Travers said. His bloodshadow snapped Jean-Claude's shackles and flung the bits into a corner. "True incarceration exists in the mind."

Jean-Claude pushed himself up to his knees. "Monsieur Travers, Ivar is up to something. Quaestor Czensos said—"

"Silence!" Travers's bloodshadow yanked Jean-Claude across the floor, splayed him facedown in a position of absolute submission, and held him pinned there. The grip of the bloodshadow was like having his skin fastened to the deck by a thousand needles.

"My slaves are raised from birth to be perfect servants, obedient and unquestioning, devoid of curiosity, ambition, anger, or passion: emotions to which they are not entitled. They desire only to serve, to be filled with the will of greater beings. So will it be with you."

Jean-Claude tried to let go the pain while Travers blathered. Fighting would only make it worse, to no good end. His one consolation was that Travers could not make a bloodhollow out of him in order to learn what he knew. The creation of a bloodhollow suppressed all memory from before the transformation, leaving behind an empty space for the Sanguinaire to fill. Jean-Claude must play along with this for now. At some point Travers would start asking questions, and Jean-Claude would tell him everything Jean-Claude needed him to know.

"We begin at the beginning," Travers said, and Jean-Claude prepared several different servings of horseshit depending on which question he asked first.

"The soulless have nothing that is not given to them by their master, not food, not water, and certainly not clothing." With a sudden rip, Jean-Claude's clothes exploded off him, everything from his doublet to his boots, bits of cloth and loose thread flying every which way.

Jean-Claude cursed inside his head if nowhere else, but to his relief the pain suddenly eased and the bloodshadow retreated.

Jean-Claude didn't move or make a sound. Clearly Travers wanted obedience, and Jean-Claude saw no reason not to give it to him. It wasn't as if he could spring into action and stab the spindly git to death with his own rabbit teeth.

Travers turned and made his way to his chair, his canes giving him a wobbly four-legged gait. He sagged in his seat, breathing heavily, and his officers sparked two very bright alchemical lights. The heat of them washed over Jean-Claude's goose-pimpled flesh, but this was not being done for his comfort. Those were the same sort of floodlights used in shadowpults. Even through clenched eyelids the reflected light burned his eyes.

"Now, speak," Travers said.

What sort of test was this? There was no way to tell what this nutter actually wanted him to say, so he'd best at least make it interesting.

"Czensos means to betray you," Jean-Claude said. A sudden pain burrowed into his head, like a corpse worm gnawing on his brain. Fear rose from the black places deep inside. Had Travers bought Jean-Claude just to kill him?

"It's true," he said. Something had to get through to the man, but what? The fear only grew worse. Panic welled and his heart raced like a kicking rabbit in the jaws of a wolf. If he said anything wrong, the vile venomous snake uncoiling in his head would strike.

"He served the Skaladin . . ." The snake loomed before him an endless coil, glistening with poison. His throat constricted and he shied away, but he still had things he needed to say. He had a hook to set. "Killed the Savior . . ." The black beast sank fangs into his mind. Dismay shattered all reason and vaporized his words. The Ravenous Gate opened and shrieked his name.

He must make Travers listen, but when the words formed in the back of his mind, courage failed. To even think of speaking brought on cold sweat and shivering. Pushing the words forward plunged him into nightmare, shriving him of all thought and intent. His tongue shriveled like a rotten carrot. He curled in on himself, but he could not escape the fear.

"You see," Travers said, "there is no thought, no word that will ever again be vital enough for you to brave the shackles of terror on your tongue. The soulless should be silent. Language is not a gift you have earned. Words are treasures that do not belong to you. Fear is the only emotion you are allowed. In due course, terror will break down your mind, destroy that corrupt and cracking edifice you dare to think of as yourself. When the terror has done its work, I will remake you into something worthy of serving me. Only then will I extract from you the truth of Czensos's schemes. You will present those facts to me as a gift, carefully arranged to please me and served up with utmost respect, entirely untainted by whatever poisonous deception you were no doubt planning."

Jean-Claude wanted to curse him, to throw his arrogance back in his face, but his voice rebelled. A wave of horror drove him back into the cave where ancient man had once huddled from the terrors of the night.

He railed against his own cowardice. His voice was his tool, his greatest weapon. Insults to the flesh he had survived, but this . . . Everything he did depended on speaking, yet even the most desperate need could not lure him out of the cave.

"Playing with broken toys again, cousin?" came a new voice. Jean-Claude dared roll his head far enough to see the newcomer, on his blurry left side. It was a bloodhollow; that much he could tell from the underwater way it moved even if he couldn't see its face.

Travers said, "They come to me broken, and I take some small pleasure in repairing them. It is the Builder's work, but why are you here? I did not expect to receive you so soon after your failure aboard the *Thunderclap*."

The cousin made a dismissive noise. "Failure? I extracted the relic, the shard, and the guide. It's true the *Thunderclap* didn't fall out of the sky, but I can be forgiven for that, since nobody knew how powerful the capitaine's sorcery was. Meanwhile, what have you done except sit in your cabin and brood?"

"You have spent too much time amongst the mongrel breed, and it has corrupted you. You forget to whom you are speaking. I am the purest and most holy. My line is unbroken and my blood undiluted, and it is through me that the Savior will manifest. Forget that at your peril."

Jean-Claude, intrigued by these intrigues, lay perfectly still. He pictured the Savior rising from the Vault of Ages and being presented with Travers as a vessel. He could only imagine disappointment on a truly epic scale.

"Then you will be happy to know that I have removed another obstacle from your path," the cousin said. "I convinced Madame to issue a recall order for Capitaine Isabelle. Given that the capitaine had her personal favor, this will be a great embarrassment to her, which will further erode her support amongst the great houses."

"You think that is a favor," Travers said. "La reine's capitaine was the weakest link in the whole expedition. You have done them a favor getting rid of her. And as for Madame, l'Empire might as well have a goat sitting on its throne. What do I care what the great houses think of her? After my apotheosis, all worldly power will be swept away, replaced at last by divine command."

It was all Jean-Claude could do to remain inert. He would have their hides for attacking Isabelle. There was enough treason here to stretch a hundred necks. A sniff of dust got up Jean-Claude's nose and tickled. He tried to blow it out quietly, but his huffing only made it worse.

The cousin said, "Or you could find nothing at all out there, and be forced to return empty-handed, in which case you may find the collapse of la reine's authority quite useful."

Jean-Claude's sneeze escaped like a cat bolting through a hole in the fence.

Travers scowled and called for porters. A brace of aeronauts with dull, incurious eyes came in. They hauled Jean-Claude to his feet and towed him away. They hauled him to the ship's manger, shackled him by his neck to the wall in a stall next to a hog, and left him in the stinking dark. He was too cold and weak to fight them, his vision was a blur, and he could not even talk his captors into being gentle.

Jean-Claude was not the sort of person to wallow in misery. He'd been wounded before. He understood pain, but he'd never met anything like this Torment that tied his tongue. Again and again he tried to speak, to utter even a single syllable, but each attempt brought another wave of terror and paralysis.

He wept. His throat could still make noise, because the frustration and humiliation came out in an animal whine. It would only get worse from here. If Travers could lock his voice away so easily, how long would it be until he lay waste to courage and reason?

Jean-Claude could not withstand another round of such torture. He must escape. But how? If he could have talked to a crewman . . . but he must put that thought from his head.

One thing about having been raised a peasant was he knew how to push on. Winter didn't care if he starved, so he pushed on with the plow after his father died. He was barely tall enough to reach the handles and not strong enough to make the furrows straight, but he turned the soil and planted the seed and tightened his belt and did not die. When the drought came, he dug the well deeper and carried water for months on end, and when the floods came he dug ditches and built dams, and it never occurred to him to give up or give in. Quitting was a luxury only the rich could afford, knowing they could always sacrifice someone else to survive.

Jean-Claude tugged at his collar. It was fastened with a padlock, which he might have picked if he had a wire. The hold was dark, but there must have been light leaking in from somewhere, for his wounded eye could make out the vague shape of the chain where it looped around a stanchion and was fastened to itself by another padlock. If he had some kind of leverage, he might break the lock. Alas, this pigsty suffered from a lack of convenient crowbars.

The chain wasn't long enough for him to reach the door, but he could reach the sides of the pen. He peered through a gap between the planks. On one side were bales of straw and on the other a massive pig. It slept leaning against the boards of Jean-Claude's stall, its bulk enough to bow the wood. Its back was lined with scars, and its snores made the deck vibrate. There was two hundred kilos of muscle if he could figure out how to use it. An enraged hog could easily demolish the stall, but that wouldn't get Jean-Claude out of his collar, and then he'd be stuck here with a quarter ton of angry pork chops. Even so, the bowed-out planks gave him an idea.

Jean-Claude worked his way along the plank until he found where it was nailed to the upright. In the weird half-light, he could make out the nail heads. He ran his fingertips over them until he found one that hadn't been hammered flat. He gripped it with his fingertips, but it was not loose. He grabbed the edge of the plank and pulled. It refused to budge. He might be able to work it out eventually, but time was not his ally. Travers could have him fetched at any moment, and Builder only knew how much of himself he'd lose. The idea filled him with the sort of animal fright that made rabbits hide in their burrows even when the floods came to drown them.

Yet that fear was normal, not the sorcerous terror that Travers had inflicted on him. This was fear he knew how to work with. He scooted to the center where the bulge was greatest, reached through to the hog's bristly back, and gave the great beast a really good scratch. The pig stirred in its sleep, grunted with porcine pleasure, and leaned into the scratch. The plank creaked in protest. Jean-Claude kept scratching until he heard the unmistakable squeal of a nail being dragged through wood. With a sharp pang, the board came loose. Jean-Claude worked one of the exposed nails and pulled it free. It was too thick to use as a lock pick, but that could be remedied.

His pulse running quick, alert for the sound of anyone approaching the pen, Jean-Claude pulled his chain tight, placed the iron nail against it, and began filing it down.

—

Isabelle found that she could paint details within details on the canvas of the everdream, like a mathematical spiral that curled in on itself but never logically reached a center. Into the memory of her father's bloodshadow she etched echoes of betrayal. Once she had been a man named Elia, doge of Udina, betrayed when his great uncle murdered his wife with the thought of replacing her with a woman more closely tied to his branch of the family.

Elia's revenge, which Isabelle painted into the smoke and fires of a burning city, was . . . excessive, even by Fenice standards. She remembered his coldness, the careful scraping away of every human emotion, the excision of every human virtue as he let his uncle's plan develop. He married the substitute, he got her with child, and framed his uncle for their gruesome murder. He had watched, empty and triumphant, as his uncle burned at the stake. Isabelle's presence in the everdream grew sick and chilled. Elia's pain she could absorb, but swallowing his hatred was like swallowing a sewer: loathsome, poisonous, corrupting.

Isabelle's phantom fingers trembled and she painted the bloody corpse of an innocent child onto the role of her misdeeds, for as she tamed the memory and took it in, she participated in it. Her many lives were the strangest sort of reincarnation. It was not as if her soul passed forward through time from body to body, but rather that it passed backwards to its origin and root. She could not choose which parts of the past she kept, only how she would cope with them going forward.

Other experiences, while not so vile, were equally hard to place within her current incarnation. She had little experience with carnal pleasures. She had no idea what to do with the brain-fogging, jittery urgency of a young man's lust, or the nervous exhilaration of a young woman's first sexual encounter. Touching these feelings kept bringing up thoughts of Bitterlich, and by thoughts she meant wholly indecorous and downright libidinous fantasies. Surely it was shameful to conscript him into her lickerish daydreams, especially given his stated disinterest in reciprocation.

Nonsense. It was less a word and more of an emotion tugging on her from one of her greater grandmothers, Lissa the courtesan.

Having these ghosts in her head was like having a whole pack of willful hounds, each dragging her toward their particular obsession. Lissa had been a consort of doges and generals, and had proved an inveterate matchmaker, breaking and bonding couples in her attempt to reshape the Vecci system of house alliances.

Isabelle reeled in Lissa's tether, bringing her close enough to the present moment that she appeared as an apparition, giving the woman enough breath to form new thoughts and speech. She looked no more than Isabelle's age, though far more flamboyant, with luscious flesh and a great plume of blue-black feathers.

"What do you mean, nonsense?" Isabelle asked.

"The beast-man hangs on your every word," said Grandma Lissa. "Primps, preens."

Isabelle bristled at the insult to Bitterlich's dignity, but arguing with her ancestors was about as futile as yelling at a gravestone.

"Bitterlich says he's not interested in me." Isabelle took him at his word.

"He said it was only a moment," Lissa said. "You know better. For months he stood beneath your window and serenaded you like a tomcat, but in the end, when you asked for clarity, he slunk away a coward."

"Bitterlich is no coward." Isabelle had witnessed his bravery many times. She snatched away Lissa's air, and the matchmaker drifted away to thump against the end of her tether. Whatever the truth of Bitterlich's feelings, his answer had closed a door and she was not going to sit outside in the rain pounding on it.

In the end she painted her romantic inclinations into the graveyard with all her other vain hopes: the university she'd wanted to build, the family she'd wanted to have.

The everdream became dull and gray around her. Her thoughts came more slowly, haltingly. She was all but out of air herself. She needed to breathe.

She let go her anchor and turned her face to the breach. The shape of it had changed, in her perception, from a crumbling barricade to a very deliberate opening, a gateway through which she could pass at will. She glided through it.

She heard a groan, and realized it was her own noise, her own body. She hurt everywhere, but her fever had broken. Some tipping point had been passed, much as the moment when a great storm blew out leaving ruin in its wake, but before rebuilding commenced.

She wasn't dying anymore. Which meant her transformation must have completed.

Isabelle opened her eyes. It was like trying to shift a door on rusted hinges, and she found her face covered with a thin parchment that let in light but not shape.

A hushed voice said, "Isabelle? Can you hear me?" It was Marie, still tending her, thank the saints.

"Yes." Isabelle's tongue was as dry as an old potato and she felt like her face had been covered in rice paper. A powerful thirst gripped her. "Water."

She reached up to brush the parchment from her eyes. Bending her arm felt like breaking a twig in two. Her bones felt like sharp-edged quartz, and her skin . . . her hand came away with a death mask of dried skin. She'd pulled her face off!

Only her parched throat and dried tongue stifled her shriek. She tried to sit, but lacked the strength and fell back immediately to the sound of crunching, like she'd fallen into a patch of dried leaves. More dead skin.

Dismay filled her at the sight of her dermis cracking and crumbling. Except . . . this had happened to her dozens of times, through many lives. It was all part of the process of transformation.

Beneath the shedding skin was new flesh covered in pale gray down except for her legs below the knees, her arm below the elbow, and the patch around her mouth and chin, all of which were covered in gray scales like a bird's legs. Her fingers ended in curved talons stronger than steel and sharper than razors, the promise of power to come.

Marie hovered into her range of vision. "There's water here, but I have to tell you not to be afraid. Quill said your skin will come off like a wheat husk and you are not to be alarmed."

Marie lifted Isabelle and bolstered her into a sitting position. The change in elevation was all but enough to make her faint. Her heart fluttered like the last clinging leaf of autumn.

Peeling off Isabelle's old skin was like pulling off a scab, sickly and disgusting, but oh what a relief not to itch anymore. Her hair came out in clumps. The detritus smelled like moldering leather.

Her body was nearly skeletal, as if she'd suffered a prolonged famine. Her new skin sagged on her aching bones. Her body had emptied every warehouse of fat and pillaged the land of muscle to get her through the transition. And now would come the work, on top of everything else, to replenish those stores.

"I admit," said Marie, scrubbing her clean with a wet bit of cloth. "This looks even weirder than Quill described."

"It's called sloughing to down," Isabelle said. "It's a rite of passage. I'm a grown-up now. There's usually a big feast to celebrate." Gorging gave the fledgling the strength to thrive.

Once it had happened to her at her elder sister's betrothal ceremony, quite stealing her thunder. She'd been saved from sisterly wrath only by her father pointing out that it might have been her wedding day instead, which would have been worse.

Generally the down lasted a few days before her *cappotto di piume* came in. Of course, there was that one time . . . She'd been a boy named Jacopo. His belly down had lasted a whole year, merciless cousins calling him a dandelion the whole time, though thankfully he got his proper feathers with his first molt.

Marie said, "If you're an adult, does that mean you'll finally start acting like a big girl?"

"Only after I get my party," Isabelle said sulkily, digging for humor in the dark.

"You'll have soup and like it," Marie said, spooning up a bowl of hot broth.

"What's been happening?" Isabelle asked. This small bare room gave her no clues as to the state of the world.

"You eat while I talk. Ask questions later." Marie said.

Isabelle dutifully slurped the tepid soup.

Marie went on in her grave-whisper voice, "Quill left yesterday on the *Thunderclap.*"

The news that the *Thunderclap* had departed stung. It marked the absolute end of Isabelle's ambitions.

Her ancestral chorus stirred and Capitana Falconé shimmered in the breach like a reflection on the surface of a still pool. *There are players in the game besides l'impératrice. Many would pay for your services.*

Isabelle splashed the plane of the breach, like throwing a stone into the water. The space rippled and Falconé disappeared. Isabelle thanked the saints she could do that now. She would not betray l'Empire or its great project. Grand Leon had envisioned a world where all sorts of saintborn could coexist in one culture, under one crown. It was a vision Sireen had continued and expanded, and to which Isabelle had attached rights for the clayborn. That dream, fragile as it was in the face of concerted, ruthless opposition from the entrenched nobility, was worth defending. As long as Sireen promoted it, Isabelle supported her.

Oblivious to Isabelle's internal debate, Marie continued, "Bitterlich has taken over Rebecca's lessons and is teaching her how to use her sorcery. Djordji has been swapping shifts with me and swapping old war stories with Commandant Turenne, a man who is very impressed with all the battles he would have won if only he'd been in the right place at the right time instead of captaining a desk."

"Rear admiral of the Wingchair Fleet," Isabelle said. She'd encountered that kind of officer often enough. In at least one past life she'd been such a man. The memory was worthy of a good cringe.

"According to Djordji, Turenne is a man without faction in Rocher Royale.

He hates all politicians equally, and he's not fond of clayborn, Seelenjägers, Fenice, Glasswalkers, or any sorcerer without a bloodshadow."

"So how is this very special person our problem?"

Marie hesitated as if looking for the right words, then settled on the blunt ones. "Turenne apparently intends to treat the recall order as an arrest warrant, complete with armed guards, restrictions on your movement, and limiting your access to allies. According to Djordji, he is angling to take some credit for your arrest and capture."

Isabelle bridled at that. "Is he insane? The whole point of a recall order is that you are supposed to present yourself voluntarily to the Crown. Does he imagine Sireen will be pleased?"

"No, but there are plenty of people in Fleet Command who were unhappy with your promotion. It's them he seeks to impress. He's been trying to convince Djordji to support him. A good word from an Old Hand can make a career, and he's hoping to be promoted off this rock."

"And what has Djordji said to this?" Isabelle asked.

"Djordji hasn't said anything. As long as Turenne thinks Djordji might help him, Djordji has leverage."

Isabelle put the empty soup bowl aside. For the first time since her transformation had overtaken her, she stretched herself not into the past, but the future. As a woman under orders it was her duty to present herself to Sireen and place herself at la reine's mercy. If Sireen followed historical precedent, her mercy was likely to consist of Isabelle retiring to a quiet life somewhere out of the way but under close supervision. Defiance, on the other hand, would earn a charge of treason and the certainty of being hunted to the ends of the sky.

Isabelle asked, "Have we learned anything about Jean-Claude?"

"No," Marie said.

The thought of Jean-Claude plummeting into the Gloom hurt like someone had ripped out Isabelle's heart. All her life he had been the arms that held her, the dire joke that undercut terror and made her laugh, the guide star that showed her the way. He could not be dead. Must not.

Yet dwelling on her dread benefitted no one. Her duty, whatever was left of it, lay in outcomes she could actually effect. "So what is our next move?" Isabelle asked. Clearly Marie had been active in keeping a space open for her, preparing for a future Isabelle could not currently imagine.

"That will depend on you, but you should consult with your privy council."

"I have a privy council?"

"Me, Djordji, Rebecca, and Bitterlich," Marie said.

"Shouldn't Bitterlich have sailed with the *Thunderclap*?" Isabelle asked. Djordji and Marie had been Isabelle's guests on the ship, and Rebecca had been Isabelle's cabin girl, but Bitterlich had been assigned to the ship itself.

"Vrain ordered him to escort you home. Bitterlich thinks Vrain was purging the ship of your loyalists. Djordji agrees."

"Do you trust Djordji?" Isabelle asked. "He's an Old Hand. He should be the first one to tell Turenne I'm awake."

Marie said, "Being an Old Hand means he makes up his own mind about things. For what it's worth, he doesn't think you're completely hopeless, which is more than he has to say about Turenne."

After ladling a second bowl of soup down Isabelle's throat, Marie slipped out.

Djordji arrived in short order, his long coat and his wide-brimmed hat making him look more than ever like a bird scare. He took Isabelle in without comment, and closed the door.

"Good seeing you awake," he said. "Marie says you questions my loyalties."

Of course Marie would've been that blunt. It certainly preempted any maneuvering Isabelle might have wanted to do. Isabelle said, "Is it not your duty as an Old Hand to ensure I obey l'impératrice's recall order?"

Djordji broke into a coughing fit, spitting up flecks of blood and black matter. His bloodshot eyes streamed, and his hands trembled as he wiped them on a handkerchief. When the fit had passed, he produced his pipe and loaded it with dragonweed, loyal to his own assassin. The oily reek of the smoke did nothing to improve the atmosphere in the sick room.

After deliberating on his answer, he said, "Who does you serve, taking on this expedition?"

"I serve l'Empire," Isabelle said. "I was to bring Sireen a craton."

"Nay." Anger tinted his voice and hot sparks rose from his pipe. "That's the lie at the storm's eye. You swears to serve l'Empire, but you thinks first of yourself. You knows you're not fit, but you does it anyway because you thinks you has no other chances. That's what Marie tells me when she asks my help."

Isabelle winced. The lie she'd told to Sireen, the worry, dishonesty, and guilt had unsettled her heart this whole journey.

"Yes," she said. "I was wrong. I should have turned the commission down. And the need for secrecy tainted my judgment almost as much as the madness. Yet I'm far past the pale now. There's nothing I can do to make amends. If I run, I will be a fugitive, so I ask you again why help me? Unless by help you mean to make sure I bend to the law."

"You saves my life, twice. You saves the ship. You saves Sireen's crown and Grand Leon's project. That's worth something."

Isabelle might have accepted this from a lesser man, but Djordji had been a champion and confidant of Grand Leon.

She said, "Justice is fundamentally asymmetrical. One good deed cannot redeem you from a lifetime of horrors, but one evil deed can destroy a life of good works."

A wreath of smoke had accumulated under the brim of Djordji's hat. He said, "Thing is, the law sees no difference between evil, stupid, and scared. All it sees is action and it punishes the one the same as the other. Evil, well, that's got to be put down. Stupid needs teaching, and scared needs a second chance. You're not evil. You never hurts anyone apurpose. You already knows your mistake, and from what I hear tell you learn fast. That just leaves scared." He coughed into his hand, a racking sound that left his papery face pale.

While he recovered, Marie returned with Rebecca and Bitterlich in tow.

Bitterlich's gaze caught Isabelle's and his whole posture softened as if some great tension had been released. Her heart swelled in response, and Lissa appeared in the reflecting pool that filled the breach. *Just because he fawns over you doesn't mean he deserves you.*

Capitana Falconé appeared alongside Lissa. *That doesn't mean you can't use him.*

Isabelle splashed both of their reflections away. Just because she wasn't sure what she wanted to do with her feelings toward Bitterlich didn't mean she wanted their cynical solutions.

Rebecca's blue-green scales glittered. Her eyes grew round at the sight of Isabelle. "Piss me. You look like a chicken!"

"Bad case of chickenpox," Isabelle said. "Has me a bit down." She teased some of the fluffy stuff on her shoulder.

"It was too much to hope that your sense of humor would improve," Marie said.

Rebecca hopped up as if to land on the bed, but just kept going until she floated halfway between floor and ceiling. Her white mane rippled as if on an ethereal breeze.

Isabelle's eyes rounded and she gasped, "You can fly."

Rebecca grinned at Isabelle's astonishment. "Yep." She bounced from wall to wall, doing somersaults in midair. "Major Bitterlich showed me." Rebecca twirled like a ballet dancer and then she hovered over the bed, upside down. "It's getting easier with practice too."

Marie said in her deadpan, "I invite you to imagine about eight hours of maniacal cackling on the wing."

"And I can spit fire," Rebecca said.

"Not indoors," Bitterlich said. "We're here to discuss our next move with Isabelle."

"I thought we were going to look for Jean-Claude," Rebecca said.

"Isabelle has to agree to it," Marie said.

Isabelle yearned to say yes. To shout it and embrace these four who would help her find her heart-father. There was no place in the sky she would not go to find him if he was lost, and no foe she would not challenge to save him if he needed her help . . . but she would not ruin other lives to do it.

"No," Isabelle said. She went to rub her face but reconsidered, given the presence of sharp talons. Eventually she'd be able to retract them, to tuck them away in that esoteric space that sorcery seemed designed to exploit, but for now putting out her own eye was a real danger.

She took in all of her would-be conspirators with her gaze. "Of course I want to find Jean-Claude, but if I run away from Sireen's recall, I will be a fugitive. If you aid and abet me, then you will all be complicit."

"We have a plan to get around that," Marie said. "As long as Turenne thinks you are still in a coma he won't try to deliver the summons. As long as you never receive the summons, you aren't bound by it."

"You're mad," Isabelle said. "If you think Sireen is going to be taken in by such a flimsy excuse—"

"Of course she isn't," Djordji said. "That's nay the point. Look at it the other way around. Impervia tells Bitterlich about the summons days afore it happens. Do ye thinks ye'd get so much warning if Sireen didn't wants ye to act on it? She's given ye all the lead time she can without being obvious about it."

Bitterlich said to Isabelle, "If not for you, Sireen wouldn't even have a crown, and she's grateful to you. She also knew you wouldn't be happy being an ornament at court. The more I think about it, the more it seems to me that she gave you the expedition as a personal gift and justified it vis-à-vis politics rather than the other way around."

Isabelle licked dry lips with a raspy tongue. "Let's assume you are correct and Sireen wants me to avoid this summons. What exactly do you imagine she wants me to accomplish? And why me? All of you are perfectly competent."

Marie and Djordji exchanged a look. Marie said, "Isabelle is congenitally incapable of accepting the idea that anyone in a position of power might actually like her enough to bend the rules in her favor. It's one of those weird blind spots I keep telling you about."

"Blind spots?" Isabelle spluttered indignantly.

"It's right up there with her indifference to food and the fact that no one else speaks math as a first language."

Isabelle glowered, which took just about all the energy she had. "Are you quite finished?"

"I could go on for days," Marie said.

"We knows the risks of what we proposes," Djordji said.

"Perhaps," Isabelle said, "but does Rebecca?" Isabelle lifted her gaze to the youngster, who was now standing on the ceiling, her white mane hanging down.

"I'm in," Rebecca said.

"Are you? If Djordji is wrong, or if we get caught by people unsympathetic to our plight, they will not take mercy on you for your youth."

Rebecca shrugged. "Been a thief my whole life. Could've got my hands cut off, but I didn't. Never thought to be anything but a thief until Jean-Claude came along. Then I was a cabin girl and an aeronaut." She flipped over again and floated cross-legged over the foot of the bed. "Now I'm a Seelenjäger, and I'll stick with them what's been good to me. Also what gets me off this rock."

Isabelle let her head sink back into the bolster. Rebecca couldn't know what she was getting herself into, no twelve-year-old could, yet Isabelle didn't have the right to make her decisions for her, not anymore.

Isabelle had learned early on that life was dangerous, and Jean-Claude had made it clear that her first and best defense was to be competent. Rebecca, being who and what she was, needed the same sort of education.

"Very well," Isabelle said. "But this doesn't get you out of reading lessons."

Rebecca rolled her pupilless eyes. "No miracle's that big."

Which meant the only honor Isabelle might save via capitulation was her own, if slinking off to commit political suicide could be considered honorable. If Djordji was right—and he'd been doing this longer than she'd been alive—Sireen was giving her a chance, one more shot at the dice, and leaving up to her as to where to place the bet.

She'd put her last token on Jean-Claude.

CHAPTER

Nineteen

There was never a time and nary a place on a ship that was not busy. Things had to be moved from port to starboard and starboard to port. Anything that wasn't painted needed to be painted, and anything that was painted needed to be stripped of paint. Even the manger where Jean-Claude was being held was not free from intrusion. The animals were kept just forward of the gun deck, and though the spaces were separated by a bulkhead, aeronauts kept circulating through on their way to somewhere else.

Some hours earlier, a flat-eyed gang of aeronauts had come by and fed the chickens, milked the cow, and scraped out the pens. One beast keeper even put down a ship's biscuit and a wooden mug of water for Jean-Claude, all without saying a word.

Travers's aeronauts were exceptionally quiet. There was none of the boisterousness he expected from sailors, no laughter, no arguments, and none of the singing that kept the men in both good spirits and steady rhythm while they worked.

Le Comte Travers didn't want his men in good spirits. He didn't want them in any spirits at all. Likely his whole crew had been born and raised in his county, and broken down until there was nothing but a blank page onto which Travers could scrawl his own pathetic screed. They weren't quite bloodhollows, but they had been starved of all imagination and ambition. Travers reserved such qualities for himself and then wasted them by his contempt.

Travers was, in his own sick way, even worse than Isabelle's late un-lamented father. Le Comte des Zephyrs had cared only that his subjects feared him and fed him, but had otherwise taken no interest in their lives. Travers, conversely, wanted to control every aspect of his subjects' lives, to deprive them of hope and will in the interest of perfecting them.

Jean-Claude finally popped the padlock holding his collar. He threw off the shackles and rubbed his abraded neck. His battered arm throbbed, and his left eye felt as if someone had stuffed his eye socket with an iron thistle, but he was past the first hurdle.

The problem was the second hurdle. There was no damned way off a sky-ship that did not involve plummeting to one's death. Even if he launched an escape skiff, sailing it required people who knew things about knots and sails. He'd just bob around in open air until Travers turned around and picked him up.

That left Jean-Claude precious few options. He could not stow away. Once his absence was noticed, the ship would be searched down to the caulking. His only hope, ghostly as it was, was to seize the snake by its head. Le Comte Travers was the only man on this ship that actually mattered. Take him and Jean-Claude could take control.

Jean-Claude removed the loop of cord that had been used to hold his pen shut. The pig in the next pen made a strange low grunt. The creature, which had hitherto been facing away from him had woken up and turned to watch him.

It had a human face.

Jean-Claude recoiled in surprise.

The human-faced swine had close-set eyes as dark as drops of oil. Its face was deepest blue and fringed with fleshy lumps and spikes. Its expression was doleful and resigned.

The Seelenjäger was chained to the wall as Jean-Claude had been, but instead of a shackle around his neck he had a ring through his nose. The metal piercing his flesh stopped him from being able to shape-shift and escape.

On closer inspection, the scars on his flanks were butchers' marks, old butchers' marks, marking the frontiers of regenerated flesh.

Normally Jean-Claude was not given to horror, but a sickness grew inside him as the truth of the Seelenjäger's plight dawned on him. This poor fellow had been harvested for meat while still alive. Then, thanks to the restorative powers of some animal he had absorbed, the missing portions had regrown, only to be harvested again and again, like the livestock of the gods in some of the oldest legends from the Bleaktimes.

Approaching footsteps drew Jean-Claude's attention. A gang of aeronauts entered the manger. Fear ran cold in Jean-Claude's veins. Had they come to fetch him back to Travers? He snapped his collar back on, but left it unlocked. Surprise was his best weapon, if his cold, aching body could make any use of it.

The aeronauts began manger chores, feeding all the livestock. Jean-Claude cowered as they looked into his pen. He prayed they followed the same routine they had last time. Feeding, watering, and cleaning.

One by one the aeronauts finished their tasks and drifted away, until the only man left was the one mucking the stalls. Jean-Claude huddled to hide his hands and twisted his cord into a loop with a slipknot. He clenched and relaxed his stiffened muscles, trying to work some warmth and flexibility into them without leaving his submissive crouch.

The mucker came into Jean-Claude's stall with rake and broom. He scraped out the foul old straw and tossed in fresh. He never even looked at Jean-Claude. At last he turned his back.

Jean-Claude pulled off his collar and rose. It was supposed to be one smooth motion, but his back creaked, his knees locked, and it turned into an awkward lurch. The aeronaut turned, dropped his rake and bucket with a clatter, and raised his hands, but then Jean-Claude was on him. He cast his noose over the man's head and around his neck, then kicked the mucker's feet out from under him. The aeronaut hit the end of the cord like a snared rabbit. His nascent cry collapsed with his windpipe. Jean-Claude kneeled on his throat and kept the line taut. The man bucked and thrashed, bludgeoning Jean-Claude about the thighs and groin. Jean-Claude flicked his gaze to the manger's entrance. He could hear nothing over the thundering of his own blood, and his heart felt ready to burst, but no shadow crossed the light.

At last the struggling ceased. Man became corpse. Jean-Claude allowed himself only two deep breaths to recover before he dragged the body into his pen. Keeping one eye on the manger's entrance, he stripped his victim for his clothes.

Alas, his victim was smaller than he. Jean-Claude could barely get the fellow's drawers on, the shirt made him feel like a sausage, and the coat buttons were out of the question. Shoving his feet into man's shoes felt like crushing his toes in a vise. Sitting down or bending over were likely to shred his cover.

He crept into the pen with the Seelenjäger. Maybe they could help each other. If this Seelenjäger could fly, he might be able to save them both.

The fellow whined and huddled up against the far end of the cell.

Jean-Claude wished he could proffer words of solace, but his voice clotted in his throat. Instead, he pointed to the Seelenjäger, hooked his thumbs together, spread his fingers in a fair imitation of a bird, and had it fly away.

The Seelenjäger pawed its nose ring with a trotter.

Jean-Claude pinched his nose and then made a clipping motion and threw the ring away. Then he made the bird gesture again.

The Seelenjäger's dull, beaten-down eyes did not exactly light up, but he leaned forward slightly and let Jean-Claude approach. The ring had been pinned and welded. It was too thick to file through and would have to be cut.

Jean-Claude pointed to the Seelenjäger then to himself, cradled his arms as if holding an infant, and made the fly away gesture.

The Seelenjäger looked hesitant, but bobbed his head in what Jean-Claude chose to interpret as tentative agreement. Else this might be the most short-lived escape in the history of flight.

Jean-Claude crept out into the aisle between pens. He needed tools. He peered around the corner into the gun deck. No one seemed to have noticed his little tussle. There might be something on the gun deck he could use to cut the Seelenjäger's nose ring, but he'd have better odds down on the orlop deck where the workshops were.

Jean-Claude hefted a large sack of chicken feed onto his shoulder. Even on a ship as dread bound as this one, no one wanted to meet the gaze of a man with a heavy load lest they be asked to share it.

The ladder down to the lower decks was between the manger and the gun platform. He entered into the public space with all the confidence he could muster, then descended carefully.

The problem with hitching a ride with the Seelenjäger was that shapeshifters could only get so big and carry so much, and Jean-Claude was no lightweight. Without a nearby place to land, they'd fall, or at least the Seelenjäger would be forced to drop him.

Yet what other chance did they have?

On the orlop deck, laughter and conversation rolled out of the surgeon's bay. Several Sanguinaire officers gathered round the table, playing cards. A handful of flat-eyed clayborn attended them.

"Would you look at this?" said one of the Sanguinaires. "That meat puppet Thirdeye brought Father used to be a King's Own Musketeer."

Jean-Claude felt as if he'd been gut punched. One of the officers had his letters pouch, the one he'd carried for decades and contained his certificate of authority, his passport. The bastards were pawing through his identity.

"Filthy clayborn," said another Sanguinaire, who might have played second nostril to Travers's virtuoso sinuses. "No piece of paper can give the soulless power over the Builder's chosen. Burn them."

That suggestion made Jean-Claude's blood run to ice.

"Not until I've made use of them," said the first officer.

One of the flat-eyed clayborn turned toward Jean-Claude, and he hastily retreated down the corridor. Truly the papers were a matter of least concern . . . but if he recovered them they could identify him to any Célestial agent he could find, even without his voice.

First he had to find a tool to free the Seelenjäger—nothing mattered unless they could get away—but if he could snag his papers too . . . Well, he'd never not overextended himself before.

Jean-Claude ducked into the first uninhabited bay he found: the carpenter's workshop. There had to be something for ring cutting in here. There were lockers and tool chests, all locked down. He offloaded his sack and started in on the largest locker with his lock pick.

He dared not light a lantern to guide his work, but as dark as it was, his left eye seemed to pick up the edges of things. The chests and the locks and even his pick were backlit like the horizon just after the Solar had disappeared for the evening. He prodded his eye, but discovered only the raised tender flesh of a stitched-up wound. He'd heard of men who'd come to see ghosts or auras around people after they'd been hit in the head. This phantom lacework limning of objects must be akin to that.

The locks seemed to have been built to deter casual pilferers rather than determined burglars, for the tumblers yielded quickly. The door opened to display racks of files, bits, rasps, and chisels. Jean-Claude grabbed a knife-size chisel and a hammer.

The ship's bell sounded. The boatswain's whistle signaled all hands on deck.

Jean-Claude's pulse thundered in fear. Had the murdered aeronaut been discovered? The first thing they would do if they found a dead man and a prisoner missing was account for everyone onboard.

He peered into the passageway in time to see the Sanguinaires leave the surgeon's bay and head for the ladders, their clayborn escorts in tow.

"Prepare to receive visitors," shouted someone on the deck above.

Nostrils, leaning on his cane, glanced up at the ceiling and said, "It's a mistake to deal with the Skaladin. Every word is a lie."

"It doesn't matter what he says as long as he brings us the Windcaller and the relic," said the other officer, dropping Jean-Claude's pouch in his jacket pocket as he climbed. "When the moment is right, we'll be rid of him, too."

Jean-Claude's mind reeled. Was Hasdrubal bringing Hailer Dok here? Could Jean-Claude somehow steal Dok back from them?

Jean-Claude tucked his tools into his belt and climbed after the clayborn escort, just like any other aeronaut responding to orders. He ascended the ladder. His old legs didn't like the climb, not with the rest of him wounded. His lungs felt like they were working for nothing. Had the ship risen into thinner air? It could happen if they were trying to leap over a storm.

On the gun deck, the Sanguinaires were forced to pause by the press of aeronauts on the companionway ahead of them. The clayborn jostled, trying to clear room for the officers.

Sphincter tightly puckered, Jean-Claude stumbled forward, bumbling into one escort, who bumped into the other. They both scowled at Jean-Claude, who turned to duck his head and tip his hat by way of apology. His hand dipped for the officer's pocket.

He was not as good at this as Rebecca, who could, by all accounts, steal a man's peg leg without him noticing, but the press worked to his advantage. His fingertips brushed the wallet's ancient leather. It helped that he had handled this pouch hundreds of times. He knew its weight without testing. He teased it up and out.

The officer turned and frowned at him. Jean-Claude palmed the wallet and kept going, expecting the merciless lash of a bloodshadow. He brushed between two aeronauts and joined the general flow. No shouts of outrage followed him. Gangs of aeronauts continued to ascend.

Heart thudding with the awful thrill of escape, Jean-Claude squeaked out of the queue and hustled to the manger. With the crew distracted, this would be their best chance to sneak away through the turvy hatches . . . but what about Dok? It was maddening to think that the Windcaller could be within reach, but he could do nothing to snatch the man back.

Yes, his first priority must be escape, to get back to Isabelle, to warn her and Impervia about this treasonous conspiracy, but that was simply shifting the problem to their shoulders.

He hustled into the Seelenjäger's pen and fished out the chisel and hammer. The Seelenjäger squealed and backed into the corner. He cast Jean-Claude a look of betrayal.

Jean-Claude put the implements on the floor. Travers's butchers must have used such tools on the Seelenjäger before, chisels to crack off ribs for consumption. Jean-Claude raised empty hands in a mollifying gesture. He pinched his nose and then pantomimed striking the ring with the chisel.

After several more calming gestures, the Seelenjäger finally lay his head down on the deck, his nose ring touching the boards. Jean-Claude placed the edge of the chisel against the ring and hefted the hammer. The pig closed his eyes and whimpered.

"Hey, waster. What are you doing there?" shouted the marine sergeant who appeared that moment at the pen's gate.

Jean-Claude slammed the chisel with the hammer. The blow jolted up his arm like a tree being hit by lightning. The iron ring split. The sergeant drew his sword and blew his whistle. Jean-Claude reset the chisel halfway round the ring and struck again, cleaving the wicked device in two. He yanked the ring from the Seelenjäger's nose. The Seelenjäger squealed in pain and huddled in the corner, shrieking in fright.

The sergeant threw open the gate. "Down on your face! Now."

Jean-Claude twisted as hard as he could and hurled the hammer. It caught the sergeant square on the chin and staggered him.

Jean-Claude plunged after him, bellowing a wordless war cry. A gang of marines rushed into the manger.

Time seemed to thicken as he lunged, his attack all rage and pain and time-honed habit. He flicked the chisel from his weak left hand to his right, and rammed its tip through the gaps in the sergeant's ribs. Jean-Claude felt the thunk all the way to his shoulder. The man huffed, his eyes wide with shock.

Jean-Claude captured his sword as he fell, but the other marines fell upon him. He caught a slash on the flat of his blade, but another sliced his thigh. His leg buckled and he crashed to one knee. A marine knocked the sword from his hand.

All the desperate hope that had upheld Jean-Claude these last few hours passed out of him like aether from a burst balloon. Yet he would not yield to Travers and his horrors. Let come the end.

Then the deck shook and there came a blast of sound like someone firing a broadside from a pipe organ. The Seelenjäger exploded from the stall, cracking the stanchion and shattering the bulkhead. He had doubled in size and sprouted tusks like scimitars. Thick armored plates covered his back and flanks.

The Seelenjäger plowed through the marines, crushing one under his hooves and goring another with his tusks, tossing him to the ceiling to rain down in a shower of blood.

Jean-Claude snatched up a sword and lurched to his feet, shouting defiance as hope returned. His fresh wound was shallow but painful. He limped after the Seelenjäger, who had finished off the marines and was looking around for something else to kill.

Jean-Claude tapped him on the flank, and leapt back as his head whipped around. The fire in his eyes cooled when he saw Jean-Claude.

Jean-Claude pointed to the companionway. Down was escape. He swung himself onto the ladder and prayed his new friend would follow his lead. A Seelenjäger in close quarters was a terror to behold, but there were still several hundred aeronauts and saints only knew how many Sanguinaires on this ship. It would take only one touch from a bloodshadow to end the rampage.

He hit the orlop deck and nearly crumpled. The Seelenjäger swarmed down behind him as a massive six-legged, blue-skinned lizard. Shouts came from above and down the passageway. Jean-Claude rounded the bulkhead and took the ladder down through the hold to the turvy deck.

He hit the lowest walkway with a hip-jarring thump and startled a turvyman who was just climbing up from the rigging below. Jean-Claude clocked him with a blow from the pommel of his stolen sword and laid him out flat.

Open hatches in the floor looked down through the turvy rigging to the deep sky. Jean-Claude checked himself before he slipped over the edge. Damned vertigo made him dizzy. He averted his gaze.

The Seelenjäger had assumed a shape that was a bipedal version of his hexapedal lizard, with four arms and a long tail. Must be his erstepelz.

The Seelenjäger grabbed him by the shoulder. "I can carry you, but not far. Is there someplace nearby to land?"

Jean-Claude hadn't the foggiest idea where they were. The odds against them being anywhere near a safe landing spot were enormous. For the Seelenjäger to carry him was just suicide with a better glide path. Yet a new idea blossomed like a canker sore, inescapable and maddening. He pointed to the fallen turvyman then to the Seelenjäger, and made carrying motions. He pointed to the ship and then to his eyes and held up two fingers.

The Seelenjäger's lizard eyes rounded. "You want them to see two people flying away."

Jean-Claude nodded vigorously, handed him his wallet, and jabbed the thundercrown embossed on the front. If he could get this to any Célestial authority and tell his story, at least Isabelle would learn what he'd done.

The Seelenjäger took the wallet. "I understand."

Jean-Claude saluted him and ran, climbing a ladder into the hold. He'd just pulled his feet up when a Sanguinaire lieutenant leapt down onto the turvy deck.

The Seelenjäger had picked up the turvyman. He shouted, "Hold on, my friend!" and leapt out the turvy hatch. The Sanguinaire's bloodshadow lashed the space where he'd just been.

Jean-Claude drew back farther into the shadows as the Sanguinaire raced to the hatches with a whole squad of marines.

"Shoot them!" he shouted. "Don't let them get away!"

The marines raced to the gun loops and opened fire. Smoke filled the chamber, but judging by the Sanguinaire's increasingly agitated shouts, not one of them scored.

He shouted, "Sergeant, get topside and light the shadowpults. Breaker be damned!"

Jean-Claude retreated from the hatch and crawled deeper into the hold, to the long-term stowage, where the rats and the cats lived but men seldom ventured.

If Travers believed Jean-Claude had gotten away, he might not have the ship searched down to the rivets. If Jean-Claude could empty out a crate, he might hide out for some time, and if Dok was brought on board, he might find a way to save them both.

CHAPTER

Twenty

"What can I do for you, Lieutenant?" Bitterlich asked Malgiers, who had sent for him down at the dock, where he stood in conversation with the capitaine and crew of a recently arrived fishing vessel.

Malgiers saluted. "Major, Capitaine Elliott here has information I think you'll be interested in."

"Good news would be welcome for a change," Bitterlich said, although, on second thought, interesting and good were not often synonymous.

Capitaine Elliott was a spare man with a brush-bristle beard who smelled of aerofish as if they had anointed him their king. He goggled at Bitterlich as one might who had never seen a Seelenjäger before.

Bitterlich nodded to him and said, "Capitaine Elliott, I am Major Ewald Bitterlich, Her Imperial Majesty's Marines. What news do you have for l'Empire?"

Elliott gave a nervous bow. "Major. Not news for l'Empire so much as a message for Capitaine Isabelle of the *Thunderclap*, which I understand just sailed off."

"It has," Bitterlich said. "But she is my capitaine, and I will deliver the message." He didn't know enough about Elliott or who he might be working for to divulge that Isabelle was still on Joubert's Folly.

Elliott fidgeted as a man wrestling with a choice. At last he said, "I was told to give it to her, but I suppose she's out of reach now." He gestured to one of his crew, a boy of perhaps fifteen, who stepped forward and held out a battered white hat with a dilapidated plume pinned with a silver hatpin in the shape of an imperial thundercrown.

Bitterlich's breath caught and his eyes grew wide with hope and excitement. There was no mistaking that bashed and battered piece of head covering: Jean-Claude. The hat by itself did not imply he was alive, but someone had to have told Elliott to bring it to Isabelle.

Bitterlich calmed his body and gently accepted the hat from the boy's hand. "Thank you," he said. "How did you come by this?"

Elliott's face puckered a little. "There was a man at the cloud market. Asked if anyone was coming this way. No one I'd seen before. Not anyone I'll likely see again."

"I see," Bitterlich said. Cloud markets were gatherings of ships on the deep sky where sailors gathered to trade news and cargoes of dubious origin. It would not be fruitful to press further in that direction. "Does the hat come with any news attached?"

Elliott relaxed slightly again and said, "Yes. I'm to say he says he's hunting the missing trinket. That's it. I don't know what it means."

Bitterlich laughed. "Hunting . . . Of course he would be." Isabelle was scared to death that he was dead, but instead he was off chasing the trinket, but did he mean the *Conquest* shard or the key?

"Thank you," Bitterlich said again, tipping his hat to the man. "Malgiers, make sure this man gets rewarded for his service: an imperial for him and each of his crew from my personal account." A gold coin each was more money than the man probably saw in a year, but it was a dividend of gratitude Bitterlich could afford.

Elliott's mouth fell open. "Thank you, monsieur."

"Now I must be off." Bitterlich tossed Jean-Claude's hat in the air, transformed into a wolf, caught the hat gently in his jaws, and dashed for the infirmary.

Just outside Isabelle's room he resumed his erstepelz and adjusted his jacket. Hopefully Isabelle was awake, but if not, Marie or whoever was watching her would appreciate the news.

The door was closed. He knocked politely. There came no response, but given that the plan was for everyone to pretend that Isabelle never regained consciousness, this was not entirely surprising.

He opened the door and eased himself in.

Isabelle lay on the bed, her arm across her chest, eyes closed. Covered in a pale-gray Fenice hatchling down and deep-gray scales, she might have been mistaken for a Seelenjäger. Her spark-arm had reappeared and her glittering mote swarm had regained strength. As emaciated as she had become, she no longer radiated sickness. A tightness in his chest eased to see her so improved.

He closed the door and softly spoke, "Isabelle? It's me."

Isabelle's lavender-and-rose eyes came open and she smiled. She had a devastating smile. It quite stunned him.

"Major," she said in a voice still dry. "Good to see you."

He nodded dumbly. It would be unseemly and inappropriate to scoop her up and wrap her in his arms. He'd have to settle for something she'd actually appreciate.

"I have good news," he said, and held out the hat. "He's alive, and he says he's out hunting the missing trinket."

Isabelle snapped up faster than a catapult, her eyes as round as two full moons. "Alive." She received the hat and hugged it to her chest, bowing her head over it and weeping tears of joy. "Oh, thank you. Thank the saints. Where did you get this?"

"A fisherman brought it in. He got it at a cloud market along with the message."

"Which trinket?"

"I don't know. Presumably the one Hasdrubal stole."

Isabelle rubbed at her eyes with the back of her hand so as not to drop the hat. "Well, I guess that narrows our focus a little bit. To find Jean-Claude, all was have to do is find Hasdrubal."

"Whom the entire Hoary Fleet is already chasing toward the City of Gears," Bitterlich said.

"So all we have to do is get there first," Isabelle said.

"The power of oversimplification in action," Bitterlich said.

"Without oversimplification, no great deed would ever be accomplished. When I took Sheerface Castle . . ." Isabelle paused and scowled as if she wanted very badly to scold someone. "That is to say when Primus Maximus took Sheerface Castle, he had no idea how it was to be done until he had already committed himself to doing it."

Her shoulders slumped. "The story loses its punch when I can't make up my mind who's telling it."

Bitterlich tilted his head and his whiskers twitched forward, a tension on his lip. "How are you feeling?"

"I'll live," Isabelle said.

Bitterlich put on an expression so attentive that it very nearly had its own notebook.

After a moment Isabelle added, "I have a whole head full of distant and opinionated relatives. I suppose the best thing is, I can tell them apart now, keep their hands off the rudder. I'm still me, but I remember them, and when I remember what they did, especially when it comes on me while I'm facing the present world, it's like I'm the one living their lives, thinking them, feeling them. I have to remind myself it's not me, that I didn't really do some of the awful things I remember doing."

She kept turning the hat around in her hand like some sort of talisman. "The nice thing is that my ancestors all used the power of the ancestral chorus, and so they know how the power works and what it can do, which means now I know too. I can either step into the everdream and look at their memories and talk to them, or I can pull them out of the everdream and wear them like a sort of cloak, in which case I gain their skills, but I also have to deal with their personalities."

"That sounds very useful," Bitterlich said.

"Very," Isabelle said. "Although there are some caveats. My mind may know how to do a backflip, but my body doesn't. I'll need to practice."

"That doesn't sound so bad," Bitterlich said.

"It's a shortcut to new skills," Isabelle said, "but with as many lives as I've lived, even the best shortcut won't let me absorb them all. I run the risk of spending the rest of my life trying to become who I was in past lives."

"Is that what your other past lives did?" Bitterlich asked. That might explain why forward-facing Isabelle was afraid of the idea.

"Oh yes. They all worshiped their ancestors, craved the legendary skills, the unbeatable warrior, the ultimate strategist, the most cunning merchant, and the most passionate lover. You name it and there was someone in the past who did it better."

Bitterlich dusted nonexistent lint off his cuffs. "Better mathematician?"

Isabelle snorted. "No, thank the saints. None of them were ever interested in math outside counting coins, soldiers, and bedposts."

"So that's something you can keep for yourself," Bitterlich said.

Isabelle bestowed him a thankful smile. "Yes, but that's only a fraction of it."

"I see what you did there," Bitterlich said.

Isabelle actually laughed, sort of a raspy croak, but he'd take it.

She went on, "When I pull on my ancestral cloak to practice these skills, there's no way to avoid absorbing a bit of the personalities that go with them, becoming a little more like them, and most of them were murderous bastards, swindlers, slavers, rapists, and worse."

"I see," Bitterlich said.

Isabelle raised her spark-hand to make a point. "It gets worse. My most famous ancestor is Primus Maximus, and not only did he have an overpowering personality, but all of his descendants thought of themselves as his rightful successors. They immersed themselves in his memory, absorbed him down to the bone, so there's almost no one back in the menagerie who hasn't been marinated in Maximus, and it's a flavor I don't particularly want running through my own mind. I finally begin to understand why Fenice vendettas are so thorough: because each new generation is subject to the will and the wants of the previous one."

"So you run the risk of becoming one of those crazy old people who stands in the forum yelling at the youth about how things were better in the old days."

"I can think of no worse fate," Isabelle said.

"I don't suppose you can just ignore them—your ancestors, that is."

"I don't know," Isabelle said. "I survived my transformation, but I was still damaged, and I may never heal completely. They can still force themselves into my thoughts at least enough that I can hear them muttering, and the ghost stains haven't stopped entirely. I don't know if rejecting them will make them weaker or stronger. I feel like I have been brought to a banquet where all the food is poisoned."

"Maybe you can nibble at the edge of the feast," Bitterlich said. "The smallest possible doses, build up an immunity to their horseshit."

Isabelle gave him a doubting look. "I'm not sure the metaphor extends that way."

"Maybe not," he said, "but you're not helpless to change your own mind either. If they try to make you cruel, you can practice being kind. Maybe you can even change them. Who says this is a one-way ratchet?"

Isabelle tilted her head at him and one corner of her mouth curved up. "You give me hope, Major. That's a precious gift."

Bitterlich doffed his hat and said, "Thank you, Capitaine." He hesitated. This was not the right time to apologize to her, or unburden himself. She didn't need any more burdens.

"I sense a 'but' in there somewhere," Isabelle said. Her expression was open and inviting.

If this was a bad time to apologize, it was also true that there would never be a better time. It would never be the case that Isabelle didn't have a hundred things on her mind.

"I . . ." Bitterlich said. "I just wanted . . . I need to apologize."

Isabelle looked perplexed. "What for?"

"For lying to you, back on the ship. You asked me what my intentions toward you were and I said I didn't have any." His tongue seemed to have taken on a life of its own and it had decided to babble. "I did have intentions. Ever since we met. I want you. I love you. I don't know how else to say it. You are so true. You have such courage. You are kind, merciful, and brilliant, and I want the curiosity in your eyes, the compassion in your heart."

He stumbled to a halt, and stuffed his hat back on his head. "I sound like an idiot. I'm sorry I hurt you. I'll go now."

"Wait." Isabelle grabbed his arm. Even with her light touch her needle-sharp talons stung his flesh through coat, cloth, and fur.

She shook her head, looking bewildered. "Why? Why did you say no if you wanted to say yes?"

Bitterlich deflated like an empty sack. Some things were harder to say than others. Some wounds bled, but if he didn't speak his shame now, he never would.

"Because I'm not a man," he said, and his voice caught. With an effort he unhitched it and stumbled on like a drunkard down a dark alley. "Eulalie didn't just shadowburn me that night. Her father pinned me with his bloodshadow and she used her power to unman me. She cut all the nerves, gelded me like a bullock, and tossed me in the gutter." The world went blurry and his voice broke, but he refused to fall apart. He must be calm, dignified, civilized, not howling in pain like some beast.

"Nothing to be done about it now, of course," he said with a would-be casualness that wasn't to be. "I mostly just got on with my life."

Isabelle looked appalled, though for him or by him he was in no shape to tell. He was adrift in a fog.

"And you thought I wouldn't want you because of that?" Her eyes shone and her l'Étincelle flared up, pink and purple motes wicking up from her skin along downy feathers and leaping into the air in great clouds, like a firework fountain.

Bitterlich shrank before her anger, even if it was friendly fire. "You said you wanted children of your own someday. You deserve someone who can give them to you."

She arrested his gaze with her own, eyes he could drown in.

"Did you ever think to ask me about that?" Her voice was calm, sad, disappointed.

Bitterlich winced, for if there was one thing Isabelle could not abide it was other people making decisions for her. She'd take advice, even take orders if she'd agreed to, but never without consent beforehand.

"I'm sorry," he said in a very small voice. "I was afraid."

Isabelle let out a long slow breath then patted the bed beside her, gesturing for him to sit. She moved Jean-Claude's hat out of the way.

It occurred to him, in his daze, that she'd let go of Jean-Claude's hat to clutch his arm. Of course, that was only practical. She only had the one solid arm.

But she could have let him walk out.

He sat; the rope weave under the mattress creaked.

"After you've issued your apology, it's up to me to decide whether I accept it. This may take time, and it is a decision with which you should not interfere."

"Ah." Bitterlich eased away. "In that case I should be going."

"Stay," she said, and he subsided.

"You hurt me, you know, ripped my heart right out. I don't think you meant to, but you did. There ought to be some penance for that."

"Whatever you command," he said, but what could he do that would atone for such a grievous wound as he'd inflicted?

"I used to say I didn't understand revenge, but now I have a long line of ancestors who thrived on it. I do understand it now, but I reject it. Suffering is not commutative or conserved."

"Which means?"

"Spreading it around just makes it worse. I don't want to hurt you."

"So . . . what happens next?" Bitterlich asked. It was damnably hard to take direction if she wouldn't give him any.

She said, "A wise man once told me, oh about four hours ago, that fear needs a second chance. He didn't specify, but I'm pretty sure the second try should involve a different plan, on well-chosen ground, with appropriate advice and counsel from trusted allies. Now, speaking as your trusted adviser, I advise you that the alliance you are proposing should be built on trust."

"Am I proposing an alliance?" he asked, hardly daring to hope she was inviting him to try again. "I thought I was flopping about like a fish in a forest."

"Hush. You listen while I talk, before you step on another rake. Understood?"

Bitterlich did his best to look receptive.

"Good. Now, mistakes have been made, but not, I think, with ill intent. Your first mistake is trying to solve the whole problem all at once. This is a big complex relationship you're talking about creating. You have to do it by stages, with participation from both sides. Sometimes you may even have to solve bits of a different equation that don't even seem to be part of the one at the heart. Do you see?"

Bitterlich only nodded, for he did not trust his tongue. Babbling was his enemy.

"Good. Now the first step is apologizing, which you've already done quite profusely, so I think we can check that off the list. Then you should start building up trust, and not just in your would-be partner, but also in yourself. The fact that you don't trust yourself is at least half your problem. So what will your first overture be?"

Panic played a quick tattoo on Bitterlich's chest. He had no idea, but maybe he didn't need one. "As my trusted adviser, what would you suggest?"

A smile tugged at the corners of her mouth. "Hmmm. Would you like to kiss me?"

Bitterlich's eyes bulged; he hadn't been expecting that. Be bold. "Yes," he choked out. "Yes, I very much would."

She leaned in so that her nose was all but touching his, the twinkling lights of her spark swarm dancing around the edges of his vision.

"Ask nicely," she said.

Bitterlich licked his lips. "May I kiss you?"

"You may," she said, and her lips brushed his. He pressed against her, felt her hot breath, and her tongue. He pulled her to him and she returned his embrace with near crushing strength. It occurred to him, in between the fireworks going off in his brain, that although her muscles had shrunken in size, they hadn't withered. Instead they'd merely become more compact, strong as steel cables and with room to grow.

"You do realize I'm an abomination," she gasped when they came up for air. "And quite possibly a lunatic."

"Definitely a lunatic," he said, and stifled her protest with another kiss.

She pulled him down on top of her and got a leg out from under the covers to wrap around him. His loins were dead, but all the rest of him was on fire. He held his weight off her with his elbows, but she flattened him against her chest and got her other leg around him. The squeeze of her thighs was like to drive him mad. This wasn't a good idea. This wasn't a safe place or a good time for this, but he wouldn't have missed it for a roi's ransom or a reine's favor.

He nuzzled her neck and whispered, "May I?"

"Oh yes." She lifted her chin and he kissed her throat. Even through the feather down, his lips found a good spot and her whole body shuddered. Little gasps of pleasure escaped her lips.

Just how far down her magnificent body could he get one "May I?" at a time?

There came a rap at the door.

Bitterlich froze. Isabelle twitched away from him, fear in her eyes.

"One moment," Bitterlich called to the door as Isabelle desperately detached herself and slid back under the covers.

Bitterlich's clothes were all askew. He yanked them as straight as possible, checked to see that Isabelle was in position, and opened the door.

Malgiers stood there, looking stuffed. He saluted in much the same way a wind-up soldier might. "Major, I'm sorry to disturb"—he took note of comatose Isabelle—"whatever you were doing."

"Why are you here?" Bitterlich said, drawing on the armor of command.

Malgiers went back to looking like a bit of taxidermy. "I have word from Comtesse Impervia. In fact, I'm talking to her now. She wants to talk to you. I am to think of myself as a speaking tube, only without the annoying hollow echo."

"Come in," Bitterlich said, and shut the door behind him. Malgiers was not yet in on the secret of Isabelle's recovery. Superficially, Malgiers always seemed slightly out of his depth, but he'd risen to every task Bitterlich had given him like a natural aide-de-camp. Perhaps what he really needed was a bit more trust and responsibility.

"Malgiers," he said. "It's no doubt plain to you that this expedition has become fraught with politics and intrigue. You've done well for me so far, but I'm going to need more from you, including the keeping of secrets."

Malgiers looked rather pale for a man with a dusky complexion. "Comtesse Impervia has already informed me that if I breathe even one word of our conversations to anyone that she will personally fillet me with a dull knife."

"The comtesse is quite colorful with her language," Bitterlich said. "But if she didn't trust your discretion she would never have used your services no matter how horrible the threat." This wasn't strictly true; Impervia used the best tools she had to hand, even if what she had to work with was less than ideal, but that didn't mean Malgiers couldn't grow in her esteem. All he had to do was prove trustworthy.

Bitterlich said, "My point being is that I trust that nothing you are about to learn gets repeated to anyone except Impervia. Can you swear to that?"

"Yes, Major," Malgiers said. "I survived at home by being, well, unobtrusive."

Bitterlich was by no means sure bringing Malgiers into the center of their little secret society was safe, but then no course of action was.

"Isabelle," Bitterlich said, "this will be a lot easier if you can talk to Impervia directly."

Isabelle's eyes opened and she said, "Or at least at one less remove." If she distrusted being thus exposed, her expression gave no sign of it.

Malgiers's expression brightened and he saluted. "Capitaine, thank the saints you're awake."

"Either that or the rest of the world has joined me in a fever dream," she said. "What does Comtesse Impervia have to say to us?"

"Uh, she wants to know what's taking so long for Bitterlich to say something useful. Or is he just hacking up a hairball?"

Bitterlich discreetly removed a bit of down from his tongue.

"Security protocols," Isabelle said. "Please tell her that I am en route to being recovered and to proceed with her briefing."

"Ah. She says it's about time you stopped malingering. Uh, is she this rude to everyone?"

"Only people she likes," Bitterlich said. "She's painfully polite to people she hates."

Malgiers said, "I see. Impervia thanks Major Bitterlich for his most proper report. She also says that she has lately increased her counterintelligence pressure on the Maze of Eyes's network within Rocher Royale and found it in unexpected disarray. Apparently several quiet but important Skaladin agents have been recently killed."

"Which agents?" Bitterlich asked. It was an odd piece of information to pass downstream, but Impervia only sent facts she wanted him to follow up on.

She called them "Dogsbody, Whistler, and Milk. Does that mean anything to you?"

A cold trickle ran down Bitterlich's spine and made his whiskers itch and twitch. "It means someone has crippled the tyrant's spy network in Rocher Royale."

"Would you like to unpack that?" Isabelle asked.

"Dogsbody, Whistler, and Milk were our code names for the tyrant's spy handlers in Rocher Royale. They were the ones who passed information back to Skaladin."

"So it's a good thing they're gone?" Malgiers asked uncertainly.

"Not at all," Bitterlich said. "We never moved on them because it was far better to know who they were and to feed them the information we wanted them to have. This is a blow as much against Impervia's network as the Maze of Eyes's. Did she say who killed them? Or when?"

"She says the last time her people saw any of them alive was a red month ago." That was the length of time it took the red moon Threin to make its orbital circuit. "That was before we left Rocher Royale."

"Sacred saints," Isabelle muttered, "Hasdrubal killed them."

"What makes you think that?" Bitterlich asked.

"A few things," Isabelle said. "If Impervia's people didn't do it, who else could have? As a premier agent of the Maze of Eyes, Hasdrubal would have had access to all three of them. That gives him opportunity."

"What about motive?" Bitterlich asked.

Isabelle spoke more carefully, as if picking up finer threads. "We believe the tyrant sent Hasdrubal to help Lael overthrow Grand Leon. It must have seemed like a very economical way to disrupt l'Empire. But the first time I met him, Hasdrubal told me that Lael had rescued him from a cruel master. That could have just been a ruse, but what if it wasn't? What if Lael really did set him free from the tyrant's influence?"

"So let's says he's gone rogue," Bitterlich said. "He knows he's being watched, so he kills the spy marshals to make a break, but a break to where and for what purpose?"

"Consider the consequences and work backwards," Isabelle said. "He kills the handlers and the Maze of Eyes suddenly looses all contact with its operations in Rocher Royale. Then very soon thereafter the whole Hoary Fleet starts charging toward the City of Gears. Our fleet believes it's chasing a Skaladin spy with a stolen relic, but the tyrant doesn't know that. All he sees is an enemy fleet winging its way toward his capital, and his spy handlers, the people who might have warned him, are all dead. To the tyrant, this looks like an invasion."

With a sudden groan like he'd been punched in the gut, Malgiers doubled over. His olive complexion went even paler and his eyes bulged.

"Oh saints!" he said, his hand grasping at the air. His bloodshadow rippled and darkened as if a great shadow had passed over it. Then just as abruptly the shadow departed and he was left standing with his hands on his knees, sweating and looking bewildered.

"It's gone," he said. He looked up at Bitterlich and said, "Sir, my bloodhollow is gone. It felt like . . . I swear something took it, just ripped it away from me. I tried to hold on but it was too fast, like a falcon snatching away a rabbit from a snare."

"That sounds like what happened to Sireen's bloodhollow," Isabelle said. "Someone hollowjacked it."

Worry rumbled in Bitterlich's mind like the thump of distant drums. "Unless we are to believe that Hasdrubal or his agent in Rocher Royale just now found out we have been communicating with Impervia by way of Malgiers's bloodhollow, we must assume they've been listening to everything we've said. They now know that Isabelle is not dead or dying. She's still in the game."

"How did this become about me?" Isabelle asked. "I'm not l'Empire. Vrain has the *Thunderclap*."

"Yes, and Vrain is a competent capitaine, a scion of the nobility, born and raised for duty, with honor to uphold and glory to win. Hasdrubal will play him like a fiddle. You, by way of contrast, have been known to upend entire kingdoms and change the course of successions to get your way."

"A reputation I could happily live without," Isabelle grumbled.

Bitterlich snorted. "So that's what a blind spot looks like."

Isabelle narrowed her eyes at him. "What's that supposed to mean?"

Bitterlich decided that discretion was probably the better part of valor and redirected the conversation. "It means that we can no longer consider this place safe. I'd bet my stripes and spots word is even now being delivered to Commandant Turenne that you are awake and recovering, which means the recall letter will be on its way, along with whatever precautions he deems necessary to ensure compliance: an honor guard, for example."

Bitterlich turned to Malgiers. "Lieutenant, find Marie and Djordji. Tell them we're decamping under fire, and they need to collect Rebecca. Then have the men assemble at the docks, muskets loaded, swords loose, but look casual."

Malgiers saluted and hurried off.

Isabelle rolled stiffly out of bed. "I'm glad you have a plan. Mind telling me what it is?"

"We're going to steal the brig."

"The one we just shot full of holes? Is it even skyworthy?"

"It hasn't fallen out of the sky yet, and I've had the shipwright aboard making repairs in order to present it to the prize board. It's the only ship in dock right now. Plus, it comes with its own crew, none of whom want to be hanged for piracy."

"And who will turn on us at the first possible chance," Isabelle said. "I don't fancy being murdered in my sleep."

"That's why we're going to collect their capitaine. I'm hoping to make a bargain with her to drop us at a neutral port. Also, she'll be our hostage against the crew's good behavior."

"This is a fantastically bad plan." Isabelle said, and laughed. "Jean-Claude will be sorry he missed it."

On an instant's reflection Bitterlich decided to take that as a compliment.

Isabelle hauled her sky chest from under the bed. "There are a few things in here I need."

Bitterlich considered that the whole of her material life, including some irreplaceable quondam artifacts, were in that trunk, and hoisted the whole thing in one hand.

"No need to choose," he said.

Isabelle's eyes rounded in apparent appreciation. He was so used to striving to be normal, to appear safe to people who feared him, that he rarely made such a display of his strength, but now was not the time for that sort of subtlety.

"Actually, I do need to choose clothes," she said. "We'll be a lot less conspicuous if I'm not lurching around in my unmentionables."

"Ah, yes." Bitterlich put the trunk on the bed and Isabelle fished through it, pulling on a skirt, a blouse, and a mantle with a cowl. Shoes were out of the question, considering her toe talons.

In the end she was only inconspicuous by Isabelle's standards. Being taller than most men, barefoot, surrounded by a cloud of pink and purple embers and possessed of a spark-arm, she still stood out like a parrot in a convention of crows, but at least she didn't look like someone who'd been dug up from the grave.

"Lead on," she said, and they slipped into the hallway.

CHAPTER
Twenty-One

Getting into the depot's stockade wasn't hard. There was a postern door made of heavy wood with a stout lock that gave way instantly to Isabelle's l'Étincelle. Bitterlich made an unconscious heap of the one guard they encountered.

Isabelle opened the door to the small, dark, tilted cell where Capitaine Similce was being held. The Skaladin capitaine rose to meet her, her eyes wary, her expression set, her body balanced, under stress but not coiled to spring.

Captivity had not been kind to her. Her eyes were sunken but still held a banked fire. Her skin was the washed-out gray of someone recently shadow-burned. She was not much older than Isabelle but her face might have been eighty for the erosion of her features.

That's the sort of face that wants revenge, Primus whispered. *That gives you a hold on her.*

Like grabbing a hot iron, no doubt, Isabelle replied. She splashed him back into the everdream. Yet the ghost was right. A wounded person might easily lust for revenge, or be goaded into it, but if Similce hadn't already chosen that path for herself, Isabelle wouldn't point it out to her. Jean-Claude said it best: *Revenge is a knife fight in a coffin.*

Isabelle eased into the cell, and Bitterlich came in after her, dragging the unconscious guard.

"What do you want, *hespta*?" Similce said. From the tone alone Isabelle knew it was an insult. One of her past lives whispered, *whelp.*

Excitement intruded upon Isabelle's mind. All she had to do was pull on the ancestral cloak and she could speak Skaladin. Unfortunately, Forenzio, the miscreant who possessed that skill, had been a slaver, trading flesh and souls up and down the Forbidden Coast, a man who delighted in cruelty. She did not need him staining her mind. Yet she could not live in fear of the mob, either. If Bitterlich was right, she might rehabilitate them, make them her honor guard.

Plus, she needed all the speed she could get. Soon Commandant Turenne must discover her missing, and the hunt would be on. Isabelle's own fear was already a mist in her mind, casting doubt on the source of shadows and sounds.

She pulled Forenzio forward, wrapped his memory around her mind. It was like fitting into someone else's clothes.

In Skaladin she said, "Is that any way to greet your rescuer?"

Similce looked surprised, but only briefly. "You are the one who put me in here, killed my crew, stole my ship, and tried to kill me. Now you say you are going to rescue me. You will forgive me if I think you a liar, soulless Breakerborn."

There was plenty of anger to work with here, rage to exploit.

No. Isabelle clamped down hard on the slaver. *We don't hurt people if we can help it.*

Isabelle marshaled her words and inspected them to make sure no traitors had slipped in. "I would point out that your crew are being treated as prisoners of war, their hurts tended and their needs met, and your ship is being repaired."

That took Similce aback. Her eyes glinted and her cheeks showed a bit of color.

Isabelle went on, "We, like you, wish to be quit of this skyland. We can get you to your ship and slip the harbor without being shot from the sky. In return all we ask is to be delivered to a neutral port, at which point you would be free to go and take your ship with you."

Similce's eyes narrowed. "So what you are saying is you need me more than I need you. If my crew are prisoners of war, the tyrant will claim us, and I need give you nothing."

Isabelle's irritation rose at this petty bluff. Everything about the brig and its crew suggested they were outcasts and unlikely to be aided. Even so, having staked out that position, Similce was likely to stick to it. Best for Isabelle to go around.

Isabelle said, "Perhaps you are right. Maybe you think Hasdrubal will bring you home in triumph, but even if the tyrant ransoms you, that still means you lose your ship. It also means you choose to sit in this hole and leave your men in cages for months on end when you had the chance to set them free. Now, will you accept my bargain or not?"

From outside the alarm bell sounded. She'd been missed.

"Time's up," Bitterlich said.

Similce scowled, but shifted. "To a neutral port of my choosing."

"To a neutral port upon which we can both agree," Isabelle said, and extended her taloned hand, palm out and open in the Skaladin way of closing a deal. "Offered in truth."

The line of Similce's mouth nearly buckled under some internal pressure. "The soulless cannot make contracts."

"Isabelle," Bitterlich said. "We need to go."

Isabelle said, "Oh, the soulless make contracts all the time. I've traded . . . merchandise all along the Forbidden Coast, in Hetchiva and Bu'el, and a hundred ports without names." Indeed, Forenzio-Isabelle knew of several ports where she could get a good price for Similce and her crew.

No, curse you. Isabelle thwarted Forenzio's impulse and went on, "My kind make contracts with your kind, it's just that the magistrates won't recognize our claims in court, if we were ever fool enough to take such claims before the law. Now I am done arguing. Are you?"

Similce made a face as if she were being asked to eat a dung worm still dripping from the cesspit, but held up her palm and said, "Accepted in trust."

"Let's move!" Bitterlich whispered.

Isabelle touched her fingers to her forehead and Similce mimicked the gesture. Bending Similce to her will once would make her more tractable later on.

No. Isabelle shucked off Forenzio's cloak, and her next breath of air hit her lungs like she'd just stepped out of a dusty coal mine into spring air.

Still the slaver left ash on her soul, stains that would be a long time coming out. Shepherds were not cruel to sheep because they did not have to prove to themselves that they were better than their livestock. Slavers needed constant proof and found it in wickedness of all sorts.

The three of them stepped out of the cell, and locked the guardsman in.

The alarm bell sounded again. The escapees hurried to the end of the corridor and slipped out the service door.

They emerged into a dark, cold, and windy evening. The depot had turned out to be even bleaker than Isabelle had imagined, just rank upon rank of low buildings with canted walls devoid of any decoration. She felt rather like a mouse in an unkempt graveyard, scuttling amongst the mounds.

The bell rang again. Reason suggested that most of the people responding to the alarm still didn't know what it was about—Isabelle's little band could still make it to the ship—but fear cared little for logic. Her ears sifted the wind for any shouts of excitement or outrage that would mean the hunt had fallen upon them.

Bitterlich hefted one end of Isabelle's crate, which they'd left by the door, and had Similce take the other. He could have carried the whole thing by himself, but this kept Similce occupied and attached to the group. He led them down the alley between warehouses on the way to the harbor. The stone slab road was pitched more than twenty degrees to the right.

The trio did not creep or sneak or attempt to dart from shadow to shadow, but simply made themselves as unremarkable as possible as they hustled toward the docks. Isabelle carried an alchemical lantern in her spark-hand, the device turned up brighter than her ember swarm, the best way to hide one light being to drown it in another.

From all over the depot, men swarmed toward the central square. Anyone not having an assigned emergency-duty post would assemble there. Fortunately, the base personnel were mostly intent on getting to where they were supposed to be. Only a few people even took note of Isabelle's group, and if they noticed anything unusual, it did not give them pause.

They reached what passed for the depot's main street, a wider lane that divided the ranks of warehouses in half. On the other side was a straight run to the docks.

Isabelle looked down the street to the square just as a large man with a neck like a bull mounted the reviewing stand. Already there under the flagpole stood a thin figure in a long coat, puffing a pipe.

"Djordji?" What in all ten thousand little Torments was he doing?

Isabelle kept walking, Djordji and Bull Neck exchanged words, too distant and distorted for Isabelle to hear.

Bitterlich had no such trouble. His expression became very fixed, his whiskers twitching forward and a strangled snigger echoing out through his nose.

"What'd he say?" Isabelle asked.

They reached the far corner, and Bitterlich gave a snort that was nearly a sneeze. "Oh saints. That was the commandant, he was just asking Djordji why he'd sounded the alarm, and Djordji said, 'I checks the logs, and I sees its a dog's age afore this place has a proper fire drill.'"

Isabelle's mouth fell open in astonishment. "He's mad." Sounding a false alarm without the base commander's permission would get anyone else whipped, but Turenne was hoping for Djordji's help in promoting his career, and was likely to be given all the leeway he could ask for.

Jean-Claude had once said, *An Old Hand's power is based on the "because they can get away with it" principle.*

Grateful for this spanner in the enemy's gears, Isabelle and her crew hurried to the end of the row, where it gave out onto the dock. Stevedores carrying heavy bundles hurried back and forth along the pier at which the Skaladin brig was tied, and a crane swung slowly outward with a huge pallet of goods while Bitterlich's marines stood guard.

Whose doing was this? Isabelle was amazed with her friends' ingenuity and efficiency. And they were doing this for her, not for any greater purpose. She didn't even have a grand goal toward which she could lead them. She hoped to locate Jean-Claude somewhere in the vast sky, but then what? She did not have the resources to make a play for the Craton Auroborea. She was in no position to hunt down Hasdrubal.

Part of her wanted to dig in her heels and yell, "Stop!" There was no reason for them all to make themselves criminals and outcasts. But there was another part of her, so quiet and eager, that wanted nothing more than to grab the west wind by its tail and see how far it would take her.

Which if any of these thoughts were her own? It would be easy for one of her past selves to slip an unsolicited urge into her head, especially in moments of confusion when she had the least time to stop and think about it.

She hurried up the gangway. Marie stepped out from behind a pile of crates. She glowed in the gathering light like a spirit of the moon. "Welcome aboard, Capitaine."

"I am the capitaine of this ship," Similce said in la Langue. "The deal was that I am to transport you to a neutral port."

"And then I give you your ship back, with all goodwill," Isabelle said. "Until then I am capitaine and you are my lieutenant."

Marie looked up at Isabelle and deployed her perfect deadpan, "I see you've managed to make things complicated again."

Isabelle ignored this jibe. "Where's Rebecca?"

Marie gestured skyward. "Keeping watch on Djordji."

"Good," Isabelle said, relieved. Up in the night sky, she'd be almost impossible to see.

"Malgiers is in the warehouse keeping the supplies coming."

"Well done," Isabelle said. "Carry on." She followed Bitterlich and Similce belowdecks to the cells, where a pair of marines guarded the prisoners in their makeshift holds. Bitterlich opened the first cage and said, "Lieutenant, if you will explain the situation to your men."

Similce glanced up at Isabelle with an expression that suggested she was contemplating rash action, but she squared her shoulders, lifted her chin, and said in Skaladin, "My friends, I have struck a deal with the heretics . . ."

Similce did not bother to hide her contempt for the Célestials, but neither did she say anything that suggested mutiny. There would be plenty of time for that later, Isabelle suspected. Right now Similce wanted to escape this skyland every bit as much as Isabelle did, and her men hurried to make the ship ready to sail.

Out in the square, the bell sounded an all-clear. Base personnel would be heading back to their regular duties. Eventually someone would notice the brig getting ready to sail or Turenne would find Isabelle gone and that bell would sound again, but human nature being what it was, everyone would be slower to react the second time around.

"We need to open the magazine," Similce said.

Isabelle hesitated. The last thing she wanted was to start a firefight with the base, but there was no point in having guns she couldn't use.

She glanced at Bitterlich, who nodded ever so slightly, then said, "Very well, but you will not fire without my permission. Agreed?"

It was Similce's turn to pause. "I did not agree to die without fighting back."

"Noted, but I'm not starting a fight if I can help it."

Similce said, "Agreed."

Isabelle left Bitterlich to open the powder magazine and keep an eye on Similce. She ascended to the quarterdeck and found Marie keeping order there.

"How far along are we on the supplies?" Isabelle asked.

"They unloaded almost everything in order to do repairs," Marie said. "Malgiers says we'd need about eight hours to get a full load. On the plus side we've got plenty of lumber."

Isabelle's nerves stretched a little tighter. They would be better off if they could launch before the alarm went up, but that would do them no good if they starved before they reached a port. It did not help that the wind had died.

She turned her gaze to the base, all the people returning to their normal routine. Who would be the first to notice all the unusual activity around the brig?

Djordji appeared from the same alley down which Isabelle had come, walking casually as if nothing was amiss. Isabelle scanned the sky for Rebecca.

The alarm bell sounded again, a frantic arrhythmic bonging as if the rope were being pulled by an irate gorilla.

Out on the review stand stood Commandant Turenne, shouting at the backs of stragglers leaving the square. Isabelle could not make out his words, but his outrage rang through.

"That's done it," Marie said in her ghostly voice.

Isabelle turned to the crew. "All hands to your stations. Prepare to loft!"

The stevedores aboard tossed their final loads in a pile and made for the gangways. Djordji, who had been raised on a clan balloon, hopped the gap between dock and ship and monkey-climbed the deadeyes as if that were the standard method of boarding. Malgiers bolted from the warehouse directly opposite the ship, running for the gangway as if the Breaker's Torments nipped his heels.

"Go, go, go!" he shouted.

A squad of base marines erupted from the warehouse doors behind him. At their head ran a Sanguinaire lieutenant with a battle lantern who set his bloodshadow flying after Malgiers.

Malgiers stumbled, his bloodshadow tangling with the marine's. Isabelle turned to Marie and her triple brace of pistols. "Can you hit that Sanguinaire from here?"

"A long gun would be better," Marie said, but drew her pistols.

With a whoosh and a flash, a great serpent swooped from the sky and spat a bright sheet of blue-and-green flame at the marines, who shrieked and leapt back. The fire lit the Sanguinaire's bloodshadow as if it were made of oil. He howled and fell, rolling back and forth to try to put it out.

"Good girl, Rebecca," Marie said.

Malgiers regained his feet and sprinted for the ship. Rebecca slithered skyward. The marines broke formation in confusion, some aiming muskets at Rebecca, but the flaming metal barrels of the front rank's weapons turned ghostly and fell right through their wooden stocks to clatter on the cobblestones. The sergeant bellowed at the rest. They leveled muskets at Malgiers and pulled triggers.

A great dark shape bore Malgiers to the ground. It resolved into a creature that looked like a cross between a bear and a turtle: Bitterlich. The muskets barked. Bullets thudded into the brig's wooden stays and rattled off the stone pier. Several musket balls ricocheted off Bitterlich's chimera, who then hoisted Malgiers and galloped toward the ship, becoming longer and leaner until he vaulted clean over the rail and landed as a mountain cat, dropping the stunned lieutenant on the deck.

"Saints preserve," Malgiers gasped.

Similce erupted from belowdecks and yelled in Skaladin, "Cast off!"

With a great lurch, the brig came away from the dock. Slowly, ever so slowly, the ship drifted away from the shore, wafted outward by warmer air rising along the skyland's turvy face and welling up into the cooling night.

The base marines reloaded and fired again, but the ship had risen above their level and the bulwarks absorbed their fire. The Sanguinaire officer regained his feet. Half his body was burned black from Rebecca's ghostfire, but he turned his battle lantern up as bright as day and hurled his bloodshadow at the hull. Creepers of crimson shadow wriggled over the bulwarks and flowed onto the deck, blindly seeking human shadows to gnaw. Malgiers lit his own lamp and beat them back. A telegraph tower flashed over the headquarters on shore and was answered by the shore batteries on the horns of the harbor.

"I hope the Breaker's given you some way of dealing with the harbor guns," Similce shouted over the clatter of muskets. "Those are giant killers."

"Shore guns has crews," Djordji said, joining their conclave. "We has sorcerers who can get to them."

More troops arrived dockside. Squads of marines piled into harbor skiffs. They unshipped their feather oars and pulled into open air. Still more soldiers rolled up with a gun carriage and wheeled it into position. Isabelle glanced up at the pennon dangling from the topmast, willing it to catch wind.

"More pressure to the chamber!" Similce shouted, and the boatswain carried the message down to the keelmaster. Higher up there was a better chance of wind if they didn't drift over land and crash.

Rarely had Isabelle felt so useless, so much like a damned passenger. She hated fighting and violence of all kinds, but she did not appreciate being a sitting duck either. Her ancestral chorus yammered at her with suggestions, and Primus Maximus loomed like a shadow at the edge of her vision. *Downing those skiffs will buy us time.*

No. Isabelle splashed Maximus, but could not banish him completely. Those marines were her countrymen, misled by a cabal of traitors.

They offer you no such mercy, Primus pointed out. *Nor will they offer it to any of your friends. Your inaction betrays those whom you love most.*

Primus's words carried with them the fog of doubt. The skiffs scudded closer. Marines readied grapnel guns. What sense did it make to wait until they came aboard to repel them? She risked the death of her own for nothing.

Shoot them down.

No. There had to be a better way. Isabelle rushed to the rail opposite the incoming fire. In the distance on the horns of the bay, the great shadowpults that were part of the shore batteries were lighting up. Their carminite reflectors magnified the power of a bloodshadow many times over so they could reach out nearly a kilometer and peel ships like grapes. The clouds drifted listlessly high overhead, portending no good wind to be had by climbing.

If not up, down. Isabelle peered through the turvy rigging, still naked of sail. Down there was the aetheric vortex created by the upwelling aether deflecting around the skyland. One could not see it with the naked eye, but it had to be there. The reason Joubert's Folly wobbled was that the aethercoral cone underneath the skyland was unusually flat and shallow, and the deflection very strong.

Isabelle pictured the forces in her mind, then turned and shouted to Similce, "Capitaine. We need to dive!"

Similce looked at her like she was mad. "There's no wind down there."

"No wind, but there is aether current. Lots of it. This rock is flat as a griddle cake and it deflects the aether at a really high angle. If we can get the keel athwart the flow, it will shoot us out from under the rim."

"That's insane. We'll get scraped on the skyland's belly."

"It's not insane, it's algebra. Even if we catch a breeze up here, do you think we're going to make it past those shore guns?"

A half dozen reports boomed off the landward side and grapnel hooks came shooting over the rail. Djordji and Marie flicked several back over before they could find purchase, but several more caught and the marines hauled the skiff closer. Bitterlich shouted for Rebecca, who spat fire at the hooks, turning two of them ghostly. They slipped through the wood as if it was no longer there.

Isabelle said to Similce, "Dive." She raced across the deck. She reached for the last grapnel with her spark-hand, intending to bend it out of the way, but Primus bulged into her awareness. Her right hand flashed down, talons extended. The sorcerous weapons sliced through metal and wood like they were soft bread. Thin slices of railing fell away. The skiff drifted off, unmoored.

Isabelle shoved back against Primus, slamming him through the breach. *Don't you ever—*

You are a Fenice, he roared. *It's time you started acting like one. Listen to your elders. I have survived more battles than you will ever see. Heed me and I will lead you to victory.*

Just like you led the Kindly Crusade to victory, Isabelle retorted. *As I recall, that is the greatest military disaster in history.*

I was betrayed, Primus insisted. *We stood on the very threshold of conquest.*

Yes, you were betrayed, Isabelle said. *And you were also betrayed in Forenzio's life, and Falconé's, and Elia's. Do you think it is coincidence that you are betrayed in every lifetime? The only common factor is you.*

Isabelle shoved him back into the recesses of memory. He would be back. He was part of every life she had absorbed, which made him impossible to contain.

"Gas the keel!" Similce shouted. "All hands prepare to dive. Dive. Dive!"

Isabelle faced ashore just as the carriage gunners cocked the flintlocks on their cannons. Similce stood exposed at the helm. Isabelle bore her to the deck just as the cannons roared, spitting fire and smoke and grapeshot. Iron shot took out several spokes of the ship's wheel. Several aeronauts screamed.

The ship shuddered and began to descend. Isabelle sank her talons into the rail and hung on as the weight left her feet. Marie grabbed Djordji and clung to the mast.

Djordji was splattered in red. He wasn't moving.

The brig fell past the skiff, past the level of the docks. Cannonballs flew by overhead.

Down and down fell the brig, the aethercoral cliff wall streaming by. Far below, the choking Miasma rushed up to meet them.

Suddenly there was no cliff wall. They'd slipped below the skyland. It hovered above them like a great stone ceiling.

"Heel us to port and charge the keel!" Isabelle shouted over the whistling wind of their descent. Similce repeated the order, and cursed all soulless sorcerers. The ship rolled to port, wood and rope groaning under the strain. Unsecured supplies slid across the deck and smashed into the bulwarks. Malgiers clung to the foot of the mast.

The ship's fall slowed. Every stout board bent around the aetherkeel's cradle as the aetheric current grabbed it.

The brig slowed, stopped, and began to rise. The aetherflow deflecting around the skyland changed direction, the push up became a push sideways and the brig flowed along with it. Up toward the skyland they rose but also out toward its edge. The upside-down forest of aethercoral cones raced by above them, a ceiling of stalactites getting closer and closer like down-thrust spears even as the inverted horizon grew wider before them.

Isabelle's heart raced so fast that she thought it might leap out of her chest. The jagged roof was less than a cable away. Half a cable. Two long stakes of aethercoral jutted down like grasping claws ahead of them. There was no way to steer.

With an almighty crash, the coral spikes sheared off the top spars. Taut ropes snapped. The whole ship quaked. Isabelle sank her toe talons into the deck to keep from falling. The whole world seemed to lurch and suddenly there was sky overhead. Stars winking in the darkness as night captured the world in its embrace.

Isabelle hauled herself up and looked around. They'd come up on the side of Joubert's Folly opposite the harbor. The coastal ridge was tilted up so they could still see the turvy side of the skyland, but they were completely out of sight of the base. Turenne would be some time figuring out what happened to them even if he didn't assume they'd plummeted into the Gloom.

The aeronauts, finding themselves in calm skies and with no enemies in sight, scrambled to their feet and let out a great cheer, all except Similce, who looked as wooden as the mast.

"Heel her up!" Similce shouted. "Level the ballast. Steady the keel! Get that spar down."

The aeronauts abandoned their celebration and got to work setting the ship aright. Everything about her posture thrummed with fury, like a pressure vessel on the verge of explosion. Isabelle could almost hear her rivets groaning.

She's dangerous, Lissa whispered. *She's married to this crew and she sees you as the other woman.*

Isabelle feared the ghost was right.

"Surgeon." Marie raised her voice. It was loud but lacking human urgency. Djordji lay in a smear of blood, clutching his side. Marie knelt beside him, holding his shoulders.

"Surgeon!" Isabelle shouted, and raced to Marie's side.

The surgeon appeared from belowdecks. He was a grizzled man with a burn scar on his chin that made it look like he'd put his beard on sideways. "Let me see."

"Damned ricochet," Djordji wheezed, his face white and his lips pale. "It skips off the rail and cracks my rib."

"Cracked? You mean shattered," the surgeon said, peering at the wound. "Blasted it to bits. There's pieces of it . . . Torments. Get him up on the table and get me some light!"

A gang of sailors slipped a canvas under Djordji and hustled him to the surgeon's bay belowdecks, with Marie and Isabelle in tow.

The surgeon got Djordji on the table just as the Old Hand was overtaken by a coughing fit. Fresh blood spilled from the wound, and black matter sprayed from his mouth. The surgeon cursed.

Horror filled Isabelle. Had the bullet broken up? How deep did the bone shards go? The surgeon tore his coat and shirt off. They were leather and silk as most fighters wore, materials that held together and didn't easily get caught in wounds.

The surgeon called for a knife and men to hold Djordji down. They gave Djordji a belt to bite on and then pulled back the edges of the wound to get a better look.

Djordji bucked and screamed into the leather belt.

"Do you have any poppy milk?" Marie asked.

"Cursed Célestials took my stores," the surgeon snapped. "Now, be quiet."

Djordji whined as the surgeon probed the bone, and teased out yellow-white slivers. Isabelle had seen such wounds before, horrible, hot, and swollen. Repairing them was like trying to unmake sausage.

Isabelle snaked her arm around Marie's shoulder and pulled her tight for comfort. Marie leaned into the embrace.

The surgeon was still working when Similce came up behind Isabelle and said, "Soulless, the ship is ready to get under way. Now we must agree on our destination. The closest neutral port is San Fortunado."

Isabelle searched her memory, but neither she nor any of her ancestors had heard of it.

"No," Djordji coughed from the table. "Fortunado is a slave port."

Isabelle was astonished that Djordji had the presence of mind to heed his surroundings during the surgery, much less respond.

Similce frowned and said, "Around here every neutral port is a black one: they trade in slaves, contraband, vice, and other people's secrets."

"Not all," Djordji whispered. "Marie. Pouch. Little wooden box. Give it to Isabelle."

Marie detached herself from Isabelle, rummaged through Djordji's pouch, and handed Isabelle a flat box of polished wood about the size of her palm. It looked like the sort of thing someone with more money than sense would store specialty toothpicks in. She flipped it open and found therein a needle of chartstone, black as onyx and salted with silver grit.

"Where?" Isabelle asked. It wasn't the *Conquest* shard; that was made of bone.

"Flotsam," he said.

Similce's eyes rounded. "The Gyrine city? And you complain to me about black ports?"

"Not a black port," Djordji said. "A refuge for Gyrine."

"Where no one else is allowed," Similce said. "Where stolen cargos are the only kind? Where kidnapped children go?"

"You makes port," Djordji wheezed. "Under Tall Clouds protection."

The surgeon said, "This is not the time for talk."

Djordji was not likely to give up the argument, so Isabelle said, "Let's discuss this in the chartroom, see if Flotsam is even close." The vagabond city was said to move about the sky. It wouldn't do them any good if it was down at the equator.

Marie appeared at her side, solving the problem of who she should take with her to discourage Similce from trying anything rash.

Marie accompanied them to the chartroom. Similce gave her a wary look. Marie's expressionless porcelain-doll face and unnerving stillness made people leery. Even men who would scoff at the idea that she might be a top-notch fighter gave her creepiness a wide berth.

Similce opened the orrery's sympathetic matrix. From somewhere up her sleeve she produced a tightly rolled bundle of chartstone needles and began slotting them into the hyperbaric chambers.

"Where did you hide those?" Isabelle asked.

"Someplace a roll of needles should never go," Similce said with the edge of a woman trying not to snarl, then she rounded on Isabelle. "Dropping us out of the sky was a cursed foolish thing to do. Could have broke the keel or smashed us to flinders on the aethercoral."

"It was either that or face the shore guns and the shadowpults," Isabelle said. "We'd have been sitting ducks. I prefer to go where my enemies aren't."

"I figured that about you," Similce said. "You're one of them. Don't mind long odds because you think you're more clever than the Builder, so you try one maggot-headed stunt after another, and you get away with it, right up until you don't and you manage to get everyone around you killed."

Marie said, "You sound like you speak from experience."

"You should have let me open fire on that longboat," Similce said.

"I won't open fire on my countrymen unless I have no other choice," Isabelle said.

Similce's dusky face turned red with anger. "Are you the capitaine of this ship, or aren't you? Because if you're capitaine of *this* ship then *your* sailors deserve better than to be made targets because you're too squeamish to defend them."

Similce's accusation hit Isabelle like a spear to the gut. Even if she didn't quite think of the Skaladin aeronauts as her men, she'd still let Djordji get injured.

Isabelle shook out her stunned tongue. "You are correct. I thought we could get away without killing anyone. I was wrong to make that my priority. Thank you for pointing it out."

Similce's face still bloomed red, but her anger stumbled in the absence of any resistance. "You are wise to listen . . . and I must thank you for saving my life."

"You are most welcome," Isabelle said.

Similce returned her attention to the orrery. "Let's have Flotsam's stone."

"Let's see what you already have, first." Isabelle said. With no pictorial vaporgrams to go by she'd have no way to tell one blip in the tank from another without a before and after.

Similce grunted and slammed the matrix shut, turned the orrery's main valve, and pressurized the sympathetic chamber. When it was charged she sparked it to life with a galvanic inducer. Waves of green light rippled through the tank and caught on scores of motes of light. It wasn't immediately obvious what each blip represented.

"The big glow bug in the middle is the *Saint Asne*, us," Similce said. "The rest are skylands familiar to me."

Isabelle glanced to Marie, who nodded; she'd memorized the pattern.

Isabelle handed over Djordji's chartstone. Similce discharged the tank, put the Flotsam stone in the matrix, and charged it up again.

"No telling where it will be," Similce said. "We've only got about a week of supply, and I'll not go hungry chasing phantoms."

Yet when she sparked the orrery to life, there was a new blip that there hadn't been before. It was very nearly the closest thing to them.

"Three days out," Similce said with huff of disbelief. "It's a cursed sort of luck you have, Soulless."

"You agree, then?" Isabelle said.

"The deal was a neutral port, not one friendly to you," Similce said.

"As if all these other ports aren't friendly to you," Isabelle said.

Marie stepped to the fore. "Lieutenant, as you pointed out, you have only limited supplies and no trade goods. If you want to keep flying you need more of both, but you'll have no leverage if you try to bargain for work, and likely you would find yourself indebted to any employer who would hire you."

"That doesn't change at Flotsam," Similce said.

"Except that it does. The Gyrine take care of their own. Djordji has been sending money home for decades. His clan will fill this ship to bursting without anybody getting hurt."

Isabelle noted that Marie tactfully left out the possibility that Similce's plans included betraying Isabelle's crew and selling them for slaves or turning them over for a bounty.

"If he lives," Similce said.

Marie said, "Even if he dies, the Tall Clouds will honor me as his daughter and heir."

"You're not Gyrine," Similce said.

"The Gyrine do not see lineage as a matter of birth, but of choice. Djordji has been everything to me a father should be. I'm honored to join his clan. I will carry on his memory, and I will sing his endsong."

"And what will this do for you?" Isabelle asked.

Marie said, "It gives me a line of retreat, if ever I should need one. It gives me a way to help my friends and finish the mission and find Jean-Claude." She squeezed Isabelle's hand reassuringly. "It's what I want."

Isabelle had no idea what this portended for Marie's future, but for now it was the wind her sails needed.

She returned her attention to Similce. "Will you ever have another chance to step foot on the vagabond city?"

Similce looked up at her. "You think that's tempting for me?"

"Am I wrong?" Isabelle asked.

Similce snorted. "Very well. We will go to Flotsam, but only because I'll still have enough supplies to get to a safe port, and it will get you off my deck the sooner."

CHAPTER

Twenty-Two

The *Potencia*'s hold was dark, and the inside of the empty crate Jean-Claude had chosen for his shelter was even darker. The fact that he could see with his left eye therefore made him rather suspicious.

The edges of his crate looked like pale green knife cuts in the cloak of darkness. Harder things like the iron ribs of a barrel seemed to glow from within like burning coals. Softer things like rope and canvas were fuzzier, and he'd be cursed if he couldn't see right through some of the flimsier materials and perceive the shadows of objects beyond them, individual potatoes in a sack, for instance.

At first he'd thought the strange limning of objects had been a consequence of the blow to the head Hasdrubal had inflicted on him, but no wallop could explain how he was able to see in pitch-darkness, or see through things that weren't glass.

The problem with this peculiar power, apart from the fact that he didn't understand or trust it, was that it gave him ice-pick headaches whenever he relied on it, and he could hardly keep his left eye open for more than a few minutes in the dark. The pain, and the odd awareness of edges and hardness, disappeared whenever he had light to work with.

Fortunately, his stowaway status had given him time to slow down and think on the problem. Whatever had affected his vision had happened between the time Hasdrubal had knocked him off the *Thunderclap*'s launch and the time he'd woken up with greasy vision on Ivar's ship.

So was this thing through which he was seeing really his eye?

Ivar had Sedgwick working for him, a Goldentongue glamour weaver who could make anything look and sound and feel like anything else. He said that his job aboard the *Dame Formue* was to keep it concealed, but why volunteer that information? He certainly didn't expect Jean-Claude to be impressed by his particular contribution to piracy. Yet as misdirection, the revelation worked. Jean-Claude hadn't thought to question what else he might be up to.

Saints, but Jean-Claude prayed the dwarf had carried through on his promise to deliver his hat and his message to Isabelle. More lives than his depended on it.

Jean-Claude waited for night to fall and the ship to go quiet. There was never a time when a ship under sail truly slept, but the night watch was quieter than the day.

He crept out of his shelter into the narrow confines of the hold. Every muscle he owned ached from being cooped up all day. He sparked a hooded lantern to life, shortening the wick until it gave off no more glow than a candle. He worked his way through the stacks of stores and sneaked up to the orlop deck. Muffled conversations came from the quartermaster's office toward the stern, and the surgeon was asleep in his own bay, but there by the companionway was a water barrel.

If Sedgwick had put some sort of glamour on him to conceal whatever had been done to his eye, water should reveal it. The barrel had a hole in its lid for dipping a ladle, but it wasn't big enough to show his reflection.

Jean-Claude tested the fit of the lid and pulled it carefully away, gritting his teeth when the sodden wood scraped and squeaked. With a last recalcitrant groan, the lid came away.

Jean-Claude leaned over to take a look at his reflection.

Horror and dismay stole his breath and balance. Light-headed, he dropped the lid with a clunk and nearly fell. His eye was gone. Hasdrubal's blow had opened a gash from the bridge of his nose, across his eye socket, and through the thin outer bone of the orbit. That whole quarter of his face was a chasm of half-healed wounds, proud flesh, and scar tissue.

Where his eye should have been was a bronze-colored clockwork eye. Wires out the back of it had embedded themselves in his flesh and threaded themselves along the whole remaining surface of his eye socket. The mechanical iris opened and shut, and the artifact eye tracked with his real one.

Saints, but he looked like Kantelvar. That clockwork parasite had tried to breed the Savior using Isabelle as his divine broodmare. It was he who'd cut off her arm.

What would Isabelle think when she saw him like this? It would be like looking in a twisted nightmare mirror of a memory.

More pressingly, why had Ivar done this to him? On the one hand, it seemed like a cruel prank. On the other hand, the eye worked. It was clearly a quondam artifact left over from before the Breaking of the World. Even broken artifacts were rare and valuable. Working ones like this, devices so arcane and complex that they could replace living flesh, were treasures beyond compare. Ivar could have bought a bigger ship with this thing, or maybe a fleet of ships. Yet he'd stuck it in Jean-Claude's skull and sent him off to be tortured by Travers.

He tried splashing water in his eye to dispel the glamour, but the illusion remained, for he could feel no metal in his face. The glamour itself must be attached to a charm somewhere nearby, but where? Travers had removed everything he'd brought with him.

This was too much to think about out here in the open. Jean-Claude filled a waterskin to carry him through the next day, then replaced the lid and hurried back to his crate. Once safely ensconced, he began examining the rest of his battered body. The surgeon had fitted him with the prosthetic eye, taking advantage of a wound that was already there. Why not do the same with the charm? His body was, after all, the thing he was least likely to lose.

Within his left forearm, lying just below the skin, his mechanical eye spied a heavy shape, like a metal pin had been sewn into him when his arm was stitched up. Jean-Claude pinched, poked, and prodded it, grimacing in pain. He would have to cut the thing out.

A knife proved surprisingly easy to procure from the sleeping surgeon's bay. Much harder was the effort of will to cut into his own flesh. He washed the site as Gretl insisted, and made the short incision while biting down hard on a leather strap. Fortunately the splinter was not deep, and he tweezed it out without ripping any big holes in himself. The charm itself was a needle made of twisted gold-and-silver wire, with the eye at one end filled with a tiny onyx stone: representing blindness, he suspected. Blood didn't dispel charms like water did, so Sedgwick had put the charm in the one place it was never likely to get lost or wet. Funny that the eye itself had showed him where it was.

Jean-Claude poured water over the needle and scrubbed it clean. Pain etched its way across his face. The glamour had prevented him from noticing the eye, or from feeling it as anything but normal. Without sorcery to suppress it, the ache, burn, and itch of his wounds rose to the surface. He imagined he would never again lose a game of who has the better scar.

Also, the smear across Jean-Claude's vision vanished and the world snapped into focus more crisp and clear than it had ever been, even in the days before he'd needed spectacles. Moreover, his head no longer ached when darkness descended and his clockwork vision took over. Most likely the power of the artifact to give him vision had been fighting the power of the glamour to convince him he couldn't see in the dark.

Without the glamour getting in the way, the absolute darkness of the hold appeared in shades of black and green. Cloth and rope were all but transparent and he could even see shadows moving behind wood. Once he held that idea in his mind, it even worked with the lantern turned on. He doused his light and looked up through the ceiling. The boards were too thick to see much past them, but he made out two blobs moving about in the space where the purser's office ought to be.

This would definitely come in handy, and it explained much about why Ivar had given him to Travers. The alliance between Hasdrubal, Czensos, and Travers was never meant to last past the end of mutual need. Czensos had put Jean-Claude on the *Potencia* ostensibly because he knew where the *Conquest* shard was, but that was a ruse. In fact, Czensos had put Jean-Claude there as a spy. Even if Travers turned Jean-Claude into a bloodhollow, he'd still have the eye.

The thing about eyes was, they generally came in pairs. Jean-Claude was willing to bet that this eye had a counterpart somewhere and Ivar was using it to watch every single thing Jean-Claude did.

You'll see, Ivar had said, the bastard. He planned to use the eye to show him the way through the Bittergale. The good thing was, Jean-Claude now had a lever to pull, if he could just figure out where to put the fulcrum.

Jean-Claude pinned the now-inert needle inside his coat and promised himself next time he encountered Sedgwick, he'd shove it someplace painful.

It took Jean-Claude several hours and two more stealthy excursions into the ship to collect paper, pen, and ink from unoccupied cabins. His clockwork eye helped him see aeronauts coming before they saw him.

He propped a board across the top of a barrel, lit his lantern, and put quill to paper:

Capitaine Thirdeye, you pestilent, goat-bothering bootlicker, I write to inform you that your plan to insert a spy on le Comte Travers's ship has succeeded, quite possibly beyond your wildest expectations.

I understand, now, just how you intended to learn the path through the Bittergale. I suspect you will be horrified to understand the fate of your entire endeavor rests in my hands.

Jean-Claude paused to savor that thought. He could almost hear Ivar's ulcer forming.

As it so happens, I am willing to assist you. I await your response to discuss terms. I assure you, my rates are reasonable.

He read the missive several times to make sure Ivar got it, then wrapped a brass plate in a strip of linen and tied it in front of his eye. It blocked off his vision nicely.

He put away his writing utensils, doused the light, and then leaned back to wait. It was possible that Ivar couldn't actually reverse the flow of information. It was equally likely that Jean-Claude had gone mad and this whole attempt at communication was based on delusion.

More though, he thought about Isabelle. Where was she now? What was she doing? Please let her be safe.

⸺

Dawn came and with it the end of Bitterlich's shift. He and Isabelle had divided the watches into day and night so that they could both keep an eye on Similce and her crew. Isabelle got the day watch, though she'd stayed up late sitting with Marie, who was tending Djordji. The Old Hand's condition was dire. He was old, his body was already weakened by his blackened lungs, and the surgeon had none of his medical supplies. The wound festered. If they could get him to Flotsam, they might find powders to draw out the poison and antiseptic salves to stop more getting in.

Bitterlich found Isabelle in the chartroom, dressed for the day in what could charitably be called a tent—a shapeless robe, an oversized mantle, and a cavernous hood that swallowed her whole. He would not have immediately known it was her but for her spark-arm and her firefly swarm, both of which ignored the fabric.

She leaned on the orrery, apparently tracking the *Saint Asne*'s progress toward Flotsam, or perhaps just lost in thought.

"Good morrow, mon capitaine," Bitterlich said, making his smartest salute.

Isabelle straightened up, but paused without returning the gesture. Worry leaked into her voice. "Are we back to formal distance and barely speaking to each other?"

"No," he said, "but we are far from our charted course, and our crew will follow our cues. As we maintain discipline, so will they, and we will only do so by keeping in the habit."

"That is one of the many reasons why I appreciate you, Major." She returned his salute, her spark-hand trailing motes like a comet. "Report."

Bitterlich assumed a parade rest. "The watch was uneventful. Similce slept through the night and her second gave no sign of mutiny. Djordji's condition . . . has not improved."

Bitterlich could not see Isabelle's grimace under her cowl, but he could feel it.

He said, "Marie is still with him. Asleep, the last time I saw her."

Isabelle let out a long breath, as if she was forcing herself to exhale. "It must seem a fever dream to her, moving from one sick bed to another."

Bitterlich could not contradict that. "Rebecca fell asleep around midnight after eating enough for three men. Malgiers and I spent most of the night talking to the Skaladin crew, listening to their stories. We found out how they came into Hasdrubal's service."

"Do tell," Isabelle said.

"It seems they ended up on the wrong side of a civil war. From what I gather, conflicts between factions are fairly common. The power structure gets reshuffled, the people on top end up on the bottom and vice versa."

"So the same cursed story every kingdom tells: rebellion against an intolerable master, only to become an intolerable master."

"So it would seem. Similce and her crew belonged to a faction that was burned to the roots and who consequently had no home to return to. They survived by becoming deniable assets for whoever would hire them, but without a home port, it's not a sustainable path. Similce kept her people alive and her ship aloft, but eventually the Breaker takes her toll. Aeronauts were killed. Contracts became fewer and farther between. When Hasdrubal approached with the promise of being repatriated in the tyrant's service, they jumped at the chance."

"Where they tried their luck against us," Isabelle said. "And lost the little they had left. I imagine that makes them ripe for mutiny."

"Perhaps not as much as you think. By sheer accident, we're playing by their rules. You beat them, but instead of killing them or selling them into slavery, you asked them to join your side. That means you think they were a worthy and honorable opponent. That sort of personnel salvage is a long and established tradition in Skaladin."

Isabelle's cowl tilted skeptically. "You learned all that in one night?"

Bitterlich tugged his cuffs. "Not me alone. My marines have been talking to them for days. It's easier and safer to run a prison when you treat your prisoners like people. Also, Malgiers has several collections of Skaladin tales. Conquest and defeat are a common theme. I directed my inquiries with that in mind."

"Similce doesn't seem enthused with the idea of being on our side," Isabelle pointed out.

"I imagine she doesn't like being displaced."

"I'm not displacing her," Isabelle protested.

"Yes, you are," Bitterlich said firmly. "Even if only for a few days. Part of winning is taking charge of the consequences of victory. You've always imagined that you can rise to the top without hurting anyone, without pushing aside the people already there. That's how you reconcile your ambition with your compassion. Similce doesn't like losing her position, but she'll feel even more betrayed if you treat it like it wasn't worth having in the first place."

Isabelle shook her head under the cowl, as if trying to dislodge this idea. "So I'm just like everyone else. I win the fight. I take over until someone knocks me down, and nothing changes."

"Every leader changes the rules of the game at least a little. Most ambitious people seek to consolidate power and protect themselves. You serve justice."

"Mercy," Isabelle said. "I serve mercy, and compassion, and reason. What society calls justice serves none of those things. It's just revenge by committee."

"You are merciful," he said. "More so than anyone I know."

She huffed a laugh. "I suppose I want to give people the gift my family never gave me."

"Speaking of your family"—Bitterlich tapped the side of her head—"how are they adjusting to their new head of household?"

"Primus is a problem," she said. "The rest of them are like ghosts, obsessed with some narrow fragment of their lives, but all of them took pieces of Primus, so there's more of him, spread around through all of them. He's not really alive, but he's more self-aware than the rest of them. During the escape, when the grapnels came over the rails, he took my hand"—she extended her taloned hand from her capacious sleeve—"and it was like my hand was his glove. He reached through me and slashed the chain like butter, something I never would have thought of doing on my own. If he can do that, what else might he make me do?"

The idea of Isabelle possessed by a malevolent memory unsettled Bitterlich to his core. "Can you block him?"

"Can you stop the next odd thought that pops into you head?" Isabelle asked. "He wants to live, to be the master of his own body, and the architect of his own destiny, to win great victories and conquer deadly foes. My past lives worshiped him and gave him what he wanted. He's not used to being opposed."

"It makes him angry?"

"More like he's incapable of comprehending it. He is like water. He'll never stop trying to run downhill—if there's a crack, he'll find it—but it's not because of any intrinsic desire to reach the bottom. I don't know what will happen when he finally finds a way through."

"We'll have to make sure that never happens," Bitterlich said.

"And how are we going to stop it? There's no manual for this. None of my ancestors have any idea how to stop it. They were too busy inviting him in and basking in his glory to ever consider how to kick him out again."

"Can you reason with him?"

She shook her head. "It's like trying to reason with a character in a play. He's got his part, his carefully crafted lines, his certain destiny, except now he's dragged me up onstage. I can't leave the stage, but I'm not cooperating with the direction."

"You'll just have to rewrite his lines. You are the woman who invented Lord du Journal, adventuring mathlogician, and then you managed to overturn analytical geometry. The tired lines from some ancient and inferior playwright should be simple to revise."

Isabelle laughed and strolled toward him around the orrery. "I did not overturn analytical geometry. It was only one proof."

She opened her arm. He embraced her. Her new strength was crushing, but in a good way. Her body against his was urgent and alive. The graceful arch of her back was a sublime pleasure to his touch, but his greatest satisfaction was feeling the tension melt out of her body.

Reluctantly he allowed the hug to end. They drifted to arms' length, though he still held her hand.

He said, "If I may be so bold, why are you wearing a cowl?"

Isabelle ducked her head just in case something was showing. "Because I look ridiculous. I'm fledging. My feathers started coming in, but I still have my down. I've never been pretty, but this . . . Saints, I just feel like the Builder is mocking me."

"I imagine you look adorable." Bitterlich asked.

"Adorable," Isabelle said pointedly, "is a word reserved exclusively to describe rosy-cheeked toddlers."

He tipped his hat to her. "Point taken, Capitaine. My apologies."

She squeezed his hand reassuringly. "Someday, we'll both get to see all of each other—see and touch—just not today."

He kissed the back of her hand in the manner of a formal courtship, and noted that her gray scales were warming into a rich purple with pink highlights. The finished effect was likely to be stunning.

She took back possession of her hand and he adjusted his cravat. Both of them, he suspected, were looking for an excuse to prolong the encounter.

There came a rap at the door. It was Malgiers, who seemed destined to intrude upon their privacy. At least this time they were upright, fully clothed, and breathing normally.

Malgiers's expression was dour. "Sirs, Monsieur Djordji is asking for you. The surgeon says you should come."

Bitterlich's heart dipped at his dire tone. He assumed his place at Isabelle's side and accompanied her to the surgeon's bay.

The bay itself was crowded. Djordji lay on a cot, his skin ghostly gray. The dressing on his wound seeped yellow. The stink of the wound reached down Bitterlich's throat and tried to choke him.

Marie sat by the bedside. Around her stood several off-duty marines. Rebecca had woken up, and even Similce was there.

The surgeon was talking low and fast to Similce in the Skaladin tongue. At the sight of Isabelle, Similce gestured her over.

The surgeon switched to la Langue and said, "Mistress, I—"

"Capitaine," Isabelle said, firmly but without malice.

The surgeon glanced at Similce, who scowled, but nodded.

"Capitaine," he said. "I've done all that's possible, but the Célestials took my supplies. I have no wound powder, no sepsis formula, nothing stronger than willow extract for the pain."

"I understand," Isabelle said. "Thank you for your efforts. How fare the other wounded?"

The surgeon looked as if this was an unexpected question. "One man lost a hand. Everyone else is back on duty."

"I'll visit the amputee later," Isabelle said. "I know what it's like to lose an arm."

"Capitaine," Djordji whispered from the cot. "A word."

Isabelle approached him. Bitterlich noted Similce and the surgeon watching her, weighing her worth as a new leader against the standards of their own.

"Help me sit," Djordji said to Marie. She propped him up and loaded a pipe, which he drew on weakly. For all that it was poison, the dragonweed brought some color back to his face.

"What would you say to me, Monsieur Djordji?" Isabelle asked.

Djordji looked up at her. "You looks like a cast-off monk."

"It's a bad habit I got into," she said, and he made a noise that was half laugh, half cough.

"I never knows defeat in battle until now. It humbles me."

Isabelle said, "That would be a shame. I would rather see you celebrated."

He coughed black flecks into his hand. "Remember that after I tells you about Flotsam."

Djordji took another draw at his pipe. It was hard to tell if he was lost in thought or merely nursing his strength.

Finally he spoke in a voice as old and tired as the last breath of winter. "It's an old story, goes back afore any of you is born."

Everybody leaned in to better hear. Even Rebecca was rapt.

"Ever since we is declared anathema, the Gyrine are free. Every clan votes their own choir and their own capitaine. Sometime the clans work together, sometime they don't. There's really only two rules. One is that the Gyrine bows to no king: you picks your own leaders, and no one needs to serve a capitaine they doesn't pick. The second is, no Gyrine ever kills another."

"What happens if your clan picks a capitaine you can't abide?" Bitterlich asked.

"You leave. You gets off at the nearest port. Maybe you finds yourself another clan who'll take you in. Maybe you makes your own way."

Djordji coughed again, long and racking, then lay back and sipped air like it was hot tea.

At length, he gathered enough breath to speak. "I is a young man when there comes a time that all the Gyrine are under threat. The dirtborn downs our balloons. Whole clans are lost. Enemies close in from all sides. A great gyre moot is called. All the clans gather at Flotsam and the capitaines tries to work out how best to respond. You imagines how that goes."

Isabelle had no trouble picturing the dickering.

"My brother is capitaine and choir leader of the Tall Clouds. Kalo is his name, but the world knows him as Solitaire."

Similce said, "Solitaire the pirate? The one who sacked Tyrant Xerxas's tomb?"

"Aye," Djordji said. "'What's the point of burying all that gold?' he says. 'The dead has no needs.' We also whips the Vecci pirate hunters at St. Oppus, and takes the Aragothic treasure fleet out of San Corvus."

"I can't imagine why the powers of the world were mad at you," Bitterlich said.

Djordji shrugged unrepentantly. "Gyrine say if you can't keep it, you shouldn't have it. Kalo, he argues that the clans should elect a storm king, one great leader to unite the Gyrine and take war to the dirtborn, put them in their place. He says we rules the skies and we should expect tribute from those who trespass in our domain. Never again will we lets them build warships. If they wants to use our skies they pays for the privilege."

"That sounds . . . implausible," Isabelle said.

"He makes it sound good," Djordji said. "Takes him some time. Takes blackmail and bribery, but all the clans take the bait. They plans a vote. Thing is, I finds out why we has so much trouble with the dirtborn. Kalo feeds the dirtborn kings information about which clans are where and in what numbers, so no matter where we turn, the dirtborn are always there to meet us. He does all this to afright the clans and make them name him king."

Djordji's head wobbled weakly side to side, as if he still could not believe it. "That night I decides who I serves. Not my brother, not my clan, but all Gyrine. Breaks my heart. Nearly breaks my mind. See, I can't prove what I knows about Kalo's plot. Can't beat him with words, either, and no one else stands with me. All I has is steel. All I has is the one choice I can't make. Gyrine don't kill Gyrine.

"In the end, I does what I has to do. The Gyrine bows to no king, and I gets named Jackhand, kinslayer. They don't kill me, but there's none who will grant me aid or succor."

"What does this portend for us if they won't give aid to you?" Isabelle asked.

"They won't give it to me, but they will to her." He twitched his nose at Marie. "I adopts her as my daughter and my heir. None may offer me shelter, but there's no bad blood as we say. My crime doesn't touch her.

"I means to introduce her to the choir at Flotsam. Stake my claim in her. Tall Clouds takes her in. Fellhand Marie is she, once she makes her challenge. Learns in a month what it takes me a year to teach others. She'll do.

"Thing is, it's two days to Flotsam, and I cuts my triumphant return a bit too fine. It may be Marie makes her case without me." He tugged at a leather thong about his wrist. It was braided with beads in shades of blue and green. Marie helped him remove it.

"Clan token," he said. "Not quite a passport, but close. Make sure she gets to the choir and makes . . . her challenge." His strength waned and he sagged again onto his pillows.

"What challenge?" Isabelle asked.

Marie answered, "To be named fellhand, I must challenge the champions of all clans present. If I can defeat their champions, they'll be able to save face by admitting Jackhand Djordji trained me, and that I am one of them."

Isabelle stiffened. "How many clans are there?"

"We don't know," Marie said. "There are twelve clan berths in the city. They're the ones who maintain the place."

Isabelle's voice grew tight. "So you could be fighting twelve duels?"

"I am a fellhand. If I can't win twelve duels, I don't deserve the title," Marie said.

"Are not the other champions also likely to be fellhands?" Isabelle asked.

"Yes, and most of them were trained by Jackhand Djordji, and he's trained me to beat them." She presented the bracelet to Isabelle. "I need you to hold this for me. Anything I wear for any period of time turns white, and that would spoil the effect."

Isabelle received the bracelet as if it were as delicate as a flower petal, but with all the weight of a ship's gun. "I will keep it safe."

"Boy," Djordji whispered. His eyes were only half open. "Major."

Bitterlich had not expected to be called on. He knelt beside the cot. "Monsieur."

"I remembers." His breath was as thin as the edge of a knife. "When he sends me to fetch you . . . Leon . . . He says . . . make sure the Temple doesn't get you . . . Don't know why."

"Thank you," Bitterlich said, though he had no way to make that fit with what he remembered of his boyhood rescue. The Temple was usually very good at granting sanctuary to saintblooded orphans, and delivering them to relatives or other sponsors. Bitterlich didn't recall seeing any Temple folk during his flight, but then he'd been eight, and there was a lot he didn't remember.

Djordji's pipe fell from his hand. He still breathed, but his fever burned hot enough to feel from a foot away.

Bitterlich picked up the pipe, extinguished it, and tapped out the bowl before placing it back in the small trove of things Djordji had chosen for the last leg of his journey. His dragonweed, his flask, his weapons, hat and long coat, a few talismans and mementos whose story he would take with him through the Ravenous Gate.

"Marie," Djordji whispered. His eyes did not open this time.

"Yes, Father," Marie said. Her voice was always flat and devoid of affect, but she knelt by the cot and clutched his hand.

"Remember to breathe," he said, and Bitterlich felt the life go out of him, his last breath rising like mist off green fields on a summer's morning. When his chest fell back, what lay there was no longer a man, but a memory.

Marie could not cry, but she lay across Djordji's chest and hugged him tight.

Isabelle knelt, placed her arm round Marie's shoulders, and wept for both of them.

CHAPTER
Twenty-Three

Night moved toward its darkest nadir. Jean-Claude had received no response from Ivar, but there was no way to tell if that was because he was unwilling to reply or unable to reply.

Jean-Claude eased out of his crate and carefully stowed the small cache of needful things he'd pilfered. Whether his epistolary gambit bore fruit or not, he still needed to find out what he could about Hasdrubal. He knew the Skaladin Seelenjäger had come aboard, but had he brought Dok or the relic with him, and if not, where had he left them?

Jean-Claude checked to see if the passage in the orlop deck was clear. He found that if he closed his right eye, the transparency of the wood above increased until he could make out stanchions, barrels, boxes, and beams in the level above. The ship's off-duty junior officers were asleep in the cabin, their bloodshadows horribly wet and distinct to his clockwork vision.

One of the first things Jean-Claude had stolen as a stowaway were clothes that fit. He could almost pass for a crewman now, save for the fact that he was older and fatter than any man aboard, not to mention the great gaping scar and clockwork eye. He adjusted his coat and pulled his hat down to cover his face, then ascended the ladder.

Jean-Claude climbed through the lower gun deck to the upper. Footsteps from above warned him in time to stuff himself in a locker. He squeezed between boxes and bags as a gang of aeronauts hurried by.

Where to go from here? On the main deck above, aeronauts busied themselves keeping the ship on course. A brace of marines, easy to distinguish by the bright edges of their steel weapons, guarded the officers' cabins.

Jean-Claude peered through the ceiling into the cabins, but there were too many layers of things in the way to make out useful details. He saw motion but could not make out who it was. If he could get underneath it . . .

Directly aft of him were the officers' stores. One Sanguinaire officer resided within, sitting on a sky chest and slumped over a crate, a bottle of liquor clutched in his hand. The glass of the bottle shimmered like a soap bubble in Jean-Claude's vision.

Jean-Claude tried the door and found it locked. The drunkard preferred his privacy. Jean-Claude attacked the lock with his makeshift pick. The clockwork eye didn't let him see through the metal workings, so he had to go by feel, praying no one came up behind him.

Sweat beaded on his brow despite the chill air. The pick slipped and he had to start over. Footsteps echoed up from the deck below. The lock clicked and the bolt slid free. The companionway shook as someone ascended. Jean-Claude opened the door only far enough to squeeze through. The hinges creaked. The drunkard stirred. Jean-Claude eased the door shut and crouched behind the crate the potted officer was using for a table. The men outside kept going.

Peering through the crate, Jean-Claude saw the drunk lift his gaze and sweep it slowly side to side. He stared at his bottle for a minute, tried it, and found it empty. He bestirred himself and searched his immediate vicinity for another. Jean-Claude espied a bottle in a basket, plucked it, and scooted it onto the crate while the officer was checking between his shoes.

The officer looked up again, saw the new bottle, squinted at it suspiciously, and decided not to look a gift horse in the souse. He pulled the cork and proceeded to embalm himself.

Jean-Claude imagined that somewhere, far away, Ivar was laughing so hard he couldn't breathe.

Jean-Claude stared up through the ceiling into the great cabin. It had been partitioned off into a master chamber, a small guest room, a chartroom.

In the first room was a knot of Skaladin aeronauts at their ease. In the other much larger chamber, Travers with his oily bloodshadow and metal leg braces stood in conference with Hasdrubal with his curving horns. And there was a third person barely apparent to the clockwork eye. Saints, what he wouldn't give to be a mouse in that wainscoting.

There came a soft thud and some ragged snoring as the drunken officer passed out again.

Travers, Hasdrubal, and the other stepped out onto the ship's stern gallery.

Carefully, quietly, Jean-Claude stood up and eased around to the back of the store to get a better view of the goings-on above. Behind a stack of crates stood a bank of windows.

Jean-Claude's blood rushed with the thrill of a good sneak, the urge to get closer and the fear of being caught. He worked his way around the edge of the crates. It was like squeezing a slab of bacon through a clothes wringer, but there was a crease of space between the boxes and the windows. There was not enough space for him back there, but he got his fingers on the window catch. The window creaked open, loud enough to make his skin shrink, but neither the drunk nor the conspirators on the gallery seemed to notice.

A chill breeze flowed in, carrying with it voices, sounds but not words. Just now he wished he had a clockwork ear to go with his eye, though it was probably unwise to tempt the Breaker with such a request.

He sucked his gut in tighter and pushed his head out the window.

The void opened up below him. The distant Miasma roiled like swarms of gnats to his clockwork eye. He squeezed his eye shut before his dizziness could take him. This had the desired effect, though it occurred to him that his left eye didn't actually have an eyelid anymore, so in a sense the clockwork eye was just being polite to his wishes.

From the gallery, a conversation drifted down.

Travers's nasal voice said, ". . . have the relic, Thirdeye has outlived his usefulness."

A wispier, more hollow voice replied, "Not necessarily. I have received word that Capitaine Isabelle hijacked the *Saint Asne* and escaped."

Jean-Claude could hardly believe his ears. Gentle, thoughtful Isabelle had hijacked a ship? And whom was she escaping from?

"You said she was dying," Travers said.

Wispy Voice said, "I said I'd heard she was deathly ill. It seems the rumors were exaggerated."

Jean-Claude could well guess what that was about. Isabelle's head troubles had finally boiled over.

"How do we know you're not wrong about her escape as well?" Travers asked.

"That message has been relayed to the Célestial Fleet. They've declared her a fugitive."

"Then let the fleet take care of her."

"That might not be a good idea," Wispy said. "She has worked out that Hasdrubal isn't working for the tyrant. If the fleet catches her first she may convince them not to engage the Skaladin and—"

Jean-Claude squinted at the wispy figure through the floor of the gallery. It was barely there: a bloodhollow.

"You give her far too much credit," Travers said.

"No," Hasdrubal said, the same goatlike bray that had taunted Jean-Claude aboard the launch. "Your cousin is correct. Capitaine Isabelle should be destroyed. Right now, neither the Célestial Fleet nor the Skaladin know we have the relic. If the Célestial Fleet catches Isabelle, she will surely tell them."

"I'll tell Ivar to send her to the Gloom, shall I?" Wispy said. The bloodhollow went back inside, ensconced itself in a locker, and went very still.

"That one is not as clever as she thinks she is." Hasdrubal's voice pierced the wind.

"Women never are," Travers said.

Behind Jean-Claude, the drunkard grunted and began muttering unintelligibly. Fear kicked Jean-Claude's pulse to a gallop. He wriggled out of the crevice, shut the window, and hurried toward the door.

The officer snorted and woke up.

"Hey, mongrel. What you doing here?"

Jean-Claude did not break stride, but opened the door and slipped out into the passage before the officer could react. He'd been seen, but what had the officer made out? Just the back of a man in a sailor's uniform.

He hurried down the companionway, expecting shouts of outrage and a call to arms. None came. Even so, he did not take a full breath until he'd reached his hiding spot and found it undisturbed.

Had Isabelle gotten his message? Even if she hadn't, she'd be heading north, hunting Hasdrubal. She'd run right into Ivar.

Might Jean-Claude turn him aside? Ivar hadn't responded to his missive, but had he really needed to? After all, he could see everything Jean-Claude could see whether Jean-Claude wanted it or not.

But what Jean-Claude had seen wasn't as important as what he had heard.

He spent a moment surveying as much of the ship as he could see, just to assure himself no excitement was about to find him. Then he lit his lantern, readied a sheet of paper, and dipped his quill.

> *Capitaine Thirdeye,*
> *By now, you will have received a visitor in the form of bloodhollow who will have directed you to attack and shoot down a ship called the* Saint Asne. *If you want to know why that is a bad idea, contact me.*
>
> *J-C*

—

"Capitaine," Similce said, "I need to speak to you."

Isabelle, weary beyond words from Djordji's death, led Similce into the chartroom, out of the increasingly bitter wind.

Inside, Similce actually saluted Isabelle, albeit with a closed fist over her heart in the style of the tyrant's navy. "Capitaine, I believe entrusting the fate of my . . . of the *Saint Asne* to that girl's dueling ability is a mistake. We don't need to make port at Flotsam. With the supplies we have, we can make it as far as Gabbering Cove."

Isabelle's temper rose at this disrespect for Marie, but she tamped it down. Similce was being a proper second-in-command, playing by the rules, and it behooved Isabelle to do the same.

She said, "I agree that putting all our lives on Marie's shoulders is a risk, but we don't have any better options. We could make it to Gabbering, yes, but then what? We still have no trade goods and not enough supplies to reach anywhere else. If you follow each choice to its possible conclusions, the only one where we actually get what we need lies in Marie's hands."

"She just seems so . . . young," Similce said.

"That *woman* is actually a year older than I am. Marie looks young because she spent twelve years as a bloodhollow. She's the only living person who's ever been brought back from that, and she revived with her sanity intact. She was trained by the greatest duelist of the last century, who made her his protégée even before he adopted her as his daughter. She has never failed me, not as a friend, adviser, or guardian. I trust her judgment, and her abilities."

Isabelle hoped she sounded confident. She did trust Marie's prowess, but still the thought of sending her to the dueling courts terrified her.

Similce said, "I did not think it was possible to come back from being a bloodhollow."

"Neither did anyone else," Isabelle said. "It's an alchemical process. I've been trying to duplicate it."

Similce's eyes narrowed. "You don't like bloodhollows?"

"Bloodhollows are a loathsome grotesquery, a blight against all that is good."

"And yet you are loyal to the queen of bloodshadows," Similce said.

"Yes," Isabelle said. "She is amenable to reason. She would rather use her Builder-given power to heal than to harm, and she lets me fight the fights that she can't touch politically."

Do not confide in this woman, Primus said, tripping up her tongue. *However subdued she is now, she is your enemy, the enemy of all saintborn.*

Isabelle swatted his apparition, splashing his reflection so violently that it would hopefully be some time before the waters calmed enough for him to return. Bitterlich was right. If she couldn't rid herself of Primus Maximus, she must find a way to rewrite his motive.

Yet he had a point, and it needed addressing.

To Similce she said, "You call me soulless. In Skaladin, all of my kind are slaves, and yet I am your capitaine. Does that trouble you?"

Similce looked uncomfortable. After a moment, she said, "You spared my life, and then you saved my life. I owe you a debt of honor."

"That's one way to square a circle," Isabelle said. Badgering Similce for a more favorable answer would only make her resentful. It was time to move on to other things. "We still have work to do. Have you finished the inventory of foodstuffs?"

Similce relaxed almost imperceptibly and said, "Yes. If you can call that stuff you eat food . . ."

⟶

Bitterlich and Rebecca sat on the gull's stoop, the lowest platform on the turvy mainmast, with the whole ship above them and nothing but deep sky below, several kilometers of thin scudding clouds above the green-tinged Miasma. He'd spent the afternoon working with her on partial transformations, teasing individual strands out of the soul threads, coiling and knotting them and releasing them and twisting them back into their original shape. So far she'd succeeded in turning her lower body into a wyrm's tail without scrambling her organs or blocking her bowels.

It was grueling work, but her training as a pickpocket had given her focus aplenty.

Yet neither the hard work nor the difficulty of the task explained the moody silence with which she sat and chewed her ration of ship's biscuit and pork. Bitterlich was used to dealing with impulsive, reckless Rebecca, not silent, pensive Rebecca.

"Is something bothering you?" he asked in his most neutral tone.

She shook her head and continued eating the nigh-inedible biscuit with the same patient determination of a termite attacking a doorpost.

Bitterlich waited.

After a long minute she said, "Why does it matter that Djordji adopted Marie? I thought she was a nob. They all have big families."

Bitterlich suspected that the question being asked was not the one that wanted an answer. Rebecca was quite capable of understanding the plan to get them resupplied on Flotsam, so her curiosity must concern the filial arrangement itself. "When Marie was turned into a bloodhollow, her parents treated her as if she'd died. After Isabelle revived her, twelve years later, she sent a message to her parents, but they could not bear to see her again. She found a father figure in Djordji and he found a daughter in her, so they made it official."

"What about your parents?" Rebecca asked.

"They died when I was eight," he said, "killed by rebels in an uprising against le roi."

"My parents abandoned me," Rebecca said in her let's-pretend-this-isn't-important voice. "Left me on the street."

Bitterlich's heart ached in sympathy. "That's hard."

"S'okay," she said, taking a bite of salt pork. "I can take care of myself. I mean, when I was little . . . I used to dream they'd come find me. That's the kind of things little kids do, like tell ghost stories."

"Which you are, of course, far too old and sophisticated to do," Bitterlich said, but that wasn't really the point. She wanted to know who she was and where she fit, as if those answers might come from outside.

Yet she was a saintborn noble; she had a family somewhere. There was no guarantee they were good people, but there was also no guarantee they were bad. Noble children were at particular risk of being kidnapped, and out-of-wedlock births were a leading cause of foundlings.

"Would you find your parents if you could?" Bitterlich asked. It was a natural desire, but also a huge emotional risk.

Rebecca shrugged defensively. "Dunno."

"If you ever decide you want to," Bitterlich said, "I have an idea where to start looking."

She turned to face him for the first time during the conversation. Her expression was wary but her gemlike eyes held the hope of ages. "Where?"

"I'll show you." He pushed himself from the platform, slipped into a bird suit, and circled up to the quarterdeck. Rebecca alighted beside him and they stepped into the chartroom, where Isabelle and Similce were taking measurements on the orrery.

"Capitaine Isabelle," Bitterlich said, "might Rebecca and I have a private moment of your time?"

Isabelle's head came up under her cowl, though not far enough for him to see more than the tip of her chin. The scales there had taken on the color of a rose.

"Of course," Isabelle said, and gestured them into the capitaine's cabin. Similce watched them in, but asked no questions.

Once the door was shut and latched, Bitterlich said, "Rebecca is curious about her parents, and I thought you and your little friends might be able to give her some idea where to look."

"My little . . . you mean the blood ciphers." She looked to Rebecca and back again. "I see what you're asking, but that's not necessarily going to work."

"You never know," Bitterlich said.

"Never know what? What's not going to work?" Rebecca asked, distrustful of circumlocution.

Isabelle dragged out her sky trunk and plunged her spark-arm through the wood in order to unlatch it from the inside. She pulled out a wooden box about as big as a loaf of bread, decorated with bare, branching trees. Inside lay her blood ciphers.

Isabelle selected one and displayed it for Rebecca. In that moment, in her deep cowl, with her spark swarm surrounding her, her luminous arm glowing, and one talon-tipped hand extending the rod to Rebecca, she might have been a forest witch in some ancient tale, delivering a talisman of hope and woe to some young adventuress.

"This is a blood cipher. It can take a sample of your blood and compare it to samples it has from other people. If the ciphers have taken a sample of any of your relatives; parents, grandparents, aunts, or uncles; this can tell you who they are. The catch is, there's no guarantee that any of your relatives have been recorded. In fact, it's pretty unlikely. Moreover, learning who your parents are won't necessarily make your life any easier, and it will definitely make it more complicated. When my blood was taken, I discovered my father wasn't who I thought he was and met a sister who tried to kill me."

Rebecca stared at the blood cipher, sizing it up like it was a scorpion guarding a purse she meant to cut.

"If I find out nothing, that's what I already know," she said. "So I can't lose by trying. How do I make it work?"

Isabelle let go a held breath and handed her the device. "Press the round end to your finger. It will sting."

Rebecca complied. The needle bit. Rebecca flinched. Isabelle took the cipher back and examined the raised lettering on the side.

"Hmmm . . ." Isabelle said, adjusting the first register so it would display Rebecca's name.

"What does 'hmmm' mean?" Rebecca asked.

"It says you're a Seelenjäger, which we already knew, but some of the tertiary glyphs are unusual."

"What about my parents?" she asked.

"Just getting to that," Isabelle said. She gave the cipher's tail a twist and set it in the box with all the others. The ciphers buzzed and stirred. Seams in the metal appeared where none had been before. The cylinders sprouted insect-like legs and milled around one another, touching horseshoes to knobs at random until they came to a collective conclusion and began hooking ends together and blooming into the shape of a bifurcating tree.

Isabelle stared at the writing on the trunk, and Bitterlich heard her sharp intake of breath. The pit of his stomach fell. What awful connection had she discovered? His brain belatedly reminded him that the capital city was notorious as a breeding ground, so to speak, of sexual indiscretion, and chief amongst the indiscreet had been the last roi, Grand Leon, a man with so many bastards that half the upper nobility was ineligible to intermarry. But . . . Grand Leon was a Sanguinaire, not a Seelenjäger.

"Major," Isabelle said. "You need to see this."

Bitterlich hurried to her side.

"Hey," Rebecca protested, popping to her feet and then flitting up to the ceiling, trying to see over Bitterlich's shoulder. "What about me? It's my parents."

Bitterlich leaned in to see the writing. Rebecca's cylinder was the base of the trunk and only one branch led away from it, indicating the ciphers only recognized half her lineage. The cylinder above hers read: Ewald Bitterlich, Seelenjäger—cull.

Bitterlich's head felt light and his lips went numb. A strange, dead tingling spread from his fingers and toes.

He was Rebecca's father?

Bitterlich sat down. He aimed for the chair but missed and landed hard on the floor. The pain barely registered.

He was Rebecca's father! But that was . . . just barely not impossible. Eulalie had gelded him, but not until after they'd had sex. She'd gotten pregnant. Abandoned the child. She'd stolen his child from him and didn't even tell him.

"What's the matter with him?" Rebecca asked, her voice shrill.

"He's just become a father," Isabelle said.

"What?" Poor Rebecca was bewildered.

Isabelle said, "You didn't know who your parents are, but at least you knew you had parents. Major Bitterlich had no idea he had a daughter, much less that it was you."

Outrage boiled up in Rebecca's voice. "How could he not know?"

Bitterlich sat doubled over, his head in his hands, trying to hold it all in. "She never told me. Your mother never told me she was pregnant, much less that she'd had you."

"Why not?" Her anger faded to confusion.

Bitterlich could not speak through his shock. His head and heart felt like they were going to explode. He'd known Eulalie was a selfish, evil harridan, but this . . . she'd thrown away her child. His child.

Isabelle spoke in more soothing tones. "I can't speak for your mother, but Major Bitterlich never would have abandoned you if he'd known you existed."

Bitterlich looked up at Rebecca. His vision blurred from tears. None of this was her fault. He took several very long breaths. How to go on from this? Rebecca. She was the important one here. Her needs must be attended first.

He knelt before his daughter. "Rebecca. I am so sorry. I did not know. If I'd known you existed, I would have searched to the end of the world to find you. I would have taken you in, raised you. I would have been a father to you. I still will if you will let me."

Rebecca recoiled, befuddled by this sudden proclamation.

Isabelle touched his shoulder lightly. "Ewald, I'm going to take Rebecca outside. I'll be right back."

Bitterlich clenched his jaw and tried to rub the blinding tears from his eyes, his whole reserve shattered. Eulalie had wrecked him at last, from half a world away and without even trying, she'd taken the daughter he didn't even know he had and tossed her in the gutter.

Yet outrage had no place in his relationship to Rebecca. She was such an amazing child. He'd taken her as a student. Would she want him as a parent?

—

Isabelle led Rebecca onto the quarterdeck where no one else was standing. The girl was shivering, and not from the cold. The shock of this late discovery had capsized Bitterlich's world, and he needed some time to right his ship. Rebecca needed help making sense of it.

"What are you feeling?" Isabelle asked Rebecca.

She hunched her head down. "I don't know. Why was he so upset?"

"He isn't upset at you," Isabelle said. "He is upset at what was done to you, to both of you. Your mother left him the night they conceived you, and he never knew she was pregnant." Trying to explain the mess Eulalie had made of Bitterlich to a twelve-year-old was not in her wheelhouse. "As he said, if he'd known, he would have taken you in and raised you, he would have been your father in heart and deed as well as body, but he never had that chance."

"Instead she left me at the orphanage," Rebecca said. "Why?"

"I don't know," Isabelle said. She was more than inclined to think the worst of Eulalie, but there were many reasons a woman, especially a saint-born noblewoman, might abandon a bastard newborn, chief amongst these being self-defense. Eulalie had gotten married shortly after conceiving Rebecca, and her husband would have been within his legal rights to divorce her and take her dowry if she presented him with a bastard. Better to give the child away. Indeed better not to tell Bitterlich lest he use that knowledge against her. Rebecca was profoundly lucky Eulalie hadn't broken her neck and called her stillborn.

Which means you can use this child against her mother, Primus said.

I am not using a child as a pawn, Isabelle replied, indignant.

But you would use her as a soldier on a warship, Primus said.

Isabelle's teeth gnashed, but she had no instant rebuttal.

Rebecca, not privy to this aside said, "Does that mean I have to be the major's daughter?"

"Any more than you already are?" Isabelle asked. "The only thing that has changed between giving that drop of blood and now is that you've learned a little bit of your own story, and how Major Bitterlich was there at the beginning. In a way you're lucky. You already know him, and you've seen what he's like. I'm sure he'd be delighted to be your father, but ultimately your relationship will be up to the two of you to decide, and yes, that means you get a choice."

"Capitaine, Rebecca," Bitterlich said, emerging from the chartroom, walking slowly like a man in a fog. He'd regained his composure and fixed his clothing up to his fastidious standard. He doffed his hat and bowed to Rebecca. "Mademoiselle, I'm sorry I frightened you."

Rebecca's face scrunched up in indignation. "I wasn't scared."

Bitterlich tilted his head. "In that case, I'm sorry for embarrassing myself in front of you. Is that better?"

"A little," Rebecca said, suddenly sheepish.

Isabelle sensed a long series of awkward moments in the immediate future that she didn't need to be part of. "I'll leave you two to work things out." To Rebecca she said, "There is no need to commit yourself to anything immediately." To Bitterlich she said, "Take as long as you need, but when you're done, we have other business."

She returned to her cabin and the Rebecca/Bitterlich family tree, and brooded about its implications. She pulled out her genealogical journal, and carefully added in Rebecca and Bitterlich, and traced the branches backward. None of these were names she had ever seen before. When she had them all down, she reset the tree from its topmost level, following the branches backward in time.

She was still scribbling when Bitterlich returned.

"How was your talk?" she asked, patting the bench seat beside her.

He sat. "Awkward. We agreed just to go on as we have been and see what happens."

Relief bubbled up in Isabelle's soul. "Good."

"Except how can I, knowing what I know now? She's my daughter."

"And your responsibility is to do what's best for her," Isabelle said, "especially if it's hard for you. She's a very smart child who's had a very rough life. You can't go back and change that, no matter how much you'd like to. All you can do is the hardest thing: wait and see."

"Very hard." He stared into some irretrievable past or unobtainable future.

"It turns out, you also have a new cousin," Isabelle said. "To be precise, an eighth cousin twice removed."

He snapped out of his meditation and bestowed her a bewildered look. "What? Who?"

"Me," she said, and pointed at her journal. "About two hundred years ago we share a several times great-grandfather."

Bitterlich blinked and stared at the name. "But that's the book where you track all of Kantelvar's breeding experiments . . ." His expression drooped into shock. "You mean . . ."

Isabelle held up the blood cipher with his name on it. "I never took a sample of your blood. We knew who your parents were, so there was never any point, but here you are."

"So I was part of the breeding program. And he labeled me a cull." For the second time that day, Bitterlich looked ready to faint. "My parents. Wolfgang's raid on my house. He was trying to kill me."

Isabelle hadn't made that leap. "We can't know that. There was a lot of unrest at the time—"

"But Grand Leon sent Djordji to rescue me in particular with instructions not to let the Temple get their hands on me. He must have known. He must have had some idea of what Kantelvar was up to, trying to breed the Savior. He saved me."

Isabelle's heart wallowed under the weight of dismay. "Then, against all normal protocol, Grand Leon assigned you to protect me, who Kantelvar meant to bear the Savior. He said he hoped that we would get along."

Bitterlich said, "He was trying to breed the Savior on the sly. That's insane, it's—"

"Exactly the sort of underhanded yet grandiose thing he would do," Isabelle said. "Grand Leon really did want to make l'Empire Céleste a place where all different types of sorcerers could live together, and what better way to do that than crafting a child in possession of all the sorceries, and then naming that child as his heir: the Savior as king. That's why he never named an heir, but said he had one in mind. At the same time he knew I'd never go along with it, so he put us together to see what would happen, but he didn't know about your disability—"

"Wait, he can't have been planning this all along," Bitterlich protested. "My parents were killed more than twenty years ago. You nearly married Príncipe Julio."

"Yes, and he tried to trick me into giving up my potential children from that marriage too," Isabelle said, frowning. "The bastard. The point is, I don't suggest that putting us together and hoping we'd fall into bed was his only plan. He had lots of schemes going. He knew most of them would never amount to anything, but once he saw the chance to put us together, it was at very low cost to him with a small chance at a very large reward."

They both fell silent, digesting the totality of this revelation.

Bitterlich said very softly, "I'm glad he threw us together."

A band of tension released from around Isabelle's heart. "So am I."

An alarm bell rang, loud and fast. Isabelle and Bitterlich sprang up, overturning the bench and nearly tripping over it. They bolted outside in time to hear the lookout cry. "War balloons! War balloons starboard and high!"

CHAPTER

Twenty-Four

Isabelle gawped at the war balloons, one painted red and black, the other blue and yellow.

These were not the lesser-clan balloons Isabelle recalled from her youth, but massive structures, each a wooden tower with several tiers of platforms all bristling with guns. These aerial fortresses hung suspended below vast armored gasbags. They moved through sky at the direction of their Wind-caller choruses, as fast as any warship, and indifferent to the natural wind.

They will burn, Primus said, old hatred flaring to life like banked coals. He still remembered how the Gyrine betrayed him at the Battle of Treacher's Coast, how he'd watched helpless and outraged from the shore when the clan balloons that had been protecting his supply fleet opened fire on it instead. The Windcallers stole the breeze from some ships and left them helpless, and dashed others against one another with hurricane winds.

If Isabelle was going to reconstruct Primus's personality into something she could live with, she couldn't just dispel him every time he showed up.

That was four hundred years ago. Everyone involved is long dead, she pointed out.

It is not over, Primus insisted. *Not until the last clan balloon falls flaming into the Gloom, the vermin aboard sent to the Halls of Torment unredeemed.* Out of the corner of her eye, she could almost see him standing by her shoulder.

Clearly, reason was not the optimal tool for this job, at least not in its most direct form.

We are not going to start a fight, she said.

Of course not. We are outnumbered and outgunned. What we will do is scout, collect intelligence on the leaders, find out their vices, their secrets, and their closest, most intimate enemies. We will turn them against each other, shatter their alliances, and isolate each clan in fear of the other. Only then, when they are alone and unwilling to call for aid, will they be ripe for annihilation.

Primus retreated before Isabelle could retort.

Isabelle ordered all the sails taken in, save those needed for maneuver. The Gyrine could deaden the wind to make sails irrelevant, or they could send in a gale to shatter the masts of a ship under full sail. Furling all but a few of the smaller sails obviated the first approach and mitigated the second.

The blue-and-yellow war balloon opened the shutter on an optical telegraph and flashed a message. Isabelle's Skaladin signalman translated, "They say they are the First Owl clan. We are to surrender immediately and prepare to be boarded."

Similce said, "We're stuck in it now."

Isabelle looked to Marie. "You have the helm. Steer us true."

Marie said, "Signalman, send, 'This vessel is a Tall Clouds prize, but the descent of Jackhand Djordji welcomes you aboard as guests.'"

The First Owl took their time answering, "The jackhand has no children. Surrender or be taken by force."

Marie said, "Send, 'I am Fellhand Marie, daughter of Jackhand Djordji by his choice and mine. You are welcome aboard as guests.'"

While the signalmen fenced, the black-and-red war balloon glided around the *Saint Asne*'s stern. It was like being sneaked up on by a heavily armed circus tent.

The Gyrine signaled, "You will be boarded. If you resist, you will be killed."

Marie said, "Send, 'Gyrine do not kill Gyrine.'"

Fear made Isabelle's stomach quiver. Had bringing them here been another mistake? Just because Djordji took their traditions seriously didn't mean other Gyrine did.

Bitterlich shouted to Malgiers, "Form the men up for parade."

Isabelle turned to Similce. "Prepare to receive guests."

"Aye," Similce said grimly, and began shouting at the crew in Skaladin.

Rebecca floated up to be at eye height with Isabelle, and said in a no-no-I'm-really-not-nervous tone of voice, "So . . . what happens now?"

Isabelle said, "The Gyrine are going to come aboard, and Marie is going to talk them out of killing us. You stay with me."

The war balloons settled into position, one to larboard and the other to stern of the *Saint Asne*. Around the waist of each armored tower were belts of cannons on gimbals that allowed them to aim down at the sloop from an angle where it could not possibly return fire.

"Remember to breathe," Marie said to Isabelle.

Primus said, *Even if your friend fails, you can present yourself as a hostage. You are valuable enough that they will not harm you. Once they have taken you in, then you can prey on their ambitions, fear, and greed.*

Isabelle clenched her teeth and replied, *I will not be the instrument of your revenge.*

Primus asked in a milder tone, *Even if so doing saves your friends' lives?*

Isabelle felt paralyzed, caught between loathing the ancestral parasite and the sure knowledge she would do much worse than manipulate a few Gyrine to save the people she loved.

Down from the war balloons dangled long ropes like a spider's threads. Dozens of Gyrine leapt from the platforms and swung down to alight in the *Saint Asne*'s top rigging like so many monkeys. They unslung muskets and took aim, ready to unleash a lethal hail of lead on the *Saint Asne*'s crew.

"I never realized they were so . . . agile," Malgiers said.

"Throw down yer weapons!" shouted a man from the rigging.

"We hold no weapons," Bitterlich replied, showing empty hands. Not that he personally needed a weapon, but his marines were likewise disarmed. Everything rode on Marie's play.

Down from the First Owl war balloon descended a launch loaded with Gyrine. It swooped slowly in on a course to meet the *Saint Asne* amidships. On its prow stood a rakish-looking Gyrine with silver rings in his ears and gold teeth in his grinning mouth.

"I need that bracelet now," Marie said. Isabelle handed it over. Marie slipped it on her wrist and then hopped up on the larboard rail and stood there like she was nailed to it.

"Ahoy, the skiff," she said, voice raised but her tone still flat. "I am Fell-hand Marie, daughter of Jackhand Djordji of the Tall Clouds clan. This ship is my prize. We welcome our First Owl kin aboard to feast with us."

"I am Conductor Feng, vote captain of the *Finale*, and you are no Gyrine, certainly no fellhand. If that kinslayer Djordji be aboard send him to talk, and you sit down to be counted."

"My father is dead," Marie said. "He succumbed to wounds received in battle two days ago. But I wear his token, and I have his homeshard, or did you think I came to Flotsam by chance?"

Feng hesitated, but only for an eyeblink. "Tokens and shards may be stolen."

"If you wish to challenge my claim, send your champion. Otherwise, come aboard as my guest."

Feng's expression hardened. "I've no need of yer permission. I can slaughter you where you stand, and every lubber aboard."

"But then what do you gain?" Marie asked. "An old bucket of a ship, a dead crew, no hostages, no booty, no prize worth having. You gain nothing by fighting. Killing us would cost you more in powder and shot than you'd ever recoup. Come aboard as my guest. Send to my clan that you've rescued one of their own adrift and you collect the salvage fee, and then I have to answer to them for the cost."

Feng's eyebrows were pierced with gold and silver rings that flashed when he lifted them. "You thinks like a Gyrine. I gives you that, but you are no fellhand, for I know their names."

"I have come to make my challenge," she said. "By ancient tradition, it is up to the clans to prove me wrong."

At that moment, gangs of Gyrine burst up from belowdecks and spread out amongst the terrified aeronauts.

One of them swaggered up to within speaking distance of Feng and hollered, "Ship's clear and secure, Cap'n. No surprises."

"My father's body rests in the turvy hold," Marie said.

Feng shot a questioning look at the boarding leader, who said, "Aye, there a corpse down there, Tall Clouds motley, made ready for the sky."

Feng grunted and returned his gaze to Marie, then after a thought pause he said, "In that case, permission to come aboard, Fellhand Marie."

In the end, only Isabelle was allowed to accompany Marie to Flotsam. It took less than half a day to get there on the *Finale*. The war balloon dove into a cloud bank so thick that it turned day to night. Isabelle imagined the choir of Windcallers who provided the vessel's motive power must be reading the currents in the air to keep them from colliding with anything.

They emerged suddenly into a great sphere of clear, calm air, a pocket of peace in the center of the storm. It was still dark, but before them floated several wide concentric rings of flickering lights. As Isabelle's eyes adjusted to the gloom, she made out dozens of ships' hulks stripped of their masts and lashed together like the spiral of an immense spiderweb. The decks were covered in bright canvas tents and lit with colorful lanterns that made the whole thing look like a fairy market. Gyrine in wildly colorful garb walked the decks, and several clan balloons were tethered about the edges of the outer ring.

"It's amazing," Isabelle said.

"Which is why yer folk tries to destroy it all regular-like," Feng said.

His kind betrayed the Enlightened and left the goodlands open to rape and pillage by the Skaladin, Primus growled.

Isabelle had no desire whatsoever to take either set of bait, so she kept her mouth shut and her inside voice quiet.

They were shoveled onto a skiff and then shuttled across to a hulk that had once been a galleon, one of the earliest types that still resembled a waterborne vessel, complete with rounded bottom and overbuilt sterncastle.

Feng marched Isabelle and Marie along a series of rope-and-plank bridges to the center of the spiderweb. At the hub, three hulks were joined, stem to stern, in a tight triangle. A deck had been erected between them, and on it was built a wooden theater, ascending circles of bench seats around a central stage.

Under the wide tent roof were strung scores of cables in a complex crisscrossing pattern. Each line was hung with the flags of other nations and navies; most of them tattered and burnt. They were the banners of captured ships. Trophies of the clans displayed for all to see.

Clearly word had been sent ahead of their arrival, for Gyrine flowed into the theater from all directions.

Feng took Isabelle and Marie to a room beneath the seats with an entrance leading out onto the arena floor. Isabelle's trepidation grew the closer they got, like frost on the spars growing into crippling sheaths of ice. Marie showed no sign of stress, but she couldn't even if she needed to.

"Conductor Feng," came a woman's indignant voice. "What trickery is this, calling a challenge in my clan's name?"

Isabelle and Marie turned to see a stout woman with reddish-brown skin and eyes like chips of onyx come floating in on her own personal updraft. She wore a clan motley of the same pale green and aquamarine blue as Djordji's token.

Feng said, "Fellhand Marie, be known to yer clan's vote capitaine, Solo Preetah. Solo Preetah, meet Jackhand Djordji's daughter, Fellhand Marie."

Preetah took in the sort of breath that might have been the prelude to an epic aria. "Is he here? Does the jackhand return?"

"In spirit," Marie said. "He died two days ago, to my great sorrow. I've brought him home. I also mean to prove myself a fellhand, champion of the Gyrine."

To Isabelle's immense surprise Preetah's anger deflated. "Leave it to Djordji to play one last trick. I've heard of you, child. I get word on the wind that Djordji's taken one under his wing, a special one they say. Still, the sky's full of special folk, and trained as you may be by him who's seen the best of all, you want no part of this challenge. Gyrine don't kill Gyrine, but you see that gate?" She pointed to the arena entrance. "That's the Ravenous Gate, sweetling. Once you go through it, you're already dead and those rules don't apply. There's twelve fellhands waiting for you out there, all seasoned and deadly, who's seen many a keen upstart bleed out on their blades."

"Djordji also told me about you," Marie said. "He said you'd try to talk me out of it. He's been gone for sixty years, but he always paid his share, and I've come to draw on that."

Preetah snorted. "His stash is of little worth. Certainly not to get yourself killed over."

"I have his log book," Marie said. "And I know how to add. If you're willing to accept me as his rightful daughter and hand over my share, then I'll have no need to walk through the Ravenous Gate."

Preetah looked like she'd just sucked the queen of lemons. "Even winning doesn't prove you're Djordji's heir."

"That depends on how I do it," Marie said.

Preetah flipped her hand in a dismissive gesture. "It doesn't matter. I does right and tries to warn you, but you doesn't listen. You chooses death over life, which no Gyrine ever does. Still if you change yer mind afore they call you out, let me know. I arranges for you to leave Flotsam with your ship and your crew. Else they be treated as plunder."

"I decline your offer," Marie said. "And I will come when the battle is over to retrieve my father's clan share. Builder keep you safe from harm."

The line of Preetah's mouth wriggled like an earthworm on a fishhook. "Savior come and take you home." She retreated, the whirlwind at the base of her updraft kicking up dust behind her like a dog burying a turd.

Isabelle turned to Marie. "Just how big is Djordji's share?"

"More than Preetah has on hand, most likely," Marie said. "He's been sending money home ever since he left, sort of like his dues, and so he's always been entitled to a clan share. He just couldn't collect it because he was banished. That's sixty years' worth of clan share built up."

"And Solo Preetah spent it, because she thought he'd never be able to collect," Isabelle surmised. "But why? I mean, why send money home?"

Feng, who had watched the entire exchange with wicked amusement, said, "He's Gyrine all the way up. Everyone knows what he does is wrong, but they also knows it's necessary. He has to go, and he never returns, and none may offer him aid, but there's not a Gyrine born since who wouldn't buy a bottle and leave it out where he might steal it, or tickle his ears with the four winds' gossip. He can't come home, so we takes home to him."

"A hero in exile," Isabelle said, and wished she known him better.

It took some time for the stadium to fill. Clans of folk in matching motley gathered in what seemed to be designated sections.

Flotsam's governing Windcaller choir gathered atop a raised platform directly opposite the floor entrance. They were a dozen men and women dressed in riotous couture with dagged hems, ripped sleeves, and warring color choices. One wore a cloak sewn with hundreds of glittering glass beads. Another displayed a hat that looked like someone had detonated a peacock. Bitterlich would have fainted dead away at the crimes against fashion.

Isabelle hugged Marie and wished her farewell, then joined Feng in the First Owl section.

A herald stepped forth to the sound of trumpets and said, "Behold, the Choir of Flotsam, blessed by the Builder, beholden to the Canticle of Law. Er Barnabus sets the stage."

Barnabus stepped forward. He was a man of middling height, built like a barrel with a thick beard and a flat nose. His voice rolled out like thunder. "Behold the arena, the land beyond death, the court of the powers divine. Today comes before us a spectacle most strange, for one unknown to us steps forth to claim our names of honor. Let the claimant step forth, Fellhand Marie, to defend her claim to that title."

Marie stepped into the sand-strewn arena. She looked so small and fragile, no matter that Isabelle knew she was as tough as seasoned oak. She strode to the center of the circle and stopped dead, so still that she might have been standing there since the Breaking of the World, as white as the great moon Kore and just as eternal.

After giving the stillness a moment to settle Marie raised her voice and declared, "I am Fellhand Marie of the Tall Clouds clan, daughter of the great pirate Jackhand Djordji. Are there any who dispute my claim?"

Despite her terror, amusement tickled Isabelle's brain. Marie had tied her legal paternity into the outcome of the duel.

"I challenge," came a ragged chorus from around the ring, and twelve champions entered the arena, each standing by their respective clan sections as the chorus boomed out their names:

"Fellhand Adelus of the First Owl clan!" He was a large man with shoulders like a ship's beam, and carried a pair of longswords so lightly they might have been feathers.

"Fellhand Holden of the Stooping Falcon clan!" He was shorter and stouter with a thick black beard, armed with cutlass and a hook on a chain.

This went on, one fellhand after another, confident, experienced, and armed to the teeth.

"Fellhand Vexatious of the Lost Horizon clan!" She was the first woman on the list, as lean and tightly coiled as a new cable. She was armed with a rapier, and a dozen knives hung about her body.

After eleven were named, the last champion stepped onto the killing floor. He was a man Isabelle would not have picked out of a crowd. His clan colors were muted nearly to gray, and his long coat looked to have seen the service of many years. His expression was neither eager nor bored, contemptuous nor fey. He was but watchful, and though he shook neither his sword nor his fist, the crowd hushed when he stepped into the light.

The choir sang, "Fellhand Ghetorix of the Moon Catcher clan, champion of champions and lord of the arena!"

"Fellhand Marie," said the choir. "There are twelve here who challenge your right to that title. Which one will you meet first?"

Marie slowly turned, surveying her selection of opponents.

Isabelle, trying not to squirm in her seat, asked, "How are there any fellhands at all with trials such as this?"

Feng said, "There are usually not trials such as this. Usually by the time someone claims the title fellhand they have already faced other champions in the ring. They are known and respected, and when they make the claim, only one or two will challenge them, and then mostly to demonstrate the challenger's skill. No such courtesy is to be extended to an arrogant outsider who seeks to claim a famous father and a title she has never earned."

Marie raised her finger and pointed at the huge man with the two swords. "Adelus."

Adelus stepped forward into the ring. Isabelle's stomach clung to her spine.

The chorus sang, "The challenge begins with the champion of—"

"Vexatious." Marie pointed to the woman, who looked startled. The whole crowd muttered in surprise.

"And Gath"—Marie pointed to another fellhand, bare-chested and bedecked in tattoos—"for the first round."

The muttering intensified.

Barnabus sounded perplexed. "You can't hope to defeat three fellhands at once."

Marie called, "If I have to beat them one at a time, we'll be here all night."

The crowd guffawed with laughter at her bravado.

She's getting them on her side, Primus said.

It's going to take more than a joke, Isabelle replied. It would take her beating three of her would-be peers at once. If she could manage that, the rest of the duels would seem superfluous.

Marie drew two short curved swords and took up a wide stance. "Begin!"

The other three fellhands looked at one another with a degree of wariness, then approached Marie from three points of a not-quite-equilateral triangle. Isabelle bit her knuckles in worry.

When the noose had constricted and the fellhands were almost within striking distance, Marie began to sing. She did not have a practiced voice, and her rhythm was that of a chanty, but it gave her opponents pause:

Hear the life of Jackhand Djordji
Champion of the Tall Clouds clan
He fell from grace, no king afflicts thee
Thus he earned his wicked brand

Her opponents approached even more cautiously, keeping a weather eye on one another.

Solitaire sailed the deep sky
Bold was he upon the wind—

Adelus pounced, his sword a blur to the eyes. Marie dipped away into Gath's path and he swept his quarterstaff to take out her legs.

Marie tucked and tumbled over the quarterstaff and came up with a kick at Gath's knee. He dodged, but the move took him into Adelus's path and fouled the big man's follow-up cut. Vexatious circled to get out from behind them.

Isabelle's heart hammered against her ribs, and a terrible hope filled her mind. Marie had spent weeks and weeks fighting men in bunches, but the fellhands weren't used to working together. She'd got them to cut each other's wind, making her own kind of home ground.

Still singing, Marie pressed Gath, her short blades flashing, driving him back into Adelus, who shoved him aside with one hand and slashed at Marie with the other.

Marie spun away from the blade. Vexatious hurled a throwing knife.

Marie fell. No, *ducked*. The blade shot by and nearly hit Gath. Adelus's blade sliced for Marie's head, but found only the space where it had been. Around and around she harried them like a sheepdog herding a flock so none had the space they needed. The crowd roared to shake the stadium when blades crashed.

Adelus scooted free of the crowd, "She's mine!"

Alone at last, he lunged at Marie, his blades a whirlwind, he drove her back and pinned her against the edge of the arena. Nowhere else to run. He stabbed; a killing blow.

Marie moved like oil on water, a shimmer on a ripple, untouchable. Adelus's blade pierced the wood of the arena wall and lodged.

Marie slithered by and slashed her blade along his belly. He yelped and leapt back. The crowd gasped, but there was no blood.

Marie showed him the flat of her blade. "Next time I use the edge."

Adelus drew himself up and bowed to her, "I yield."

The crowd hooted and jeered and applauded. Isabelle let out a shuddering breath and gripped the rail before her. One down, only two to go . . . or eleven, and Marie was breathing hard. Worse, her advantage waned the more foes she eliminated.

Marie resumed her song and took the battle to her foes. Isabelle could hardly follow the blur of bodies and weapons. Suddenly came an awful thud. Fully extended like a gymnast doing the splits, Marie's heel rammed up through Gath's chin with a blow that would have laid out a dray horse. He went over backward like a felled tree and landed hard.

The crowd gasped and cheered, but Marie came up limping. Somewhere in there she'd twisted an ankle.

Vexatious pounced. Her rapier zipped like a hummingbird, her line quick and long, darting in and retreating where Marie could not follow. Marie's leg crumpled with every step.

Vexatious lunged and Marie twisted aside, but not fast enough. The blade sliced her shoulder and her colorless blood soaked her sleeve. The tip of her sword dipped and wobbled.

"Well, she almost did it," Feng said.

"She's not done yet," Isabelle said.

She is lost. It is time for you to start negotiating your own future, Primus said.

Shut up. Isabelle splashed him hard.

Again the women clashed, and again. Vexatious opened a wound on Marie's other arm. When Vexatious darted out of range, Marie sagged to one knee to relieve her ankle. Her face held no expression, but her body quivered in agony.

"Yield," Vexatious commanded, her voice like a hunting hawk.

Marie pushed herself to her feet. "No." She readied her defense.

"As you will." Vexatious whipped her sword up in salute, then approached, testing Marie's defense with the tip of her blade. Marie, wounded and weary, retreated and circled, making no attempt to retaliate.

Isabelle gripped the rail so tightly that the wood bent and splintered. She prayed Marie had some strategy—

Vexatious lunged, her whole body extended like a spear. Marie missed the parry, the blade hit her ribs. The blade lanced out the back of her blouse. She fell.

"No!" Isabelle shot to her feet.

But as she fell, Marie twisted, locked her arm around Vexatious's sword arm, bore her to the ground, and elbowed her in the face. Vexatious lost her sword and tried to squirm away, but Marie twisted her arm and locked it, driving her face into the floor of the arena.

"Yield," she demanded breathlessly.

Vexatious strained against the hold but could not break it. "I yield."

The crowd whooped and hollered, delighted to be entertained. From the Tall Clouds section, came a chant, *"Fellhand Marie. Fellhand Marie!"*

Preetah looked like a game hen that had been chocked too full of stuffing.

Marie stood up and extended an arm to Vexatious, who took it and rose to her feet. Then Marie stretched up and whispered something in the other woman's ear that made her laugh.

Only then, from a better angle, did Isabelle see the rent in Marie's blouse, and the glittering corset of chainmail she wore underneath.

"Only nine more to go," Feng said.

As Vexatious left the arena, and Gath's clansmen dragged his still-unconscious body away, Marie limped to the center.

Barnabus said, "Three victories to Fellhand Marie, but who would you challenge next? Three more, or shall you attempt four?"

"Just one," Marie said. Slowly she turned, lifted her chin, and said, "Fellhand Ghetorix of the Moon Catcher clan, champion of champions and lord of the arena!"

The watchful champion stepped into the arena. Isabelle thought she understood what Marie was about, and prayed she had judged the situation aright. Ghetorix faced the choir and in a low voice that somehow filled the room said, "I have no objection to Fellhand Marie, daughter of Jackhand Djordji. I withdraw my challenge."

The stadium erupted in pandemonium.

Twenty-Five

Isabelle barely had time to congratulate Marie on her victory before the ebullient crowd swept her up and carried her off to a great bring-what-you-can feast. She'd won Flotsam's heart, at least for today. Isabelle made sure Marie's wounds were tended and that Preetah acknowledged her as Djordji's heir, but then got out of the way and let Marie enjoy the adoration of her newfound clan.

The *Saint Asne* arrived in port. Isabelle went to guarantee landing rights for her crew before setting them loose to join the party. The resulting evacuation left the ship very quiet, which suited her mood. Her skin had grown as tight as a sausage casing. Past life experience suggested this meant that the long, aggravating transformation was approaching its conclusion.

Alone with her thoughts and those of her relations, she stood in the *Saint Asne* chartroom. Jean-Claude's hat lay on the flat top of the orrery. Saints, but she missed him so hard she wanted to weep.

There came a rap at the doorframe and Bitterlich strolled in. "Good evening, Capitaine."

Isabelle found herself smiling behind her cowl. "Ah, Major, why aren't you out celebrating?"

"Because it is loud, and because the person I'd rather spend time with is here." Bitterlich's golden eyes smiled at Isabelle's in their smug feline way. She much preferred seeing him primly self-satisfied than moping about.

He is a toy, whispered Lissa. *A pleasant diversion. Enjoy yourself, but remember that a house is only as strong as its weakest pillar.*

Isabelle stirred the courtesan's reflection and dispersed her into her brain's baggage car. She'd sooner trust her heart to loyalty and honesty than wealth or power.

He betrayed your trust once, Primus put in. *A broken sword may be mended, but it will always snap again.*

Isabelle made to banish his manifestation, but he retreated before she could dispel him. Leaving on his own terms: a master tactician indeed.

"Where is Rebecca?" Isabelle asked.

"Passed out in her rack after picking half the pockets in Flotsam, and packing her guts like a pickle barrel."

"You let her pick pockets?" Isabelle said, appalled. "What if she'd been caught?"

"She'd have to give up her sack to whoever caught her, and start over. All Gyrine children are taught to pick pockets, and to practice on their fellows. They aren't allowed to rob shops or merchants in Flotsam, but anyone on the planks is fair game. It's expected."

"And how did you find all that out?" Isabelle said.

"From the urchin who tried to rob me," Bitterlich said. "I sought out independent confirmation after his preliminary testimony. It really helps to know what questions to ask. Once Rebecca was apprised of the rules of engagement, she cut a swath through the festivities."

Isabelle shook her head in dismay. "Just when I thought this place couldn't get any stranger. Dare I ask how much Rebecca absconded with?"

"In value or weight? She clinked all the way back to her rack, I'm going to make her spend most of it tomorrow."

"Are you sure that's the kind of lesson you want to be teaching her, though?"

Bitterlich said, "She didn't stop being an impulsive twelve-year-old pick-pocket just because we found out she's my daughter. More to the point, she did behave herself. She waited until she learned the rules of the game before joining in, and picking pockets is a useful skill."

Isabelle wanted to dispute this, but every argument that came to mind boiled down to "But she's a child!" which was never a good reason for withholding vital training. The world could not be made safe, so the child must be made capable.

Bitterlich gestured to the hat. "Thinking about him."

She rubbed the hat brim between her thumb and fingers. "I get the feeling he was trying to send me a message. 'I'm off hunting the missing trinket.' Those were his exact words, yes?"

Bitterlich said, "Yes, but was he talking about the relic or the shard? Or was the fisherman I got it from not repeating the message properly?"

"Which one?" Sudden hope bloomed in Isabelle's breast, rising on wings of inspiration. "And he sent me his hat."

"It's a very identifiable hat," Bitterlich said.

"Oh, it's unique. I need a mirror." She led him to the great cabin and drew a hand mirror from her trunk. "About two years ago, Jean-Claude went mirror walking with a Glasswalker and lost his hat's reflection. It's never had one since." She held the battered headgear up to the mirror so she could see where its reflection should have been. "He said he was hunting the missing trinket."

"Which means the other one isn't missing," Bitterlich said.

A grin split her face as she found the gift Jean-Claude had sent her. The hat itself was not visible, but there, floating in approximately the place the feather was pinned, was the *Conquest* shard.

Isabelle resisted the urge to cackle gleefully as she turned the hat around, unpinned the ancient feather, and drew the bonekeel needle from its hollow shaft. "Thank you, Jean-Claude. We are back in the hunt. Hasdrubal is making his way to the Vault by way of the *Conquest*, so that's where Jean-Claude will be."

"The only problem now is how do we get there?" Bitterlich asked. "Your bargain with Similce doesn't include challenging the Bittergale."

"You could put it to a vote with the crew," Similce said, stepping through the door. Her expression was rigid and her voice flat, as if she were facing a judge or a hangman.

Surprise and wariness bubbled up in Isabelle's breast and her ancestral chorus shouted warnings of danger and treachery at her, but she put on her diplomat's face. Everything about Similce's posture said she was pushing herself past some personal limit.

"I could," Isabelle said. "But you're not obligated to us after we get to a neutral port; why would you put your crew in that position?"

Similce snorted and a smidgen of contempt gave life to her voice. "You think you're the only one who can talk to the crew? My 'nauts have been talking to yours since before we lofted."

"And what did you learn?" Bitterlich asked, his whiskers bending forward with curiosity.

Similce shrugged as if trying to loosen a knot in her shoulder. "That you treated them well. That some are alive who wouldn't be if you'd left them to rot. Also that Hasdrubal lied."

Her mouth worked hard for a moment, as if her tongue had become a stone, and then she said, "He never told us about the *Conquest,* or the Vault of Ages. He was never going to take us home." She fixed her stare on Isabelle as if daring her to make something of this.

"Soldiers aren't enemies," Isabelle said. "They are opponents." History was crammed with examples of foes becoming allies at need. Harder to forgive was Similce's attack on Fishers Point and the slaves they'd tried to take, but if Isabelle meant to die on that hill, she should have done it back on Joubert's Folly.

"Then put it to the crew," Similce said stiffly. "We've got nowhere to go, no safe port, no other jobs, but there's still the *Conquest*'s treasure, enough to set us up for life."

Isabelle considered this proposition and the obvious strain it put on Similce. What wasn't she saying?

"Exactly how does this vote work?" Isabelle asked.

"You make a proposal to the crew. Tell 'em what you have planned. Take a vote. If they say yes . . . that's where we go."

"Isabelle, a word," Bitterlich said. He drew her into a corner and whispered in her ear, "She's offering to make this arrangement permanent, which means giving up command."

"Oh," Isabelle said, feeling the fool for not having tripped to it herself. She'd heard some pirates operated that way. Similce was suggesting what she thought was best for her crew, even at a high cost to herself. That raised her immensely in Isabelle's estimation.

Isabelle returned to stand before Similce. "I will put it to the crew, on one condition. You must stay on as my second; it's part of the deal."

Similce couldn't have looked more surprised if someone swatted her with a fish. "Why?"

Isabelle placed her taloned hand carefully on Bitterlich's shoulder. "As a good friend once told me, 'You're already a hero, you don't have to be a martyr.' This ship is your home. This crew is your family. I have no wish to take them from you."

After a moment Similce saluted and lifted her chin. "Thank you, Capitaine."

—

The weather had gotten so cold that Jean-Claude had to keep his waterskin under his clothes to keep it from freezing. He'd stolen as many clothes as he could wear while being able to move and still wasn't entirely sure he still had toes.

The aeronauts were now engaged day and night with clearing the ship of ice. Their boots thumped along the hull, the wood groaned, and the crack of shearing rime had become a constant refrain. The ship tossed in turbulent skies, straining the keel braces and the rigging.

He'd lost track of the days he'd been cooped up in this stygian icebox. They blended together in a mismatched pastiche of fitful sleep, ratlike skulking, constant hunger, and worry. He'd taken to rereading his message to Ivar every few minutes on the notion that the pirate probably only checked in on his eye occasionally. After all, the things he needed to know from Jean-Claude were not things Jean-Claude was in a position to see just yet.

Either that, or Jean-Claude was completely wrong about the eye and its function.

And where in all the endless sky was Isabelle? He prayed she had found the *Conquest* shard and was on her way north. For his part he must distract and delay Hasdrubal and Travers, but his chances for that were few and slim. There were any number of ways he could sabotage the *Potencia*, but he had a strict moral objection to the downing of any ship he happened to be on.

Jean-Claude was staring at his missive again when vision faded from his clockwork eye to be replaced with a view from somewhere else. At last, a response! The double vision with his ordinary eye made him dizzy. The sensation of the metal orb being physically inside someone else's head was uncanny.

Before his bifurcated vision hovered a sheet of paper covered in writing. It remained directly before his left eye no matter which way he turned his head, as if someone had stuck the thing to his spectacles. He squeezed his right eye shut to stop the world from reeling and read the message written there, in a large sloppy hand:

> *Monsieur Jean-Claude:*
>
> *I bid you recall I saved you from plummeting to your death, tended your wounds, and even replaced your missing eye with an improvement the likes of which would bring a king's ransom. A measure of gratitude would be in order.*
>
> *I have indeed received a request to down a particular airship, and I am interested in hearing your argument against the proposition.*

Jean-Claude had time to read the message twice before it disappeared and his own vision returned . . . if he could consider it his own. If Ivar could turn it off whenever he liked, it made that much of him Ivar's puppet, and that he would not stand. It was too useful to get rid of just now, but when the time came, he'd either find a way to wrest control of the artifact from Ivar or dig it out with a spoon.

Fortunately, Jean-Claude had already worked out and written down what he wanted to say. He held up another piece of paper:

> *If you down that ship, you will never obtain the* Conquest *shard.*

It was, he thought, a delicately balanced sentence, allowing the reader to believe the shard might be on the ship, but not allowing them to be sure of it.

He stared at the message until a new, freshly inked message manifested before his eye:

> *It should occur to you that I can very easily inform Le Comte de Travers that you are stowed away aboard his ship. You should consider very seriously telling me where the shard is.*

Jean-Claude waited until that faded. He covered the clockwork eye with a plate of bronze stolen from the ship's stores and took the time to write out his reply before uncovering it again.

The new message read:

> *Capitaine Ivar:*
> *You could indeed end my life with a word, but then what? You still won't have the* Conquest *shard, nor will you have a spy aboard this ship. If you kill me out of anger or wounded pride, you will cheat yourself out of the prize that you came to claim. Worse, you will have spent considerable time and expenses, not to mention enduring the likes of Travers, only to return empty-handed, a fact I doubt your backers will appreciate.*

This last was a guess, but not a difficult one. Ivar was never one to work for one payout when several were available. He would have promised first access to the Craton Auroborea to as many people as possible before he ever lofted. He might have even sold shares in the venture, money on which his clients back on Craton Massif would expect a return.

———

In the dim light of morning under Flotsam's perpetual fog bank, Isabelle stood on the quarterdeck of the *Saint Asne*, with the ship's crew gathered on the main deck below. They were not her crew, not until they voted, and she'd given them as much to fear as to hope for. Such was the cost of honesty.

She'd told them all of the *Conquest* treasure, of the Vault of Ages. She laid out the deadly risk of the Bittergale, of their lethal and determined competition, and, of course, the insects that had driven off Hailer Dok's expedition.

"The dangers are many," she said. "But the rewards are great. Who is with me?"

She would not be surprised if they voted no, even less so if they thought her mad.

You should have phrased it as a choice between courage and cowardice, Primus said. *People such as these will risk much to avoid being named a coward.*

Which is why it is a threat I will not make, Isabelle replied. *I will not have my people abandon reason for the safety of fear.*

They aren't your people, yet.

"Let the vote be taken," Similce said. "All in favor!"

"Aye!" came the shout, and every member of the crew threw their fist in the air, albeit some only after seeing everyone else do it.

They are now, Isabelle thought grimly. *My crew. My responsibility.*

"Capitaine," Similce said, "what are your orders?"

"Fill her belly and make ready to sail," Isabelle said.

Drawing on Marie's account, Isabelle and Similce bargained and hustled and swapped for supplies all morning.

Isabelle gave Similce the lead. She'd been keeping her own crew aloft on breadcrumbs for the last two years, and she drove a bargain like a carpenter drove a nail.

Isabelle was just about to duck into a tent where supposedly they could find a man who could sell them cheese in bulk when Marie's voice caught up to them.

"Capitaine!" she called, limping along the boardwalk with the help of a staff and a brace on her sprained ankle.

With her came a large blue Seelenjäger with four arms and the aspect of a lizard.

"Fellhand Marie," Isabelle said, striding to meet her. Isabelle really wanted to ask about what she'd been up to all night, but that would have to wait for a private chat. "Who is your companion?"

"Capitaine," Marie said, "meet Heinrich von Keisle, who has news you want to hear."

"Herr von Keisle," Isabelle said. "What news?"

"I have apparently met a friend of yours," he said, and presented her with a leather documents wallet that Isabelle would have recognized anywhere.

Nearly breathless, Isabelle received it from him. "Jean-Claude! Thank you for this. Where did you meet him? Where is he?"

"He rescued me from captivity aboard le Comte de Travers's flagship *Potencia*, where I had been kept in bondage for many months. He helped me to escape, but he remained aboard as a stowaway."

Isabelle was stunned, but not entirely surprised. "Did he say why?"

"He actually said nothing at all. When I met him he was voiceless. I suspect le Comte de Travers stole his speech."

Isabelle was horrified. Jean-Claude's voice and his wit were his busiest and most accomplished tools. Without them . . . he would improvise, just like he always did. She'd always envied his ability to adapt to any trouble without breaking stride. Still, what a horrific blow.

She'd heard of the Travers family, a purity cult in which first cousins were considered distant relations. They weren't known to be militarily adventurous, but if he had a flagship . . .

"How many in Travers's fleet?" Isabelle asked.

"Five that I counted," Heinrich said. "An old galleon and four smaller ships. I was mostly concerned with flying away at the time, so it is hard to be sure."

"How long ago?" Isabelle asked "How far away?"

"I flew for two days until I stumbled upon this place. It's been another two since."

Isabelle weighed the pouch in her hand. "I owe you a debt for this."

Heinrich raised all four hands to demur. "Your Jean-Claude saved my life and sanity. Bringing you this costs me nothing and gives me joy."

"Then let me make you a different proposition," Isabelle said. "Please, come with me."

She took Heinrich back to the *Saint Asne* and into the chartroom, where she pointed out Flotsam on the orrery. "We are here." She pulled out a compass and made a measurement into a blank space on the map. "Joubert's Folly is about here. It's an imperial supply depot. If you could deliver Jean-Claude's papers there, and tell the base commandant what you told me about your escape from Travers, I would be immensely grateful and make it worth your while. Just don't tell him about me or Flotsam."

Heinrich examined the orrery. "Why not tell them about you?"

"Because the commandant wants my neck in a noose," Isabelle said. "On the other hand, he has nothing against Jean-Claude, and this will alert him to divert fleet resources to Jean-Claude's aid. If he asks, tell him that Travers is headed for the Bittergale."

"If this helps Jean-Claude, then I will do it," Heinrich said. "He saved me from such torture as you cannot imagine."

Twenty-Six

Jean-Claude felt the noose of time tightening around his neck. He reckoned Hasdrubal would wait until the last possible moment to bring Dok aboard the *Potencia,* and now that moment was at hand. The galleon drew up on a Skaladin sloop, one of the ships from the raid on Fishers Point, and the smaller ship sent over a launch.

Watching with his clockwork eye through the hull of the ship, Jean-Claude could make out few details, though the vortex of Dok's Windcaller sorcery glimmered like ripples on a lake. Jean-Claude watched from one deck down as they chained him in a cell newly partitioned off from the great cabin.

Hasdrubal's people also brought aboard a large iron-bound chest. It was the sort of thing Jean-Claude did not expect to be able to see through even with his artifact eye. But something in the center of it glowed in his sight like a single star shining through a cloudy night.

The key. Hasdrubal didn't have it on his person, probably because he could not shift it away when he changed shape.

That meant the ring was at least possibly in reach, if Jean-Claude could figure out how to get into a locked trunk surrounded by guards in a secured room without being cut to pieces.

Whatever he attempted it must be soon. If Dok could get the *Potencia* through the Bittergale, then no pursuit could reach them. For days on end, Jean-Claude had evolved and discarded plans for killing Travers and Hasdrubal, to cut off the head of the snake, but both men were personally powerful and very well guarded. He might kill either one of them, but the chance of getting both was vanishingly small.

Dok, on the other hand, was vulnerable. His captors had muffled his powers, and the guards they'd placed around him were inward-facing, to keep him from escaping. Without the Windcaller, passage through the Bittergale was impossible, and the conspiracy would fail. If that didn't work, he might seize the key and toss it into the Gloom.

With these thoughts in mind, Jean-Claude acquired a rope and harness of the kind the aeronauts wore when they were knocking around the hull of the ship. He ascended to the main deck. His only consolation for the unbearable cold was that with bulky clothes came a greater level of anonymity. With his girth covered and his eye concealed under a hood, he dared venture up on the main deck in daylight.

If you could call it daylight. Behind him the Solar was barely two hand spans above the cloud horizon even at midday, so that every upright thing cast long shadows along the deck. The dome of the sky was gray and dead, as if all the color had drained south for the winter, and a dreadful churning noise like the rumble of a rockslide rolled down constantly from the north.

Some way ahead of the *Potencia*—distances aloft were always hard to tell—the sky ended in an immense vortex of wind-borne ice, snow, and debris: the Bittergale.

The sheer scope of it beggared Jean-Claude's imagination.

It stretched up from the Gloom, carrying with it streaks of lightning from the Galvanosphere. It stirred the Miasma like a witch's cauldron, drawing the noxious brew into itself, and it reached so high into the sky that it seized the uppermost clouds and dragged them screaming by their tails into its maw. It stretched out to devour the horizon on either side.

Jean-Claude turned from the Bittergale's snarling menace. He could not linger on deck. Everyone not needed for steering the ship and keeping it clear of ice was huddled below, but those who remained would surely notice if he did not immediately make himself busy.

He shuffled toward the back of the ship. Ice rained down around him, kicked loose by topsmen from the spars and rigging. Even more men scraped and shoveled it off the deck.

He passed two safety launches athwart the ship and just forward of the wheel. If he could get Dok into one of those and launch it, they'd be adrift in a freezing sky in a tiny boat in the middle of deadly winter. It was a terrible plan, but it was the only one he had. Conditions would only get worse from here.

Unfortunately, the marines in charge of keeping uninvited guests out of the cabins remained at their posts, or at least as close to their posts as could be managed whilst sheltering behind crates and barrels.

Trying not to think too hard about what he meant to do, Jean-Claude stumped up the outside stair to the poop deck, directly above the great cabin. Through the thick wood he could just make out Travers and Hasdrubal sitting down to supper with most of the other officers likewise invited. The edges of their silver plates and utensils stood out strongly in Jean-Claude's clockwork vision, and the various Sanguinaires' bloodshadows looked like red honey on diaphanous linen.

In a smaller cabin next door, Hasdrubal's Skaladin retinue gathered around an alchemical stove, sharing several bottles of liquor amongst them.

Beyond that, in a cell that was barely more than a locker, sat Hailer Dok, chained to a wall. The gritty edges of the iron shackles glittered, and the air around Dok shimmered, as if the clockwork eye could see the ripples of his sorcery leaking out into the world.

The only door into Dok's cell faced the Skaladin cabin, but it did have a window facing the gallery. All Jean-Claude had to do was go over the back of the ship on a rope, drop down onto the gallery without being noticed, and hope the window had hinges.

It was the first step that terrified him most. Even approaching the rail made him queasy, and looking over the side would undo him. *L'appel du vide* had never stayed its hand or granted him the slightest reprieve. It made him sick to his stomach and light in his head. It called him to let go and fall. This time he had a rope, a harness, and if he fell straight down he'd land on the damned gallery, but as he approached the rail his belly flopped and his lips went numb as if he was going to vomit.

Above him, aeronauts swung along slick frozen spars, knocking off ice sheets before they could snap the wood. Jean-Claude could barely bring himself to imagine the poor souls clambering amongst the turvy masts.

If they could do it, why couldn't he? Why had the vertiginous urge of the deep sky always defeated him?

He eased astern, and the world seemed to bend around him, funneling him toward the fall. He closed his eyes and groped his way forward until his hands found the wooden rail.

He opened the clockwork eye and imagined he was seeing the world as he did when it was dark, only catching the edges of things. To his relief the eye complied, and the urge to fall receded slightly. He tied a knot that might not instantly fail if he put his weight on it.

"Hey, you!" shouted the boatswain, striding in his direction.

Fresh fear seized Jean-Claude. He must not be singled out. Recognition was death. He fumbled his ropes through the clasps on the harness. Was that bit supposed to go over or under the other bit?

"Get down to port side abaft the mainmast, clear the ice dam!" the boatswain yelled.

Jean-Claude's first instinct was to bluff, but he could not press words into his throat, much less out his mouth. The black snake poisoned his mind and tied his tongue in a knot.

Desperate, he spun, gave a salute sharp enough to split wood, and pressed his hood down to cover the mechanical eye. He made a show of recovering his rope. The boatswain turned to harangue someone else.

Jean-Claude squeezed his eyes shut and, giving himself no time to think, hauled himself up and over the rail. His toes scrabbled for purchase. His weight hit the harness and it held. He played out his line, opened his clockwork eye, and rappelled onto the gallery. His heart beat so fast that it seemed to buzz in his chest. He pressed himself into a corner out of sight of the officers' partition and forced himself to breathe slowly until he could stand without the wall to brace on. He'd faced cannon fire, royal displeasure, and Impervia's wrath with less reaction.

As soon as he could make his hands work, he turned his attention to the window. Jean-Claude deployed his knife and worked it between the window frame and the jamb, cracking ice until he found the latch—a simple one, thank the Builder—and slowly worked the stubborn thing free.

The process was not silent, but the howl of the wind gave him cover. He chipped away the ice all the way around the frame before pulling the window open. None of the Skaladin in the next cabin showed any inclination to barge in, but someone had to come in at least occasionally to feed and water their prisoner, especially given that they needed him at full strength to try the Bittergale. If they came in and found Jean-Claude, he was dead and all this work for naught.

Dok, chained to the wall like a dog, huddled under several layers of blankets. His face was encased in a leather mask that covered eyes, mouth, and ears. Only by the vortex that circled and the visible bits of his clan motley could Jean-Claude even be sure this was him.

He clambered in through the window and shut it behind him, but the Windcaller shrank away as he drew near.

Jean-Claude wished he could whisper some reassurances, but his tongue remained a dead eel in his throat. Instead, he captured Dok's head and unbuckled the mask as swiftly as possible. The leather case came away with a sucking sensation and a cloud of dank reek.

Hailer Dok drew a breath that very nearly voided the cabin of air. He looked like a man who'd been ground up into sausages and then slapped back into shape by an unskilled sculptor. His face was nearly fleshless, raw skin stretched tight and covered in blisters and sores, his nose nearly crushed by the ill-fitting mask. He squinted and hissed at the cabin's dim light.

Jean-Claude's fear climbed a notch. Would he even be able to see, or had his time in the dark made a blind cave fish of him? Worse, would he scream and smash the place to bits with a windstorm, or just alert the pirates in the next room?

Streamers of air spiraled about his head, whispering winds murmuring in his ears. Jean-Claude could not make out the words, but he thought he heard several voices. After a few moments the whispers faded and he subsided, letting out a long sigh.

Jean-Claude shook his shoulder. He needed to get those manacles off him and get him on the move. Off this ship was the only chance they had.

Dok blinked blearily and said in a low, rough voice, "Monsieur musketeer, either I goes to Torment or you comes back. Can't tell which. Or is that still you behind that thing of gears?"

Jean-Claude pulled from his coat a sheet of paper and showed it to Dok. It read: *We need to leave. We take the quick launch.*

Dok mouthed the words out, then shook his head. "Nay. I'm staying. I fetches Aria."

Jean-Claude gave him his most incredulous look and swept his hand to include the *Potencia* and every wicked thing aboard.

Dok returned his look bemusedly. "Lost your tongue? That be a point in favor of paradise, by my reckoning."

Jean-Claude cast an exasperated look at the heavens, then gestured to the cabins full of enemies, then to Dok and made a throat-slicing gesture.

"Kill me? Nay. They needs me to get them through the Bittergale. I gets 'em through all right, but I don't brings 'em back."

Jean-Claude leafed through the other notes he'd written. *We will rejoin Isabelle.*

Dok looked skeptical, "But she's not here, is she? I hear she loses her ship, has to steal a new one. So now l'Empire's own navy hunts her, and Travers sends some pirate to shoot her down. Your lass is a fine woman, I gives her that, but I don't fancy bobbing about in a punt with the grubbiest lubber who ever lived while Travers, Hasdrubal, and their whole cursed squadron tries to get us back. If you want to win this, you has to see it through. Gets the bastards through to the craton, see. The closer they gets to the treasure, the less they wants to share. That's when they're ripe for plucking."

Jean-Claude hated to admit it, but Dok was right. If Dok could get them through the Bittergale and Jean-Claude could get on land, then he might defeat his enemies in detail.

The door creaked. Jean-Claude's attention whipped round like a snake. If he were caught, he'd at least make his enemies pay a price for his blood. But the noise came from someone brushing against the door on their way by.

His pulse rushing, Jean-Claude pointed in the general direction of Travers and his allies. He mimed slashing throats. Then he pointed to Dok and then to himself. He put them in an invisible basket and made his much-practiced flying-away gesture.

"Aye," Dok said. "You kills them, and Aria and I brings you home."

Jean-Claude had no idea how Dok might manage such a feat, but he imagined the Windcaller had no desire to die and no intention of staying trapped on the Craton Auroborea. He folded his piece of paper so it just said *Isabelle,* and showed it to Dok, then he mimed whispering and sending that whisper on its way.

Dok nodded slowly. "Aye I can do that."

Jean-Claude motioned him to hurry up. Dok sang very softly, a light breeze gathering about him. The zephyr tugged the words from his mouth and wound them up in its flow, a braid of sound that looped round and round until it finally flew to the window, where it circled and scratched like a cat until Jean-Claude let it out.

"And now I sings to Aria," he said.

He built up a slower, longer string of music. The words were opaque to Jean-Claude, but the melody spoke of longing and affection.

Motion outside caught Jean-Claude's attention. Travers's bloodshadow slid across the wall like a monstrous tongue. With le comte came Hasdrubal, entering the Skaladin cabin.

Jean-Claude's bowels nearly gave way in fright. He stuffed Dok's head back in the leather mask, cutting him off mid-song. Dok struggled, so it was like trying to shove a piglet into a sack two sizes too small.

Fortunately Jean-Claude had been raised on a farm. He got the hood on in a wink, buckled it tight, and toppled through the window just as the cell door unlocked. He pressed the window shut and held it closed while crouching under the sill.

Through the boards he watched Travers and Hasdrubal enter the cell. A pair of Skaladin aeronauts secured Dok and removed the hood Jean-Claude had so gently replaced.

The wind shrieked and moaned, but Jean-Claude made out Travers's voice, "what you . . . brought here . . ."

They unhooked Dok's chain from the wall, heaved him to his feet, and dragged him away.

Jean-Claude watched them leave the room and he waited until they'd shut the door, then ever so carefully jiggered the latch back into place. He hurried back into his harness. He had to shake new ice off his own ropes. He dreaded the ascent to the poop deck, but at least he didn't have to look back or down. He hoisted himself onto the rail and then up the side.

The Bittergale loomed above him, the wall of the vortex nearly straight up, and its roar had become a thing to menace the Builder himself. It sounded like all the Halls of Torment let loose, endless streams of shriven souls sent shrieking into the sky.

Jean-Claude could only stare in awe. What fools they were, what arrogant nits clinging to the short hairs of the world. This wonder stood as a warning against the folly of mortalkind, and they sought to challenge it.

"Hit the deck!" shouted a lookout.

Jean-Claude threw himself flat behind a bulwark.

The storm must have noticed them, for it flung out a long whip of ice and snow to crack against their ship. The sky to port grew suddenly dark. A swarm of hailstones the size of lemons blasted the *Potencia* like grapeshot, sweeping unlucky aeronauts from the deck and the rigging. The Bittergale tore even their dying screams away. The barrage snapped lines and shredded them.

Yet somehow through the scream came another song, low and thrumming. It did not oppose the wind but danced with it, turning and twisting, looping and curling until the wind swooped and rose, leaping over the ship and diving below, leaving no more than a stiff breeze to fill the wounded sails.

Down on the main deck, Dok had been chained to the mainmast. Hasdrubal and Travers's helmsman stood over him while he sang. Once he had the melody going, he gave the music its own hook and took a breath to speak, "I can't keep this up overlong. If you wants to live through this you has to steer as I say."

"What are we steering toward?" the helmsman asked.

"The Gray Runners. There!" He pointed his bound hands into the whiteout haze.

Through the thickening sheets of snow loomed a vast dark shape. Like a mountain in the fog, it tumbled in the shearing wind.

"There be our escorts, lads. Seems we don't die today," Dok's voice filled with a joy that transcended his captivity. "Run hard abreast her, ride her vortex, but don't let her cut your wind."

The helmsman shouted orders to the boatswain, who passed them on to the crew. Aeronauts ran every which way, scuttling through the rigging like ants from a kicked nest. Jean-Claude hurried below lest he be noticed.

Hours passed in the dark of the hold. The hammering on the hull slowed but never stopped, and twice they came under the storm's full bombardment. Hailstones like cannonballs cracked the strakes. Jean-Claude could not help but imagine some Breaker-cursed missile smashing through the hold and splattering him all over the far wall. Yet there was nothing he could do but wedge himself between a bulkhead and a barrel and hang on for the ride.

Isabelle stood on the foredeck of the *Saint Asne*, willing the ship to go faster, chasing disaster and wondering what she would do when she caught it.

A thin breeze got in under Isabelle's hood and ruffled the feathers on the back of her neck. She shivered as the zephyr stuck its tongue in her ear and whispered. "Capitaine Isabelle, this be Hailer Dok. You'll be pleased to know yer friend Jean-Claude has found me."

Isabelle's heart soared and she held her breath as if that might help her listen better.

Dok's whispering wind continued: "We're aboard the *Potencia*, about to go through the Bittergale. We rides in the lee of the Grey Runners."

The wind died and the voice faded. Isabelle strained her hearing against the wind, but there was nothing more to be had. Jean-Claude was still alive, or at least he had been when Dok sent the message. They'd gone through the Bittergale, but what was a Gray Runner? And if they were through, what chance did Isabelle have to catch them? Travers and Hasdrubal had an unimpeded path to the Vault of Ages.

Only Jean-Claude stood in their way.

The wind shifted more to the west the farther north they flew, and above the far horizon rising beyond the curve of the sky, a dark smudge blurred the heavens as if part of creation had been rubbed out. The taste of the air had changed as well. This far from land, all traces of grit and soil had faded, and the coppery tang of the deep sky darkened to bronze on her tongue.

We're made for the sky, Forenzio said, churning up memories of open air and distant ports, strange and exotic lands. They might have had much in common if only his holds had not been filled with human chattel and his mind with the sort of rot that reduced every human thing to its value in coin. In life, he judged every interaction as a struggle for power. His only joy was in making other people lose.

Forenzio scoffed, *You're no better, grasping for authority wherever you can get it, princess, ambassadress, capitaine. You want power, but you're afraid of it. You haven't learned to seize it. You don't know how to win.*

Isabelle sensed much of Primus Maximus in the slaver's words. Had the slaver always been so twisted and bitter, or had his worship of Primus made him so? She turned her attention into the everdream and plunged down into Forenzio's memories. By his side she slithered through the slave markets, the whorehouses, and the gambling dens of his career. The memories were none of them complete, and not even in any particular order. She climbed up a companionway in his ship and emerged on a clifftop on the coast of some nameless skyland, and when she turned around to retrace her steps, she found herself in a great villa atop one of the marble cliffs at Om.

Yet her trek was not without direction, for she sought his earliest memories, the very first enshrined in his vitera. The people and the buildings all grew taller as she delved into his memories as a half-grown man-child. Where had the corruption begun?

She remembered with him his own coming of age, his transformation into a fully fledged Fenice. Oh saints, how he hated the scruffy stage. His sisters laughed at him. He remembered with relief that great, full-body sneeze as he put away his *cappotto di piume* for the first time.

After he came into his power, girls had been more impressed, especially Cassandra, who was his same age and who had feathers of gold and bronze and a voice that could soothe the souls in Torment.

Then he received his first vitera. He had hoped to receive his father's vitera, but instead he'd been told he'd be receiving one from some great-uncle he'd never heard of. His annoyance turned to awe when that distant uncle brought him Primus Maximus. He was never to tell anyone whose memories he carried, but with Primus's help, he would gain everything he ever wanted.

It came to pass that Cassandra was to be married to a wealthy salt merchant in a distant city. All of their elders considered it a good match, and Cassandra was willing to at least meet the man, but the boy who would become the slaver was heartbroken.

Fortunately he had Primus. *Never give your enemies anything but at a cost,* he said. *If they want this girl, make them pay, and it may well be they find the price too high.*

Isabelle remembered vividly the argument Forenzio had with Cassandra. He explained how they could void the offer of alliance and lay the blame on the salt merchant, but she was appalled at the idea of betraying her family and threatened to reveal his plans to them.

The boy might have backed down, but Primus was his guide: *If you cannot hold a bridge, a field, a town, always make sure your enemy can get no use from it either.*

Her family never found Cassandra's body, never knew what prize he had claimed from her beforehand.

Isabelle withdrew from the memory and surfaced in the real present world, in her own body with its scruffy feathers and overtight skin. She could blame no one but Forenzio for his actions, but there was no doubt Primus had urged him on, and every other ghost in her ancestral chorus, and he'd never stop trying to get to her.

How could she use her ancestors' knowledge and skills without likewise being corrupted? Could the dead be rehabilitated, or was she stuck forever with rotten, bloodstained advisers?

She reached into the everdream and pulled Forenzio on as her ancestral cloak. His perceptions colored her awareness. She found herself more keenly aware of the currents in the air, the precise tint of the Miasma, the temperature of the wind. Many more years had he spent on the sky than she. She turned to her crew and called for an adjustment to the sail even before the helmsman did.

The *Saint Asne* surged beneath her feet as it picked up speed.

Together we're stronger, Forenzio said.

Not yet, Isabelle said. She could appreciate her ancestors' skills, but they would not truly be allies until she could trust them.

She sought out Bitterlich, who was giving more shape-shifting lessons to Rebecca, an activity with which they both felt comfortable.

Forenzio's gaze lingered on Rebecca. Young and fresh, that one. Get an iron ring through her nose and she'd fetch a hefty price at market. He imagined the rush of power he'd feel at capturing such a prize, of breaking her spirit, a hot surge of triumph.

A paltry prize, Isabelle said. *A rush like a drug that sweeps everything away and leaves you emptier than before. Your victory is not victory if it destroys your prize.*

Then she pulled Forenzio into her memory, into the first time she'd met Rebecca and how impressed Isabelle had been with her poise and powers of observation. She opened up the memory of the amazement she'd felt at Rebecca's transformation and her delight at seeing her bond with Bitterlich.

Feel that, she said. *Those are the emotions that matter. They are the ones that last and build and become more than the sum of their parts.*

Her ancestral cloak seemed to fray about her, Forenzio's perceptions unraveling and leaving her mind clear of his prejudice, but in possession of his skills. In the depths of the everdream, a young man who made an evil choice began to weep.

—

"Cabin crackers," Bitterlich said to Rebecca. He sat on the starboard rail, and she floated before him in her ghostfire wyrm form.

She snapped her tail once in determination and said, "Sathin thathers. Sa-thin Tha-thers." She swam around in a circle in frustration, then unfolded into her mostly human erstepelz. "Cabin crackers! So there."

"Try it again," Bitterlich said.

"I hate this," she snapped.

"Hate what, exactly?" Bitterlich asked. She'd become more volatile in the last two days, ever since she learned he was her father. Failures she once would have gritted her teeth at provoked outbursts now. She was trying to get a reaction from him, but he doubted even she knew what she wanted that reaction to be.

"This," she gestured at herself. "All of this." She threw her arms out toward the sky.

"It must be hard to hate so much, especially all at once."

She glowered at him and he expected her to declare her hatred for him most of all. He readied himself for it like he would for a deathblow; it would hurt that much.

"How come you can talk as an animal and I can't?" she said.

"Because I practiced for about a year," he said. It wasn't the first time he'd told her this, but they'd been going over a lot of ground twice or thrice today. "You can make the sounds; you just have to figure out how."

"You said you'd teach me," she said. "Not just say 'again,' again and again."

"Sometimes that's what teaching is," he said. "Making you keep trying something you don't want to do."

"You can't *make* me do anything. I don't have to listen to you."

Here Bitterlich thought she'd gotten as close to the root of her frustration as she could without exposing her fear.

"Just because I'm your father," he said.

"That doesn't mean you own me," she said.

Bitterlich could only wonder at the dizzying chain of reason that had brought her to that declaration. Take some perfectly ordinary fear and multiply by twelve-year-old.

"Do you want me to go away?" Two days ago she had been keen to find her family, but perhaps wishful-thinking fathers were better than the real thing. They were certainly easier.

Rebecca looked uncertain. "Just so you know, I don't have to do what you say."

Bitterlich normally avoided any overt display of emotion, especially ones that could be construed as barbaric or uncivilized, so it was with a very deliberate effort that he drew his hand down his face with frustration. She needed to see it.

"You're right. Being a daughter is not like being a cabin girl. You never swore an oath to me, but I'll tell you a secret," he said, and gestured her to come closer.

Warily she drifted in.

He spoke in a conspiratorial whisper, "I don't want your obedience."

She twitched away, surprised. "You don't, but—"

"I want your trust," he said. "When I tell you to do something, I want you to do it because you know I'm older and more experienced and have your best interests at heart, not because I might punish you if you don't."

Her face adopted the same expression of concentration that it did when Isabelle presented her with a puzzle. "So . . . what would you do if I just said no?"

"I would have no choice but to shake my head and be very disappointed. Like so." He shook his head sadly and let slip his most disappointed sigh.

"Ungh. Why? Why is that somehow worse than being yelled at?"

"Because you don't want me to be disappointed," Bitterlich suggested. "Now, are you going to try your speech exercise again, or must I shake my head at you?"

Rebecca rolled her eyes, flipped over backward, and transformed into her ghostfire wyrm form. "Sathin thathers."

"Sails!" hollered the lookout. "Sails on the horizon!"

Bitterlich and Rebecca joined everyone else in staring in the indicated direction. Bitterlich turned his head into an eagle shape for the sake of its incredible vision.

A sloop of war sailed course crossways to the *Saint Asne*.

Isabelle, still in her cloak and cowl, stepped up beside him. "Is it anyone we know?"

"The sloop's nameplate says *Dame Formue*."

"Ivar Thirdeye," Isabelle said. "It's too much to hope they haven't spotted us."

A bright light on the *Dame Formue* flashed in their direction.

"They say they want to parley," Bitterlich said.

CHAPTER

Twenty-Seven

The *Saint Asne* and the *Dame Formue* eyed each other across the top of a small barren skyland, a floating rock barely a musket shot in diameter. Isabelle and Marie made land in a rowed skiff, but the coastal precipice proved unstable, made mostly of aggregate that crumbled and bobbed like bits of cork in water so that the aeronauts had to leap out and drag the skiff half again its length onshore until they found rock solid enough to hold them.

Primus crept into her awareness, as if he were standing just out of sight behind her shoulder. Forenzio had regressed into his old habits of mind, but brought with him an awareness of the world that might have been, and a desire for the fulfillment Isabelle had shown him. The road home was long, but at least he had taken the first steps. If he could be rehabilitated, what about the others? If she could repair enough of her ancestors, she could rob Primus of his strength, deny him refuges in which to hide.

Why do you fight me? Primus asked. *You need me.*

I would find your skills useful if they served my purposes, Isabelle replied. *Perhaps you should exert yourself to see to it they do.*

One the far side of the skyland, three pirates disembarked. There was a bulky man with a bronze beard, a leather long coat, and a patch over his left eye. He was a Tidsskygge sorcerer surrounded by half-glimpsed images of himself. The most solid part of him flickered from time shadow to time shadow, like a candle flame jumping between wicks. That would be Ivar Thirdeye: pirate, scoundrel, and capitaine of the *Dame Formue.*

His first companion Isabelle recognized by reputation if not by sight. Sedgwick the Goldentongue, short of stature, but strong in sorcery. Jean-Claude called him a tricky bastard, which was a compliment to his skills if not his character. When she looked directly at him, his Gloriole convinced her eye that he was clad in thick furs and supple leathers. When she looked away she caught a glimpse of a rather less glamorous layering of fair-weather clothes and an overlarge winter coat.

The second companion made Isabelle's skin crawl: Quaestor Czensos, though not as she had seen him in his few appearances at court. The desecrated raiment of a Last Man fluttered about him like a mustard-yellow shroud, the black-embroidered gear train on his mantle ripped to shreds that fluttered like telltales on the Ravenous Gate itself. The tattooed symbols on his head spoke of fury and a rejection of order and reason. He carried in one hand a staff of some black metal that hurt the eye to look upon. His presence clarified much, but raised even more questions. If Czensos had been working with Hasdrubal, that went a long way to explaining why the latter had known about the reliquary of Saint Cynessus. Did he know where the Skaladin was now?

Isabelle and Marie trudged toward the center of the skyland. Marie was still limping, but not badly, and she carried her full kit of weaponry.

As forlorn and abandoned as this hunk of rock was, someone had crowned it with a large cairn of stones surrounded by a low wall, an area some ten meters across. The space was demarcated but not marked in any way as to signify its purpose or provenance.

Ivar and his company angled away from the cairn, and Isabelle aimed to meet them.

"Do you see any more of them?" Isabelle asked. She'd only agreed to this parley because she couldn't outrun or outgun the *Dame Formue.* She imagined Ivar had more men hidden about; she certainly did. Bitterlich was making his own approach, unobserved.

Marie said, "No, but they do have a Goldentongue, so who knows how much of what we see is true."

"That's comforting," Isabelle said dryly.

"It wasn't meant to be," Marie replied.

The parties stopped within hailing distance of each other.

"Capitaine Ivar, you asked for a parley," Isabelle shouted.

"Aye, Princess." The title was an insult on his tongue.

"I am Capitaine," she said.

"Sure you are," Ivar said, "of a wee toy boat, with some wee toy sailors. You're no match for the *Dame Formue* and definitely not for me. Now, because I'm a gentleman I'll give you a chance to get off easy. You have something that was promised to me: a shard of bonekeel from the *Conquest*. Hand it over and that'll be the end of your troubles. You run along home and I'll go about my business. Otherwise, you end real messy."

Marie stepped forward, two of her pistols already in hand, and raised her voice flat but forceful. "Before you act, be aware that I am Fellhand Marie of the Tall Clouds clan and my father is Jackhand Djordji. If you fight me you fight him, and there was never a sorcerer who stood against him, not even a Tidsskygge."

Ivar's eye narrowed to a slit. "I know all about the jackhand, missy. Wastrel and a cheat he is, good with a blade, but you're not he. I see's what's coming and I'll have those irons from your fists afore you can think about pulling the trigger, so mind your place." He returned his attention to Isabelle. "Not that I have to touch you at all. I have it on good authority that you put some value in that reprobate Jean-Claude."

Sedgwick winced at this, and Ivar went on. "Turns out he's aboard the *Potencia*, right under Travers's nose. Travers doesn't know it yet, but I could let him."

Fear flooded Isabelle's mind, and anger like a ball of hot iron.

Call his bluff, Primus said. *Threatening a hostage means that his position is otherwise weak. He means to make the hostage your problem. Make it his.* He pulled her attention down into his memory, to a lonesome hill outside a burning town the name of which history had forgotten. There she stood as Capitana Falconé, and the man before her held a knife to her unfledged daughter's throat.

"Throw down your weapons or she dies," said the man.

Falconé's pulse thrummed. She remembered fear and excitement, a gamble for the highest stakes.

She put ice water in her voice, cocked her head to one side, and said, "And then what?"

The man looked uncertain. "Did you hear me, I said—"

"She dies, I know," Falconé said. "And then I kill you and your family, the whole nest of rats down to the last naked kit, and I leave them out for the crows. Do we have a bargain?"

Isabelle returned to herself as quickly as she'd left. The whole memory had come upon her and gone again as quickly as an eyeblink. She could not gamble with Jean-Claude's life . . . yet if he were here, he'd hand her the dice.

She squared her shoulders, took a breath and said, "And then what?"

"And then Travers turns him into a damned bloodhollow."

Isabelle forced a thin smile. "But you still wouldn't have the shard. Besides, I've brought people back from being bloodhollows before." She pointed at Marie with her nose.

Ivar squinted at Marie as if he couldn't quite see her properly. "You?"

"You couldn't tell from my weather-baked skin tone?" Marie asked.

Isabelle said, "You've said your piece. Now consider an alternate arrangement: You sail away and no one gets hurt. You might be able to take us, but the Skaladin will make you pay for it, and I'll drop the shard in the Gloom before I let you have it. There is no victory here for you, only shades of loss."

Ivar glowered. His fist slammed into Isabelle's jaw so hard that she left her feet and fell backward. She hadn't even seen him move. Stunned and dizzy she flopped on her side to see him holding Marie's guns, and aiming both at her head.

"The jackhand you aren't!"

Bang!

Terror tore at Isabelle's throat even as she lurched to her feet, "Marie!"

But it was Ivar who stumbled backward, the smoking pistols clattering to the ground, clouds of gray smoke swirling around his face. Ivar's time shadows ran out in all directions, or tried to; they shattered into a hundred incoherent fragments before they left his skin.

Marie stepped forward, spit out a metal tube, and blew a thread of gun smoke as if she were a human cannon. "You didn't think I'd give you loaded guns, did you?" With two swift blows she brought him to his knees and then to the ground. The gray smoke resolved into a fine spray of silvery particles coating Ivar's face and upper body. She pulled another pistol from behind her back a shoved it in his mouth.

"Be warned," she said. "I don't need you alive."

"What just happened?" Isabelle asked.

Marie said, "He can't see the future while he's shifting time. He can't shift time while he's holding anything denser than bone. Grabbing my decoys slowed him down, which gave me the chance to fire my bite gun. Now he's got a gram of iron dust embedded in his face. It'll be weeks before he sweats it all out, if I don't empty out his skull first."

Ivar made a furious helpless noise around the barrel of the gun.

"You actually hid a gun in your mouth," Isabelle said, incredulous.

"Only a small one. I like my teeth."

"Have I mentioned lately you are an absurdly dangerous person?"

"Not since Flotsam."

Isabelle dragged her attention back to the skyland. Sedgwick and Czensos had closed ranks, or at least Sedgwick had eased up to take cover in Czensos's shadow. The Last Man quaestor leaned on his staff, looking surprisingly unperturbed by Ivar's defeat.

Isabelle stepped forward and said, "You two go back to your ship and sail downwind. Once you're out half a day, we'll maroon your capitaine here. You can come back and pick him up."

Czensos chuckled. "Don't you want to pay your respects first? Or don't you have any idea where you are? This is the most sacred, most profane ground in all the world." He swept his arms to encompass the skyland.

Isabelle kept a corner of her gaze on him as she looked around. The wall was unmarked, the cairn unremarkable except for the fact of its existence so far from anyplace inhabitable.

"I don't understand," she said.

"Pity," he said. "Everyone should know about this place. It should have been a point of pilgrimage, come and gaze upon ultimate folly, but of course the Temple kept it secret from all but their most trusted agents." The word "trusted" dripped with acid. "As well they must. For anyone not completely committed to their lies must surely see this place for what it is, the utter refutation of their dogma."

Isabelle eased away from Marie, just to make it harder for him to watch both of them. Czensos's prologue gave her the impression of a man who preferred to begin with his conclusions and work his way back to whatever facts he needed to support them.

Sedgwick, perhaps sensing Czensos's pressurized rage, backed away from him.

"All I see are stones," Isabelle said.

"Think about it," he said. "I've heard that you're possessed of a genius spirit. Surely you can figure it out. You have come from Craton Massif. You are heading toward the Vault of Ages. That is not just a jaunt across the sky; that is a voyage back in time. Or perhaps you simply can't see what this place once was." He turned and pointed his awful staff at Sedgwick. "Go ahead and show them, master sorcerer. Show them a city with towers of crystal, topiary plants that walk amongst the people, water that flows through the air, and a great golden dome."

Sedgwick swallowed hard and raised his hands as if to conjure some image into being, but the wonders Czensos described belonged to only one tale of Legend, one place in this broken world.

"Rüul," Isabelle said. "You're saying this is the city of the saints." The desolation of the place hollowed out a cold spot in Isabelle's soul.

"This is all that remains," Czensos said.

"The rest fell into the Gloom then," Sedgwick said.

"No," Czensos said. "The saints built a city in an attempt to re-create the Primus Mundi, and it was full of wonders. Yet the city was not enough for them. They sought to repair the world and put it back to the way it had been. It was from here the masters of Rüul reached into the Vault of Ages to awaken the Savior and complete the Prophecy, but the Breaker caught them and with her long arm, destroyed them. The annihilation was said to be complete, but ever imperfect is the Breaker and she left a bit of herself behind."

Czensos produced a small device that looked a bit like a top but with a wide disk around its equator. It was made of the same purplish bronze stuff that was the signature of the Builder's workshop. He held it in the palm of his hand and blew on it. It began to spin and remained suspended in the air when he took his hand away.

The wind pushed the little device toward the cairn. Isabelle resisted the urge to chase after it and catch it. How was it levitating? What made it spin? The materials alone possessed properties barely dreamt of.

The spinning object floated over the boundary wall and for a few heartbeats nothing happened. Then it wobbled. Its spin slowed. Its color faded to gray. It fell from the air and shattered on the ground, first into pieces and then into dust, which the wind blew away.

"That was a whirling speculum," Czensos said. "It survived the Breaking of the World, being buried under a mountain, and a thousand years of neglect without the slightest hint of wear or aging, but it cannot survive the Breaker's touch."

Isabelle shivered into the depths of the everdream. Even her ghosts feared that space.

Czensos said, "This is what the saints found when they reached into the Vault of Ages, not salvation, but annihilation. There was never a Savior. There was never a true Prophecy. Don't you see? Iav let the Breaker in and she crafted this world in her own image. This is Torment. We are shat into being twixt our mothers' legs, and every moment thereafter is suffering. Those who seek to improve the world only corrupt it. Those who seek knowledge discover only lies. The only realization that matters is that the world cannot be saved. The only true act of faith is to end it."

"You're barking mad," Marie said, more succinctly than Isabelle could have.

"Perhaps, but at least I do not pretend to be sane." Czensos tapped his wicked staff on the ground. A pulse like silent thunder throbbed through Isabelle and she nearly fell. Her body felt wrong, heavy, lopsided. She clamped her left hand to her stump. Her spark-arm was gone. Her scales and feathers too. Even the voices in her head had vanished. She had all but forgotten what it was like to have a silent mind. The sudden silence captivated her despite the circumstances.

Sedgwick reeled, his gloriole vanished. Even Marie staggered back, her color returning, black hair, brown eyes, and clothes of mismatched motley hues that put the loudest Gyrine to shame. She doubled over, gasped in pain, and bawled. Isabelle guessed all the emotions she'd been unable to express had come welling up at once, a geyser of pent-up fear and delight and anger and joy.

Released from Marie's grip, Ivar lurched to his feet, looking around baffled as if the whole world had changed. His time shadows were gone and he was as stuck in the moment as everyone else.

"The reliquary of Saint Iav," Czensos said. "Just a taste of oblivion, a sense of what is to come. It wears off in a few minutes." He jabbed the tip of the staff into a bewildered Ivar's chest. "Unless I give you the full dose."

Ivar's last sound was a gasp. And then he was gone, as if he'd never been.

Czensos pointed the tip of the staff at Isabelle. "Take comfort in knowing that your death serves a greater purpose."

"Annihilation is not a purpose. It's a capitulation." Isabelle dashed away from him, circling. She'd spent most of her life unhallowed, without any manifest sorcery. Readjusting ought to be easy, but her body was queasy and slow.

Something blurred in the corner of Isabelle's vision, a small black bird swooping in at tremendous speed.

Bitterlich, no!

Bitterlich hit the frontier of the reliquary's power and his sorcery sloughed away . . . but not his velocity. As a clayborn man he smashed Czensos like a cannonball and plowed him into the boundary wall. Both men fell, stunned. Isabelle rushed toward them.

Czensos recovered more quickly and stood while Bitterlich discovered the nausea that came with losing his sorcery. Czensos's flesh arm dangled, broken. His clockwork arm raised the awful black staff to strike.

A gun cracked, and another, and another. Blood sprayed from Czensos's chest. Marie, her eyes streaming with tears and her expression twisted in rage emptied all her remaining pistols into him. "Die, you son of a dog!"

Blood flowing from his wounds, life draining from his body, the hate in Czensos's eye still burned bright. His clockwork arm cared nothing for the expiration of his flesh.

"Breakerspawn!" He stabbed at Bitterlich.

Isabelle crashed into the quaestor, her shoulder to his chest, and flipped him over the wall. He landed with a thump, then rolled to his side even as obliteration claimed him. His body unraveled. Skin, muscle, and bone flayed away. The reliquary and his clockwork arm were the last bits to go.

"Isabelle?" Bitterlich tugged her teetering body away from the wall.

Breathing like a bellows forge, she faced him. So this was what he looked like as a clayborn. He had a square face, long hair the color of chestnuts, and dark eyes. The eyes had the same soul in them.

She smiled and said, "I see it now. Rebecca has your cheeks and your nose."

Bitterlich looked down at himself. "This is very strange. I can't feel my Seelengewölbe. And your arm—"

"Still missing."

"I meant your l'Étincelle."

"Gone, along with all the ancestors in my head." Was that a trade she would take? A week ago she would have given anything, including her other arm, to get rid of her ancestors, but now . . . now she was making progress.

Marie sat on the ground, hugging her knees and weeping. Isabelle hurried to her. "Are you hurt?" It was a stupid question, but her heart ran away with her tongue.

Marie looked up at her, her face red with crying. "I'm . . . I'll live. I forgot how much it hurts not to be able to weep, to laugh, to blush. It's like living in a box. I can only talk to people by shouting through a wall. No one can really hear me. No one can feel me."

Isabelle pulled her up into a hug. "Oh saints, I'm so sorry."

Marie snuffled into Isabelle's cloak. "And I forgot what a relief it is to be able to forget. There's so much I want to forget. So much, and now I have to go back to that. I have to go back in the box."

Grief filled Isabelle's chest, if Czensos had been telling the truth, everything would return to the way it had been: a relief for the sorcerers, but an entombment for Marie.

"What can I do for you?" Isabelle asked.

"Just . . . just keep being my friend. It's having friends that makes it worth living."

"Ahem," said Sedgwick, approaching cautiously. "As much as I hate to interrupt, we've still got business."

"What else do you have to say?" Isabelle asked flatly.

"A few things," he said. "First, I had no idea what Czensos was up to."

Bitterlich said, "Because you couldn't find out, or because you didn't want to?"

Sedgwick tried a friendly smile. It came off slightly pained. "That hardly matters at this juncture, does it? What's important is that I know about your friend Jean-Claude."

Twenty-Eight

The *Potencia* lurched and groaned, waking Jean-Claude from a fitful half-sleep. Once, in his army days, he'd slept through an artillery barrage, but his side had been the one delivering it. Being on the receiving end was considerably more harrowing.

Bells rang and pipes sounded for some kind of maneuver. Jean-Claude dragged himself out of his niche to have a go at the chute. It was only then he realized the hailstone bombardment had stopped. He stood rapt, listening to the benign creaking of the hull, waiting for another almighty bang, but even the howl of the wind had faded. They'd made it. Somehow against all good sense they'd made it through the Bittergale.

He stole out of his hiding place and peeked out a gun loop on the turvy deck. It was full night outside. Even so, to starboard he could see the inside wall of the Bittergale. The wind whipped by with a receding howl.

Out the larboard side of the ship, in the distance, a great dark smear, barely more than a smudge against night, stretched left and right as far as the eye could see: the Craton Auroborea.

He focused on it with his clockwork eye. A landscape of high cliffs and narrow fjords curved away at a distance even the quondam prosthesis could not make out. Beyond the coastal bluffs, jagged mountains loomed.

Isabelle would love this.

Voices from above warned him of officers coming his way. The beaten-down clayborn aeronauts rarely talked, but their saintborn masters almost never stopped.

He'd just gripped the ladder that led up into the hold when his clockwork eye suddenly opened from inside Ivar's eye socket. No missive appeared to him this time, just a flat plain under a gray sky. Marie scooted to his right, but Jean-Claude could not follow her for the whole of Ivar's attention was fixed on . . . Quaestor Czensos? Jean-Claude barely had time to register the apostate cleric when he jabbed Ivar with his staff.

A snap of galvanic fire lit up the inside of Jean-Claude's eye socket and the eye went completely dark. He reeled and bumped against the ladder, barely holding himself upright.

The officers descended the companionway forward of his position. Jean-Claude swallowed his gorge and scrabbled up the ladder, his feet slipping from several rungs. Fortunately the officers seemed too engrossed in their own conversation to notice him.

He huddled in a crevice out of sight in the hold, and tapped on the clockwork eye, trying to get it to wake up, to signal Ivar. To his dismay, it merely rattled around in its cage. What could have caused it to fail? Back in his academy days, he'd seen artifacts like this shot with cannons and not take a scratch.

What had happened on that skyland? If Marie was there, could Isabelle be far away? Jean-Claude had hoped his message to Ivar would stave off violence, or at least make the man think, but he hadn't counted on Czensos.

Stunned and nearly numb with dread he clambered back to his feet. The whole world seemed lopsided and narrow now that he truly could not see on his left side, and the closed-in space of the hold was much tighter since he could not see shadows through the walls.

Worse, he had no way to find out what happened to Marie or Isabelle.

Morning came at last, with no sign of the eye coming back to life. His whole body felt hollow and numb with worry for things he could not know. He had no choice but to carry on with the handful of ideas he was calling a plan, which mostly involved waiting until the ship made land somewhere and sneaking out at the earliest opportunity. Once he had room to maneuver, he

374 — CURTIS CRADDOCK

could work out how to put an end to Travers and Hasdrubal with at least the chance of not getting himself dead.

He took care exiting the hold and peered out the gun loops on the landward side. Most of the coastline consisted of tall cliffs or reefs of aethercoral that would make landing difficult. Yet beyond the edge was green. The very tops of immense trees waved above the cliff tops. Long leafy vines hung down the granite faces and draped over the aethercoral. The smell of earth and mulch drifted down, and even a few insects found their way to the ship.

It was warmer this side of the Bittergale vortex, though where the heat came from he could not guess. The Solar still hung low on the horizon, and the scant daylight had to filter through the Bittergale, and yet there was enough heat that the officers shed their wool coats, and spent the day on deck, basking like pale lizards. This had the fortunate effect of leaving their quarters unoccupied. Jean-Claude needed to arm himself, and many officers, even these chinless inbreeds, kept weapons in their private storage.

A thief's anxiety gripped him as he slipped into one vacant chamber. With only one eye, he kept his head on a swivel trying to look everywhere at once even as he picked his way through sky trunks and lockers. He found a decent dagger in the first trunk he looked in, but swords were harder to come by. Most Sanguinaires relied on their bloodshadows in combat, and carried clayborn weapons only as symbols of military status, useful for bolstering flagging pride while strutting through ballrooms. The first two blades he came across were costume quality, and the third was badly rusted, having been improperly stored and promptly forgotten by its owner.

He squirted out of the room unobserved just as two Sanguinaire officers descended into the passage from above with half a dozen marines in tow.

The lieutenant snapped orders to his sergeant, ". . . stem to stern. Search every deck, every compartment, every single bag, barrel, and box. I want him found."

Fear gripped Jean-Claude in an icy fist. Somehow they'd learned he was here. He must get off the ship. The quick launches were on the main deck, several levels away, plus there was a whole complement of marines loose in the corridors, and Builder knew how many Sanguinaires and Hasdrubal. He needed to give them something else to think about.

He sneaked into the carpenter's bay, looking for something to burn. His disinclination to sabotage the ship he was on yielded to the more urgent need for a distraction. He needed tar, or wood small enough to be kindling.

He pulled the top off a barrel and found nails, in another one paint. He tripped over a bag and nearly fell. It was filled with sawdust.

He thanked the saints, cut open the bag, and shook it hard, filling the air with dust from one end of the cabin to the other.

He snatched a lantern from its hook, turned up the pressure, and sparked it to life as he ran out the door.

He nearly barreled into a half dozen marines.

"There he is!"

Jean-Claude hurled the lantern back into the cloudy room with all the force he could muster. Glass shattered. He sprinted away. A bloodshadow slicked across the floor, caught his shadow and tripped him to the ground before he'd taken three steps. Pain gouged furrows in his mind. The marines reached for him.

Bright light. Fire. A sound so loud that it deadened the air. The wall of the carpenter's bay blew outward. Flame filled the corridor. The pressure bowled Jean-Claude to the end of the passageway and slammed him into a wall. He couldn't breathe. Blackness crept in where light had been. His lungs felt like they'd been run through a sausage grinder.

Finally his chest heaved and he drew breath. The air was hot, dry, dead, and dusty. The corridor was littered with corpses and men who might as well be. He managed to topple forward, crawl to the companionway, and fall down to the turvy deck. The air was cooler here. Strength eked back into his limbs.

Diversion accomplished. Alarm bells pealed. The ship was definitely on fire. Turvymen swarmed up from the turvy masts to help fight the blaze. Jean-Claude levered himself to his feet. Unfortunately, the fire was now between him and the part of the ship he needed to get to.

The companionway above him was choked with smoke. Aeronauts with wet blankets swatted at the fire, but it pushed them back. Men came coughing, stumbling back out of the hole, hands burned and eyes blind from the smoke. Jean-Claude shoved his way through the press of bodies and joined a knot of men racing toward the stern. Through the gun loops, he saw cinders falling toward the turvy sails. Beyond the bottom hatches, the Gloom yawned and beckoned to him. It would be so much easier just to fall.

Halfway down the turvy run, two marines stepped in front of the panicked mob and started shoving aeronauts back toward the fire, whipping them with swords, their faces red with rage.

"Get back. Back to work, or we all burn."

Jean-Claude, in the middle of the pack, got low and shoved, driving forward so the press of bodies simply could not stop. They broke over the marines like a wave and forced them back. The first marine shrieked as he stepped back over a turvy hatch and his foot came down into thin air. The second lurched to the side and came at Jean-Claude with a cutlass. Jean-Claude surged inside the blow, stabbed the man in the gut with his stolen knife, and relieved him of his cutlass when he fell.

He ran to the aft companionway, climbed the ladder past the hold and the orlop deck to the lower gun deck. The whole place was bedlam, with men shouting and shoving to no purpose Jean-Claude could see. He climbed again, but the hatchway to the upper gun deck was closed and locked. He was trapped. Forward lay the crew cabins. Aft was the officers' stores.

Blowing like a winded bull, he bashed his way into the stores and tore down the stack of chests covering the windows. He flung the window open with a thought to reaching the gallery and Dok, but he had no rope or harness, and the ship bobbed and rolled. The fantail rudder swung, the copper mesh stretched between long spars bending the aetherkeels' aura. Smoke billowed from the side of the ship, and enemies hunted the decks for him.

He faced into the ship, sat down on the sill, and reached for the lintel. He focused his one eye on his grip and pulled himself out and up until only his toes were still on the sill. The wind tugged at his coat and the ship shuddered over a ridge of turbulence. His feet skittered like water in a hot greased skillet. Every muscle he had clenched tight. He must move, but the only muscle that let go was the one in his bladder.

He stared at his hand and the space around it. The side of the ship was covered in fretwork, a processional scene of clayborn descending into Torment while the Savior received the saintborn in Paradise.

Jean-Claude snarled his anger at the arrogance, the sneering superiority of Travers and his ilk. He reached out and grabbed a fretwork saint and pulled himself straighter. He kicked in a windowpane and climbed up the muntins. The wood creaked and cried out under his weight, but he grabbed another loftier saint and hauled himself up. Curse Travers and all his spiteful, wicked kind. Curse the Temple for putting them above clayborn folk. Curse the clayborn for putting up with it. Up and up he climbed, one curse at a time until he found himself halfway between the windows below and the buttresses for the gallery above. He groped for a toehold and wheezed with terror as the ship bobbed again. He dared not look down. His strength withered as the wind tried to lick him from his perch.

"You are the one called Jean-Claude, yes?" said a measured alto voice from his blind side.

Jean-Claude turned his head so fast he lost one handhold, flailed, and somehow managed to grab a fretwork cloud and hug himself to the hull.

There was a woman hanging on the fretwork beside him. A vortex of wind skirled around her: a Windcaller. Given the circumstances, the only person this could possibly be was Dok's wife, Solo Aria. She'd been trapped on Craton Auroborea for months, and must have been keeping a sharp lookout for ships. She knew Dok was coming back for her.

Jean-Claude turned his head as far as he could without letting go of the fretwork. She was a thickset woman with brown skin, brown hair, and sky-blue eyes. She braced with one foot and hung by one hand, watching him with evident disdain.

"Where is Hailer Dok?" she asked.

Trying not to let go of anything, he pointed to her, pointed to himself, and then pointed up. He bestowed her with the sort of pleading look as a begging hound dog.

"But you does so well," she said. "Another hour and maybe you makes it to the next deck. 'Course, by then they either has the fire out or crashes, and that does no one any good."

She grabbed him by the collar and peeled him off the ship. For an instant he fell and then Aria sang a cold, clear note and a column of air lifted him to the gallery.

"Where?" she asked.

Jean-Claude opened the window to Dok's cell, but he was gone, his chain detached from the wall.

The next door down on the gallery flew opened and a trio of Skaladin barged out, pistols and cutlasses in hand. Jean-Claude raised his weapon, but Aria made a piercing whistle and a gust of wind answered her call. Like a thin slice of hurricane it whipped the men from the deck and hurled them into the deep sky.

"Feast well, Deep Mother," she cried. Then to Jean-Claude, "They must have taken Dok to put out the fire."

Jean-Claude saw an opportunity and rushed through the open door, making incoherent noises and gesturing Aria to follow him. Would she heed him?

Inside, two of the Skaladin hoisted Hasdrubal's iron-bound crate, one had opened the door, and the last one fired his pistol even as Jean-Claude caromed off the doorframe. The shot shattered glass. Jean-Claude lunged at the rearmost porter and hacked his cutlass deep into the man's neck. The thunk of the blade hitting bone jarred all the way to his shoulder. The man fell, spraying blood, taking the crate with him. Jean-Claude kicked the slumping corpse toward the one who'd shot at him. The man gave way, but Jean-Claude followed up quick. The Skaladin blocked Jean-Claude's cutlass, but blood from the blade sprayed in his face as Jean-Claude got under his guard and gutted him with his dagger.

Jean-Claude spun, trying to see the whole room with only one eye. The last two Skaladin both grabbed the trunk and tried to pull it from the room.

There was a high, shrill noise, then a blast like a cannon shook the room and both men went flying, pieces of them in different directions. Solo Aria stepped up beside Jean-Claude. She must have seen his stunned expression because she said, "Press air in a tight enough space and it goes off like a bomb. Now, why in the Deep Mother's hungry cunt are we here?"

Jean-Claude banged on the crate. The reliquary of Saint Cynessus was in there. He sheathed his dagger wet and whipped out his picklocks.

"Takes too long." Aria whistled up a needle of wind, tossed in a handful of grit from a pouch at her belt, and drilled through the lock until it popped. The lid came up, and inside Jean-Claude found the fancy wooden box in which the reliquary had been stored before it was stolen. He opened the catch and found the quondam ring reunited with the skeletal hand that had worn it in life.

"They're after the chest!" shouted a Sanguinaire into the chartroom just beyond the door. His bloodshadow flicked toward them, but Aria's wind gust kicked the chest through the door at him. The bloodshadow caught the chest midair. Jean-Claude slammed the door shut, threw the bolt, and ran.

"Over the side, lubber!" Aria shouted, and boosted him into the air. Above on the poop, men appeared at the rails shouting and raising muskets. Aria sang a warbling note, and she and Jean-Claude shot away in a fast, high arc like an arrow. Musket balls whizzed around them.

Jean-Claude hurtled through the sky, tossed from one updraft to another. Aria took them toward land and swooped through a crack in the cliff wall to a cave large enough to stand in. There she dropped him off like porter lumping a sack of grain. He sprawled on the ground, aching, dizzy, and sick.

To his dismay, the ground seemed to tilt and sway beneath him. He never got his sky legs, but still his land legs abandoned him.

Aria set down lightly across from him. Her clothes were stained but well mended, her feet bare as Gyrines' tended to be. The cave was only about two paces wide, but extended into the cliff face out of sight. A rivulet of water gurgled along a channel in its rounded floor.

Slowly, so as not to alarm his rescuer, and also because every inch of him hurt, he rolled into a seated position, and mimed tipping his hat to her.

She snorted. "Hailer says not to kill you straightaway. Says you're more useful than you looks. I doesn't realize that's such a low hurdle."

Jean-Claude, too tired to think of a good pantomime, and still incapable of speech, made hand sign: "You don't see me at my best." At least she'd know he'd heard her, even if she didn't understand.

To his utter astonishment, she signed back, "Where did you learn silent song?"

Jean-Claude's sprit lifted like smoke from a prayer fire. "I have a deaf friend." Saints, it was good to be able to talk, even if this was not his best language. "How did you learn it?"

"Ha," her fingers flashed more quickly than his could, and she put her whole body into the interpretation. "Gyrine invents it. When you works in a chorus chanting up a long wind, you can't speak with your mouth, so you talk with your hands. Your friend probably learns it from us. Since we go everywhere, we teaches it to deaf people all across the sky. They always likes to talk to us when we come back, and they knows more than people think."

Jean-Claude nodded in appreciation. They'd created an informal network of informants just by being willing to talk to people whom most other people ignored.

Buoyed by open lines of communication, he stood and signed, "How did you know who I was?"

"Hailer tells me to look for a fat cyclops. He says you're a blunt instrument, but no friend of Travers and the Skaladin."

"I'm sorry we couldn't fetch your husband."

She glowered at him. "Don't go hunting honey after you've riled the bees. I means to slip in, grab him, and go afore anyone knows I'm there, but some lout sets the ship on fire."

"We'll get him back," Jean-Claude replied.

"Aye, we will," Aria said. "And you does as I say if you wants any part of it. What's that trinket you risked our necks for?"

Jean-Claude considered Aria had been the vote capitaine of her clan before getting stranded here. She'd boss him if he let her, but this needed sharing.

Jean-Claude opened the reliquary and liberated the ring from the dead, dry fingers.

He set the ring on a stone and signed, "It's the true reliquary of Saint Cynessus the Blind, gatekeeper of the Vault of Ages. Travers and Hasdrubal think the reliquary is the key."

Aria grunted. "The Vault of Ages? You means that quondam ruin that's just hinter the *Conquest* crash site? I've been there. There's not a door in the place still standing."

Jean-Claude shrugged. "That's their story, not mine."

"So, they wants to wake up the Savior does they?" Aria said. "Can't imagine he's happy with the likes of them prodding him up."

"Travers wants to be the Savior's vessel."

"Humble little tit, is he?"

"No one has ever been more humble than him, and he'll spend hours bragging about it."

"What about the other one?"

"The last time I saw Hasdrubal, he said he would complete the great unfinished work."

"Which is?" Aria asked.

"The Breaking of the World," Jean-Claude said.

"That's daft."

It was an assessment with which Jean-Claude wholeheartedly agreed.

———

Isabelle held Marie's hand tight as Saint Iav's curse passed. Marie's flesh cooled and her color faded away, bleaching back to white. Her expression froze once again into its porcelain mask. Isabelle ached for her, trapped in a bleak and endless winter of the soul.

Bitterlich's body regained it feline aspect, all luxuriant fur and expressive whiskers and warm golden eyes. He shuddered in relief from tip to toes and immediately shifted into his domestic cat form except at the size of a tiger.

Isabelle's own sorceries erupted into her awareness like a pack of relatives lurching through the door in the midst of an argument. Her spark-arm flared to life and her half-fledged coat returned. A quick survey of her ancestors ascertained that none of them were aware they had, in that brief eclipse, ceased to exist.

These facts made Isabelle's skin crawl. She had learned much about sorcery, the organs it lived in, and the organelles in the brain that controlled it. It was a physical thing that lived in the body and was part of the world . . . or so she'd thought.

This taste of oblivion was something else. It was a divine blight, an anti-miracle that had no process, no root in the world. It was as if everything she knew about the workings of nature was a dream on the surface of a soap bubble. Hasdrubal meant to erase those rules, wash away the world she knew like a chalk painting in the rain.

Similce received them at the *Saint Asne*, "Capitaine, what happened?"

Rebecca was there, too, wide-eyed but uncharacteristically quiet.

"We knocked a fanatic through a hole in the world," Isabelle said. If it had just looked like a hole, perhaps she would have been less unnerved. Instead it looked like nothing. "I also found out how to get through the Bittergale." Sedgwick had been useful for that much, at least. "Set our course for the *Conquest*."

"Aye, Capitaine!"

A day passed, and another. The Bittergale took shape before them, wild and wicked, but as terrifying as the storm was, she begged the wind to be her ally and get them there faster. More than being bashed to bits, she dreaded the thought of a sudden unraveling, and all the world unmade as if it had never been.

The wind and ice offered the *Saint Asne* no quarter. Aeronauts banged rime off the spars, the hull, and the rigging. Rebecca tried using her ghost-fire, only to discover that it had no effect whatsoever on water.

Isabelle stood on the quarterdeck, spyglass in her spark-hand, notebook strapped to a reading stand before her, and her timepiece in hand. She'd seen a shadow in the wind wall this morning. Sedgwick had explained how Ivar had fitted Jean-Claude with one of his spy eyes, and how Jean-Claude had witnessed Hailer Dok's "reliable route" through the Bittergale. Sedgwick said, and observation confirmed, that massive stonebergs circled within the Bittergale in such a way that a ship riding in the lee of the stone could get an escort through the wind wall.

From first light to midday, Isabelle watched for the shadows that indicated an escort mountain pressed up against the edge of the storm. She timed them, calculated their speed, and measured how long they stayed at the cusp of the storm before receding into its depths.

They came at calculable intervals, each a function of the velocity and duration of the one before it. Whether this relationship was derived from some natural principle or was the product of design she could not tell.

"Sails!" called the lookout, but Isabelle dared not look away from the storm wall. It was just about time for the next measurement. She checked her timepiece and counted down two . . . one . . . Another shadow appeared. With compass and point rule she tracked its flight.

"Capitaine," Similce said, cutting herself off when she saw Isabelle scribbling notes and resetting her timepiece.

"Whose sails, Lieutenant?" Isabelle asked without looking up.

"Travers's squadron," Similce said. "A frigate and three sloops of war on a course to intercept us. They flash, 'Surrender or be destroyed.' They'll catch us before we reach the storm wall."

Isabelle ticked off marks in her journal and calculated timing and position of the next escort. "We're already on our best wind. At our current speed we have just enough time to reach the wind wall before the next escort window. We have to be at the point of contact, moving in the right direction at the right speed when it does, or we might as well scuttle ourselves."

Similce squinted at the towering squall. "How much room for error?"

"A minute. Two at the outside."

Similce's expression grew grim. "That's no time at all."

"It's worse than that," Isabelle said. "We have to hit it at speed to slot into its vortex."

Similce faced the storm wall, an endless smear of wind that sounded like a roaring waterfall even at this distance. "How can you even tell where it's going to be?"

"Trigonometry," Isabelle said. She gathered her gear and led her lieutenant into the chartroom, and adjusted the orrery, increasing the pressure and decreasing the scale until only the two charted objects closest to the ship were visible. The *Saint Asne* was the bright mote in the center.

"This one is the beacon we dropped on Rüul, and that one is the *Conquest*," Isabelle said, and thanked Jean-Claude for getting the shard to her. She spread a large sheet of rice paper across the orrery and ruled in those points. Then she pulled out her trigonometry tables, did some quick calculations, and ruled in a fourth point.

"That's our entry point," she said. "As long as we can keep these two points of the triangle on our beacons, we know exactly where it's going to be. I just need you to put us at that point in exactly"—Isabelle checked her timepiece—"one hour and five minutes."

"Ask for the moons while you're at it," Similce grumbled.

"That's tomorrow," Isabelle said.

Similce saluted and stepped outside. "Beat to quarters and clear for action!"

The crew made the ship ready for battle. They brought up lumber from stores and hammered together an extra layer of armor for the port side, where the Bittergale would hit them. Bitterlich made sure his marines got as fed and rested as possible. Every cannon aboard was checked and rechecked, every loose thing doubly secured.

Through it all, Isabelle stood fast, refining her calculations. The *Saint Asne* would have to pull up alongside a runner at the very tip of its turn, running the wind at full sail, and even that didn't guarantee they'd have enough momentum to stick in the vortex hole.

The hour crept by and the Solar skulked along the southern horizon like a fox scuttling across a road. Isabelle tracked the *Saint Asne* in the orrery as it drew closer and closer to the point of influx, checking her timepiece and counting down. They had nothing to spare.

Similce leaned into the chartroom. "Capitaine, they're almost on us. They're going to cross our stern."

And rake us to bits. Isabelle's pulse kicked up double time. She turned the knob on her timepiece and set the race hand running.

To Similce, she said, "Ten minutes to insertion." Their window for success had never been wide, but every thump of turbulence, every cannon shot or punctured sail only narrowed it further.

Similce cursed in fluent sailorese and hurried below to give instructions to the gunners. Travers's sloops came in staggered and stacked, one high

384 — CURTIS CRADDOCK

and two low. Their gun ports opened. The frigate sweeping in behind them sported a quartet of shadowpults. When they got in range they'd cast bloodshadows strong enough to peel the *Saint Asne* like an orange. The little brig would have no chance against any one of them, much less all four.

"Major Bitterlich! The top sloop!" Isabelle shouted. "Get it to turn." She hated sending him unescorted out of the range of covering fire, but she couldn't afford to be bracketed above and below.

He snapped a smart salute, gave her a heart-fluttering wink, and leapt over the side.

Eight minutes. Isabelle's heart rattled like a snare drum and her mouth was desert dry.

The forward sloop crossed into firing range, close enough that Isabelle could see the buttons on the officers' coats.

"Hard a larboard!" Similce shouted, spinning the wheel and turning the ship to protect her vulnerable stern.

Isabelle clutched the rail and mourned the loss of speed, of ticking seconds they could not retrieve.

The sloop opened fire. It guns spat fire and smoke. Cannonballs whizzed by. Most missed entirely, but a few smacked the boards twixt tops and turvy. The *Saint Asne* answered with double-loaded chain shot into the sloop's rigging, snapping lines and rending sails. The ship shook, slowed again by its own cannonade.

The frigate's shadowpults threw open their shutters.

"Hit the deck!" roared the boatswain. Isabelle ducked into the shadow of a bulwark as a great crimson shadow licked over the ship.

Explosions rippled along the *Saint Asne*'s port side as Similce set off the smoke pots. Thick, black, oily krakensmoke boiled up over the ship's bulwarks, fouling the shadowpults' grasping beams.

The bloodshadows tore at the smoke, punching through like the crimson rays of a bloody dawn. Malgiers, amidships, with a dozen lesser lanterns at his back, strove to keep them from creeping onto the deck, but it was like trying to hold back a river with a teacup. A crimson bloodshadow beam ravaged the topsails. Cloth and rope frayed and faded toward shadow. Topsmen fell like swatted flies, paralyzed and unable to scream.

At the stern, Marie braced a twist gun in a gun loop. The bloodshadow washed over her, scrabbling futilely to find a shadow that wasn't there.

The *Saint Asne* hit the top of its turbulent pitch. Suspended at apogee, Marie pulled the trigger. Flash and recoil. A shadowpult turned from red to white as its Sanguinaire gunner's brain matter sizzled on the overheated reflector.

Six minutes.

The frigate opened fire from long range. It shots fell short. The forward sloop fired another broadside. Her deck guns sprayed grapeshot at the *Saint Asne*'s main deck. One of the bow gunners went down in a spray of blood. Marie's loader handed her another twist gun. She braced to the loop and fired again.

Musket fire erupted from the high sloop. Everyone with a gun blasted away at the twisting, darting bird that was Bitterlich. Sanguinaire officers' bloodshadows reached for him, but he swept under the ship out of sight. The sloop's turvy guns hammered the air in his wake.

Bitterlich swept up the stern, turned into a monstrous hybrid of bear and snake, and twisted the rudder spines into a knot. The ship lurched out of control.

Isabelle shouted down the hatch to Similce, "Charge the keel! One-point pressure!" The *Saint Asne* dared not alter course any farther, but she could lift at least a mast length and still stay on target.

The ship had barely begun to lift when the forward sloop delivered a broadside. Wood cracked and splintered. The frigate fired, the shots went low. Something bucked and the ship started to drag.

Sail's loose, Forenzio said.

A horrible dread filled Isabelle's chest and packed it tight so she couldn't breathe. They must not lose speed. Isabelle ran to starboard and leaned over as far as she could to see the damage. A lucky shot had snapped some shrouds. The sail got backed to the wind, and a spar was twisting, threatening the whole mast.

Isabelle leapt through the hatch onto the gun deck. Rebecca was shifting powder with the other powder monkeys.

Isabelle grabbed her by the shoulder. "Turvyside!" she yelled to be heard over the gunfire. "There's a loose spar with a sail. Cut the sail loose and fix the shroud! Understand?"

Rebecca's eyes were as wide as dinner plates. "Cut the sail, fix the shroud. Aye!"

Rebecca flew down the ladder and out the turvy hatch. Isabelle launched herself up from the hold to the main deck in one great leap, her Fenice strength a wonder even in this chaos.

The *Saint Asne* sailed through the gap where the second sloop had been, firing as she went. The third sloop came about to run alongside the *Saint Asne*, losing way. The frigate made to pass her stern.

A sudden crash shook the ship, flinders sprayed through the sterncastle, the great cabin, and chartroom. Isabelle dashed inside and stopped in horror. The orrery was smashed, ripped completely from its pedestal. The emergency valves had slammed shut, and no aether leaked, but she'd lost the inflection point . . . unless she found another fixed point to steer by.

No, Primus said. *The time has come to surrender while you still can.*

Be quiet. Isabelle splashed at him and scrambled through the room picking up her navigational tools: sextant, triangle tables, timepiece.

Enough of your foolishness, Primus snapped. *You claim to value evidence and reason. If so you must know you have lost. You must live and regroup. You are valuable as a hostage—*

Suddenly his memory was beside her in her head, seizing control of her limbs. Her instruments clattered to the deck and she collapsed to her knees.

Isabelle grabbed him and hauled him into the everdream. *We don't have time for this.*

You are correct, he said. *We don't have time. If you don't surrender now, your foes will down this ship. Yield to me and I will save you.*

No, Isabelle insisted. What had made him this way? She threw herself into his memories, entangled with his descendants through scores of lives and hundreds of years. She strode with him across battlefields and through the wide marble court of the great senate in Om. With him she plotted the conquests of nations, the sacks of cities, the ruin of enemies. And always his need was the same. He must have power. He needed control.

She found herself in a villa. A great mosaic floor ran the length of the hall and the call of shorebirds echoed down the pillared corridor, but it could not drown out the sound of sobbing, of screaming. Mother was there. Mother, who laughed with him and held him when the night terrors came. Mother, whose plumage was swan white with tips of black. And Father was there. Father, who led the army, who was master of the fleet. Father, who beat Mother with a rod of steel, covered in hooked barbs that tore out her feathers and left her bloody with every blow.

"This is my house!" he screamed. "My city, and there is nothing in it that does not belong to me. I will do with you as I wish."

"Stop!" Primus wailed, terrified, scampering on short legs to get between his parents. "Father, please stop!"

But his father's rage towered like a storm cloud. "Do not tell me what to do!" He swatted Primus aside with the club. "You belong to me, too, boy, and don't you ever forget it. I am the master, and if you ever think otherwise, my scourge will remind you."

His mother's funeral was very well attended. Everyone was sorry for his father's loss. How tragic and unexpected.

Father's next wife had no use for Primus or his twin, and they had been sent away to live with relatives who had no use for them, either, but who did owe their father a debt.

And Primus had sworn, on the day he came of age, no one would ever have power over him again . . .

No one ever found out who'd beaten his father to death with his own scourge, or who poisoned wife number three, but by the time all other claimants to the family lands and fortune turned up dead, people had learned not to ask questions.

Isabelle ached for the child Primus had been, even as she loathed the bitter, grasping thing he had become. There was no experience of hers that could help him. He could not see any reality but his own.

But maybe that was the key. She pulled him into Forenzio's memory and showed him the wreck he had made of the boy's life.

Is this what you wanted? she asked. *Did this make you safe? Did it give you control?*

Then she pulled him into Lissa's memories and all the relationships he'd ruined grasping for influence, and the merchant he'd destroyed trying to crush all his enemies. She showed him the senator he'd wrecked trying to make him a king, the clergyman he'd corrupted trying to become Omnifex.

Then she took him back and showed him his father, his face twisted in rage.

How many times are you going to let him win?

Primus's pain unraveled like a tornado in Isabelle's soul, blowing everything flat, leaving her empty and spent. Yet somewhere in the deepest part of her long memory, a child faced away from an angry father, and embraced his dying mother.

Isabelle surfaced into her own body with a gasp. She checked her timepiece.

Five minutes left.

She scooped up her tools and raced to the stern. She needed a longitude. She kicked open her sky chest and whipped out her Solar navigation book. She needed the angle of the Solar, and the precise time. She needed more hands.

Inspiration struck her with a clear, cold note. She needed all hands.

She turned to the breach of the everdream and shouted, *All hands on deck!*

Her ancestors rose at her command, gathering in a throng.

Forenzio, she said, *man that sextant; get me azimuth of the Solar.*

Aye, Capitaine, he said. *But how?*

Like this. She seized his ghost, grabbed the sextant with her spark-hand, and pushed his awareness into the instrument along with enough of her l'Étincelle sorcery to let him animate the device. She stuck it on its tripod and aimed it at the hole in the hull where the windows used to be.

She pushed another ancestor into her timepiece and another one into her compass. She explained to the rest what computation she wanted each of them to perform. She opened her navigation book and sped through the tables until she found today.

"Four minutes," chimed the timepiece. They might already be too late.

Another barrage rocked the ship, sloughing time. *Faster.*

"Give me numbers!" Isabelle commanded, touching the devices one at a time, feeding the numbers to her waiting throng of ghostly computers.

Twenty-seven point nine five three, said Capitana Falconé, who had been selected to give the final result.

"Three minutes," chimed the timepiece.

Isabelle checked her previous calculations. Her soul felt like it had been ripped out. *Too late . . . unless . . .*

She sprinted for the quarterdeck and the wheel. "Hard to starboard!" she shouted. "Take us straight at the wall! Pressure to the keel!" They needed speed that wind couldn't give them.

The helmsman threw himself into the wheel. The rudder flexed and the ship turned. Isabelle peered through the smoke at the shrieking veil of wind, looking for the escort. Logic insisted it was a good thing she could not see one yet.

A great dark shape cast a shadow over her. She looked up just as Bitterlich landed beside her, all black wings and sinewy body. He shifted down into his ordinary shape.

"How are we doing?" he shouted.

"That depends on how much you trust my arithmetic!"

The light dimmed. The sky closed in and a wall of sleet turned all shapes into shadows. The frigate kept up its fusillade, falling behind. The *Saint Asne* hooked into the Bittergale's outer wall and began to accelerate. The third sloop gained on them.

Hailstones whipped across the deck, clawed at the rigging, and pummeled the strakes. Where in all the uncharted skies was that cursed escort? Had she miscalculated?

Rebecca popped up from belowdecks, flush with victory. "Did you see me catch that spar?"

The sleet tapered off as an enormous shape emerged from the fog on their larboard side. Isabelle's breath caught at the sheer immensity of it. The escort was like a mountain tumbling through the sky, but no mere rock was this. Isabelle's l'Étincelle spark swarm flared in its presence, recognizing a quondam artifact, albeit one layered in accretions of ice, snow, and stone.

"Larboard!" Isabelle shouted to the helmsman. "Vent the forward keel chambers!"

Similce looked at her like she'd gone mad, but relayed the order without delay.

The *Saint Asne* drifted sideways, sliding into its vortex. The timbers groaned as the ship tilted nose down and fell forward, accelerating. Ships were never supposed to be pitched down like this. Sliding forward under gravity not only risked backing the sails, but if the forward tip of the keel dipped too far, the ship would flip vertically and javelin into the Gloom.

The Bittergale shook the sails and bent the masts. Turbulence threw aeronauts up and smashed them down. One man's tether snapped and he whisked away, shrieking into darkness.

Isabelle clung to a stanchion with her talons. The mountainous escort filled the whole sky. The vortex boundary had to be here.

The ship leapt up and dropped. And settled. The turbulence suddenly abated.

"Come to starboard! Ride the ridge!" Isabelle commanded. "Charge the keel!"

"Down!" Bitterlich shouted.

Isabelle threw herself flat just as a hail of grapeshot sprayed the deck from starboard. One sloop had followed them into the storm, but it came in too wide, out of the escort's shelter. The Breaker's own wind caught it. Lines snapped and masts sheared. It rolled over like a wallowing pig before vanishing in the storm.

"Help!" shrieked Rebecca.

Isabelle turned. Her heart nearly stopped.

Bitterlich had borne Rebecca to the deck and covered her with his body. He'd given himself an armored shell, but the grapeshot had torn right through it. Blood poured from a dozen wounds and soaked into the sand on deck in a widening pool.

CHAPTER

Twenty-Nine

Jean-Claude and Aria lay in the cover of brush atop a ridge overlooking Travers's headquarters camp. Le comte had managed to anchor the stricken *Potencia* to the edge of a coastal plain near the mouth of the *Conquest* fjord. The sky cliff was rough and rocky, but the land rose from there in slow stages to the feet of some ragged hills. His men had spent two days clearing the ground and erecting a palisade as if they might be suddenly assailed by an infantry regiment.

This gray morning they rang the ship's bell and fired a shot from their cannon, apparently in an attempt to get Aria's attention. Then they dragged Hailer Dok out, chained him between two stout pales, and stripped him to his skin.

A herald, stationed atop a large stone at the edge of Travers's encampment, cried into the wilderness, "For the crimes of piracy, murder, theft, and heresy, the criminal Hailer Dok, anathema of the Risen Kingdoms, is hereby condemned to death by excruciation."

Jean-Claude's skin crawled. Excruciation was a slow dismemberment. The victim was rendered into a carcass one joint at a time over the course of several days. Greatest care was taken to keep the victim alive, awake, and aware through the entire process, ostensibly so they would have ample opportunity to repent their wickedness. Only when a great confession was extracted was the victim allowed a swift and relatively painless death. Thus could the condemned sorcerer be permitted into Paradise Everlasting instead of condemned to Torment with the clayborn.

Aria gnashed her teeth. Her personal whirlwind bent the shrubs and grasses around her.

The herald continued, "Yet the Builder and his true servants may be merciful. Let the heretic witch Solo Aria present herself, the traitor Jean-Claude, and the relic they have stolen to the most excellent justice and mercy of le Comte de Travers, eighteenth of that name, pure of blood and the true heir of the Risen Saints. Do this by nightfall, and your crimes may be forgiven."

Aria started to sing in a low, soft voice, and what felt like a mountain of air built around her. Jean-Claude imagined her flinging one of her air bursts down there and blowing the herald to bits. He tapped her on the shoulder and shook his head vigorously.

"No," he signed, sliding back from the ridgeline to converse without risk of being seen. "You can't take the whole camp."

"Can't I? We sees how they deal with a hurricane."

"How long can you keep that up, and what will you do once you've exhausted yourself?" Jean-Claude asked. "We still don't know where Hasdrubal is. They know you're here. They know I'm here. They'll have prepared for both of us. We have to present them with something they aren't prepared for."

"Unless you has someone else down your trousers, you and me is all we has."

Jean-Claude found himself grinning as he sometimes did when he felt a really bad idea coming on.

"That's not quite true," he signed. "We have them." He gestured toward the encampment. "It's time I went and had words with them."

"Far be it from me to point out you can't talk."

"One problem at a time," he signed.

It was barely an hour later when Jean-Claude marched out of the wilderness carrying a long pole with his white shirt tied to it like a flag. His pace was steady, but his heart worked double time. Travers's sentries could see him from the palisade by now, and no doubt word of his approach had raced up the chain of command. There was a small chance Travers would simply have him shot and thereby cut his opposition in half. Yet any sensible person would realize Solo Aria was far more dangerous, and they would want to drain him of information about her plans, or so he prayed.

"Halt!" shouted a soldier from the rampart, and several more came out to deprive him of weapons that he'd already discarded, bind his hands, and march him through camp. Hundreds of flat-eyed aeronauts went about routine tasks, showing no interest in the procession.

Dok knelt on bare, hard ground, staked out between the pales, naked but for the mask on his face, his skin bearing the colorless pallor of one who had been shadowburned into submission. Jean-Claude would not be surprised if Travers had excised Dok's voice to make him useless if he was captured. Travers had implied at the beginning that he could give Jean-Claude's voice back, no doubt he could do the same for Dok.

In the center of the encampment stood Travers's pavilion, all white with red trim and emblazoned with the Travers's coat of arms, which was, in grand irony, a black tree of many branches bearing blood drops for fruit. The tent glowed from within like a paper lantern, with bright lights to make strong bloodshadows.

Inside, Travers sat upon a throne on a platform, his canes folded across his lap and his bloodshadow in a wide pool around him. To one side stood a small cadre of officers. Jean-Claude recognized most of them from his eavesdropping aboard ship. They were the ones who called Travers father-brother, and they shared his chinless, beak-nosed aspect.

To the other side stood Hasdrubal, short and broad of shoulder, wearing red robes and a hood with black tassels over his caprine head. His eyes, red as garnets, watched Jean-Claude intently. Also present in the back was a bloodhollow, though Jean-Claude could not tell if it was the one belonging to Travers's cousin.

Jean-Claude's escorts forced him to his knees and made him touch his forehead to the ground. If Hasdrubal could smell fear, he'd be getting a snoot full. Travers might well kill him now out of spite and wounded pride. Jean-Claude had planned for death—to do otherwise would have been malpractice—but he had no wish to meet the Breaker yet. He must find out what had happened to Isabelle and stop these miserable schemers in their tracks.

The question was how to separate them. Hasdrubal's place in the conspiracy had to be precarious. His contributions to the cause had been Dok, who was now in Travers's control, and the relic, which he'd lost. Yet he must still have some value to Travers or he would have already been killed or fled.

Travers, on the other hand, wanted to draw his prize to him in the center of his power, like a spider in his web. He despised anything he did not control absolutely.

"So, my property has returned itself," Travers said, his sinuses providing him with his own personal echo. "Is there any sign of the wind witch or the reliquary?"

"No, monsieur," said the escort.

The bloodhollow came to life. Jean-Claude could see nothing but its feet. The body was male, but the way it glided when it walked suggested the rider was a woman.

"You didn't expect there would be?" said the bloodhollow. It had the cousin's voice.

"No," Travers said. "I expect base trickery. Take it out, lop its head off, and stick it on a pike outside the gates. Let the wind witch know that we are not to be trifled with."

Jean-Claude began to consider the notion that he might be in slightly more trouble than he had originally anticipated. Fortunately, his hands were tied in front of him rather than behind, so he was able to pull a slip of paper from the seam of his coat and extend it out where someone might see.

"It appears our captive has a note," Hasdrubal said, his voice a bray. "Bring it here."

A guard stooped and reached for the paper, but Travers snapped, "Do not."

"Well, I want to see what it says," said the cousin, stepping forward and kneeling.

"Eulalie, do not!" Travers snapped.

Jean-Claude knew that name. Comtesse Eulalie was one of Sireen's confidantes, a founding member of the Order of the Succoring Shadow.

"Mind your tongue," said Eulalie. "I'm your cousin, not your slave." She took the paper from Jean-Claude's hands and read it, "Solo Aria is willing to exchange the reliquary of Saint Cynessus for her husband. I have been sent as her emissary to arrange time and place so that all further violence may be prevented. If I am not returned safely within the hour, Solo Aria will toss the reliquary into the Gloom."

Eulalie said to Travers, "Useful to know, don't you think."

"It is a lie," Travers said. "She will not endanger her husband."

Hasdrubal said, "Is that a chance you need to take? The reliquary is the only important thing. It matters not how we obtain it, only that we do, and barter is less fraught with danger."

Jean-Claude took the opportunity of their infighting to rise as far as a kneeling position. Though his hands were bound, he tried signing to Hasdrubal, "Aria talk you." He hadn't any idea if Hasdrubal could understand hand speech, but it was worth a try.

Hasdrubal nodded and said, "Yes, I see."

Travers caught the exchange and glowered. "What did he say?"

"Restore his voice if you want to find out," Hasdrubal said, which suggested to Jean-Claude that he hadn't really understood the hand speech but knew how to roll with an opportunity.

"It is clayborn," Travers said. "It will only lie."

"And you think we can learn nothing from lies?" Eulalie asked. "Let him talk."

Travers glowered at her. "You will regret this, I guarantee it."

Attendants rearranged several of the large alchemical lanterns to cast bright beams on Jean-Claude, and Travers's bloodshadow lanced his shadow like a needle into a boil. Even though he was prepared for it, the pain made Jean-Claude whimper and whine. Travers peeled his shadow into several layers and found within them threadlike veins or nerves that spread through his whole body. Several of these had been cut and looped into knots that would have impressed a sailor. Travers ripped the knots loose—it was like having his fingernails ripped out over and over again—and tied them into new positions. The only reason Jean-Claude did not pass out was that the bloodshadow would not give him leave.

Yet for all the agony, Jean-Claude might have sung with joy, for the black snake in his mind recoiled deeper and deeper until it finally yielded its grip on his tongue.

"Yes." The word slipped past his lips. He could speak, bless the Savior. Now he must make his words count.

Travers's bloodshadow twitched out of him with all the gentleness of a leviathaner yanking a harpoon from his prey.

Travers leaned forward. "Well, clayborn, what do you have to say?"

Though dizzy and weak, Jean-Claude shrugged off the attendants and stood.

He bowed slightly to the assembled group, tested some words on his tongue and felt no impediment to moving them forward. "Solo Aria sends her greetings. She has entrusted me to negotiate on her behalf for the safe and unharmed return of her husband."

Travers said, "In that case, she should do as directed and return the stolen reliquary to me before nightfall."

Jean-Claude bobbed his head in Travers's direction. "She will be happy to do so if we meet on neutral ground."

"We will meet here," Travers said. "That is nonnegotiable."

Jean-Claude said, "If your infirmity makes it difficult for you to travel, perhaps one of your compatriots would be open to the idea. Surely it doesn't matter which one of you makes the transfer and receives the reliquary."

Hasdrubal said, "How would you guarantee my safety if I were to accompany you?"

Jean-Claude made a gesture of nonchalance. "Bring as many men as you like. Follow me in the form of a hawk so high up that I can't see you. Once we're at the meeting place, you can leave Dok in a place where you can watch him. Once Aria is satisfied she will not be ambushed, she will take her husband and leave the reliquary in his place. I will note that she has every reason to uphold her end of the bargain. The reliquary is of no use to her, and once Hasdrubal has it, he gains nothing and risks much by pursuing her."

"I forbid this," Travers said. "Dok is my prisoner."

"You forget who captured him," Hasdrubal said. "And who obtained the reliquary."

Eulalie said, "Neither of which could you have done without me."

"Messieurs, mademoiselle," Jean-Claude said, "there is no need to bicker. As I have said, Solo Aria's only concern is getting her husband back safe and unharmed. If neither of you wish to go, you could send your bloodhollow."

"I could do that," said Eulalie.

"No," Travers said. "A hundred times no. Can't you see, he's trying to make us fight amongst ourselves."

Fear coursed through Jean-Claude's veins, but it was the clear, cold type that sharpened his senses to their keenest edge, and the mad joy of being handed the perfect straight line was the spark on the edge of the blade.

He grinned inside and aimed a wedge at the heart of their conspiracy. "Oh, you don't need my help for that. Betrayal was always the endgame. You, monsieur, want to rule the world. Monsieur Hasdrubal wants to destroy it. The only reason you haven't already killed each other is that neither of you has the reliquary and you need the other one to get it. At this point Hasdrubal already has what he wants. He was using you, monsieur, to lure me in, to give him a thread he can follow back to the reliquary. It took me a while to figure out what you still needed from him, but then I remembered the locked trunk in his quarters, and it occurs to me that you've never actually seen the reliquary. That was his last bit of leverage. You don't know what it looks like or how to tell if it's real. It turns out I can help you with that. Indeed, I can give either one of you what you want, but only one of you. The question is, which will it be?"

Hasdrubal cast a sideways glance at Travers, whose face had taken on the cast of a judge about to render a verdict. His bloodshadow did not ripple but its crimson took on a deeper hue.

Jean-Claude caught Hasdrubal's gaze. "Time's up."

Travers's bloodshadow licked toward Hasdrubal, quicker than an eyeblink.

But Hasdrubal was gone, his cloak drifted down, empty. Travers's bloodshadow caught the cloak and whipped it aside. "Where—" he snarled, furious and bewildered, but there was a mole hole in the ground where Hasdrubal had been standing.

Jean-Claude lunged backward between his guards and bolted for exit. One marine seized his arm, but he squatted, twisted, and stuck out a leg, throwing the man to the ground.

Jean-Claude surged upright just as the ground split behind him, filling the air with dirt and toppling the tent poles. Travers sent shadows winging at the monstrous shape churning the earth, but the tent dropped on top of him, dust and fabric fouling all shadows.

Jean-Claude lunged through the collapsing flap and bowled over a guard outside. The other guard cocked his musket and took aim. Hasdrubal erupted from the ground as a monstrous six-legged, mole-blind thing with scales like a crackback and rat teeth the size of garden shears.

The marine screamed in fright and tried to bring his gun around, but Hasdrubal bit down hard, severed his arm, and flung his body away.

Jean-Claude lengthened his stride. Hasdrubal paced him easily.

Jean-Claude shouted, "You want the ring. Aria wants Dok!"

The pavilion's canvas ripped like sailcloth in a storm, torn to bits by Travers's bloodshadow. Jean-Claude darted down a tent alley before the enraged Sanguinaire could draw sight to him. Hasdrubal leapt into the air and took wing as a falcon, racing ahead.

Travers's shouts woke the camp to danger, horns sounded, and marines mustered. Jean-Claude huffed into the torment square with a stitch in his side. Hasdrubal landed next to Hailer Dok and switched into something huge and hairy with arms like an ape and tusks like a loxidont. He ripped the chains from the post, scooped up Dok and Jean-Claude, and bounded toward the ramparts, breaking the perimeter faster than the circle could close. It was all Jean-Claude could do to hang on and not be torn limb from limb like a rag doll in the mouth of a terrier. Sentries on the outer wall fired at them. Guns barked. Bullets thunked into the soil and scattered off rocks, but Hasdrubal was moving too quickly and erratically to make a good target.

Just as they crested the first ridgeline, Hasdrubal dropped Jean-Claude. Jean-Claude bounced and tumbled through the alien foliage until he fetched up against the bole of a very thick but stunted tree.

Hasdrubal's chest heaved with his exertion and the inside of his flaring, horse-sized nostrils burned pink with his effort. Through a mouth full of great flat teeth, he said, "You tell the Windcaller I have her husband and will meet her at the wreck of the *Conquest*."

Jean-Claude fought for breath and said, "I can take you to her," but Hasdrubal had already turned and loped away.

Horns from the camp strongly suggested pursuit being organized.

Jean-Claude levered himself up and hurried to find the cache where he'd left his weapons. He rooted them up and, with the dagger braced on a rock, cut the bonds that held his hands. His fingers ached and burned as blood flowed back into them, but he managed to assemble his kit and lurch over the next ridge into thicker brush just as the first hunters poured from the gates of the palisade.

—

The *Saint Asne* rumbled and shook, every line vibrating and every timber creaking as it hurtled through the Bittergale. Isabelle had locked them into a stable eddy in the lee of the quondam escort, which towed them along in its wake. The storm raged outside their bubble of relative calm. Only the lightest debris, sleet, and pea-sized hail got bent enough in the escort's vortex to spray across their hull. The ship's lanterns turned the racing slurry into a smear of gray tinged with green and red.

Down in the surgeon's bay, the wails and moans of injured men rose above the hammering of the storm. Rebecca hovered in the doorway, her eyes still wide and wild with shock. Isabelle stood with teeth clenched and knuckles white with helpless fear as the surgeon and his loblolly boys dumped Major Bitterlich on the cutting table. He'd already lost so much blood.

The surgeon took one look at his perforated shell and said, "I can't cut through that. He needs to change."

"Can't," Bitterlich muttered, his voice withered. "Bullets."

"Get him off the table for someone I can help," the surgeon said.

"No," Isabelle commanded. His wounds were deep and sore, but a mature Seelenjäger had more than one body to draw on. He could disperse the wounds. Plus he had a healing form. Her talons could cut his shell, or . . .

"Rebecca!" Isabelle shouted over the storm. "Turn into a wyrm."

Rebecca looked at Isabelle through eyes brimming with tears. "Wh-Why?"

"Burn him with your ghostfire. It'll make the metal fall out of him." She'd seen the ghostfire wash over living men without hurting them. It only burned things like stone and metal.

Rebecca took several rapid breaths, closed her eyes, and stretched out into her wyrm form, a sinewy ribbon of blue-green scales and mother-of-pearl horns.

She whipped up into an *s* shape and spat green fire, sweeping Bitterlich from one end to the other. Isabelle clutched her hand to her chest and prayed for the Builder's mercy. Bitterlich gasped once, and the now-ghostly grapeshot dropped out of him, falling like hailstones through his flesh, through the table, and through the deck.

"Perfect!" Isabelle shouted to Rebecca. She bent over Bitterlich and urged him, "The metal's out. Change into a healing form."

But his eyes were staring sightless and his breath came only in hiccups.

"Bitterlich!" Isabelle cried, taking his face in her hand. "We got the metal out. You can change! Please! Please. Oh saints. Don't go." Tears streamed down her face and she shook him. "No. No. No."

"Ssmme," he mumbled.

Isabelle took what felt like the first breath of her whole life. "Bitterlich?"

"Kiss me," he muttered.

"Are you out of your mind? You need to change!" Relief, disbelief, and sputtering outrage turned her voice into a wail. But she locked her lips to his and kissed him as if that one touch must last until the end of time.

His body unraveled and wove itself into a new shape, shrinking and twisting. He mumbled into her mouth. "Bring me home."

His lips disappeared from hers and shrank into a chimeric form she had not seen before. It was the size of a large dog, but had the general shape of a lizard, if a lizard had no face, feet, or claws. Its color and texture were that of a reef star. It occurred to her that both reptile and reef star were masters of regeneration.

Rebecca, back in her regular form, landed across from Isabelle, looking shaken. "What happened to him? Will he live?"

"I think so," Isabelle said, her analysis driven more by need than logic. She opened her arm in invitation and Rebecca stuck to her side like a limpet. "You saved him."

As rattled as she was, Rebecca looked at the strange hybrid lump that was her father and said, "He saved me first."

———

Hounds bayed on the scent behind Jean-Claude. Hounds, because of course the cursed nobles brought their dogs with them halfway across the deep sky. What self-respecting snob wouldn't be ready for a foxhunt at a moment's notice on any Breaker-be-damned deserted skyland? Of course, le Comte de Travers was the same man who'd kept a porcine Seelenjäger on hand just in case he got peckish for pork chops.

Jean-Claude climbed off the coastal plain into the rocky hills, heading for his rendezvous point with Aria. If he could reach her before the hunt caught up with him, she could fly them someplace safe to work out how to deal with Hasdrubal.

On the tumbled slopes of these hills grew a forest like none Jean-Claude had ever seen. The trees were short and thick with dome-shaped canopies that were too tall to see over and too short to walk under. Between there was an undergrowth of plants with thick woody stems that branched out into long slender leaves like the thatch of a broom, if brooms came in blue, purple, and red. They were also spiny and sticky and exuded a milky resin that gave him a rash. It was probably a good thing no one was going to put him in charge of naming things, or everything in the canopy panoply would be named "scratchweed," "itchy bastard," and "burn-on-sight bush."

Every plant seemed to be in bloom just now, their arms and stems bedecked with big waxy flowers in every conceivable shape, each of which had its own species of bothersome insect. The whole place was full of bugs. Everything he'd seen in Lael's specimen collection didn't amount to a fair sample of all the different types he could count, even without slowing down. At his pace, he couldn't go three steps without crushing some undiscovered species underfoot.

Jean-Claude's lungs burned and his legs ached. Still distant behind him bayed the hounds, and with them the whoops and hollers of the beating party, trying to spook him. Somewhere on the wings of the formation would be the scouts, quick men with keen eyes and a hunger for the chase.

Fortunately, Jean-Claude did not have far to go, assuming he didn't miss his turn. There was a flat-topped hill, the tallest one in the first rampart of ridges facing Travers's camp. There was no way to avoid exposure on the boulder-strewn face, and sure enough the horns sounded to announce he'd been spotted. Down below, the bushes rattled and a mob of men came on. He tried to look every way at once, but he still hadn't seen the flankers. Hopefully they hadn't gotten ahead of him. He scrambled over the narrow ridge that formed a saddle between two peaks and set out toward the left one. His lungs burned and his muscles quivered. Old he was. Old and fat.

Solo Aria ought to be around here somewhere.

He reached the huge hill-cresting boulder where they'd planned to meet. He knew it was the right one by the rock scratches he'd made before he left.

"Where's my husband?" Aria said, emerging from behind the stone.

Still out of breath, Jean-Claude wiped his brow with his sleeve and said, "Hasdrubal has him. Taking him to the *Conquest* wreck."

"You useless lout," Aria said. "You says you gets him free."

"I got him out of Travers's camp," Jean-Claude said. "That's half the job done. Now we only have Hasdrubal to deal with."

Pebbles skittered by Aria's feet. A lizard scampering by . . . but there were no lizards here.

Fear jolted Jean-Claude. He dove to shove Aria aside even as the lizard exploded into the size and shape of a bear, if a bear had armored plates and claws like scimitars. With a horrible crack Aria's head flopped forward like a rag doll's and she landed in a sprawl, lifeless eyes staring at the sky. Jean-Claude reached for his cutlass and dagger, but Hasdrubal swatted him with a backhand that lifted him from the ground, knocked the air from his lungs, and sent him tumbling down the hillside.

Jean-Claude woke to pain and the baying of hounds. He lay beneath the shattered boughs of a half-dome tree. A hole in the canopy above him gave evidence of his plunge. Saints, but he hurt . . . and Aria was dead . . . and the hunt was almost on him. He rolled to his side—each side hurt worse than the other one—and forced himself to his feet. Hasdrubal had tricked Jean-Claude into thinking he was running ahead, when in fact he'd stayed behind and followed him straight to Aria. He must have killed Dok first, or left him to die, so he could move quietly. Jean-Claude had been checking his back trail, but Travers's hunters had served as a distraction for the Seelenjäger. With the reliquary in hand, absolutely nothing stood between Hasdrubal and the Vault of Ages.

Fool.

Hasdrubal had whipped him like a mangy cur, then wiped his arse with what was left. Dok and Aria had paid for his mistakes. He hadn't much liked either of them, but they'd been good to their word, and that was something in this world.

Men shouted nearby and dogs barked. They were close enough he could hear the rattling of trees as they passed.

Time for recriminations later. Jean-Claude pushed himself to his feet, found his cutlass hanging in the branches, and fetched it down. Of his dagger there was no sign. He limped away into the brush at right angles to the direction of the chase. The hunters would find Aria's body. They'd have to decide what to make of it. That would give Jean-Claude precious minutes, but no more. In chasing Jean-Claude they would be pulled away from Hasdrubal, which explained why he'd been left alive.

Jean-Claude lurched along the crease of a narrow valley looking for a way up and over the next ridge. He had somehow managed not to break any bones in that fall, but he was so bruised he would resemble a ripe plum should he survive until tomorrow, whatever tomorrow looked like at the top of the world. He knew when his pursuers had found Aria's corpse by the sudden eruption of noise and sounding of horns.

The shadows lengthened and shifted direction as the Solar continued its progress around the rim of the sky. The light dimmed and the veils of the auroras shimmered and crackled overhead. In this gloaming, many of the bugs began to glow and twinkle, as if the stars had all come down to live in this fairy forest. Under other circumstances it would have been enchanting to watch.

Something bigger than a beetle rustled the bushes. Jean-Claude crouched, ignoring the complaints in his knees, and scuttled under a half-dome tree. He eased up against the trunk and held deathly still.

A man prowled by: one of the scouts. He was not much more than a shadow with tall boots. One shout from him and the whole hunting pack would be on Jean-Claude before he could limp to the edge of this draw.

Jean-Claude held still, barely breathing as the scout padded by. The insects buzzed louder. An itch on his leg turned out to be a large black beetle with glowing speckles climbing his trousers. Jean-Claude resisted the urge to kick and shake the thing off, for Travers's scout still hunted nearby. The beetle crawled up his thigh and then his chest. As it drew closer to his head, he noted that the beetle itself was not speckled but rather bedecked in luminescent dust or pollen. Its tiny hooked feet scrabbled for purchase on his neck, grabbed his beard stubble and jabbed a hind leg in his ear before it finally found its way onto the rough bark of the tree.

The beetle disappeared into a hole in the trunk. There was a brief flash of light from the hole, as if the beetle had stepped into a well-lit house and closed the door behind it.

Curious and careful, Jean-Claude eased up so that his eye was level with the hole. With a twig, he prodded the recess. His prod pushed aside a flap made from a leaf. The inside of the trunk was hollow, and though his field of view was like staring through a keyhole, he could see a complex structure within. Tendrils like spiderwebs crisscrossed the space, and the outer wall was covered in something that looked like pale blue honeycomb. Many different sorts of insects crept, crawled, flew, and hopped around on whatever business the Builder had given them.

Isabelle would love this. She'd spend hours staring at it and taking notes, and counting things. He'd have to show it to her someday, if he was lucky enough to ever see her again. He ached with missing her and Marie and young Rebecca. Not knowing what happened to them on that barren skyland was a weight greater than all the pains of his body.

Jean-Claude pushed the leaf-gate a little wider for a better view, and his twig poked and popped one of the honeycombs. A sickly sweet and vinegar smell puffed from the hole. Every bug in the trunk went completely insane. Beetles clamped onto his stick, buzzing wasplike things stung the tip. Jean-Claude lurched back as long segmented creatures erupted from the holes all around the crown and poured down the side in angry, venomous streams. Midge-like specks of hate swarmed from the branches to bite and sting.

Jean-Claude ducked out from under the overhanging branches. The canopy seemed to flash as if it had lightning beneath it. All around, other umbrella trees answered in kind, and swarms of insects rose from them, answering the call to arms.

Nearby, a foot crunched on a beetle. Jean-Claude dodged. A gun barked. The bullet slammed into the leaf litter. Horns sounded in response to the gunshot, and the hunting party whooped and yelled, crashing through the bushes toward him. Jean-Claude turned and charged the scout who'd found him. He was a younger man, tall, lean, and fit. He wielded a boar spear and Jean-Claude was the boar he meant to gut. But Jean-Claude had lived through more battles than the youth had years. He swatted the spear aside and slammed into the boy with his shoulder. The scout reeled back to set his stance, but Jean-Claude gave him no rest or quarter, hacking his arm with the cutlass and then cleaving his skull.

The scout fell and lay twitching, blood pouring from his wound. The umbrella trees flashed with longer pulses in red instead of blue, and the gathering swarms retreated. They cared nothing for the brawling men, only for the defeat and destruction of the stick that had prodded them.

Jean-Claude grabbed two cartridges from the scout's bandolier, fetched the pistol from the ground, and overcharged it. He snatched several rabbit snares from the man's belt and tied them together into one long cord, then looped one end around the trigger. He carefully wedged the gun in the tree entrance and cocked it. The other end he tied to a broach on the scout's shirt front and flipped him facedown.

The nearby trees shook with the rumble of the approaching hunt. Jean-Claude ran. He lumbered around the back side of a boulder just as the dogs broke cover. He kept running, or at least limping enthusiastically. His booby trap might work or not, but he wanted to be as far away as possible when—

Bang went the gun. The trees flashed blue, brighter this time. Jean-Claude imagined he'd done much more than pop a honeycomb. Chances were the trunk had exploded. He pushed himself faster until his lungs burned. Swarms of insects leapt from the canopy. White blooms on the trees opened up and glowing pollen filled the air. The ground quaked under Jean-Claude's feet, and the hillock he just stepped on shuddered and stood up, revealing itself as a beetle the size of an ox. It rubbed its wing carapaces with a sound like someone sawing down a tree and lumbered off toward the hunting party. More gunshots erupted. Men cursed and dogs yelped. Battle cries turned to shrieks of pain and terror.

Jean-Claude's legs turned to lead, but he did not stop until he'd left the last of the blue flashing trees behind him, and the forest sank back into silence.

—

The *Saint Asne* shuddered and bucked in sudden turbulence. Isabelle ran out on deck and gauged the storm, praying they hadn't slipped out of their stable eddy. Instead, she found the sky had grown lighter, the gray tunnel disappearing before them. The shaking came as they passed through the storm's inner wall into the calm air beyond. The mighty vortex, angered at their intrusion, lashed them with one last flurry of melon-sized hail before the brig slipped into open sky.

Relief washed through Isabelle so fast it made her dizzy. They'd made it. Even when she'd been in the escort's shadow, she hadn't been sure it would work. Saints only knew what other hazards waited in that storm.

Almost instantly the air grew warmer, and the green, earthy smell of the Miasma rolled up from the depths. Isabelle ordered the maneuver to take them out of the eddy and into free air, but did not draw an easy breath until they were well out of the Bittergale's reach.

The Craton Auroborea swung into view, a wide smear of hazy green in the distance. She could hardly believe the witness of her senses. Jean-Claude was there, somewhere. He'd be at the *Conquest* if he possibly could. Her dizziness increased, and the whole world went gray around the edges. Her skin tingled, and every bit of fluff and feather stood on end. Then she twitched. It was like a sneeze or a whole-body seizure.

She found herself lying on the deck, Marie and Rebecca hovering over her.

"What happened?" Rebecca asked. "Is she hurt?"

"I don't think so," Marie said. "Just doing things the hard way, as usual."

"Ungh," Isabelle said wittily, and rubbed her face with her hand. Her hand, covered in skin instead of fluff, feathers, and scales. She stared at it in wonder. Her skin had taken on undertones of pink and purple. And her face felt like skin too.

Your transition is complete, Primus said, *though you should not sheath your* cappotto di piume *in such perilous circumstances.* He remained critical of her "weaknesses" but had ceased trying to force his way into her mind.

Rebecca helped Isabelle sit up.

"Water?" Marie offered, and Isabelle took a sip. The dizziness passed with each breath.

"I see you got your skin back," Marie said.

"Yes," Isabelle said. "The transformation is finished."

"Ooh, can I see?" Rebecca asked.

"Don't you think she should get a chance to see it first?" Marie said.

"In a moment," Isabelle said. "We still have a ship to sail."

Similce said, "We're on course for the cratonic rim. I expect finding the *Conquest* will be a matter of finding the *Potencia* first."

Isabelle stood. It felt like climbing a very tall ladder. "And then we have to deal with Travers."

"If you want to get some rest, now is better than later, I'm thinking."

"Well thought," Isabelle said. She walked into the great cabin. By the time she got there, she felt less like falling over. That last step of her transformation had taken a lot of energy, like water changing to steam. She didn't recall it being so exhausting in past lives.

You've been fighting the change for days, Brunela said. *You've been bottled up too tight to let it happen.*

So she'd had a case of transformation constipation, because nothing was ever merely difficult when it could also be uncomfortable. She told herself the lie that she really didn't care what she looked like as long as it was not a flamingo, but hurried to get her mirror anyway.

She pulled off her hood and lifted the mirror to see her reflection.

Oh.

Isabelle had never thought of herself as beautiful. She had a long face, an extra helping of nose, and teeth like a horse. She still had those things, but her transformation had filled in everything her birth had left out: strong cheeks, skin dappled with lilac and rose, and where her dishwater hair had been, a crest of pink and purple feathers that fanned out or flattened back with the same ease as twitching an eyebrow. And along the edges of those feathers ran the sparks of her l'Étincelle sorcery. The motes glowed and flowed up the fringes until they reached the tips, like her crest was a fan in front of a fire. Even her eyebrows and lashes had turned to feathers.

I . . . think I can live with this.

"Lemme see," Rebecca said, bounding down and up on the ceiling.

When Isabelle turned, her eyes went round. "Ooh! That's golden! Not as good as mine, though." She shook her mane.

Isabelle laughed. "Well, I'm glad to be second best, then."

Marie stepped into the room. "Can you extend your *cappotto*?"

Isabelle queried her ancestral chorus and found a mental string. She gave it a tug. It felt a bit like pulling thread through every follicle in her body, but in less time than a finger snap she was sheathed in feathers. They lay tight and bright against her skin like a fish's scales. They added no apparent weight, but past-life experience suggested that she was now virtually bulletproof.

"Apparently so," she said, extending and retracting her talons.

"Then maybe it's time you got properly dressed," Marie said. She nodded to Rebecca.

"Right. I'll go get the package," Rebecca said, and zipped out the door.

Isabelle gave Marie a suspicious look. "What package?"

"When we were back on Flotsam, we decided that if you were going to be a pirate capitaine, you might as well look the part. Now that you've finally run out of reasons to punish yourself sartorially, it's time to get you fitted and kitted. Besides, Rebecca needs the practice."

—

Isabelle sat by Bitterlich's bedside, wondering when or if he would wake up. This healing state was so terribly quiet. She wasn't even sure by what method he was breathing. What if his body didn't have the resources to repair itself? He'd lost so much blood.

"I don't know if you can hear me," she said, as suppressed fears and hopes found their voice. "You know I'm really proud of you, the way you've taken on Rebecca. You really make a good father. I . . . I also think you'd make a good husband. I mean yes, you need to get it through your thick skull that you don't have to be perfect to be special. I don't want perfect. I want you."

Ridiculous, Primus said. *Marriage is a tool of politics. Leveraged properly, it can shift the power of kingdoms. It is not a plaything for lovers.*

There is a time and a place for your opinion, Isabelle replied. *This is not it.* She'd spent many hours playing confessor to all her ancestors, slowly bringing them around to her way of thinking, or at least her sense of priorities. It was a work she suspected would never be entirely finished, but that did not mean she had to spend every waking moment dealing with them.

"Ship!" cried the lookout, and Isabelle's pulse lifted up into a trot.

She squeezed what she took to be Bitterlich's shoulder, reassured by its warmth and life. Then, on impulse, she kissed him where his cheek might be.

His form shuddered, and his lips manifested to meet hers. Startled, she lurched back to see him emerge from his chrysalis face-first, unfolding and refolding into his erstepelz. His eyes opened and he let out a long breath. "Hello, beautiful. Have you seen Capitaine Isabelle?" His sloppy grin suggested this was supposed to be a joke.

She glowered at him. "And here I was, just saying nice things about you."

"I'm sorry I missed that. How long have I been gone?"

"About two days."

"That explains the hunger," he said. "And the headache. Why didn't you wake me up sooner?"

"Sooner? If you were recovered . . ."

"Not recovered so much as out of danger," he said. "It's still going to take me a while to mend all the pieces. The problem with the deep-healing chimera is that it's made up of a bunch of creatures who are collectively a few lobes short of a brain. My mind more or less shuts down while I'm in that state. I'll wake up eventually, once I get hungry enough, or I can set myself a trigger."

The arithmetic slowly clicked into place. "That's why you asked me to kiss you."

"And to bring me home," he said.

Isabelle groaned a little. "Saints, I thought you were just being an insufferable romantic."

"I was. I mean, who could resist such a tale, a dashing sky capitaine waking her equally dashing marine major with a kiss."

"You could have been more clear," she said, poking him in the shoulder to punctuate each word.

"Ow. Ouch. My apologies, but I was in a great deal of pain at the time. Thank you, by the way, for saving my life."

"You need to thank Rebecca for that," Isabelle said. "And I need to go capitaine my ship." Then, more gently. "I'm glad you're going to recover."

"So am I. You look absolutely stunning, by the way, and stylish."

Isabelle brushed some nonexistent lint off her new waistcoat and cravat. "Thank you, but if you're going to start judging me by my pulchritude, I'm going back in the sack-cloth."

"Saints forbid," he said. He extended a hand, almost touching her chin. "May I?"

Isabelle warmed all through her chest. She didn't have time to dally . . . much time, anyway.

"You may," she said, her voice rough.

He touched her chin with the pad of his finger and guided her mouth to his. The touch of his lips sent sparks flying that had nothing to do with her sorcery. The taste of him woke a hunger that warmed her whole body.

With a great effort she pulled away, unsated and unsatisfied. She wanted not to drink from his well but to swim in it, drown in it.

"I'll let Rebecca know you're awake," she said, and left before desire led her into neglecting her duties.

Up on deck, she called Rebecca and gave her the good news. Her eyes lit up, her scales shimmered with relief, and she flew belowdecks to talk Bitterlich's ear off.

Isabelle found Similce, who pointed out a white speck in the distance. "It's the *Potencia*."

Isabelle trained her glass on the ship. It had apparently seen them and was taking flight from the edge of an abandoned naval camp. It headed away from them.

"See that inlet?" Similce pointed to a crack in the sky cliff just beside the camp. "I'll bet that's where the *Conquest* wreck is."

"Then that's where we go. The *Potencia* is a decoy." Isabelle said. That's where Travers and Hasdrubal would go. That's where Jean-Claude would be if he possibly could.

"I don't like leaving an eighty-gun galleon behind us," Similce said.

"Neither do I," Isabelle said, "but I don't want to fight it, either, and we don't have time to chase it around the sky. We need to stop the reliquary from getting to the Vault of Ages." Memories of Czensos's annihilation goaded her on. What sort of madness seethed in Hasdrubal's brain that he would do that to the whole world?

Isabelle ordered the *Saint Asne* into the fjord, a great fissure running from the sky above to the Miasma below.

She reefed all but the smallest maneuvering sails, and sent Rebecca flying ahead to scout the mist-filled passage for reef stone and other obstacles. The helmsman held the ship steady against the vortex shear as they passed through the gap. The shadow of the canyon walls fell across them, plunging the passage into dimmest twilight.

A breath of warm mist caressed her face, the heat stinging after so many weeks of relentless winter. It brought with it the muddy smell of a swamp. Whence came this heat she could not tell, but by the time the outlet to the sky disappeared around a bend behind them, the rime on the ship started to melt, splattering the deck with an unsteady rain of heavy, wet splashes.

A light appeared in the fog ahead. Rebecca had planted an alchemical lantern on a conical chunk of rock twice the size of the ship. It spun slowly by to starboard.

The chasm narrowed. Isabelle gripped the rail tightly enough to leave finger grooves in the wood. If the fjord got much narrower, they'd have to anchor and take the launches in.

More reef stones speared from the fog, each one marked by a lantern.

All along the top deck and the turvy deck, men stood by with stout poles to fend off any stone that got too close.

From the murk far ahead shot a pair of reddish-orange lights, flying in formation. They swooped and looped and weaved in and out of the reef stones much like . . . or rather exactly like a child at play. The lights were Rebecca's hand lamps. Shooting through the air without wings or wind, she did an acrobatic tumble, used the bowsprit as an entirely redundant springboard, and landed in front of Isabelle with a smart salute and an ear-to-ear grin that said "Yeeeeeahoooooooo!" without actually making the noise.

"Capitaine," she said, without waiting for a prompt. "The channel opens up just around the next corner, and there are waterfalls, and it's green!"

Whilst not being the most professional report ever delivered, it had one of the most profound effects. Men tense with dread and uncertainty shifted their balance forward, the gleam in their eyes of victory near at hand.

"Well done," Isabelle said. She resisted the urge to tousle Rebecca's white mane. "A pistol shot off the bow if you will, and guide us in."

"Aye, Capitaine." Rebecca bounded over the side. Her body twisted in midair, stretching out into the undulating, green-and-blue glittering shape of her ghostfire wyrm. She rippled through the air, looping and making helixes while she waited for the ponderous ship to keep up.

"Helmsman," Isabelle said. "Follow that wyrm."

"Aye, Capitaine."

The *Saint Asne* rounded another bend, and Isabelle was not alone in her gasp of astonishment.

The narrow slot opened up into a great wide bowl. Numberless waterfalls bounded down from high cliffs, splashed into cliffside pools, and slid down glistening stone to plunge at last into the bottomless sky below. With the water came a profusion of greenery—creeping vines and broad-leafed plants of the type that never saw a day of frost. Below the high bluffs were a series of natural terraces down to a rocky shoreline.

"There." Similce spotted it first. Isabelle followed her pointed finger to a narrow ridge several mast lengths above the skyfall edge.

There like a cast-off carcass of some immense leviathan lay the wreck of the *Conquest*. Its aged corpse was little more than a set of bleached-white ribs and a bonekeel spine more than half consumed by the creeping greenery.

Unfortunately, they were not the first ones to arrive. Four cargo skiffs had been pulled up on the shore, but of their occupants there was no sign. Nor, despite her hopes, was there any sign of Jean-Claude.

Isabelle brought the *Saint Asne* in and anchored it to the sky cliff, then sent out landing parties to check for enemies and ambushes. They reported no people present but signs of a beaten-down trail leading off into the sweltering green.

Isabelle stepped from the gangway to the shore. After so long aloft, her legs wobbled at the sturdiness of the land. The wet heat of the green stuck to her skin, but the thing that struck her most was the quiet. Aside from the rippling of the wind, the place was silent. With a forest that thick, there ought to be birdsong or some sign of life, but the only things that moved on the rocky shoreline were glossy black beetles and other crawling things.

Travers and Hasdrubal had been here and gone, and she had no idea how much of a lead they had. She ordered an expeditionary party prepared. She would lead the vanguard ahead, with Malgiers and half the marines. Similce would bring up a supply company afterward, and a detachment would be left to guard the ship.

She had just finished dispatching orders when her perimeter scouts shouted an alarm.

Isabelle looked up with everyone else. Down a treacherous switchback path from the cliff wall came a man in sailor's garb, carrying a bloodied white rag on a stick. Isabelle lifted her glass and focused.

"Jean-Claude!" Isabelle shouted. "It's Jean-Claude!" She whooped and rushed to meet him. Her new Fenice muscles responded to her joy, and her stride lengthened until she was covering eight meters a stride. She was moving so fast, she nearly caromed off the cliff wall before hurtling up the switchback trail like a spring-loaded mountain goat.

Jean-Claude's one flesh-and-blood eye grew wide as she leapt up from the trail below to land beside him.

"Isabelle," he said, astonished. "You've changed."

"I've changed," she said, "a cocoon, a chrysalis choosing new challenges and a choir of churlish characters over catatonia and cognitive calamity, and you . . ." The alliteration game was one they had always played.

"A clockwork cyclops, crashed on a craton covered in cockroaches."

Isabelle opened her arm and they embraced, a crushing hug such that she had to take care not to crack his ribs. He was here. He was real.

"I was so worried," Isabelle said.

"So was I," he said, and they let each other drift to arms' length.

"I got your hat," she said. "And your message."

"Sedgwick proved true, then. I saw Marie facing off against Czensos just before my eye blacked out."

"Sedgwick told me about your eye. You mean it stopped working?"

"It might as well be a metal marble," he said.

The air stirred and Rebecca flew up and said breathlessly. "You moved fast, Capitaine. *Bonjour*, Jean-Claude."

"Who?" Jean-Claude asked, and then, "Rebecca?"

"Bet you didn't know I'm a Seelenjäger."

"It was not included on your list of qualifications," he said.

Isabelle said, "We've all got stories to tell, but this is not the place for them. Rebecca, go tell Similce to get ready to march."

Isabelle walked with Jean-Claude down the switchback trail, talking about all that had transpired since their parting. Isabelle was dismayed to hear about Dok and Aria.

"I got tricked," Jean-Claude said. "Sometimes you lose." But she could tell it bothered him more than he was willing to say.

They had just reached the last switchback when the world stuttered.

Between one eyeblink and the next, Isabelle found herself in a thunderstorm. Rain sheeted down, soaking her to the skin before she could even think to deploy her *cappotto*. The trees on the slopes bent in the wind.

Then just as quickly, all was as it had been, save for the water dripping from her crest feathers. Isabelle looked to Jean-Claude, also dripping wet, who returned her gaze as bewildered as she felt. On the staging ground, her aeronauts broke into excited chatter and drew weapons to aim . . . where?

It was as if reality was a candle that flickered, and might be snuffed out.

"Hasdrubal," Isabelle realized. "He's made it to the Vault." That lunatic had grabbed hold of the levers of the world and started jerking them around. How long would it be before he broke the ineffable machine?

Fear kicked Isabelle's heart, for all the good it did. "How far ahead of us are they?"

"Hasdrubal took the reliquary two days ago, and he can fly," Jean-Claude said. "What's left of Travers's party, including most of his Sanguinaire relations, landed here yesterday and set off through the woods."

"So we're going to have to get through Travers to get to Hasdrubal,"

Isabelle said. "How convenient for us. Do you have any idea how far away the Vault is?"

"Aria showed me. It's a ruin on a lake about a day's walk from here."

They rejoined Similce at the staging area. She'd gotten all the aeronauts rounded up, but they all looked as spooked as Isabelle felt.

Similce saluted. "The supply unit is ready."

Isabelle returned her salute and addressed the crowd. "My brave aeronauts, I have reason to believe that ripple in the world that we all just experienced came from the Vault of Ages. I further believe that we shall experience more of these disruptions. I know you are afraid, and it might seem sensible to get as far away from this place as possible, but there is nowhere to run. If I am right, that strange skip in the world was felt all the way to the Craton Massif and beyond. Hasdrubal, who betrayed you, has managed to find and penetrate the Vault and it is his intention to use the tools of the Builder to rend the world from its moorings and cast it into the abyss. Our only hope is to find him and stop him. So gird your souls in courage, and let that which you love be the beacon that pulls you on, for we are all that stands between the Builder and oblivion."

Isabelle was no great orator, but the aeronauts believed her. They tightened the straps on their packs and bent their shoulders into gale-force winds of fear.

Isabelle looked to Jean-Claude and frowned. "The vanguard group is going to have to move quickly." Jean-Claude, battered and bruised, looked like he could hardly stand.

"It's the end of the world," he said. "I wouldn't want to be late for it."

"Neither would I," Bitterlich said, emerging from behind a clutch of porters. His manner was easy, but his gait was stiff. He stopped and saluted. "Reporting for duty."

Isabelle shook her head. She could order them to stay. They might even obey her. It would even be the right thing to do if she thought their presence might diminish the chances of them stopping Hasdrubal.

The world shuddered again, and this time she found herself in a vast hot desert, with nothing but sand dunes and rocky upcrops in all directions. Her aeronauts variously yelped, milled about, or froze in confusion. Something that might have been a scorpion if it wasn't the size of a carthorse spun in surprise at their sudden appearance. Its tail lashed. She threw on her *cappotto*.

The world as it had been returned as if that other realm had never happened, except for the sand on her boots. Breathing heavily she looked at her men, and her aeronauts. "We'd best get a move on."

She set off at a brisk but human pace, pulled out her timepiece, and started the tracking hand. Was there a pattern to these disruptions?

Isabelle and her family, the people in the world she loved most, quickmarched into the woods along the beaten path. The canopy closed in above them and the sound of insects grew loud. This place was entirely strange enough without flickering out of existence. After confirming he could still shift shape, she sent Bitterlich ahead to scout and Rebecca with him under strict orders to follow his lead.

Jean-Claude kept tapping his clockwork eye. "I wish this thing would work. I could see through half the forest."

"What happened to it?" Isabelle said.

"After I saw you face down Czensos, it went dark."

Marie said, "Probably when Ivar died."

Isabelle tossed sparks from her fingers and said, "Do you mind if I have a look at it?"

"I didn't think we had time."

"I'll do it while we're walking."

"I thought you could only be in once place at a time," Jean-Claude said.

"That was before I had help."

Isabelle summoned up Falconé and gave her the helm of her body. *Just keep walking. No shenanigans.*

What do you think I'd get up to? Falconé asked.

You know better than I do what your worst impulses used to be. I leave it to you not to surrender to them. In fact, Falconé the spy was as close to being a woman after Isabelle's own heart as any of her ancestors, at least once she got over her infatuation with Primus. She liked being trusted.

Isabelle touched Jean-Claude's clockwork eye with her spark-hand and made the leap into the quondam metal.

The eye was slick and smooth and much bigger than it seemed on the outside. All sorcery was created by the Builder and she had for some time entertained the hypothesis that before the Breaking of the World, sorcerers of her kind had been his helpers, the forge masters and the engineers who labored on the ineffable machine. Alas, even if this were true, her ability to meld with the Builder's artifacts had not been handed down with any instructions as to how to make use of that talent.

Jean-Claude's eye was filled with gears and mechanisms to operate the iris and deform the lens. She spun these wheels and felt the eye focus blindly on nothing. As far as she could tell, the mechanism was still intact.

She made a circuit of the whole eye, following each subcontraption to whatever threadlike fiber or glimmering plate it attached to. The deeper into the eye she went, the denser the mechanism became, but the space it involved expanded for her and gave her ample room to maneuver.

Eventually all of the clockworks, springs, silver threads, subassemblies, and whatnots arrived at a single dark and unresponsive node. She hovered around the node and peeked inside it. There could be no doubt that all the information the eye gathered was funneled through here.

From what Sedgwick had told her about the way the eye worked, and from the fact that Jean-Claude had been seeing through Ivar's eye when he was obliterated, there ought to be a channel leading away.

At last she found a tangle of loose silver threads that had once been connected to a plate that just wasn't there anymore. The plate had been on a rocker. She flipped the rocker to its other position and found another contact plate. This must be how the primary eye controlled which view the secondary eye saw, but since the primary eye was annihilated, there was nothing to flip the switch back.

Carefully, she began attaching the silver threads to the newly exposed plate in the same configuration that they came out of the junction node. She had to stretch the wires a bit and weld them in place, but as the last one made contact, the whole eye began to hum and click. Gears whirled, axles turned, and springs wound.

She slipped back into her body, gave Falconé's ghost a hug for her good behavior, and turned her attention outward.

Jean-Claude shook his head. The clockwork eye tracked with his natural eye, his pupil glowing blue at its center.

"So how does it feel?" she asked.

"You did it!" He laughed. "I can see."

The world stuttered again. Isabelle clicked her timepiece. Everyone came to a halt as they found themselves in the middle of a city, but one like they had never seen. The buildings seemed to have been grown rather than built, stone teased up in trellises and twisted into living shapes. And there were people here. A man in breeches and boots goggled at them and was gone.

Or mostly gone. Images of the grown city remained, suspended like vaporgrams in the air for several seconds before fading away.

Isabelle checked her timepiece, called out the time to Marie for safekeeping, then set it ticking again.

"Was that place real?" Malgiers asked. "I mean, are all those other places out there somewhere?"

"I don't know," Isabelle said. It was one of a thousand things she didn't know.

"It looked real enough to me," Jean-Claude said.

"Keep moving," Isabelle said. There was no other choice.

They reached a branch in the trail. Bitterlich had left a marker to indicate which way they should go, but even so the new path suggested either Travers's party had split up, or they weren't the only ones making paths in the forest.

"It could be the bugs," Jean-Claude said. "I saw some that were as big as a cart."

"So we don't know precisely which way Travers went," Isabelle said.

Jean-Claude said, "We're not looking for Travers. We're looking for the Vault."

"Yes, but I don't want to end up with him behind me."

Isabelle sent a runner back to warn Similce's party about the side roads, and then pressed on. Over the next several hours the world flickered again and again. There seemed to be no pattern to the timing of the appearances, but each event was growing longer, the smoke images lingering until they seemed to be running through a haze of half-seen other places.

"Capitaine!" Rebecca's voice raced ahead of her as she swooped in under the canopy. "We found it!"

"The Vault?" Isabelle asked. "How far ahead is it?" They might survive this yet.

"Ah. Not the Vault exactly, the flower." She held up a Saint's Promise flower, only slightly crushed by its hectic flight.

Isabelle took a deep breath to stop herself from howling in thwarted hope. "Good job," she said. "How far ahead?"

"Not . . . too far," Rebecca said uncertainly. "There's a lake that's on fire. Major . . . my father is looking for a way across it."

"Father?" Jean-Claude asked.

"Later," Isabelle said. "Any sign of Travers?"

"Not a sniff or a sneeze," Rebecca said, which meant le comte had taken one of the many side paths they'd encountered.

Isabelle and her vanguard picked up the pace again. They tromped over a muddy hill drooping with tangled vines, and along a track that twisted around trees as big as castle towers. Time constricted around Isabelle's throat, making it hard to breathe. Her timepiece seemed to run fast and slow at the same time.

At last they humped it over a rocky scarp and gazed down a long smooth slope. It was absolutely covered in Saint's Promise flowers, white blooms laid out in a vast field leading down to the edge of a lake.

The Temple's *Instructions* and the tales of Legend contained no detailed description of the Vault of Ages, but in the centuries since it had been abandoned, a variety of artistic traditions had taken to depicting it as a huge mausoleum either built into or resting atop a steep-sided mountain. Most had depicted it as being made of some kind of marble or granite, though Isabelle would have placed her bet on any surviving structure being made of impervious quondam metal.

She had not anticipated a burning lake. Black water with an oily sheen spread out through fractured canyon land like a many-tentacled kraken. A heavy cloud of sulfurous vapors hung close to its surface and crept onto land. Even standing on the ridge top, the stink of it made her throat bind and her eyes water. The empty carapaces of many beetles along the water's edge warned of heavy poisonous air. All along the surface of the lake fires burned, red and angry, filling the air with columns of soot that smudged the surrounding lands to black.

Isabelle had never seen a land so inhospitable or ugly, but there could be no doubt that this was where Hasdrubal had gone, for out in deep water stood a quondam ruin. Broken towers poked up from the water's surface like the ribs of a dead man. Twisted and crumpled bridges threaded the structures and spilled out into the surrounding water.

A hawk circling above glided in and became Bitterlich upon landing. His disposition was as neat as always, but there was a strain of fear behind his eyes.

He saluted. "Capitaine. I've found no sign of any of our quarry, but I have found a causeway to that ruin."

"Thank you, Major," she said. "Lead on."

"Isabelle," Jean-Claude said. "I mean, Capitaine. Request permission to stay behind."

Isabelle was shocked. She could not imagine Jean-Claude would not want to be at the head of the hunting pack, but his face was set and grim.

"You need a rearguard," he said. "Travers doesn't know where the Vault is. He was too slow to follow Hasdrubal. I imagine he'll think he's clever if he lets you find it for him and then tries to take it from you."

"I understand," Isabelle said. He'd led Hasdrubal to Aria and she'd paid with her life.

"Fool me once," Jean-Claude said.

"I should stay with him," Marie said, and that made sense too. Of all of them she had the biggest advantage against the Sanguinaire.

"Take care of each other," Isabelle said, her throat tight.

"And you . . ." Jean-Claude turned to Bitterlich. Somehow Bitterlich had ended up holding Isabelle's hand. Or rather they held each other's.

Jean-Claude nodded slowly as if in answer to some unspoken question, and said, "Major Bitterlich, it's your turn to keep her safe."

Isabelle felt as if she were falling, for in the weight of his words was not just now, but untold years to come.

"To my last breath," Bitterlich said, his voice the steady flame of a torch being passed. He saluted Jean-Claude, who returned the gesture.

Isabelle's heart squeezed so hard that she thought it might split. This was not goodbye. Must not be. She strode to Jean-Claude and Marie, never had she missed her right arm more than when she wanted to embrace them both at once. Tears stood in her eyes as she finally relinquished her life grip on her oldest friends, her dearest family, extended her hand palm-down, and said, "May the Builder keep you safe from harm."

They replied palms-up, "Until the Savior comes to take you home."

CHAPTER
Thirty-One

Isabelle ended up leaving the marines and Malgiers with Jean-Claude as well. Travers had a force with him, and they should be able to answer in kind. Plus there were great gaps in Bitterlich's causeway that Isabelle could leap but no ordinary man could manage. The roadbed, if she could call it that, was a metal mesh in the shape of a honeycomb, with holes big enough to accommodate a man's thumb. Still, it bore her weight without complaint, and she struck out toward the ruin. Bitterlich and Rebecca guided the way. Hungry flames reached for her from the oily lake, and she held her breath and hurried through low yellow clouds when no other path was available.

Night, such as it was, fell by the time she reached the outskirts of the once-city. The auroras danced and the lake fires grudgingly illuminated her path as she traversed spaces between the buildings.

Where was Hasdrubal? Where was the Vault? What did it even look like?

The world stuttered again, but it was different this time. There was no living world on the other side of the skip, just the causeway, the ruined towers, and cold, barren rock, lifeless and airless. All the breath raced from

Isabelle's body and cold slammed her lungs. Her *cappotto* and her spark-arm vanished just as they had on the remnant of Rüul.

Rebecca and Bitterlich fell from the sky, their sorcery likewise dispelled. Rebecca fell beside the causeway, landed on her head, and lay stunned. Isabelle stumbled toward her, growing dizzy, trying to draw air that wasn't there. She hauled the child onto the causeway. Her legs gave out. She fell to her knees and flopped over on her back, reaching for Bitterlich. He crawled toward her.

Above, the aurora had vanished, but the distant stars still gleamed in their familiar patterns. That much, at least, was constant. Yet there was also a structure here, a tall stepped pyramid in the center of the ruined city that hadn't been there a moment before.

It was the Vault of Ages. Just there, but she could not breathe. Her sight dimmed and blackness crept in.

The world snapped, the auroras crackled, and breath hit her lungs, burning through the empty sacs like fire through dry scrub. Her ears popped, and for a long minute she could do nothing but cough and wheeze. Her head felt like someone was hammering it on an anvil. Still she rolled to her knees and looked around. Rebecca lay unmoving.

Bitterlich felt for Rebecca's pulse. She groaned and rolled her head, mumbling incoherently.

"Just stunned, I think," Bitterlich said with more hope than evidence.

"Keep watch on her," Isabelle said, regaining her feet and staggering up the causeway toward the chopped-off buildings.

"Where are you going?" Bitterlich asked.

"To the Vault of Ages," Isabelle said. "That world we were just in. That's the one Hasdrubal wants. The dead world. The broken world. The end of everything."

Bitterlich scooped Rebecca up lightly, cradling her head. "I'm coming."

"I don't think you can," she said. "The Vault of Ages isn't a place you can reach from here, not without the reliquary." She gestured at the towers around them. "When the world ended, four things remained: us, these ruins, the stars, and the Vault. They are constants. They are part of the original design. Everything else, our world, our sorcery, it's just . . . painted on somehow, and the Vault is painted out."

She approached one of the broken towers. They were wide cylinders packed closely together and then chopped off a few stories aboveground like rushes in a swamp. In the darkness the metal throbbed with a light that did not spill beyond the surfaces, and behind those pulses spun the shadows of gears, axles, catchments, and rockers that ticked and tocked in directions beyond the three the human mind could easily comprehend. What did you do if you didn't have enough space in your gearbox? If you were the Builder in his workshop, you just added another direction and multiplied your space, so that your gears might mesh in one place and their axles might intersect without interacting. Isabelle could see how the foundations of the math might be laid, if only the stubbornness of space could be overcome.

She touched the metal with her spark-arm and dove in. Inside the metal a whole new city spread out before her. It was a city of silver pathways that sang like harp strings and clockwork junctions that whirled driven by the Builder's limitless engine. Much of the city was broken and smashed, its chords dissonant and its pathways dark, but all of it was there. All except a hole where nothing was, a tight spiral that warped the space around and inward and then disappeared into its own center like a snake eating its tail.

Isabelle reached for the center of the spiral and found it clenched tight, held shut by something on the other side.

Found you.

Isabelle returned to her body and shook herself. Her feathers shivered. Rebecca was back on her feet but woozy.

Bitterlich asked, "What happened?"

"I found the door." Isabelle led them both up a few streets toward the center of the ruin. The road curled around a circular tower and just kept curling beyond the place where the circle should have completed. Two other roads met here at a point, like the center of a triskelion.

"It's here," she said, wafting her hand through the point in space where the door must be. Hasdrubal brought the reliquary here and it opened for him.

"Can you open it for us?" Bitterlich asked.

"I'll be lucky if I can squeeze myself through it," she said.

"But we're supposed to be helping," Rebecca said. Her voice was stronger, but she still leaned on Bitterlich.

Isabelle crouched to her level. "I need you to watch over your father for me. Make sure he doesn't get into too much trouble."

"But . . ."

Isabelle touched a finger to Rebecca's lips. "Take care."

Then she stood and took Bitterlich by the hand. His golden eyes were as deep and warm as summer sunlight. "I wish we had more time."

"So do I," he said. "But the fate of the world could rest in no better hands."

They embraced and kissed, trying to fit in the hope and care of an entire lifetime. But it could not last.

"Bring me back," she said. Then she turned and gripped the center of the spiral with her spark-hand. The nexus tightened at her intrusion, locking her out, but she did not try it force for force. She had not the Builder's strength. Instead she recalled the mechanism she found inside the vault key when she'd taken it from Quill. She remembered the pattern, the peculiar many-dimensional shape. She slid toward the center of the spiral, growing smaller and thinner as she ran along its infinite edge. She felt her way through the constricting world until she found the gap, the hole that was shaped like the key. Into it she pulled herself, until she filled the whole space.

She turned the key.

Without so much as a pop, Isabelle vanished from the world.

—

Marie helped Jean-Claude back to his feet. His lungs burned and his head ached. His whole contingent had fallen, choking in that soundless nothingness. Even men hitting the ground had made no noise. He had no words for that empty world save Torment, and for a terrible moment he'd thought Hasdrubal had won.

When the world came back, he wasn't entirely sure all of him had come with it, but Marie helped him to his feet, and all the men had survived it, though one of the marines sat weeping, inconsolable in his terror. Jean-Claude did not blame him in the least.

They had taken up a position on a ridge overlooking the point where the causeway touched the shoreline. He had scouts out in either direction and two in the woods behind just in case. There was nothing to do but wait. With any luck, this precaution would turn out to be unnecessary. Perhaps Travers had wandered into the forest and been eaten by a spider.

He looked to Marie, who sat still as only she could, like a statue, but alive inside.

"How are you feeling?" he asked.

"Scared out of my mind," she said flatly. "Life hurts, but it's also beautiful."

"If you could change anything—"

"No," Marie said, before he could even finish. "I wouldn't change anything."

"Not even becoming a bloodhollow?"

"That was twelve years of Torment," Marie said. "Worse than that airless void we were just in, because I couldn't even die. But if I had avoided that fate, what then? I was due to be married to a man I'd never met, far from friends or family or anyone who cared. Who knows, maybe I would have made a decent life. Maybe I would have been happier, but I wouldn't be Fellhand Marie of the Tall Clouds clan. I wouldn't be here, now, where it just might matter."

Before Jean-Claude could respond, one of the scouts hurried in. "They're coming, a whole parade of 'em, at least a hundred, and they've captured our baggage train."

Jean-Claude cursed and wondered if he would live to see a day when he was not wrong-footed from the start. He sent the scout back to make sure the parade didn't have a wing of scouts to catch his band from behind.

They waited as Travers's parade trudged into view. It was a ragged affair on the uneven ground, with rank upon rank of aeronauts leading the way, followed by squads of marines and a flotilla of sedan chairs, because of course Travers and his scrawny kin couldn't be arsed to hack through the rough.

Some of the porters from the *Saint Asne* had been tied together and trudged alongside the sedan chairs as human shields.

Behind the sedan chairs came a string of wagons, with teams of the rest of the *Saint Asne*'s crew hitched up to them like mules.

"Take out the Sanguinaires first?" asked Marie. "The rest won't do well without leaders."

Jean-Claude was about to give her the nod when it occurred to him that, aside from the lieutenants leading the marines, he hadn't actually seen any bloodshadows. He scanned the sedan chairs with his clockwork eye. The draperies were all but invisible to his sight. The people inside were clayborn, tied up. The one in the fanciest of the chairs was the Skaladin capitaine Similce.

"Decoys," he said, and swept his penetrative gaze over the rest of the

426 — CURTIS CRADDOCK

caravan. The wagons . . . At least three of those wagons were rolling bunkers lined with metal that he could not see through. They'd added metal slats to the wheels to make them wider so they wouldn't sink into the mud.

"The Sanguinaire are in those wagons," he said. "They're armored, bulletproof."

"So we have to get them to come out."

Jean-Claude chewed on the problem. "No. We need to get them to stay in. Marie, you're going to start the show. I need you to take out those marine lieutenants. Malgiers, you're the moat, keep they clayborn off of us." That left him with a double handful of marines. He assigned two sharpshooters to each wagon. "Shoot anything that shows its head. The rest of you come with me, cutlasses and pistols."

Jean-Claude and the six remaining marines sneaked forward as close to the path as they could manage and took up positions behind an irregular row of bushes and boulders. The caravan tromped by, the lead ranks thumping and squishing. They'd chosen the clearest path available to them, farthest from the danger of the woods. Jean-Claude and his crew would have to cross a dozen meters of open ground.

The decoy sedan chairs marched by. The squeak and thump of the armored wagons drew near. Jean-Claude checked his grenade pouch and cocked his pistol.

A gun cracked. Jean-Claude leapt from cover and charged the nearest wagon. The wagon guards turned and raised their guns. Jean-Claude raised his pistol, fired. A guard went down. Pandemonium erupted farther up the line. The caravan guards fired without aiming, a ragged fusillade. One of Jean-Claude's fellows groaned and fell. And then Jean-Claude was on the enemy, hacking with his cutlass. Steel hit bone. The guard stumbled away, dead or dying. The man riding shotgun brought his weapon around, but a twist-gun shot hit him in the chest and flipped him over backward. The cart driver whipped his hapless team, who struggled to make speed.

A panel on top of the cart flipped up, and with it the blinding light of a shadowpult. A Sanguinaire's bloodshadow slicked across the ground, but even at the speed of thought, two bullets slammed into the sorcerer before his shadow reached the tree line. The cart panel slammed back down again.

Jean-Claude ran alongside the exhausted human team and hacked at the bonds that held them to the yoke.

"Turn!" he shouted. "Push for your lives!" He threw his own shoulder into the foremost push bar and forced it to the left.

The wagon turned.

"Push!" he shouted.

The driver cracked his whip but he'd lost all control. The wagon continued its turn, and trundled onto the steep downhill slope toward the lake edge.

"Run!" Jean-Claude shouted as soon as the wagon started picking up speed on its own. He leapt out of the way and let the wagon rattle by, bouncing, rocking, and finally splashing into the water up to its axles. The yellowish clouds of poisonous air closed in around it. Both of the other carts had been similarly turned. The second one had flipped over before it reached the water.

The back panels on the upright carts opened and their Sanguinaire cargo came flopping out, splashing into the black oily water, gasping and wheezing as they struggled to shore. The heavy mud clung rather stubbornly to their fine coats and muck filled their expensive boots. The first one fell in the water and his fellows trampled right over him.

Not one of them made it farther than the rocky shore.

The rest of the battle drew to a close. With their marines dispatched, the leaderless aeronauts had no will to fight, and surrendered to a force less than a tenth their number.

From the back of the tumbled wagon came a hammering, and Travers's voice, "Guards! Guards! Get me out of here!" He coughed and choked. The lake smoke coiled around his wagon like a great constricting snake.

"All your guards are dead," Jean-Claude called back to him.

"Release me. I am le Comte de Travers, and I order you to release me."

"I'm sorry," Jean-Claude said. "But I don't answer to you."

"I am. Sanguinaire! You. Clayborn. I command. You obey. Builder. Builder . . ."

Jean-Claude waited several minutes after the last gasp died away, then lit an incendiary grenade and tossed it on the cart and watched the wooden parts go up in flames.

———

Isabelle snapped into being with a force that felt like a spring unwinding, and landed on her hand and knees. She felt like she'd left most of her innards behind. The floor was made of a metal she could not name, as were the ribs of the domed ceiling above. Between the ribs were windows that looked out into a swirling realm of different shapes and shades of light as if the chamber were suspended in the middle of the auroras.

Bubbles of light filled the room like vaporgrams in an orrery. Each bubble looked like a globe, a map of a whole world, but not the one she was familiar with. Some seemed to be covered in forests, deserts, water, cities, or some dizzying combination of them all.

In the center of the room glowed a great sphere of light and within it stood Hasdrubal, the ring of Saint Cynessus on his finger.

She'd only seen Hasdrubal in person once before, and his head had been covered in a hood. Now she understood why. His caprine face was horribly mangled, much of the flesh ripped. His tongue and his teeth showed through the side of his head as if through a ragged curtain. How there was enough of his face left to function she had no idea.

"So, the Breaker sends one last pawn against me," he brayed.

Isabelle wobbled to her feet, snapping her armored feathers in place. "You don't have to do this."

Hasdrubal hovered his hand over the surface of the sphere in the center of the room. It was Caelum. There was the Craton Massif and the crescent-shaped Craton Riqueza in the southern hemisphere. If she got close enough, could she see Rocher Royale?

"Of course I must," he said. "The saints tried to halt the destruction of the world. They gathered here and constructed this device to bind the Breaker and stop her tearing the world asunder, but in so doing they trapped the Breaker, and gave her all of mortalkind to play with. She created a place of wickedness, of depravity, a place of corruption that can never be expunged. Your Temple believes that all clayborn souls are doomed to Torment. The priests of the tyrant say that all saintborn are bound there. What none of them comprehend is that we are all born into Torment, and there is no escape from it in this life or the next."

"No," Isabelle said. "The world is full of suffering, but it is also full of hope."

"False hope," Hasdrubal snapped. "It is the hope of the mirage, of the oasis that is always just beyond reach. It is the hope that dies on the vine. In Torment, there is no human act that matters. It cannot be changed from within. The only solution, the only act that has ever or can ever have any meaning is to annihilate it, to erase it down to its roots so that it will never have existed. Only then, with the Breaker destroyed, will the Builder begin anew."

"And if you're wrong?" Isabelle got the feeling that Hasdrubal had spent a lot of time telling himself this story, repeating it over and over again until it was more real to him than the evidence of his senses.

"If our world is what the Builder intended, then the Builder is more a fiend than the Breaker ever was."

"You're insane," she said, stepping forward through a whole constellation of worlds. She needed to get the reliquary away from him.

"You are far too late to stop me." He removed the ring from his finger and pressed it against the image of Caelum as if it were a solid thing. The world sputtered and patches of decay spread across the surface.

Isabelle lunged at him, but he twisted his shape into that of a gorilla with an armored crackback shell and swatted her away. The blow would have broken human Isabelle in half, but Fenice Isabelle was tougher than iron. She bounced off the floor and slid to a halt against the wall.

"Stay down," Hasdrubal said. "You are no match for me. You should feel privileged to be here at the end, to witness the one true act in all Creation."

Isabelle rolled to her feet. Terror spread through her soul as corruption bloomed across the world, skylands crumbling into dust and then nothing, the whole world rotting away.

"You're right, Isabelle is no match for you," she said. "But Primus Maximus is."

She turned to the breach and called, *Primus Maximus, you have the helm. Get me into that ring!*

Primus expanded into her awareness, and for once she stepped out of his way. The rush and joy of battle filled her white-hot, like iron fresh from the forge. She felt her body as she never had before, every piece of her a weapon.

Primus charged, muscles like iron springs flinging them across the room so fast that Hasdrubal scarce had time to raise his guard. Sorcerous claws ripped through armored flesh and shattered Hasdrubal's forearm with a crack like lightning splitting a tree.

Hasdrubal yowled and staggered back and shifted into a leaner, faster form with many arms and stingers for fingers.

Still the world crumbled, decaying like an apple left out to rot.

Now! Isabelle cried.

Primus surged forward and thrust out her spark-hand; it passed straight through Hasdrubal and grasped the ring.

Isabelle jumped, her spark self sliding into the reliquary. It was like swimming through a river of light, sparks flying by so fast she could hardly see them. Isabelle darted through the slick, bright channel all the way to the end. She could feel where the reliquary hooked into the world.

The whole thing was made of symbols so simple that she did not see how they could have any individual meaning, but they came together into an emergent complexity that defied comprehension.

With no time to wonder she slid into the flow of symbols and fell into the world. Not just any part of it. All of it. She emerged into bottomless sky and onto the broad, flat cratons. She flowed with rivers and danced with lightning and pumped in the blood of countless millions of people.

Terrified people.

She found the edges of the rot that Hasdrubal had inflicted, spreading not from anywhere but from everywhere, her world decaying from the roots up, from cell to organ, from organ to body. Down into the rot she dove, into the decay, and found there a discontinuity, a hole in the words that made up the pieces that made up the things.

Hasdrubal hadn't needed to understand what he was doing any more than a bullet needed to know how a heart pumped blood. He'd just rooted around until he found something fundamental and ripped it out, and she had no idea how to repair it any more than she knew how to unbruise an apple or unburn a match.

She raced around the edge of the reliquary, the place where the gears of the tool meshed with the fundamental cogs of the world. The reliquary waited for her to give a message to send, words to start repairs and instructions on how to proceed. But the Builder's language was beyond her . . .

Or was it?

When the world had stuttered and the void rushed in, three things had remained. *The stars, the Builder's artifacts, and us.*

We are fundamental. She had the pattern. She was the pattern. She was built from it, and unlike the artifact world, she had not had the vital language ripped out.

Whispering a prayer to hope, she reached into the waiting mechanism. *I am part of this world. Take what you need.*

For an instant nothing happened. It didn't understand her. But then the

Builder's machine took hold of her and pulled. Terror flooded her and the gears spun, unraveling her, but she held her ground, her peace. Bitterlich was still out there, Jean-Claude and Rebecca and Marie and everyone else who had ever lived and loved.

Let them live.

There were artists with dreams yet unkindled, empiricists with discoveries yet unmade, there were children yet unborn.

Let them be!

Isabelle's thoughts grew hazy as the machine stretched her out like thread and wove bits of her into the holes in the world. The part Hasdrubal had torn out had not been complicated in the same way the first crystal of a snowflake was not complicated, but was just the beginning of an endless algorithm. From simplicity repeated with variation a great complexity emerged.

All around her the world healed, the substance filled in. The blackened bits scabbed over like a living thing and flaked away. Relief welled up within her and joy so warm and soft that she hardly noticed when she stopped noticing things.

Thirty-Two

The first thing she remembered was the ticking, a never-ending stream of clicks like a clock that never got to chime.

She opened her awareness. The world floated before her in all its wonder and glory.

It lived.

To her immense surprise, so did she, and with every passing tick she remembered more of who she was. She was Isabelle. She was inside the mechanism at the heart of the Vault of Ages. The machine wove her back together again like a tapestry that had been taken down to individual threads and then somehow put back together again. There were snarls in the design, though, and snags. Had those been there before? She couldn't remember.

There was a sudden sensation of separation, like a thread being snipped, and then suddenly she was herself again, or at least she was her spark self, the part of her that lived outside her flesh when she was using her sorcery. She pushed her perceptions up against the edge of the reliquary and peered out into the room. It was still full of bubble worlds being born and popping.

Those were, she reasoned, potential worlds, other realities that could have been or might have been after the Breaking of the World.

There were a dozen different variations of Legend, but they all agreed on this basic point: the world had been broken and the saints had tried to repair it.

This place represented their failure. The saints had made this place to try to reclaim the Primus Mundi. She imagined their frantic efforts as the world they knew literally disintegrated around them. They'd tried to fix the problem.

First step: stabilize the patient. They'd done that. The world still existed, or at least a world: her world.

Second step: perform the necessary operation to return the patient to health. That was where they'd failed, not because the patient was dying, but because they could not accept that it would never go back to the way it had been. For them, a return to the Primus Mundi was the only acceptable outcome, and so they had, in effect, left the patient on the operating table for several thousand years.

Third step: close up the wounds. Finish the operation. Let the healing begin. The saints couldn't accept the world as it was, but Isabelle could. She loved the world with its boundless skies and soaring cratons, its unexpected beauty and even the ragged edges of its horrors.

Isabelle took hold of the reliquary's machinery once again.

"Be done," she whispered. The machinery whirred and a galvanic tingle rolled through her awareness. The bubble worlds evaporated, and no new ones appeared. The thrum of the Vault died away. The world settled. She explored the reliquary and found it lifeless, the same with the deep mechanism of the Vault. At last the world lived on its own.

With no more simulacrum to attach to, the ring fell and clattered on the floor.

Isabelle looked outside the reliquary for her body. Primus stood at the edge of the room in front of a passageway that hadn't been there before. Hasdrubal's corpse lay at his feet. A long corridor led away to a platform at the far end.

Primus stepped into the corridor, and Isabelle's soul shrank in horror. He meant to take her body and leave her here, entombed forever in this ring. He would leave and grasp for power again and wreck the lives of everyone she loved.

No! Isabelle hammered on the surface of the ring, but she couldn't leap out, couldn't reach her body. He was too far away. *Please!*

Primus stopped two steps down the corridor. There was no way he could have heard her, but he looked back. His gaze rested on the ring and he grimaced.

Please.

Slowly he squared her shoulders, lifted her chin, and walked to the machine. He plucked the ring from the ground.

Isabelle leapt back into her body even before he slipped her finger into the ring.

Primus waited for her in the forefront of her mind. *Welcome aboard, Capitaine.*

You came back, she said. *Why?*

I have stolen too many lives from my children, he said. *And they let me know it.* He directed her attention to the breach, where all the rest of her ancestors stood and cheered.

Primus saluted and retreated into the throng.

"This way! This way!" Rebecca called as she shot through the entrance like a comet. Her eyes grew wide and she shrieked with delight. "She's here! I found her!"

She flew straight to Isabelle and wrapped her in a hug. "You're alive!"

Isabelle returned her embrace. Her warmth and solidity cracked the ice of unreality, the fugue of playing Builder and Breaker and saints all in one. Bitterlich swooped in as a raven, dropped into his erstepelz, and met her gaze with joy and relief before he took her in his arms and expressed with lips a love that words alone could not describe. Here was a world she wanted to live in—a larger, better world than the grandiose fears of saints and fanatics, a world that could not be compressed into a single virtue or flaw. Here was a world of friendships and family. Yes, there was pain and wickedness aplenty, but it was no longer beholden to the fears of men long dead.

"Thank you," she said when finally they came up for air. She felt she could flow through Bitterlich's gaze forever.

"For what?" he asked.

"For bringing me back."

CHAPTER

Thirty-Three

The *Potencia*, with Isabelle in command, breached the Bittergale on her outward run three months after going in.

There had been a great deal of work to do, first in collecting all of Travers's crew and convincing the acting capitaine of the *Potencia* to surrender. The *Conquest* treasure, what remained of it, had been gathered. Isabelle had planted the flag of l'Empire on a patch of land well up the coast and away from la Forêt d'Essaims, which had become the insect forest's name of record over Jean-Claude's objection. He'd wanted to call it New Buggering. And so was the colony of Ultima Thule declared and claimed in the name of Impératrice Sireen.

And then many a council had been held on what to do next.

In the end, "We go home" had won out over less practical suggestions.

Isabelle had sworn in Similce and her crew into the Célestial navy and granted them shares in the venture. Then they'd spent weeks practicing approaches to the escorts that would get them all through the Bittergale intact. They would present the whole package to l'impératrice as a fait accompli.

"Do you think all these promises will stick?" Jean-Claude asked.

Isabelle said, "I imagine Sireen will be happy enough to present this new craton to the world as her idea, and use it to cut the knees out from under everyone who has been trying to pin the expedition on her as a failure."

No one was entirely surprised to find most of the Hoary Fleet waiting for them outside the Bittergale. Capitaine Vrain invited them aboard the *Thunderclap*, addressed Isabelle as capitaine, and informed her that l'impératrice had extended her an imperial invitation to a personal audience at her earliest possible convenience. There was no mention of the recall order.

To Quill, Isabelle presented the regalia of Prime Architect Cassius, which had indeed been discovered amongst the wreckage. It was, after all, the thing he had officially signed up to find.

"And the Vault?" he asked, gesturing to the reliquary ring on her finger.

"It's empty," she said, which was literally true. "People are therefore still free to fill it up with whatever fantasies they prefer."

—

Isabelle arrived in Rocher Royale at the first cusp of autumn and presented herself to Sireen in private audience to explain herself and what had transpired. It was a story long in the telling, and lasted well into the wee hours.

"So," Sireen said, when at last she'd extracted every detail she could imagine from Isabelle. "If you are to be believed, in the time since the Prophecy was made, you and only you have emerged from the Vault of Ages. And you have set the world on its proper axis so that it might not be destroyed again. Does this make you the Savior?"

Isabelle blanched at the very thought. "Madame, I would never presume such a thing."

"Other people would," Sireen said. "The flickering of the world, as you called it, touched every corner of the world, every city, every hamlet, every charcoal burner's hut. Some people went mad. Dozens of cults have sprung up within and without the Temple claiming that it was a sign of the Savior's coming. Several charismatics have even claimed to be the Savior."

"Put them in a room and let them fight over it," Isabelle said. "The Savior isn't something anyone should be. If you think about it, the Savior's coming would be the end of the world, the end of strife, but also the end of achievement, improvement, and change."

"So you think that meaning requires suffering?"

"No, just . . . uncertainty, I suppose, room for curiosity, and the space to grow and become something more than we are. I've had perfect moments, but I couldn't keep them, and I wouldn't want to. There are different perfect moments to hunt for, surprises to be had, and discoveries to be made. I would hate to have to pick just one."

Sireen sipped her wine. The two of them must have worked their way through half a vineyard over the course of the night.

Sireen asked, "How do you come back from that; from touching the Builder's mind?"

Isabelle said, "It helps to have things to come back to, family, friends, duties. Yet even if I had none of those, my bladder would have brought me round eventually."

"In that case, if you are just Isabelle, what am I to do with you? As a mere mortal, you lied to me about your mental state, stole a ship, conspired with the enemies of l'Empire, consorted with pirates, and made promises in my name that you had no right to make."

"And saved the world," Isabelle said.

"I admit that is a significant mitigating factor," Sireen said. "I suppose I'm going to have to settle for adopting you."

Isabelle was stunned. "But . . ."

Sireen held up a finger. "I can already see the objection brewing in your mind. Don't tell me why I shouldn't do this. I am issuing you an imperial pardon and I am making you my legal daughter. Ultima Thule is a royal colony. It needs a royal governor, someone who can deal with uncharted territory and adapt to shifting needs, someone who can govern on her own with limited resources and little oversight. It also has to be someone I can trust to do the right thing even when it's the wrong thing. Besides, you scare the shadows off of most of my nobles, and putting you second in line to the throne will make people think twice about challenging Princess Josette's claims. Don't you agree, Princess Isabelle d'Auroborea?"

"I . . ." Isabelle said. "Yes, Madame. I will do my best."

"Now, there's a terrifying thought," Sireen said, but with a glint of good humor in her eye. "Making you governor is not a reward. As la reine it is my duty to put the right people in the right place. Yet I would like to express to you my personal gratitude, if there's anything I can give you that you desire."

Isabelle nearly declined by pure reflex. The things that she yearned for weren't the sort of gifts that even a reine could bestow. She had Jean-Claude, Marie, and Bitterlich . . .

"As a matter of fact," Isabelle said, "I would like a favor from the Order of the Succoring Shadow."

⌒

"Are you sure you want to do this?" Bitterlich asked Rebecca as they waited in the antechamber outside one of Rocher Royale's many retiring rooms. He was certainly not sure he wanted to face what awaited him beyond the door.

Rebecca fidgeted in her new dress. The knee-length skirt and tall boots, similar to the ones Isabelle wore, had been a fight to get her to wear, but, in typical thirteen-year-old fashion, almost as soon as she'd been adorned, she'd twirled herself dizzy making the skirt flare.

"Yeah," she said in the flat tone that he'd learned to interpret as social nervousness. "It's a favor to la reine, right? That's worth summat."

"I see you'll fit right into court life," Bitterlich said.

A doorman ushered them into a comfortable sitting room with couches at right angles, a low table, and historical tapestries on the walls.

The doorman announced, "Major Ewald Bitterlich."

Inside stood Comtesse Eulalie du Blain. The sight of her made Bitterlich's bowels turn to water and his heart shrivel, but she must answer for what she'd done, not just to him but everyone around her. Her bloodshadow spread behind her like a snail's slime trail. Darker shadows swam within it, and Bitterlich now had an inkling what they represented: the bloodhollows she managed to steal. Her face was powdered and painted as white as snow, to cover up her hated freckles, as he recalled. Her lips were painted the color of fresh-spilt blood. She caught sight of Bitterlich and her curious expression stretched instantly into the blank-faced smile that courtiers and crocodiles had in common.

"Major Bitterlich," she said. "What a surprise. I was told a message had arrived for me from home."

"Not from home," he said, his voice already rough as if he'd been shouting all day. "From your family. More precisely from your long-lost daughter. Allow me to introduce Rebecca du Blaine, the offspring of our liaison."

On cue, Rebecca stepped forward, curtsied, and said in a tone that could have frozen flame. "Greetings, Mother."

It was impossible to say if Eulalie turned pale behind all that powder, but her smile never wavered. "Don't be ridiculous," she said. "She's a Seelenjäger."

"Thankfully, yes," Bitterlich said, anger on Rebecca's behalf burning in contrast to his own deep-rooted dread. "The records show your first child was stillborn, but in fact you had her taken away to be disposed of. I spent the last fortnight tracking down the maid who did it. You told her to throw Rebecca off a cliff, but it turns out she didn't have the heart. She left the babe at the orphanage, and you pretended to be bereaved."

Eulalie scoffed. "Who would ever believe a maid's word over mine? I see what you're up to. You're trying to blackmail me, to embarrass me in front of my husband. Well, it won't work, and you won't get a wooden penny out of me. My husband knows you tried to rape me."

"I did no such thing," Bitterlich said, anger burning through his shame. "And you know it. I was young and I was dumb and I was as lustful as a stoat, but I'd never touched you except that you asked me to."

"Oh, spare me your indignation," Eulalie said. "You're Seelenjäger, barely more than an animal. If I was curious, well, I can be forgiven for that. I was young and innocent, but you . . . you should have known your place."

All of Bitterlich's fur stood on end. Half of him wanted to rip her head off. The other half wanted to run and hide in endless shame. "And then you gelded me," he spat, words of venom that had been stewing almost fourteen years.

"Of course I did," Eulalie said. "It's clear you can't control yourself. I did you a favor, like cutting a horse to tame it. Just think how much happier you are without having those urges to contend with. I think we can all agree that this was the best possible outcome for everyone. Now, if you'll excuse me—"

"You certainly enjoy forgiving yourself, don't you?" Isabelle said, stepping in from the alcove behind the tapestries. She was magnificent in her full *cappotto di piume*, feathers glittering, her spark swarm flaring like a bonfire from the fan of her crest, her eyes ablaze with fury that could have incinerated a mountain. "That ends now."

Eulalie backed away from Isabelle's unfettered wrath. "I don't have to forgive myself," she said. "I've done nothing wrong. It's Bitterlich who has to answer for all he's done. I was only defending myself. I did what was best for everybody."

Isabelle stalked forward. "And then when you were done with him, you set your hooks in la reine, drawing her into your circle with the Order of the Succoring Shadow, so that you could spy on her on behalf of your cousin, the late, unlamented Comte de Travers."

"Don't be absurd, there's nothing wrong with sharing gossip with my cousin. That's what cousins are for, and besides someone had to reach out to la reine, to warn her against the pernicious influence of people like you, abomination."

Isabelle cocked her head to one side. "Even to the point of hijacking her bloodshadow to try and kill me?"

Eulalie lifted her nose in the air. "I only did what was best for l'Empire. La reine never should have trusted you. You are an abomination. You should have been destroyed, but you had her under your spell. I had to do something. Once she hears what you've done to me, how you've attacked and threatened me, she'll have you thrown from the sky cliff."

"I think that's very unlikely," Sireen said, striding in behind Bitterlich. Bitterlich stepped out of the way and bowed deeply. Everyone else made obeisance as well, even Eulalie.

"Madame," Eulalie said without looking up. "Thank the Builder you're here. These fiends have been conspiring—"

"Comtesse Eulalie," Sireen said, to instant silence. "If I were you, I would consider cutting out my own lying tongue and making a noose of it to hang myself. I guarantee it will be less painful and humiliating than the traditional punishment for treason. Guards."

Two of the royal guards pinned Eulalie with their bloodshadows and dragged her away, at which point Sireen gestured everyone else to rise. "Thank you all. It's always a pleasure to have the chance to participate directly in all the cloaking and daggering. Eulalie's public confession of crimes against the Crown will make it considerably easier to sell the eradication of the Travers household to the other great houses."

She turned to Bitterlich. "I imagine it must have been especially difficult for you."

"I live to serve," Bitterlich said, as jauntily as he could. He felt drained, but in the way of a man who'd had a boil lanced. The wound was still there, but much of the pain had bled away.

"I do hope there is more to your life than that," Sireen said. "Being locked into duty is just as bad as being locked into anything else. Speaking of which, the remaining members of the Succoring Shadow will see you tomorrow at sunup; we should have excellent light then."

"I . . . beg your pardon," Bitterlich said.

"What Eulalie did to you is the same kind of shadow surgery that the Succoring Shadow does. We have reason to believe that what she did to you is as reversible as the damage done to Jean-Claude. That is, if you want it reversed." She cast a sly look at Isabelle. "She does."

Bitterlich's tongue seemed to take up his whole throat. Did he? Could they? He'd already discovered a world of intimacy with Isabelle that he thought he'd never have, but this? He'd never stopped wishing for it. Never let the wish get in his way. He'd packed it down so tightly that he could hardly bring himself to think it now.

"Just say yes," Isabelle said with a lopsided smile. "Don't overthink it."

"Ah . . ." he said. "Yes."

Isabelle and Bitterlich found Grand Leon at his hunting lodge, an expansive stone pile on the forested slopes in the hinterlands behind Rocher Royale. The pensioner roi had just arrived from a gallop through the woods with a pack of huntsmen, and he bade them join him at the fireside in one of his withdrawing rooms. Generous helpings of wine served to mellow the mood as they caught him up on their adventures. Isabelle was certain he'd already been briefed by Sireen and Impervia, but there was always something to be said from hearing the story from the horse's mouth.

"I do worry that the Fenice will assume I was lying to them and start up their vendetta again," Isabelle said.

"You were lying to them," Grand Leon said, "but given that they had officially canceled the vendetta by the time you disappeared, they would have to start a new one. Times have changed, and you are once again a princess of l'Empire. I doubt they will find it politically expedient to do so."

"Times have changed," Isabelle said. "Old secrets lose their sting. Just how much did you know about Kantelvar's plans for breeding the Savior when you ordered Djordji to save Bitterlich?"

Grand Leon tugged at his gray goatee. "I guessed more than he thought I did, but I was less clever than I thought. I deduced he was engaged in selective breeding, but I believed his purpose was more political than it turned out to be." He frowned into his cup and then looked at Bitterlich. "I learned that Kantelvar had arranged to have you killed. I believed he was trying to reshuffle the inheritance deck to put your cousin first in line to the family seat." He paused and shook his head. "I did not know he meant to kill your family. I rescued you to guarantee the succession would go the way that I wanted it to. Then the death of your parents diverted that plan. There was no great secret scheme to it, just petty politics. The rest you know."

Bitterlich said, "But by the time you assigned me to Isabelle, you had learned about Kantelvar's Savior-breeding scheme."

Grand Leon raised his bushy eyebrows. "Are you worried about the Prophecy? From what you've told me about the Vault of Ages, it sounds exceedingly unlikely a Savior will be born at all. As for why I put you together . . . are you displeased with the outcome?"

Almost against her will Isabelle met Bitterlich's gaze. It was so very hard not to grin like a loon, especially when his ears pricked up like that.

"Just so," Grand Leon said. "I planted a seed, but I have moved on. The orchard is yours. I will leave you two to tend it."

⁓

The deck rocked under Jean-Claude's feet. Marie's homestone had brought him to Flotsam, and her fellhand status had gotten him an audience of sorts, a skymoot they called it, with the Seven Thunders clan—Dok and Aria's people. He'd come to sing their endsong, which, fortunately, did not require any actual singing. Hundreds of people gathered round in their great stadium to listen under lightning-shot skies as he told how they lived and how they died at the last, still fighting for each other and for a future for their kin.

To his amazement, none of the Gyrine seemed to blame him for their captains' deaths. Instead, they thanked him for the tale and named him clan friend.

"Everyone dies," said Vote Capitaine Solo Dyne. "Not everyone has something worth dying for."

The wake lasted a night and a day. Toasts were made and songs were sung and Dok and Aria were woven into Legend, may they not be forgotten while the wild winds yet blow.

Jean-Claude had other business there as well, an offer of treaty from l'Empire Céleste. "I know the Gyrine bow to no roi or reine," Jean-Claude said, "but Madame Sireen would make good on Hailer Dok's bargain."

He showed them a map of l'Empire Céleste, and pointed out where there was good land recently dispossessed, that she would be willing to lease to the Gyrine on terms that did not require a subject's service to a sovereign but instead would be paid for in terms of trade for particular services, namely to provide guides and good winds for Célestial trade ships and colony ships throughout the deep sky. The Craton Auroborea was due to open up and she would help the Gyrine tame and settle parts of it as well.

The Seven Thunders gave him no answer immediately. The decision would affect all Gyrine, so it must be agreed upon by the other clans.

"Do you think they'll take the offer?" Jean-Claude asked Marie as they strolled the decks back toward the recently renamed and refitted galleon *Veritus* that was carrying the bulk of the supplies needed for the new colony.

"Do I look like a diplomat?" Marie asked. "Or a fortune-teller?"

"You look like somebody dipped you in flour. That doesn't make you a pastry."

"I hope they do," Marie said. "They can't go on as they are. This gives them the chance to change on their own terms. I'm going to go find Fellhand Vexatious and talk her into advocating the idea."

"Vexatious?"

"Tall woman. Black skin. Tried to kill me once. We're not quite friends yet."

"Sounds like you're off to a good start," Jean-Claude said.

"It could've been worse," Marie said. "She could've succeeded."

They came aboard the *Veritus* and found Capitaine Similce engaged in teaching Malgiers and Rebecca the Skaladin tongue.

Jean-Claude asked, "Is Princess Isabelle on board?"

"In the great cabin with Bitterlich," Similce said dryly. "Last I checked they had clothes on, but that was twenty minutes ago."

Jean-Claude trained his clockwork eye on the great cabin. The shadows moving behind the wall suggested that indeed a critical interval had passed and that now might not be the best time to intrude upon the young couple.

Jean-Claude dialed the eye back to normal vision and left them to their fun. He remembered being that young and vigorous, and he wished them the best of it. The intoxication wouldn't last forever, even if the deeper affection did.

He turned to Rebecca and asked, "Have you thought about how you're going to handle the immense responsibility of being somebody's big sister?"

She made a face at him. "Eh. Why?"

"Oh," Jean-Claude said. "No reason."

He leaned against the rail and contemplated how much fun it was going to be to be a grandfather.

Acknowledgments

Innumerable thanks go to Susan Smith, Carol Berg, Brian Tobias, Brian Winstead, Courtney Schafer, and Saytchyn-Maddux Creech, without whose good and abundant advice this book would not have become half of what it is. Special thanks to auntie editor Diana Pho, for all her invaluable insight, and Chris Morgan for taking me on. Thanks to Caitlin Blasdell for her skillful work and dedication.

About the Author

Curtis Craddock lives in Sterling, Colorado, where he teaches computer information systems to inmates in a state penitentiary. He is the author of the Risen Kingdoms trilogy, starting with *An Alchemy of Masques and Mirrors*.

curtiscraddock.com
Twitter: @artfulskeptic